Here is a collection of brilliant stories by the greatest writers of detective fiction. From the very first example of this genre —Poe's "Murders in the Rue Morgue"— to the present-day tales by Agatha Christie and Ellery Queen, these thirteen ingenious stories will astonish, terrify and delight.

STEWART H. BENEDICT, with degrees from Drew University and Johns Hopkins, has taught at New York University, Michigan Tech, Jersey City State College and Rutgers, and is currently at City College of New York. He has previously edited *Tales of Terror and Suspense* for Dell. His articles on modern American, English and European literature have appeared in leading scholarly magazines.

THE LAUREL-LEAF LIBRARY brings together under a single imprint outstanding works of fiction and nonfiction particularly suitable for young adult readers, both in and out of the classroom. This series is under the editorship of Charles F. Reasoner, Professor of Elementary Education, New York University.

THE CRIME-SOLVERS:
13 Classic Detective Stories

EDITED BY STEWART H. BENEDICT

LAUREL-LEAF LIBRARY

Published by DELL PUBLISHING CO., INC.
1 Dag Hammarskjold Plaza, New York, N.Y. 10017
Copyright © 1966 by Dell Publishing Co., Inc.
Laurel-Leaf Library ® TM 766734
Dell Publishing Co., Inc.

First Printing—February, 1966
Second Printing—September, 1967
Third Printing—November, 1969
Fourth Printing—May, 1972
Fifth Printing—October, 1972
Sixth Printing—December, 1973
Seventh Printing—September, 1974
Eighth Printing—August, 1975
Ninth Printing—October, 1976

Printed in U.S.A.

Acknowledgments: The following selections are reproduced by permission of the authors, their publishers, or their agents:

"THE SECRET GARDEN." Reprinted by permission of Dodd, Mead and Company from THE INNOCENCE OF FATHER BROWN by G. K. Chesterton. Copyright 1911 by Dodd, Mead and Company. Reprinted by permission of A. P. Watt & Son and Penguin Books Ltd., copyright held by Miss D. E. Collins.

"THE ANGEL OF THE LORD." Reprinted by permission of the author's estate and Robert P. Mills. Copyright © 1918, by D. Appleton and Co.; renewed in the name of the author's estate, 1946.

"THE PLYMOUTH EXPRESS." Reprinted by permission of Dodd, Mead and Company and Harold Ober Associates, Inc. from THE UNDERDOG AND OTHER STORIES by Agatha Christie. Copyright 1924 by Agatha Christie.

"MIRACLES DO HAPPEN." Reprinted by permission of the author and the author's agents, Scott Meredith Literary Agency, Inc. Copyright © 1957 by Ellery Queen. First appeared in ELLERY QUEEN'S MYSTERY MAGAZINE.

THE
CRIME-SOLVERS

CONTENTS

LIKE JAZZ MUSIC, THE DETECTIVE STORY IS ONE OF THE FEW original American contributions to the arts; it began in 1841 with the publication of "The Murders in the Rue Morgue."

1966 is an important year in the history of the detective story, for it marks the one-hundred-and twenty-fifth anniversary of the publication of "The Murders in the Rue Morgue," the first story of this type ever written. Since Edgar Allan Poe's first attempt, literally tens of thousands of detective stories have been published and, in the comparatively short span of a century and a quarter, the story involving a mystery and its solution has become one of the most popular varieties of fiction.

In addition to "The Murders in the Rue Morgue," Poe wrote three other detective stories, "The Mystery of Marie Roget," "The Purloined Letter" and "Thou Art the Man," as well as one that came close, "The Gold Bug." The first three of these, says the noted critic Howard Haycraft, "established once and for all the mold and pattern for the . . . works of police fiction which have followed." This being the case, it is certainly fair to call Poe the Father of the Detective Story.

Interestingly enough, the form did not catch on immediately, especially in the United States. France, which has always appreciated and valued Poe more than his native land, produced the next significant writer of detective fiction in Emile Gaboriau. Known mainly as a novelist, Gaboriau wrote very few shorter works. His story "A Disappearance," included here, is a typical example of the very early mystery.

The second important practitioner of this form in America was Anna Katherine Green. In establishing herself as a mystery writer, she helped to start a tradition that has continued to the present day. For, no matter what discrimination may exist against women in other fields, there has never been any in the mystery novel, as the mention of names like Dorothy Sayers, Craig Rice, Josephine Tey and Agatha Christie will remind us. "A Difficult Problem" shows clearly what the detective story was like toward the end of the nineteenth century.

Sir Arthur Conan Doyle is so widely known as the creator of Sherlock Holmes that many people have almost forgotten that he also wrote mystery stories that do not feature the man from Baker Street. Such a tale is "The Lost Special," where we can see that lively interest in deduction which resulted in his great fame later on.

Baroness Orczy was another writer fascinated by man's ability to make deductions. Her work is especially interesting because she introduced the detective who does not need to visit the scene of the crime in order to solve it in the person of "The Man in the Corner." Needless to say, this device has been copied many times.

"The Problem of Cell 13" by Jacques Futrelle is one of the most famous detective stories ever written. It also marks the high point of pure reason in the mystery: "The Thinking Machine," Futrelle's sleuth, is all mind and so carries the chief quality of detectives like Sherlock Holmes about as far as it can be carried.

Many writers known primarily for their work in other types of fiction have tried their hands at the detective story, including such respected figures as Charles Dickens and William Faulkner. Among them is Jack London, famous mainly for his tales of adventure and his novels like *The Sea Wolf* and *The Iron Heel,* which present problems of philosophy in fictional form. "The Leopard Man's Story" is perhaps his only attempt at a story of detection.

If Futrelle had taken the mastermind sort of detective to his ultimate point, two British writers opened new doors for the mystery and led it in directions still being followed today. The first of these was R. Austin Freeman, the inventor of the so-called inverted detective story and the most ardent spokesman for the idea that all of the clues available to the detective must also be made available to the reader. Much of the argumentation that goes on at the present time about the "ethics" of the mystery, that is, insuring that the writer plays fair with his audience, has its origins in some of the questions raised by Freeman.

The second of the influential figures was Gilbert K. Chesterton, with his gentle detective-priest, Father Brown. In the hands of Chesterton, the personality of the detective began to assume a certain importance in the story: no longer was he a "thinking machine," but a person. Chesterton, too, was the first to make extensive use of the detective story as a vehicle for the expression of ideas on subjects quite unrelated to crime. In this, of course, he has been followed very widely, various mysteries having presented arguments for everything from tolerance for aborigines to free enterprise in economics.

Just as Chesterton had in England, Melville D. Post in America created a crime-solver with a personality—that modern Jeremiah, that avenging angel, Uncle Abner. Even such a restrained critic as Anthony Boucher has called the tales featuring Uncle Abner "the best American detective short stories since Poe."

Probably the best-selling mystery writer of all time is Agatha Christie. At first an almost slavish imitator of Conan Doyle, she evolved a style and a method of her own and enjoy the distinction of being the only mystery writer thus far to have created two major detectives, namely Hercule Poirot and Jane Marple. Already the authoress of over seventy novels in her forty-five-year career, she seems destined for a place beside Poe and Conan Doyle as one of the greats.

Ellery Queen is actually two men, Frederic Dannay and Manfred B. Lee, and they constitute the most prolific and successful duo in the history of detective fiction. They have an even greater claim to fame, however: more than any other, they have enabled the reader to become the detective. They have mastered the technique of writing in such a way that the passive reader can enjoy going through an interesting story while the one who wants to work out the puzzle for himself is given every clue, as is the case in "Miracles Do Happen."

Such, then, has been the history of detective fiction and of some of the trends within its brief but active life-span. Naturally, like all other forms of literature, it has been the subject of parody. One hardly need say that some types of this story, especially those which feature the great brain who never makes a mistake, are almost perfect targets for humor. And who is better suited to write a parody than America's best comic writer, Mark Twain? "The Stolen White Elephant" is his contribution to the field and, hopefully, provides a fitting conclusion to this collection.

STEWART H. BENEDICT

THE MURDERS IN
THE RUE MORGUE
by Edgar Allan Poe

What song the Syrens sang, or what name Achilles assumed when he hid himself among women, although puzzling questions, are not beyond *all* conjecture.

Sir Thomas Browne

THE MENTAL FEATURES DISCOURSED OF AS THE ANALYTICAL, are, in themselves, but little susceptible of analysis. We appreciate them only in their effects. We know of them, among other things, that they are always to their possessor, when inordinately possessed, a source of the liveliest enjoyment. As the strong man exults in his physical ability, delighting in such exercises as call his muscles into action, so glories the analyst in that moral activity which *disentangles*. He derives pleasure from even the most trivial occupations bringing his talent into play. He is fond of enigmas, of conundrums, hieroglyphics; exhibiting in his solutions of each a degree of *acumen* which appears to the ordinary apprehension preternatural. His results, brought about by the very soul and essence of method, have, in truth, the whole air of intuition.

The faculty of re-solution is possibly much invigorated by mathematical study, and especially by that highest branch of it which, unjustly, and merely on account of its retrograde operations, has been called, as if *par excellence*, analysis. Yet to calculate is not in itself to analyze. A chess-player, for example, does the one, without effort at the other. It follows that the game of chess, in its effects upon mental character,

is greatly misunderstood. I am not now writing a treatise,
but simply prefacing a somewhat peculiar narrative by observations very much at random; I will, therefore, take occasion to assert that the higher powers of the reflective intellect
are more decidedly and more usefully tasked by the unosten-
tatious game of draughts than by all the elaborate frivolity
of chess. In this latter, where the pieces have different and
bizarre motions, with various and variable values, what is
only complex, is mistaken (a not unusual error) for what is
profound. The *attention* is here called powerfully into play.
If it flag for an instant, an oversight is committed, resulting
in injury or defeat. The possible moves being not only manifold, but involute, the chances of such oversights are multi-
plied; and in nine cases out of ten, it is the more concentrative rather than the more acute player who conquers. In
draughts, on the contrary, where the moves are *unique* and
have but little variation, the probabilities of inadvertence are
diminished, and the mere attention being left comparatively
unemployed, what advantages are obtained by either party
are obtained by superior *acumen*. To be less abstract, let us
suppose a game of draughts where the pieces are reduced to
four kings, and where, of course, no oversight is to be expected. It is obvious that here the victory can be decided
(the players being at all equal) only by some *recherché*
movement, the result of some strong exertion of the intellect.
Deprived of ordinary resources, the analyst throws himself
into the spirit of his opponent, identifies himself therewith,
and not unfrequently sees thus, at a glance, the sole methods
(sometimes indeed absurdly simple ones) by which he may
seduce into error or hurry into miscalculation.

Whist has long been known for its influence upon what is
termed the calculating power; and men of the highest order
of intellect have been known to take an apparently unaccountable delight in it, while eschewing chess as frivolous.
Beyond doubt there is nothing of a similiar nature so greatly
tasking the faculty of analysis. The best chess-player in
Christendom *may* be little more than the best player of
chess; but proficiency in whist implies capacity for success in

all these more important undertakings where mind struggles with mind. When I say proficiency, I mean that perfection in the game which includes a comprehension of *all* the sources whence legitimate advantage may be derived. These are not only manifold, but multiform, and lie frequently among recesses of thought altogether inaccessible to the ordinary understanding. To observe attentively is to remember distinctly; and, so far, the concentrative chess-player will do very well at whist; while the rules of Hoyle (themselves based upon the mere mechanism of the game) are sufficiently and generally comprehensible. Thus to have a retentive memory, and proceed by "the book" are points commonly regarded as the sum total of good playing. But it is in matters beyond the limits of mere rule that the skill of the analyst is evinced. He makes, in silence, a host of observations and inferences. So, perhaps, do his companions; and the difference in the extent of the information obtained, lies not so much in the validity of the inference as in the quality of the observation. The necessary knowledge is that of *what* to observe. Our player confines himself not at all; nor, because the game is the object, does he reject deductions from things external to the game. He examines the countenance of his partner, comparing it carefully with that of each of his opponents. He considers the mode of assorting the cards in each hand; often counting trump by trump, and honor by honor, through the glances bestowed by their holders upon each. He notes every variation of face as the play progresses, gathering a fund of thought from the differences in the expression of certainty, of surprise, of triumph, or chagrin. From the manner of gathering up a trick he judges whether the person taking it, can make another in the suit. He recognizes what is played through feint, by the manner with which it is thrown upon the table. A casual or inadvertent word; the accidental dropping or turning of a card, with the accompanying anxiety or carelessness in regard to its concealment: the counting of the tricks, with the order of their arrangement; embarrassment, hesitation, eagerness, or trepidation—all afford, to his apparently intuitive perception,

indications of the true state of affairs. The first two or three
rounds having been played, he is in full possession of the
contents of each hand, and thenceforward puts down his
cards with as absolute a precision of purpose as if the rest
of the party had turned outward the faces of their own.

The analytical power should not be confounded with simple ingenuity; for while the analyst is necessarily ingenious,
the ingenious man is often remarkably incapable of analysis.
The constructive or combining power, by which ingenuity is
usually manifested, and to which the phrenologists (I believe erroneously) have assigned a separate organ, supposing
it a primitive faculty, has been so frequently seen in those
whose intellect bordered otherwise upon idiocy, as to have
attracted general observation among writers on morals. Between ingenuity and the analytic ability there exists a difference far greater, indeed, than that between the fancy and
the imagination, but of a character very strictly analogous.
It will be found, in fact, that the ingenious are always fanci-
ful, and the *truly* imaginative never otherwise than analytic.

The narrative which follows will appear to the reader
somewhat in the light of a commentary upon the proposi-
tions just advanced.

Residing in Paris during the spring and part of the summer of 18——, I there became acquainted with a Monsieur
C. Auguste Dupin. This young gentleman was of an excellent, indeed of an illustrious family, but, by a variety of un-
toward events, had been reduced to such poverty that the
energy of his character succumbed beneath it, and he ceased
to bestir himself in the world, or to care for the retrieval of
his fortunes. By courtesy of his creditors, there still remained
in his possession a small remnant of his patrimony; and, upon the income arising from this, he managed, by means
of a rigorous economy, to procure the necessities of life,
without troubling himself about its superfluities. Books, indeed, were his sole luxuries, and in Paris these are easily
obtained.

Our first meeting was at an obscure library in the Rue
Montmartre, where the accident of our both being in search

of the same very rare and very remarkable volume, brought us into closer communion. We saw each other again and again. I was deeply interested in the little family history which he detailed to me with all that candor which a Frenchman indulges whenever mere self is the theme. I was astonished, too, at the vast extent of his reading; and, above all, I felt my soul enkindled within me by the wild fervor, and the vivid freshness of his imagination. Seeking in Paris the objects I then sought, I felt that the society of such a man would be to me a treasure beyond price; and this feeling I frankly confided to him. It was at length arranged that we should live together during my stay in the city; and as my worldly circumstances were somewhat less embarrassed than his own, I was permitted to be at the expense of renting, and furnishing in a style which suited the rather fantastic gloom of our common temper, a time-eaten and grotesque mansion, long deserted through superstitions into which we did not inquire, and tottering to its fall in a retired and desolate portion of the Faubourg St. Germain.

Had the routine of our life at this place been known to the world, we should have been regarded as madmen—although, perhaps, as madmen of a harmless nature. Our seclusion was perfect. We admitted no visitors. Indeed the locality of our retirement had been carefully kept a secret from my own former associates; and it had been many years since Dupin had ceased to know or be known in Paris. We existed within ourselves alone.

It was a freak of fancy in my friend (for what else shall I call it?) to be enamored of the night for her own sake; and into this *bizarrerie*, as into all his others, I quietly fell; giving myself up to his wild whims with a perfect *abandon*. The sable divinity would not herself dwell with us always; but we could counterfeit her presence. At the first dawn of the morning we closed all the mossy shutters of our old building; lighted a couple of tapers which, strongly perfumed, threw out only the ghastliest and feeblest of rays. By the aid of these we then busied our souls in dreams—reading, writing, or conversing, until warned by the clock of the advent of true Darkness. Then we sallied forth into the streets, arm in arm, continuing the topics of the day, or roaming far and wide until a late hour, seeking, amid the wild lights and shadows of the populous city, that infinity of mental excitement which quiet observation can afford.

At such times I could not help remarking and admiring (although from his rich ideality I had been prepared to expect it) a peculiar analytic ability in Dupin. He seemed, too, to take an eager delight in its exercise—if not exactly in its display—and did not hesitate to confess the pleasure thus derived. He boasted to me, with a low chuckling laugh, that most men, in respect to himself, wore windows in their bosoms, and was wont to follow up such assertions by direct and very startling proofs of his intimate knowledge of my own. His manner at these moments was frigid and abstract; his eyes were vacant in expression: while his voice, usually a rich tenor, rose into a treble which would have sounded petulant but for the deliberateness and entire distinctness of the enunciation. Observing him in these moods, I often dwelt meditatively upon the old philosophy of the Bi-Part Soul, and amused myself with the fancy of a double Dupin—the creative and the resolvent.

Let it not be supposed, from what I have just said, that I am detailing any mystery, or penning any romance. What I have described in the Frenchman was merely the result of an excited, or perhaps of a diseased, intelligence. But of the character of his remarks at the periods in question an example will best convey the idea.

We were strolling one night down a long dirty street, in the vicinity of the Palais Royal. Being both, apparently, occupied with thought, neither of us had spoken a syllable for fifteen minutes at least. All at once Dupin broke forth with these words:

"He is a very little fellow, that's true, and would do better for the *Théâtre des Variétés*."

"There can be no doubt of that," I replied, unwittingly, and not at first observing (so much had I been absorbed in reflection) the extraordinary manner in which the speaker had chimed in with my meditations. In an instant afterward I recollected myself, and my astonishment was profound.

"Dupin," said I, gravely, "this is beyond my comprehension. I do not hesitate to say that I am amazed, and can scarcely credit my senses. How was it possible you should know I was thinking of——?" Here I paused, to ascertain beyond a doubt whether he really knew of whom I thought.

"——of Chantilly," said he, "why do you pause? You were remarking to yourself that his diminutive figure unfitted him for tragedy."

This was precisely what had formed the subject of my reflections. Chantilly was a *quondam* cobbler of the Rue St. Denis, who, becoming stage-mad, had attempted the *rôle* of Xerxes, in Crébillon's tragedy so called, and been notoriously Pasquinaded for his pains.

"Tell me, for Heaven's sake," I exclaimed, "the method—if method there is—by which you have been enabled to fathom my soul in this matter." In fact, I was even more startled than I would have been willing to express.

"It was the fruiterer," replied my friend, "who brought you to the conclusion that the mender of soles was not of sufficient height for Xerxes *et id genus omne*."

"The fruiterer!—you astonish me—I know no fruiterer whomsoever."

"The man who ran up against you as we entered the street —it may have been fifteen minutes ago."

I now remembered that, in fact, a fruiterer, carrying upon his head a large basket of apples, had nearly thrown me down, by accident, as we passed from the Rue C—— into the thoroughfare where we stood; but what this had to do with Chantilly I could not possibly understand.

There was not a particle of *charlatânerie* about Dupin. "I will explain," he said, "and that you may comprehend all clearly, we will first retrace the course of your meditations, from the moment in which I spoke to you until that of the *rencontre* with the fruiterer in question. The larger links of the chain run thus—Chantilly, Orion, Dr. Nichols, Epicurus, Stereotomy, the street stones, the fruiterer."

There are few persons who have not, at some period of their lives, amused themselves in retracing the steps by which particular conclusions of their own minds have been attained. The occupation is often full of interest; and he who attempts it for the first time is astonished by the apparently illimitable distance and incoherence between the starting-point and the goal. What, then, must have been my amazement, when I heard the Frenchman speak what he had just spoken, and when I could not help acknowledging that he had spoken the truth. He continued:

"We had been talking of horses, if I remember aright, just before leaving the Rue C——. This was the last subject we discussed. As we crossed into this street, a fruiterer, with a large basket upon his head, brushing quickly past us, thrust you upon a pile of paving-stones collected at a spot where the causeway is undergoing repair. You stepped upon one of the loose fragments, slipped, slightly strained your ankle, appeared vexed or sulky, muttered a few words, turned to look at the pile, and then proceeded in silence. I was not particularly attentive to what you did; but observation has become with me, of late, a species of necessity.

"You kept your eyes upon the ground—glancing, with a petulant expression, at the holes and ruts in the pavement (so that I saw you were still thinking of the stones), until we reached the little alley called Lamartine, which has been paved, by way of experiment, with the overlapping and riveted blocks. Here your countenance brightened up, and, perceiving your lips move, I could not doubt that you murmured the word 'stereotomy,' a term very affectedly applied to this species of pavement. I knew that you could not say to yourself 'stereotomy' without being brought to think of atomies, and thus of the theories of Epicurus; and since, when we discussed this subject not very long ago, I mentioned to you how singularly, yet with how little notice, the vague guesses of that noble Greek had met with confirmation in the late nebular cosmogony, I felt that you could not avoid casting your eyes upward to the great *nebula* in Orion, and I certainly expected that you would do so. You did look up; and I was now assured that I had correctly followed your steps. But in that bitter *tirade* upon Chantilly, which appeared in yesterday's '*Musée,*' the satirist, making some disgraceful allusions to the cobbler's change of name upon assuming the buskin, quoted a Latin line about which we have often conversed. I mean the line

Perdidit antiquum litera prima sonum.

I had told you that this was in reference to Orion, formerly written Urion; and, from certain pungencies connected with this explanation, I was aware that you could not have forgotten it. It was clear, therefore, that you would not fail to combine the two ideas of Orion and Chantilly. That you did combine them I saw by the character of the smile which passed over your lips. You thought of the poor cobbler's immolation. So far, you had been stooping in your gait; but now I saw you draw yourself up to your full height. I was then sure that you reflected upon the diminutive figure of Chantilly. At this point I interrupted your meditations to remark that as, in fact, he *was* a very little fellow—that Chantilly—he would do better at the *Théâtre des Variétés.*"

Not long after this, we were looking over an evening edition of the *Gazette des Tribunaux* when the following paragraphs arrested our attention.

"EXTRAORDINARY MURDERS. — This morning, about three o'clock, the inhabitants of the Quartier St. Roch were roused from sleep by a succession of terrific shrieks, issuing, apparently, from the fourth story of a house in the Rue Morgue, known to be in the sole occupancy of one Madame L'Espanaye, and her daughter, Mademoiselle Camille L'Espanaye. After some delay, occasioned by a fruitless attempt to procure admission in the usual manner, the gateway was broken in with a crowbar, and eight or ten of the neighbors entered, accompanied by two *gendarmes.* By this time the cries had ceased; but, as the party rushed up the first flight of stairs, two or more rough voices, in angry contention, were distinguished, and seemed to proceed from the upper part of the house. As the second landing was reached, these sounds, also, had ceased, and every thing remained perfectly quiet. The party spread themselves, and hurried from room to room. Upon arriving at a large back chamber in the fourth story (the door of which, being found locked, with the key inside, was forced open), a spectacle presented itself which struck every one present not less with horror than with astonishment.

"The apartment was in the wildest disorder—the furniture broken and thrown about in all directions. There was only one bedstead; and from this the bed had been removed, and thrown into the middle of the floor. On a chair lay a razor, besmeared with blood. On the hearth were two or three long and thick tresses of gray human hair, also dabbled with blood, and seeming to have been pulled out by the roots. Upon the floor were found four Napoleons, an earring of topaz, three large silver spoons, three smaller of *métal d'Alger,* and two bags containing nearly four thousand francs in gold. The drawers of a *bureau,* which stood in one corner, were open, and had been, apparently, rifled, although many articles still remained in them. A small iron safe was discovered under the *bed* (not under the bedstead). It was open, with the key still in the door. It had no contents beyond a few old letters, and other papers of little consequence.

"Of Madame L'Espanaye no traces were here seen; but an unusual quantity of soot being observed in the fire-place, a search was made in the chimney, and (horrible to relate!) the corpse of the daughter, head downward, was dragged therefrom; it having been thus forced up the narrow aperture for a considerable distance. The body was quite warm. Upon examining it, many excoriations were perceived, no doubt occasioned by the violence with which it had been thrust up and disengaged. Upon the face were many severe scratches, and, upon the throat, dark bruises, and deep indentations of finger nails, as if the deceased had been throttled to death.

"After a thorough investigation of every portion of the

house without farther discovery, the party made its way into a small paved yard in the rear of the building, where lay the corpse of the old lady, with her throat so entirely cut that, upon an attempt to raise her, the head fell off. The body, as well as the head, was fearfully mutilated—the former so much so as scarcely to retain any semblance of humanity.

"To this horrible mystery there is not as yet, we believe, the slightest clue."

The next day's paper had these additional particulars:

"*The Tragedy in the Rue Morgue.*—Many individuals have been examined in relation to this most extraordinary and frightful affair," (the word *'affaire'* has not yet, in France, that levity of import which it conveys with us) "but nothing whatever has transpired to throw light upon it. We give below all the material testimony elicited.

"*Pauline Dubourg,* laundress, deposes that she has known both the deceased for three years, having washed for them during that period. The old lady and her daughter seemed on good terms—very affectionate toward each other. They were excellent pay. Could not speak in regard to their mode or means of living. Believe that Madame L. told fortunes for a living. Was reputed to have money put by. Never met any person in the house when she called for the clothes or took them home. Was sure that they had no servant in employ. There appeared to be no furniture in any part of the building except in the fourth story.

"*Pierre Moreau,* tobacconist, deposes that he has been in the habit of selling small quantities of tobacco and snuff to Madame L'Espanaye for nearly four years. Was born in the neighborhood, and has always resided there. The deceased and her daughter had occupied the house in which the corpses were found, for more than six years. It was formerly occupied by a jeweller, who under-let the upper rooms to various persons. The house was the property of Madame L. She became dissatisfied with the abuse of the premises by her tenant, and moved into them herself, refusing to let any portion. The old lady was childish. Witness had seen the daughter some five or six times during the six years. The two

lived an exceedingly retired life—were reputed to have
money. Had heard it said among the neighbors that Madame
L. told fortunes—did not believe it. Had never seen any person enter the door except the old lady and her daughter, a
porter once or twice, and a physician some eight or ten
times.

"Many other persons, neighbors, gave evidence to the
same effect. No one was spoken of as frequenting the house.
It was not known whether there were any living connections
of Madame L. and her daughter. The shutters of the front
windows were seldom opened. Those in the rear were always
closed, with the exception of the large back room, fourth
story. The house was a good house—not very old.

"*Isidore Musèt, gendarme,* deposes that he was called to
the house about three o'clock in the morning, and found
some twenty or thirty persons at the gateway, endeavoring
to gain admittance. Forced it open, at length, with a bayonet—not with a crowbar. Had but little difficulty in getting it open, on account of its being a double or folding gate,
and bolted neither at bottom nor top. The shrieks were continued until the gate was forced—and suddenly ceased. They
seemed to be screams of some person (or persons) in great
agony—were loud and drawn out, not short and quick. Witness led the way up stairs. Upon reaching the first landing,
heard two voices in loud and angry contention— the one a
gruff voice, the other much shriller—a very strange voice.
Could distinguish some words of the former, which was that
of a Frenchman. Was positive that it was not a woman's
voice. Could distinguish the words '*sacré*' and '*diable.*' The
shrill voice was that of a foreigner. Could not be sure
whether it was the voice of a man or a woman. Could not
make out what was said, but believed the language to be
Spanish. The state of the room and of the bodies was described by this witness as we described them yesterday.

"*Henri Duval,* a neighbor, and by trade a silver-smith, deposes that he was one of the party who first entered the
house. Corroborates the testimony of Musèt in general. As
soon as they forced an entrance, they reclosed the door, to

keep out the crowd, which collected very fast, notwithstanding the lateness of the hour. The shrill voice, this witness thinks, was that of an Italian. Was certain it was not French. Could not be sure that it was a man's voice. It might have been a woman's. Was not acquainted with the Italian language. Could not distinguish the words, but was convinced by the intonation that the speaker was an Italian. Knew Madame L. and her daughter. Had conversed with both frequently. Was sure that the shrill voice was not that of either of the deceased.

"——— *Odenheimer*, restaurateur.—This witness volunteered his testimony. Not speaking French, was examined through an interpreter. Is a native of Amsterdam. Was passing the house at the time of the shrieks. They lasted for several minutes—probably ten. They were long and loud—very awful and distressing. Was one of those who entered the building. Corroborated the previous evidence in every respect but one. Was sure that the shrill voice was that of a man—of a Frenchman. Could not distinguish the words uttered. They were loud and quick—unequal—spoken apparently in fear as well as in anger. The voice was harsh—not so much shrill as harsh. Could not call it a shrill voice. The gruff voice said repeatedly, '*sacré*,' '*diable*,' and once '*mon Dieu.*'

"*Jules Mignaud*, banker, of the firm of Mignaud et Fils, Rue Deloraine. Is the elder Mignaud. Madame L'Espanaye had some property. Had opened an account with his banking house in the spring of the year ——— (eight years previously). Made frequent deposits in small sums. Had checked for nothing until the third day before her death, when she took out in person the sum of 4,000 francs. This sum was paid in gold, and a clerk sent home with the money.

"*Adolphe Le Bon*, clerk to Mignaud et Fils, deposes that on the day in question, about noon, he accompanied Madame L'Espanaye to her residence with the 4,000 francs, put up in two bags. Upon the door being opened, Mademoiselle L. appeared and took from his hands one of the bags, while the old lady relieved him of the other. He then bowed and departed. Did not see any person in the street at the time. It is a by-street—very lonely.

"*William Bird*, tailor, deposes that he was one of the party who entered the house. Is an Englishman. Has lived in Paris two years. Was one of the first to ascend the stairs. Heard the voices in contention. The gruff voice was that of a Frenchman. Could make out several words, but cannot now remember all. Heard distinctly '*sacré*' and '*mon Dieu.*' There was a sound at the moment as if of several persons struggling—a scraping and scuffling sound. The shrill voice was very loud—louder than the gruff one. Is sure that it was not the voice of an Englishman. Appeared to be that of a German. Might have been a woman's voice. Does not understand German.

"Four of the above-named witnesses, being recalled, deposed that the door of the chamber in which was found the body of Mademoiselle L. was locked on the inside when the party reached it. Every thing was perfectly silent—no groans or noises of any kind. Upon forcing the door no person was seen. The windows, both of the back and front room, were down and firmly fastened from within. A door between the two rooms was closed but not locked. The door leading from the front room into the passage was locked, with the key on the inside. A small room in the front of the house, on the fourth story, at the head of the passage, was open, the door being ajar. This room was crowded with old beds, boxes, and so forth. These were carefully removed and searched. There was not an inch of any portion of the house which was not carefully searched. Sweeps were sent up and down the chimneys. The house was a four-story one, with garrets *(mansardes)*. A trap door on the room was nailed down very securely—did not appear to have been opened for years. The time elapsing between the hearing of the voices in contention and the breaking open of the room door was variously stated by the witnesses. Some made it as short as three minutes—some as long as five. The door was opened with difficulty.

"*Alfonzo Garcio,* undertaker, deposes that he resides in the Rue Morgue. Is a native of Spain. Was one of the party who entered the house. Did not proceed up stairs. Is nervous, and was apprehensive of the consequences of agitation. Heard the voices in contention. The gruff voice was that of a Frenchman. Could not distinguish what was said. The shrill voice was that of an Englishman—is sure of this. Does not understand the English language, but judges by the intonation.

"*Alberto Montani,* confectioner, deposes that he was among the first to ascend the stairs. Heard the voices in question. The gruff voice was that of a Frenchman. Distinguished several words. The speaker appeared to be expostulating. Could not make out the words of the shrill voice. Spoke quick and unevenly. Thinks it the voice of a Russian. Corroborates the general testimony. Is an Italian. Never conversed with a native of Russia.

"Several witnesses, recalled, here testified that the chimneys of all the rooms on the fourth story were too narrow to admit the passage of a human being. By 'sweeps' were meant cylindrical sweeping-brushes, such as are employed by those who clean chimneys. These brushes were passed up and down every flu in the house. There is no back passage by which any one could have descended while the party proceeded up stairs. The body of Mademoiselle L'Espanaye was so firmly wedged in the chimney that it could not be got down until four or five of the party united their strength.

"*Paul Dumas,* physician, deposes that he was called to view the bodies about daybreak. They were both then lying on the sacking of the bedstead in the chamber where Mademoiselle L. was found. The corpse of the young lady was much bruised and excoriated. The fact that it had been thrust up the chimney would sufficiently account for these appearances. The throat was greatly chafed. There were several deep scratches just below the chin, together with a series of livid spots which were evidently the impression of fingers. The face was fearfully discolored, and the eyeballs protruded. The tongue had been partially bitten through. A large bruise was discovered upon the pit of the stomach, produced, apparently, by the pressure of a knee. In the opinion of M. Dumas, Mademoiselle L'Espanaye had been throttled to death by some person or persons unknown. The corpse of the mother was horribly mutilated. All the bones of the right leg and arm were more or less shattered. The left *tibia* much splintered, as well as all the ribs of the left side. Whole body dreadfully bruised and discolored. It was not possible to say how the injuries had been inflicted. A heavy club of wood, or a broad bar of iron—a chair—any large, heavy, and obtuse weapon would have produced such results, if wielded by the hands of a very powerful man. No woman could have inflicted the blows with any weapon. The head of the deceased, when seen by witness, was entirely separated from the body, and was also greatly shattered. The throat had evidently been cut with some very sharp instrument—probably with a razor.

"*Alexandre Etienne*, surgeon, was called with M. Dumas to view the bodies. Corroborated the testimony, and the opinions of M. Dumas.

"Nothing further of importance was elicited, although several other persons were examined. A murder so mysterious, and so perplexing in all its particulars, was never before committed in Paris—if indeed a murder has been committed at all. The police are entirely at fault—an unusual occurrence in affairs of this nature. There is not, however, the shadow of a clew apparent."

The evening edition of the paper stated that the greatest excitement still continued in the Quartier St. Roch—that the premises in question had been carefully re-searched, and fresh examinations of witnesses instituted, but all to no purpose. A postscript, however, mentioned that Adolphe Le Bon had been arrested and imprisoned—although nothing appeared to criminate him beyond the facts already detailed.

Dupin seemed singularly interested in the progress of this affair—at least so I judged from his manner, for he made no comments. It was only after the announcement that Le Bon had been imprisoned, that he asked me my opinion respecting the murders.

I could merely agree with all Paris in considering them an insoluble mystery. I saw no means by which it would be possible to trace the murderer.

"We must not judge of the means," said Dupin, "by this shell of an examination. The Parisian police, so much extolled for *acumen,* are cunning, but no more. There is no method in their proceedings, beyond the method of the moment. They make a vast parade of measures; but, not unfrequently, these are so ill-a⹀ ⹀t⹀d to the objects proposed, as to put us in mind of Monsieur Jourdain's calling for his *robe-de-chambre—pour mieux entendre la musique.* The results attained by them are not unfrequently surprising, but, for the most part, are brought about by simple diligence and activity. When these qualities are unavailing, their schemes fail. Vidocq, for example, was a good guesser, and a persevering man. But, without educated thought, he erred continually by the very intensity of his investigations. He impaired his vision by holding the object too close. He might see, perhaps, one or two points with unusual clearness, but in so doing he, necessarily, lost sight of the matter as a whole. Thus there is such a thing as being too profound. Truth is not always in a well. In fact, as regards the more important knowledge, I do believe that she is invariably superficial. The depth lies in the valleys where we seek her, and not upon the mountain-tops where she is found. The modes and sources of this kind of error are well typified in the contemplation of the heavenly bodies. To look at a star by glances —to view it in a side-long way, by turning toward it the exterior portions of the *retina* (more susceptible of feeble impressions of light than the interior), is to behold the star distinctly—is to have the best appreciation of its lustre—a lustre which grows dim just in proportion as we turn our vision *fully* upon it. A greater number of rays actually fall upon the eye in the latter case, but in the former, there is the more refined capacity for comprehension. By undue profundity we perplex and enfeeble thought; and it is possible to make even Venus herself vanish from the firmament by a scrutiny too sustained, too concentrated, or too direct.

"As for these murders, let us enter into some examinations for ourselves, before we make up an opinion respecting them. An inquiry will afford us amusement," [I thought this an odd term, so applied, but said nothing] "and besides, Le Bon once rendered me a service for which I am not ungrateful. We will go and see the premises with our own eyes. I know G——, the Prefect of Police, and shall have no difficulty in obtaining the necessary permission."

The permission was obtained, and we proceeded at once to the Rue Morgue. This is one of those miserable thoroughfares which intervene between the Rue Richelieu and the Rue St. Roch. It was late in the afternoon when we reached it, as this quarter is at a great distance from that in which we resided. The house was readily found; for there were still many persons gazing up at the closed shutters, with an objectless curiosity, from the opposite side of the way. It was an ordinary Parisian house, with a gateway, on one side of which was a glazed watch-box, with a sliding panel in the window, indicating a *loge de concierge*. Before going in we walked up the street, turned down an alley, and then, again turning, passed in the rear of the building—Dupin, meanwhile, examining the whole neighborhood, as well as the house, with a minuteness of attention for which I could see no possible object.

Retracing our steps we came again to the front of the dwelling, rang, and, having shown our credentials, were admitted by the agents in charge. We went up stairs—into the chamber where the body of Mademoiselle L'Espanaye had been found, and where both the deceased still lay. The disorders of the room had, as usual, been suffered to exist. I saw nothing beyond what had been stated in the *Gazette des Tribunaux*. Dupin scrutinized every thing—not excepting the bodies of the victims. We then went into the other rooms, and into the yard; a *gendarme* accompanying us throughout. The examination occupied us until dark, when we took our departure. On our way home my companion stepped in for a moment at the office of one of the daily papers.

I have said that the whims of my friend were manifold, and that *Je les ménageais:*—for this phrase there is no English equivalent. It was his humor, now, to decline all conversation on the subject of the murder, until about noon the next day. He then asked me, suddenly, if I had observed any thing *peculiar* at the scene of the atrocity.

There was something in his manner of emphasizing the word *"peculiar,"* which caused me to shudder, without knowing why.

"No, nothing *peculiar,*" I said; "nothing more, at least, than we both saw stated in the paper."

"The *Gazette,*" he replied, "has not entered, I fear, into the unusual horror of the thing. But dismiss the idle opinions of this print. It appears to me that this mystery is considered insoluble, for the very reason which should cause it to be regarded as easy of solution—I mean for the *outré* character of its features. The police are confounded by the seeming absence of motive—not for the murder itself—but for the atrocity of the murder. They are puzzled, too, by the seeming impossibility of reconciling the voices heard in contention, with the facts that no one was discovered upstairs but the assassinated Mademoiselle L'Espanaye, and that there were no means of egress without the notice of the party ascending. The wild disorder of the room; the corpse thrust, with the head downward, up the chimney; the frightful mutilation of the old lady; these considerations, with those just mentioned, and others which I need not mention, have sufficed to paralyze the powers, by putting completely at fault the boasted *acumen,* of the government agents. They have fallen into the gross but common error of confounding the unusual with the abstruse. But it is by these deviations from the plane of the ordinary, that reason feels its way, if at all, in its search for the true. In investigations such as we are now pursuing, it should not be so much asked 'what has occurred,' as 'what has occurred that has never occurred before.' In fact, the facility with which I shall arrive, or have arrived, at the solution of this mystery, is in the direct ratio of its apparent insolubility in the eyes of the police."

I stared at the speaker in mute astonishment.

"I am now awaiting," continued he, looking toward the door of our apartment—"I am now awaiting a person who, although perhaps not the perpetrator of these butcheries, must have been in some measure implicated in their perpetration. Of the worst portion of the crimes committed, it is probable that he is innocent. I hope that I am right in this supposition; for upon it I build my expectation of reading the entire riddle. I look for the man here—in this room—every moment. It is true that he may not arrive; but the probability is that he will. Should he come, it will be necessary to detain him. Here are pistols; and we both know how to use them when occasion demands their use."

I took the pistols, scarcely knowing what I did, or believing what I heard, while Dupin went on, very much as if in a soliloquy. I have already spoken of his abstract manner at such times. His discourse was addressed to myself; but his voice, although by no means loud, had that intonation which is commonly employed in speaking to some one at a great distance. His eyes, vacant in expression, regarded only the wall.

"That the voices heard in contention," he said, "by the party upon the stairs, were not the voices of the women themselves, was fully proved by the evidence. This relieves us of all doubt upon the question whether the old lady could have first destroyed the daughter, and afterward have committed suicide. I speak of this point chiefly for the sake of method; for the strength of Madame L'Espanaye would have been utterly unequal to the task of thrusting her daughter's corpse up the chimney as it was found; and the nature of the wounds upon her own person entirely precludes the idea of self-destruction. Murder, then, has been committed by some third party; and the voices of this third party were those heard in contention. Let me now advert—not to the whole testimony respecting these voices—but to what was *peculiar* in that testimony. Did you observe any thing peculiar about it?"

I remarked that, while all the witnesses agreed in supposing the gruff voice to be that of a Frenchman, there was much disagreement in regard to the shrill, or, as one individual termed it, the harsh voice.

"That was the evidence itself," said Dupin, "but it was not the peculiarity of the evidence. You have observed nothing distinctive. Yet there *was* something to be observed. The witnesses, as you remark, agreed about the gruff voice; they were here unanimous. But in regard to the shrill voice, the peculiarity is—not that they disagreed—but that, while an Italian, an Englishman, a Spaniard, a Hollander, and a Frenchman attempted to describe it, each one spoke of it as that *of a foreigner.* Each is sure that it was not the voice of one of his own countrymen. Each likens it—not to the voice of an individual of any nation with whose language he is conversant—but the converse. The Frenchman supposes it the voice of a Spaniard, and 'might have distinguished some words *had he been acquainted with the Spanish.'* The Dutchman maintains it to have been that of a Frenchman; but we find it stated that *'not understanding French this witness was examined through an interpreter.'* The Englishman thinks it the voice of a German, and *'does not understand German.'* The Spaniard 'is sure' that it was that of an Englishman, but 'judges by the intonation' altogether, *'as he has no knowledge of the English.'* The Italian believes it the voice of a Russian, but *'has never conversed with a native of Russia.'* A second Frenchman differs, moreover with the first, and is positive that the voice was that of an Italian; but *not being cognizant of that tongue,* is like the Spaniard, 'convinced by the intonation.' Now, how strangely unusual must that voice have really been, about which such testimony as this *could* have been elicited!—in whose *tones,* even denizens of the five great divisions of Europe could recognize nothing familiar! You will say that it might have been the voice of an Asiatic—of an African. Neither Asiatics nor Africans abound in Paris; but, without denying the inference, I will now merely call your attention to three points. The voice is termed by one witness 'harsh rather than

shrill.' It is represented by two others to have been 'quick
and *unequal.*' No words—no sounds resembling words—
were by any witness mentioned as distinguishable.

"I know not," continued Dupin, "what impression I may
have made, so far, upon your own understanding; but I do
not hesitate to say that legitimate deductions even from this
portion of the testimony—the portion respecting the gruff
and shrill voices—are in themselves sufficient to engender a
suspicion which should give direction to all farther progress
in the investigation of the mystery. I said 'legitimate deductions'; but my meaning is not thus fully expressed. I de-
signed to imply that the deductions are the *sole* proper ones,
and that the suspicion arises *inevitably* from them as a single
result. What the suspicion is, however, I will not say just yet.
I merely wish you to bear in mind that, with myself, it was
sufficiently forcible to give a definite form—a certain tend-
ency—to my inquiries in the chamber.

"Let us now transport ourselves, in fancy, to this chamber. What shall we first seek here? The means of egress employed by the murderers. It is not too much to say that
neither of us believes in preternatural events. Madame and
Mademoiselle I'Espanaye were not destroyed by spirits. The
doers of the deed were material and escaped materially.
Then how? Fortunately there is but one mode of reasoning
upon the point, and that mode *must* lead us to a definite
decision. Let us examine, each by each, the possible means
of egress. It is clear that the assassins were in the room
where Mademoiselle L'Espanaye was found, or at least in
the room adjoining, when the party ascended the stairs. It
is, then, only from these two apartments that we have to
seek issues. The police have laid bare the floors, the ceiling,
and the masonry of the walls, in every direction. No *secret*
issues could have escaped their vigilance. But, not trusting
to *their* eyes, I examined with my own. There were, then,
no secret issues. Both doors leading from the rooms into the
passage were securely locked, with the keys inside. Let us
turn to the chimneys. These, although of ordinary width
for some eight or ten feet above the hearths, will not admit,

throughout their extent, the body of a large cat. The impossibility of egress, by means already stated, being thus absolute, we are reduced to the windows. Through those of the front room no one could have escaped without notice from the crowd in the street. The murderers *must* have passed, then, through those of the back room. Now, brought to this conclusion in so unequivocal a manner as we are, it is not our part, as reasoners, to reject it on account of apparent impossibilities. It is only left for us to prove that these apparent 'impossibilities' are, in reality, not such.

"There are two windows in the chamber. One of them is unobstructed by furniture, and is wholly visible. The lower portion of the other is hidden from view by the head of the unwieldy bedstead which is thrust close up against it. The former was found securely fastened from within. It resisted the utmost force of those who endeavored to raise it. A large gimlet-hole had been pierced in its frame to the left, and a very stout nail was found fitted therein, nearly to the head. Upon examining the other window, a similar nail was seen similarly fitted in it; and a vigorous attempt to raise this sash failed also. The police were now entirely satisfied that egress had not been in these directions. And, *therefore*, it was thought a matter of supererogation to withdraw the nails and open the windows.

"My own examination was somewhat more particular, and was so for the reason I have just given—because here it was, I knew, that all apparent impossibilities *must* be proved to be not such in reality.

"I proceeded to think thus—*a posteriori*. The murderers *did* escape from one of these windows. This being so, they could not have re-fastened the sashes from the inside, as they were found fastened;—the consideration which put a stop, through its obviousness, to the scrutiny of the police in this quarter. Yet the sashes *were* fastened. They *must*, then, have the power of fastening themselves. There was no escape from this conclusion. I stepped to the unobstructed casement, withdrew the nail with some difficulty, and attempted to raise the sash. It resisted all my efforts, as I had anticipated. A concealed spring must, I now knew, exist; and this corroboration of my idea convinced me that my premises, at least, were correct, however mysterious still appeared the circumstances attending the nails. A careful search soon brought to light the hidden spring. I pressed it, and, satisfied with the discovery, forbore to upraise the sash.

"I now replaced the nail and regarded it attentively. A person passing out through this window might have reclosed it, and the spring would have caught—but the nail could not have been replaced. The conclusion was plain, and again narrowed in the field of my investigations. The assassins *must* have escaped through the other window. Supposing, then, the springs upon each sash to be the same, as was probable, there *must* be found a difference between the nails, or at least between the modes of their fixture. Getting upon the sacking of the bedstead, I looked over the headboard minutely at the second casement. Passing my hand down behind the board, I readily discovered and pressed the spring, which was, as I had supposed, identical in character with its neighbor. I now looked at the nail. It was as stout as the other, and apparently fitted in the same manner—driven in nearly up to the head.

"You will say that I was puzzled; but, if you think so, you must have misunderstood the nature of the inductions. To use a sporting phrase, I had not been once 'at fault.' The scent had never for an instant been lost. There was no flaw in any link of the chain. I had traced the secret to its ultimate result,—and that result was *the nail*. It had, I say, in every respect, the appearance of its fellow in the other window; but this fact was an absolute nullity (conclusive as it might seem to be) when compared with the consideration that here, at this point, terminated the clew. 'There *must* be something wrong,' I said, 'about the nail.' I touched it; and the head, with about a quarter of an inch of the shank, came off in my fingers. The rest of the shank was in the gimlethole, where it had been broken off. The fracture was an old one (for its edges were incrusted with rust), and had apparently been accomplished by the blow of a hammer, which had partially imbedded, in the top of the bottom sash, the head portion of the nail. I now carefully replaced this head portion in the indentation whence I had taken it, and the resemblance to a perfect nail was complete—the fissure was invisible. Pressing the spring, I gently raised the sash for a few inches; the head went up with it, remaining firm in its bed. I closed the window, and the semblance of the whole nail was again perfect.

"This riddle, so far, was now unriddled. The assassin had escaped through the window which looked upon the bed. Dropping of its own accord upon his exit (or perhaps purposely closed), it had become fastened by the spring; and it was the retention of this spring which had been mistaken by the police for that of the nail,—farther inquiry being thus considered unnecessary.

"The next question is that of the mode of descent. Upon this point I had been satisfied in my walk with you around the building. About five feet and a half from the casement in question there runs a lightning-rod. From this rod it would have been impossible for any one to reach the window itself, to say nothing of entering it. I observed, however, that the shutters of the fourth story were of the peculiar kind called by Parisian carpenters *ferrades*—a kind rarely employed at the present day, but frequently seen upon very old mansions at Lyons and Bordeaux. They are in the form of an ordinary door (a single, not a folding door), except that the lower half is latticed or worked in open trellis—thus affording an excellent hold for the hands. In the present instance these shutters are fully three feet and a half broad. When we saw them from the rear of the house, they were both about half open—that is to say they stood off at right angles from the wall. It is probable that the police, as well as myself, examined the back of the tenement; but, if so, in looking at these *ferrades* in the line of their breadth (as they must have done), they did not perceive this great breadth itself, or, at all events, failed to take it into due consideration. In fact, having once satisfied themselves that no egress could have been made in this quarter, they would naturally bestow here a very cursory examination. It was clear to me, however, that the shutter belonging to the window at the head of the bed, would, if swung fully back to the wall, reach to within two feet of the lightning-rod. It was also evident that, by exertion of a very unusual degree of activity and courage, an entrance into the window, from the rod, might have been thus effected. By reaching to the distance of two feet and a half (we now suppose the shutter open to its whole extent) a robber might have taken a firm grasp upon the trellis-work. Letting go, then, his hold upon the rod, placing his feet securely against the wall, and springing boldly from it, he might have swung the shutter so as to close it, and, if we imagine the window open at the time, might even have swung himself into the room.

"I wish you to bear especially in mind that I have spoken of a *very* unusual degree of activity as requisite to success in so hazardous and so difficult a feat. It is my design to show you first, that the thing might possibly have been accomplished:—but, secondly and *chiefly,* I wish to impress upon your understanding the *very extraordinary*—the almost preternatural character of that agility which could have accomplished it.

"You will say, no doubt, using the language of the law, that 'to make out my case, I should rather undervalue than insist upon a full estimation of the activity required in this matter.' This may be the practice in law, but it is not the usage of reason. My ultimate object is only the truth. My immediate purpose is to lead you to place in juxtaposition, that *very unusual* activity of which I have just spoken, with that *very peculiar* shrill (or harsh) and *unequal* voice, about whose nationality no two persons could be found to agree, and in whose utterance no syllabification could be detected."

At these words a vague and half-formed conception of the meaning of Dupin flitted over my mind. I seemed to be upon the verge of comprehension, without power to comprehend —as men, at times, find themselves upon the brink of remembrance, without being able, in the end, to remember. My friend went on with his discourse.

"You will see," he said, "that I have shifted the question from the mode of egress to that of ingress. It was my design to convey the idea that both were effected in the same manner, at the same point. Let us now revert to the interior of the room. Let us survey the appearances here. The drawers of the bureau, it is said, had been rifled, although many articles of apparel still remained within them. The conclusion here is absurd. It is a mere guess—a very silly one—and no more. How are we to know that the articles found in the drawers were not all these drawers had originally contained? Madame L'Espanaye and her daughter lived an exceedingly retired life—saw no company—seldom went out —had little use for numerous changes of habiliment. Those found were at least of as good quality as any likely to be possessed by these ladies. If a thief had taken any, why did he not take the best—why did he not take all? In a word, why did he abandon four thousand francs in gold to encumber himself with a bundle of linen? The gold *was* abandoned. Nearly the whole sum mentioned by Monsieur Mignaud, the banker, was discovered, in bags, upon the floor. I wish you therefore, to discard from your thoughts the blundering idea of *motive*, engendered in the brains of the police by that portion of the evidence which speaks of money delivered at the door of the house. Coincidences ten times as remarkable as this (the delivery of the money, and murder committed within three days upon the party receiving it), happen to all of us every hour of our lives, without attracting even momentary notice. Coincidences, in general, are great stumbling-blocks in the way of that class of thinkers who have been educated to know nothing of the theory of probabilities—that theory to which the most glorious objects of human research are indebted for the most glorious of illustration. In the present instance, had the gold been gone, the fact of its delivery three days before would have formed something more than a coincidence. It would have

been corroborative of this idea of motive. But, under the
real circumstances of the case, if we are to suppose gold the
motive of this outrage, we must also imagine the perpetrator
so vacillating an idiot as to have abandoned his gold and his
motive together.

"Keeping now steadily in mind the points to which I have
drawn your attention—that peculiar voice, that unusual agility, and that startling absence of motive in a murder so singularly atrocious as this—let us glance at the butchery itself.
Here is a woman strangled to death by manual strength, and
thrust up a chimney head downward. Ordinary assassins
employ no such mode of murder as this. Least of all, do they
thus dispose of the murdered. In the manner of thrusting
the corpse up the chimney, you will admit that there was
something *excessively outré*—something altogether irrecon-
cilable with our common notions of human action, even
when we suppose the actors the most depraved of men.
Think, too, how great must have been that strength which
could have thrust the body *up* such an aperture so forcibly
that the united vigor of several persons was found barely
sufficient to drag it *down!*

"Turn, now, to other indications of the employment of
a vigor most marvellous. On the hearth were thick tresses—
very thick tresses—of gray human hair. These had been torn
out by the roots. You are aware of the great force necessary
in tearing thus from the head even twenty or thirty hairs
together. You saw the locks in question as well as myself.
Their roots (a hideous sight!) were clotted with fragments
of the flesh of the scalp—sure token of the prodigious power
which had been exerted in uprooting perhaps half a million
of hairs at a time. The throat of the old lady was not merely
cut, but the head absolutely severed from the body: the
instrument was a mere razor. I wish you also to look at the
brutal ferocity of these deeds. Of the bruises upon the body
of Madame L'Espanaye I do not speak. Monsieur Dumas,
and his worthy coadjutor Monsieur Etienne, have pronounced that they were inflicted by some obtuse instrument;

and so far these gentlemen are very correct. The obtuse instrument was clearly the stone pavement in the yard, upon which the victim had fallen from the window which looked in upon the bed. This idea, however simple it may now seem, escaped the police for the same reason that the breadth of the shutters escaped them—because, by the affair of the nails, their perceptions had been hermetically sealed against the possibility of the windows having ever been opened at all.

"If now, in addition to all these things, you have properly reflected upon the odd disorder of the chamber, we have gone so far as to combine the ideas of an agility astounding, a strength superhuman, a ferocity brutal, a butchery without motive, a *grotesquerie* in horror absolutely alien from humanity, and a voice foreign in tone to the ears of men of many nations, and devoid of all distinct or intelligible syllabification. What result, then, has ensued? What impression have I made upon your fancy?"

I felt a creeping of the flesh as Dupin asked me the question. "A madman," I said, "has done this deed—some raving maniac, escaped from a neighboring *Maison de Santé.*"

"In some respects," he replied, "your idea is not irrelevant. But the voices of madmen, even in their wildest paroxysms, are never found to tally with that peculiar voice heard upon the stairs. Madmen are of some nation, and their language, however incoherent in its words, has always the coherence of syllabification. Besides, the hair of a madman is not such as I now hold in my hand. I disentangled this little tuft from the rigidly clutched fingers of Madame L'Espanaye. Tell me what you can make of it."

"Dupin!" I said, completely unnerved; "this hair is most unusual—this is no *human* hair."

"I have not asserted that it is," said he; "but, before we decide this point, I wish you to glance at the little sketch I have here traced upon this paper. It is a *facsimile* drawing of what has been described in one portion of the testimony as 'dark bruises and deep indentations of finger nails' upon

the throat of Mademoiselle L'Espanaye, and in another (by
Messrs. Dumas and Etienne) as a 'series of livid spots, evidently the impression of fingers.'

"You will perceive," continued my friend, spreading out
the paper upon the table before us, "that this drawing gives
the idea of a firm and fixed hold. There is no *slipping* apparent. Each finger has retained—possibly until the death of the
victim—the fearful grasp by which it originally imbedded
itself. Attempt, now, to place all your fingers, at the same
time, in the respective impressions as you see them."

I made the attempt in vain.

"We are possibly not giving this matter a fair trial," he
said. "The paper is spread out upon a plane surface; but the
human throat is cylindrical. Here is a billet of wood, the cir-
cumference of which is about that of the throat. Wrap the
drawing around it, and try the experiment again."

I did so; but the difficulty was even more obvious than before. "This," I said, "is the mark of no human hand."

"Read now," replied Dupin, "this passage from Cuvier."

It was a minute anatomical and generally descriptive account of the large fulvous Ourang-Outang of the East Indian Islands. The gigantic stature, the prodigious strength
and activity, the wild ferocity, and the imitative propensities
of these mammalia are sufficiently well known to all. I understood the full horrors of the murder at once.

"The description of the digits," said I, as I made an end
of the reading, "is in exact accordance with this drawing. I
see that no animal but an Ourang-Outang, of the species
here mentioned, could have impressed the indentations as
you have traced them. This tuft of tawny hair, too, is identical in character with that of the beast of Cuvier. But I cannot possibly comprehend the particulars of this frightful
mystery. Besides, there were *two* voices heard in contention,
and one of them was unquestionably the voice of a Frenchman."

"True; and you will remember an expression attributed
almost unanimously, by the evidence, to this voice,—the
expression, '*mon Dieu!*' This, under the circumstances, has

been justly characterized by one of the witnesses (Montani, the confectioner) as an expression of remonstrance or expostulation. Upon these two words, therefore, I have mainly built my hopes of a full solution of the riddle. A Frenchman was cognizant of the murder. It is possible—indeed it is far more than probable—that he was innocent of all participation in the bloody transactions which took place. The Ourang-Outang may have escaped from him. He may have traced it to the chamber; but, under the agitating circumstances which ensued, he could never have recaptured it. It is still at large. I will not pursue these guesses—for I have no right to call them more—since the shades of reflection upon which they are based are scarcely of sufficient depth to be appreciable by my own intellect, and since I could not pretend to make them intelligible to the understanding of another. We will call them guesses, then, and speak of them as such. If the Frenchman in question is indeed, as I suppose, innocent of this atrocity, this advertisement, which I left last night, upon our return home, at the office of *Le Monde* (a paper devoted to the shipping interest, and much sought by sailors), will bring him to our residence."

He handed me a paper, and I read thus:

"CAUGHT—In the Bois de Boulogne, early in the morning of the ——— inst. (the morning of the murder), a very large, tawny Ourang-Outang of the Bornese species. The owner (who is ascertained to be a sailor, belonging to a Maltese vessel) may have the animal again, upon identifying it satisfactorily, and . paying a few charges arising from its capture and keeping. Call at No. ——— Rue ———, Faubourg St. Germain—au troisième."

"How was it possible," I asked, "that you should know the man to be a sailor, and belonging to a Maltese vessel?"

"I do *not* know it," said Dupin. "I am not *sure* of it. Here, however, is a small piece of ribbon, which from its form, and from its greasy appearance, has evidently been used in tying the hair in one of those long *queues* of which sailors are so fond. Moreover, this knot is one which few besides sailors can tie, and is peculiar to the Maltese. I picked the ribbon up at the foot of the lightning-rod. It could not have belonged to either of the deceased. Now if, after all, I am wrong in my induction from this ribbon, that the Frenchman was a sailor belonging to a Maltese vessel, still I can have done no harm in saying what I did in the advertisement. If I am in error, he will merely suppose that I have been misled by some circumstance into which he will not take the trouble to inquire. But if I am right, a great point is gained. Cognizant although innocent of the murder, the Frenchman will naturally hesitate about replying to the advertisement—about demanding the Ourang-Outang. He will reason thus:—'I am innocent; I am poor; my Ourang-Outang is of great value—to one in my circumstance a fortune of itself—why should I lose it through idle apprehensions of danger? Here it is, within my grasp. It was found in the Bois de Boulogne—at a vast distance from the scene of that butchery. How can it ever be suspected that a brute beast should have done the deed? The police are at fault—they have failed to procure the slightest clew. Should they even trace the animal, it would be impossible to prove me cognizant of the murder, or to implicate me in guilt on account of that cognizance. Above all, *I am known*. The advertiser designates me as the possessor of the beast. I am not sure to what limit his knowledge may extend. Should I avoid claming a property of so great value, which it is known that I possess, I will render the animal at least, liable to suspicion. It is not my policy to attract attention either to myself or to the beast. I will answer the advertisement, get the Ourang-Outang, and keep it close until this matter has blown over.'"

At this moment we heard a step upon the stairs.

"Be ready," said Dupin, "with your pistols, but neither use them nor show them until at a signal from myself."

The front door of the house had been left open, and the visitor had entered, without ringing, and advanced several steps upon the staircase. Now, however, he seemed to hesitate. Presently we heard him descending. Dupin was moving quickly to the door, when we again heard him coming up. He did not turn back a second time, but stepped up with decision, and rapped at the door of our chamber.

"Come in," said Dupin, in a cheerful and hearty tone.

A man entered. He was a sailor, evidently,—a tall, stout, and muscular-looking person, with a certain dare-devil expression of countenance, not altogether unprepossessing. His face, greatly sunburnt, was more than half hidden by whisker and *mustachio*. He had with him a huge oaken cudgel, but appeared to be otherwise unarmed. He bowed awkwardly, and bade us "good evening," in French accents, which, although somewhat Neufchâtelish, were sufficiently indicative of a Parisian origin.

"Sit down, my friend," said Dupin. "I suppose you have called about the Ourang-Outang. Upon my word, I almost envy you the possession of him; a remarkably fine, and no doubt a very valuable animal. How old do you suppose him to be?"

The sailor drew a long breath, with the air of a man relieved of some intolerable burden, and then replied, in an assured tone:

"I have no way of telling—but he can't be more than four or five years old. Have you got him here?"

"Oh, no; we had no conveniences for keeping him here. He is at a livery stable in the Rue Dubourg, just by. You can get him in the morning. Of course you are prepared to identify the property?"

"To be sure I am, sir."

"I shall be sorry to part with him," said Dupin.

"I don't mean that you should be at all this trouble for nothing, sir," said the man. "Couldn't expect it. Am very willing to pay a reward for the finding of the animal—that is to say, any thing in reason."

"Well," replied my friend, "that is all very fair, to be sure. Let me think!—what should I have? Oh! I will tell you. My reward shall be this. You shall give me all the information in your power about these murders in the Rue Morgue."

Dupin said the last words in a very low tone, and very quietly. Just as quietly, too, he walked toward the door, locked it, and put the key in his pocket. He then drew a pistol from his bosom and placed it, without the least flurry, upon the table.

The sailor's face flushed up as if he were struggling with suffocation. He started to his feet and grasped his cudgel; but the next moment he fell back into his seat, trembling violently, and with the countenance of death itself. He spoke not a word. I pitied him from the bottom of my heart.

"My friend," said Dupin, in a kind tone, "you are alarming yourself unnecessarily—you are indeed. We mean you no harm whatever. I pledge you the honor of a gentleman, and of a Frenchman, that we intend you no injury. I perfectly well know that you are innocent of the atrocities in the Rue Morgue. It will not do, however, to deny that you are in some measure implicated in them. From what I have already said, you must know that I have had means of information about this matter—means of which you could never have dreamed. Now the thing stands thus. You have done nothing which you could have avoided—nothing, certainly, which renders you culpable. You were not even guilty of robbery, when you might have robbed with impunity. You have nothing to conceal. You have no reason for concealment. On the other hand, you are bound by every principle of honor to confess all you know. An innocent man is now imprisoned, charged with that crime of which you can point out the perpetrator."

The sailor had recovered his presence of mind, in a great measure, while Dupin uttered these words; but his original boldness of bearing was all gone.

"So help me God!" said he, after a brief pause, "I *will* tell you all I know about this affair;—but I do not expect you to believe one half I say—I would be a fool indeed if I did. Still, I *am* innocent, and I will make a clean breast if I die for it."

What he stated was, in substance, this. He had lately made

a voyage to the Indian Archipelago. A party, of which he formed one, landed at Borneo, and passed into the interior on an excursion of pleasure. Himself and a companion had captured the Ourang-Outang. This companion dying, the animal fell into his own exclusive possession. After great trouble, occasioned by the intractable ferocity of his captive during the home voyage, he at length succeeded in lodging it safely at his own residence in Paris, where, not to attract toward himself the unpleasant curiosity of his neighbors, he kept it carefully secluded, until such time as it should recover from a wound in the foot, received from a splinter on board ship. His ultimate design was to sell it.

Returning home from some sailors' frolic on the night, or rather in the morning, of the murder, he found the beast occupying his own bedroom, into which it had broken from a closet adjoining, where it had been, as was thought, securely confined. Razor in hand, and fully lathered, it was sitting before a looking-glass, attempting the operation of shaving, in which it had no doubt previously watched its master through the keyhole of the closet. Terrified at the sight of so dangerous a weapon in the possession of an animal so ferocious, and so well able to use it, the man, for some moment, was at a loss what to do. He had been accustomed, however, to quiet the creature, even in its fiercest moods, by the use of a whip, and to this he now resorted. Upon sight of it, the Ourang-Outang sprang at once through the door of the chamber, down the stairs, and thence, through a window, unfortunately open, into the street.

The Frenchman followed in despair; the ape, razor still in hand, occasionally stopping to look back and gesticulate at his pursuer, until the latter had nearly come up with it. It then again made off. In this manner the chase continued for a long time. The streets were profoundly quiet, as it was nearly three o'clock in the morning. In passing down an alley in the rear of the Rue Morgue, the fugitive's attention was arrested by a light gleaming from the open window of Madame L'Espanaye's chamber, in the fourth story of her house. Rushing to the building, it perceived the lightning-rod, clambered up with inconceivable agility, grasped the shutter, which was thrown fully back against the wall, and, by its means, swung itself directly upon the headboard of the bed. The whole feat did not occupy a minute. The shutter was kicked open again by the Ourang-Outang as it entered the room.

The sailor, in the meantime, was both rejoiced and perplexed. He had strong hopes of now recapturing the brute, as it could scarcely escape from the trap into which it had ventured, except by the rod, where it might be intercepted as it came down. On the other hand, there was much cause for anxiety as to what it might do in the house. This latter reflection urged the man still to follow the fugitive. A lightning-rod is ascended without difficulty, especially by a sailor; but, when he had arrived as high as the window, which lay far to his left, his career was stopped; the most that he could accomplish was to reach over so as to obtain a glimpse of the interior of the room. At this glimpse he nearly fell from his hold through excess of horror. Now it was that those hideous shrieks arose upon the night, which had startled from slumber the inmates of the Rue Morgue. Madame L'Espanaye and her daughter, habited in their night clothes, had apparently been occupied in arranging some papers in the iron chest already mentioned, which had been wheeled into the middle of the room. It was open, and its contents lay beside it on the floor. The victims must have been sitting with their backs toward the window; and, from the time elapsing between the ingress of the beast and the screams, it seems probable that it was not immediately perceived. The flapping-to of the shutter would naturally have been attributed to the wind.

As the sailor looked in, the gigantic animal had seized Madame L'Espanaye by the hair (which was loose, as she had been combing it), and was flourishing the razor about her face, in imitation of the motions of a barber. The daughter lay prostrate and motionless; she had swooned. The screams and struggles of the old lady (during which the hair was torn from her head) had the effect of changing the

probably pacific purposes of the Ourang-Outang into those
of wrath. With one determined sweep of its muscular arm
it nearly severed her head from her body. The sight of blood
inflamed its anger into phrensy. Gnashing its teeth, and
flashing fire from its eyes, it flew upon the body of the girl,
and imbedded its fearful talons in her throat, retaining its
grasp until she expired. Its wandering and wild glances fell
at this moment upon the head of the bed, over which the
face of its master, rigid with horror, was just discernible.
The fury of the beast, who no doubt bore still in mind the
dreaded whip, was instantly converted into fear. Conscious
of having deserved punishment, it seemed desirous of concealing its bloody deeds, and skipped about the chamber in
an agony of nervous agitation; throwing down and breaking the furniture as it moved, and dragging the bed from the
bedstead. In conclusion, it seized first the corpse of the
daughter, and thrust it up the chimney, as it was found;
then that of the old lady, which it immediately hurled
through the window headlong.

As the ape approached the casement with its mutilated
burden, the sailor shrank aghast to the rod, and, rather
gliding than clambering down it, hurried at once home—
dreading the consequences of the butchery, and gladly
abandoning, in his terror, all solicitude about the fate of the
Ourang-Outang. The words heard by the party upon the
staircase were the Frenchman's exclamations of horror and
affright, commingled with the fiendish jabberings of the
brute.

I have scarcely any thing to add. The Ourang-Outang
must have escaped from the chamber, by the rod, just before
the breaking of the door. It must have closed the window as
it passed through it. It was subsequently caught by the owner himself, who obtained for it a very large sum at the
Jardin des Plantes. Le Bon was instantly released, upon our
narration of the circumstances (with some comments from
Dupin) at the *bureau* of the Prefect of Police. This func-
tionary, however, well disposed to my friend, could not altogether conceal his chagrin at the turn which affairs had

taken, and was fain to indulge in a sarcasm or two about the propriety of every person minding his own business.

"Let him talk," said Dupin, who had not thought it necessary to reply. "Let him discourse; it will ease his conscience. I am satisfied with having defeated him in his own castle. Nevertheless, that he failed in the solution of this mystery, is by no means that matter for wonder which he supposes it; for, in truth, our friend the Prefect is somewhat too cunning to be profound. In his wisdom is no *stamen*. It is all head and no body, like the pictures of the Goddess Laverna—or, at best, all head and shoulders, like a codfish. But he is a good creature after all. I like him especially for one master stroke of cant, by which he has attained his reputation for ingenuity. I mean the way he has *'de nier ce qui est, et d'expliquer ce qui n'est pas.'* "[1]

[1] Rousseau—*Nouvelle Héloise.*

A DISAPPEARANCE
by Emile Gaboriau

I

NOT LONG AGO, WE MIGHT AS WELL SAY YESTERDAY, ON A
Sunday, about four o'clock in the afternoon, the entire
Marais quarter was in a commotion.

People were telling that one of the most respectable business men of the Rue du Roi-de-Sicile had disappeared and
that all researches undertaken to find him had remained un-
successful.

In all the shops of the neighborhood this strange event
was being discussed; groups had gathered at the door of
every fruit-seller; every moment some housewife arrived
who, frightened, brought some new details.

The grocer on the corner, on that day, had the best and
latest news, as also the most exact, as he had it from the
very mouth of the cook of the house.

"Well," he was saying, "it was last evening after dinner;
M. Jandidier, our neighbor, went down in his cellar to get a
bottle of wine, and he has not been seen since; he disappeared, vanished, evaporated."

It happens from time to time that one hears of mysterious
disappearances; the public gets excited, and prudent people
buy sword-canes.

The police hear of these ridiculous rumors and shrug
their shoulders. This because they are acquainted with the
other side of these nicely embroidered canvases. They
search, and, instead of artless falsehoods, find the truth;
instead of novels, sad stories.

However, up to a certain point, the grocer in the Rue
Saint Louis was telling the truth.

M. Jandidier, manufacturer of imitation jewelry, had in fact not reappeared at his home after almost twenty-four hours.

M. Theodore Jandidier was a man of fifty-eight years, very tall, very bald, of passably good manners, who had made considerable money in business. He had put aside, they said, about twenty thousand francs income, in stocks or bonds, and his business yielded him, one year with another, fifty thousand francs. In his quarter he was loved and respected, and rightly so; his honesty was above suspicion, his morals severe. Married late in life to one of his poor relatives, he had made her perfectly happy. He had an only daughter, pretty and graceful, named Therese, whom he adored. She was to marry M. Gustave, the oldest son of the Banker Schmidt, of the firm of Schmidt, Gugenheim & Worb; but that engagement was broken, without anybody ever knowing why, for the young people loved one another desperately. The acquaintances of the Jandidiers claimed that old father Schmidt, who, as everybody knows, was meanly avaricious, had exacted a dowry much higher than the merchant's means could afford.

Informed by public rumors which were increasing from hour to hour, the police commissary had to go to the domicile of the already so-called victim, for the purpose of obtaining exact information on the subject.

He found Madame and Mademoiselle Jandidier immersed in such grief that it was with great trouble that he succeeded in gathering the truth.

This is what he finally learned:

The evening before, a Saturday, M. Jandidier had dined as customary with his family, however, without much appetite, having, as he told them, a very violent headache.

After dinner he had gone down to his store, had given some orders, and had seated himself at his desk.

At half-past six he had come up again and had told his wife that he was going to take a walk.

He had not reappeared.

After having carefully noted these details, the commissary asked Madame Jandidier to be allowed to speak to her alone for a few minutes. She assented with a nod; Mademoiselle Therese left the room.

"You will pardon me, madame," then said the police commissary, "the question which I am going to ask you. Do you know whether your husband had not outside of his home—again I ask you to excuse me—any lady friend?"

Madame Jandidier stood up at once, anger drying her tears.

"It is twenty-three years, monsieur, that I am married; my husband was always home at ten o'clock."

"Had your husband, madame," he continued, "the habit of going to some club, to some cafe?"

"Never; I would not have allowed it."

"Did he usually carry any bills or securities about him?"

"I do not know; I occupied myself with my household and not with business."

It was impossible to obtain any other information from this haughty woman of the middle class, who was distracted by grief.

His duty done, the commissary thought best to address to the poor woman a few every-day words of consolation.

But when he left, after having made an inquest in the house, he was very uneasy, and was beginning to suspect a crime.

That same evening the office of the Public Prosecutor took charge of the case, and one of the ablest police detectives, Retiveau, better known in the Rue de Jerusalem under the name of Magloire, was rushed on the trail of M. Jandidier, provided with an excellent photograph of the merchant.

II

THE VERY NEXT DAY FOLLOWING THE ONE ON WHICH M. Jandidier had disappeared, Magloire called at the Palais de Justice to report his achievements to the judge in charge of the investigation of the case.

"You are here, Monsieur Magloire," said the magistrate; "you must have found something?"

"I am on the trail, monsieur."

"Speak!"

"To begin, monsieur, it was not at half-past six that M. Jandidier left his house, but at exactly seven o'clock."

"Correct!"

"Perfectly. I obtained this information from a watchmaker in the Rue Saint Denis, who is certain of it, because, passing in front of his store, M. Jandidier pulled out his watch to compare it with the dial over the entrance. He had in his mouth an unlit cigar. Hearing of this circumstance, I said to myself: I have him! He will certainly light his cigar somewhere. I reasoned correctly. He entered to light it in the store of a woman tobacco dealer on the Boulevard du Temple, who knows him well. What makes this woman's memory certain is, that he, who always smokes one-sou cigars, bought some of the size they call Londres."

"Was there anything unusual about his appearance?"

"He looked as if he was worried, the dealer told me. Through her I found out that he often patronized the Turkish Cafe. I went there and they were positive that they saw him there Saturday evening. He drank two glasses of liqueur and conversed with some friends. He looked sad. These gentlemen, the waiter told me, talked the whole time about life insurance. At half-past eight our man left the cafe with one of his friends, M. Blandureau, a merchant living in the same quarter. Immediately I went to see this gentleman, who answered me that he had walked up the boulevard with M. Jandidier, and that the latter left him at the corner of the Rue Richelieu, saying that he had to look after some business. He seemed to be out of sorts and besieged by the worst presentiments."

"Very good up to here!" murmured the judge.

"After leaving M. Blandureau, I went to the Rue du Roi-de-Sicile, to find out from somebody in the house if M. Jandidier did not have any customers, friends, or a mistress;

only his tailor lives in the Rue Richelieu. At all events, I went to see this tailor. He had seen our man on Saturday. M. Jandidier had come up to see him after nine o'clock, to order a pair of trousers. While his measure was being taken, he had noticed that one of the buttons of his waistcoat was very loose, and asked that it be sewed on. For this little repairing he had to take off his coat, and as at the same time he had taken out all there was in his side pocket, the tailor noticed several hundred-franc bank-notes."

"Ah! there we have a clue! He had a very considerable sum of money with him!"

"Very considerable, no; but quite a large one. The tailor estimates it at from twelve to fourteen hundred francs."

"Continue," said the investigating judge.

"While they were repairing his waistcoat, M. Jandidier complained of a sudden illness, and sent a little boy, who was there, to get a carriage. He had to go, he said, to see one of his workmen who lived very far, near the wine market. Unfortunately the little fellow had forgotten the number of the carriage. All he remembered was, that it had yellow wheels and a big black horse. That was easy to find. A circular sent to all livery stables put me again on the trail. I found out this morning that the carriage was No. 6007. The driver, who was examined, remembers very well to have been stopped by a little boy Saturday evening toward nine o'clock in the Rue Richelieu, and to have waited for ten minutes in front of the Gouin House. The description of the citizen who took him is that of our man, and he recognized the photograph among five others which I showed him."

M. Magloire stopped. He wanted to enjoy the approving satisfaction which he was reading on the magistrate's face.

"M. Jandidier," he continued, "had him drive to 48 Rue d'Arras-Saint Victor, near the wine market. In that house lives a workman who works for M. Jandidier, a man called Jules Tarot."

The manner in which Magloire pronounced this name could hardly fail to arouse, and did arouse, the attention of the judge.

"You have suspicions?" he asked.

"Not exactly, but here is what happened. M. Jandidier dismissed his carriage in the Rue d'Arras and went up to Tarot's at about ten o'clock. At eleven the employer and the workman went out together.

The workman did not return home until midnight, and it is here that I lost my man's trail. It goes without saying that I did not examine Tarot, fearing to put him on his guard."

"Who is this Jules Tarot?"

"A worker of mother-of-pearl, that is, one who polishes shells with sandstone to give them a perfect iridescence. He is a capable fellow, who is assisted by his wife, whom he has taught his trade; he is able to earn as much as a hundred francs a week."

"Then they are well-to-do working people?"

"Not at all! They are both young, they have no children, they are Parisians, and well! they amuse themselves. Monday regularly does away with all that is earned in the other days."

III

TWO HOURS AFTER MONSIEUR MAGLOIRE HAD MADE HIS report, the police appeared at Jules Tarot's house to make a strict search.

At the sight of the officers, the mother-of-pearl workman and his wife became as pale as death, and had an attack of nervous trembling, which could not escape Magloire's experienced eye. However, in spite of the most minute researches, nothing whatever suspicious could be found, and the police were just going to leave, when the officer caught the Tarot woman in the act of anxiously looking at a cage, which hung near the window.

This was like a flash of light. In no time Magloire had unhooked the cage and taken it apart. Between two boards at the bottom he found twelve one-hundred-franc notes.

This discovery seemed to astound the workman. As to his wife, she began to scream terribly, insisting that she and her husband were innocent.

Arrested and taken to prison, they were examined the same day by the investigating judge. Their answers were absolutely identical.

They admitted that on Saturday evening their employer called on them. He seemed to be feeling so ill that they asked him to take something, which he had refused. He had come, he told them, to see them about an important order, and to propose to Tarot that he alone should take charge of it, engaging the necessary workmen. Tarot and his wife answered that they could not do it, owing to lack of money which would have to be advanced.

Their employer then said to them: "Never mind that, I will furnish you the money." And immediately he had laid on the table twelve one-hundred-franc bills.

At eleven o'clock M. Jandidier asked his workman to go with him; he had to go, he said, to the Saint-Antoine suburb. As a matter of fact, Tarot had accompanied him as far as the Bastille Square, crossing the Constantine footbridge and walking along the canal.

The examining judge asked both the husband and the wife this perfectly natural question:

"Why did you hide the money?"

Both gave the same answer.

On Monday morning, having heard of M. Jandidier's disappearance, they were seized with fright. Tarot said to his wife:

"If it is known that the boss was here, that I crossed the footbridge, and went along the bank of the canal with him, I'll be compromised. If ever this money is found in our possession, we are lost."

The woman then wanted to burn the bills, but Tarot would not allow it, intending to return them later to the family.

This explanation was reasonable and plausible, if not probable, but it was nothing but an explanation. Tarot and his wife remained under arrest.

IV

A WEEK LATER THE INVESTIGATING JUDGE WAS IN THE
greatest perplexity. Three new examinations had not convinced him.

As for Tarot and his wife, were they innocent? Had they
simply arranged with each other how to sustain a probable
fable?

The magistrate was in a quandary as to what to do, when
one morning a strange rumor reached him. The Jandidier
firm had just suspended payments. An officer, sent out to see
about it, brought back the most peculiar information.

M. Jandidier, who was believed to be quite rich, was
ruined, absolutely ruined, and for the past three years had
maintained his credit only by means of expedients. Not a
thousand francs were found at his place, and his bills due
at the end of the month amounted to sixty-seven thousand
five hundred francs.

The stern merchant had been speculating in stocks; the
virtuous husband had had a mistress.

The judge in charge of the investigation had just been informed of these details, when Monsieur Magloire appeared,
pale. all out of breath.

"You know, monsieur!" he exclaimed when he was still
on the threshold.

"Everything."

"Tarot is innocent!"

"I believe so; however, that call—how can you explain
that call?"

Magloire sadly shook his head.

"I am nothing but an idiot," he said, "and Lecoq just
proved it to me. At the Turkish Cafe, M. Jandidier had been
talking of life insurance. There was the clue to the case. Jandidier's life was insured for two hundred thousand francs,
and in France the companies do not pay in the case of a
suicide; does your honor understand?"

V

THANKS TO M. GUSTAVE SCHMIDT, WHO NEXT MONTH WILL marry Mademoiselle Therese Jandidier, the firm of Jandidier was not declared in bankruptcy.

Tarot and his wife, set free again, were assisted in establishing themselves by the same M. Gustave, and do not fear blue Monday any longer.

But what became of M. Jandidier? A reward of one thousand francs will be paid to whosoever will bring news of him.

A DIFFICULT PROBLEM
by Anna Katherine Green

I

"A LADY TO SEE YOU, SIR"

I looked up and was at once impressed by the grace and beauty of the person thus introduced to me.

"Is there anything I can do to serve you?" I asked, rising.

She cast me a child-like look full of trust and candor as she seated herself in the chair I pointed out to her.

"I believe so, I hope so," she earnestly assured me. "I—I am in great trouble. I have just lost my husband—but it is not that. It is the slip of paper I found on my dresser, and which—which—"

She was trembling violently and her words were fast becoming incoherent. I calmed her and asked her to relate her story just as it had happened; and after a few minutes of silent struggle she succeeded in collecting herself sufficiently to respond with some degree of connection and self-possession.

"I have been married six months. My name is Lucy Holmes. For the last few weeks my husband and myself have been living in an apartment house on Fifty-ninth Street, and as we had not a care in the world, we were very happy till Mr. Holmes was called away on business to Philadelphia. This was two weeks ago. Five days later I received an affectionate letter from him, in which he promised to come back the next day; and the news so delighted me that I accepted an invitation to the theater from some intimate friends of ours. The next morning I naturally felt fatigued and rose late; but I was very cheerful, for I expected my husband at noon. And now comes the perplexing mystery.

In the course of dressing myself I stepped to my bureau, and seeing a small newspaper-slip attached to the cushion by a pin, I drew it off and read it. It was a death notice, and my hair rose and my limbs failed me as I took in its fatal and incredible words.

" 'Died this day at the Colonnade, James Forsythe De Witt Holmes. New York Papers please copy.'

"James Forsythe De Witt Holmes was my husband, and his last letter, which was at that very moment lying beside the cushion, had been dated from the Colonnade. Was I dreaming or under the spell of some frightful hallucination which led me to misread the name on the slip of paper before me? I could not determine. My head, throat and chest seemed bound about with iron, so that I could neither speak nor breathe with freedom, and, suffering thus, I stood staring at this demoniacal bit of paper which in an instant had brought the shadow of death upon my happy life. Nor was I at all relieved when a little later I flew with the notice into a neighbor's apartment, and praying her to read it for me, found that my eyes had not deceived me and that the name was indeed my husband's and the notice one of death.

"Not from my own mind but from hers came the first suggestion of comfort.

" 'It cannot be your husband who is meant,' said she; 'but some one of the same name. Your husband wrote to you yesterday, and this person must have been dead at least two days for the printed notice of his decease to have reached New York. Some one has remarked the striking similarity of names, and wishing to startle you, cut the slip out and pinned it on your cushion.'

"I certainly knew of no one inconsiderate enough to do this, but the explanation was so plausible, I at once embraced it and sobbed aloud in my relief. But in the midst of my rejoicing I heard the bell ring in my apartment, and running thither, encountered a telegraph boy holding in his outstretched hand the yellow envelope which so often bespeaks death or disaster. The sight took my breath away. Summoning my maid, whom I saw hastening towards me from an inner room, I begged her to open the telegram for me. Sir, I saw in her face, before she had read the first line, a confirmation of my worst fears. My husband was—"

The young widow, choked with her emotions, paused, recovered herself for the second time, and then went on.

"I had better show you the telegram."

Taking it from her pocket-book, she held it towards me. I read it at a glance. It was short, simple and direct.

"Come at once. Your husband found dead in his room this morning. Doctors say heart disease. Please telegraph."

"You see it says this morning," she explained, placing her delicate finger on the word she so eagerly quoted. "That means a week ago Wednesday, the same day on which the printed slip recording his death was found on my cushion. Do you not see something very strange in this?"

I did; but, before I ventured to express myself on this subject, I desired her to tell me what she had learned in her visit to Philadelphia.

Her answer was simple and straightforward.

"But little more than you find in this telegram. He died in his room. He was found lying on the floor near the bell button, which he had evidently risen to touch. One hand was clenched on his chest, but his face wore a peaceful look as if death had come too suddenly to cause him much suffering. His bed was undisturbed; he had died before retiring, possibly in the act of packing his trunk, for it was found nearly ready for the expressman. Indeed, there was every evidence of his intention to leave on an early morning train. He had even desired to be awakened at six o'clock: and it was his failure to respond to the summons of the bell-boy, which led to so early a discovery of his death. He had never complained of any distress in breathing, and we had always considered him a perfectly healthy man; but there was no reason for assigning any other cause than heart-failure to his sudden death, and so the burial certificate was made out to that effect, and I was allowed to bring him home and bury him in our vault at Woodlawn. But—" and here her earnestness dried up the tears which had been flowing freely during this recital of her husband's lonely death and sad burial,—"do you not think an investigation should be made into a death preceded by a false obituary notice? For I found when I was in Philadelphia that no paragraph such as I had found pinned to my cushion had been inserted in any paper there, nor had any other man of the same name ever registered at the Colonnade, much less died there."

"Have you this notice with you?" I asked.

She immediately produced it, and while I was glancing it over remarked:

"Some persons would give a superstitious explanation to the whole matter; think I had received a supernatural warning and been satisfied with what they would call a spiritual manifestation. But I have not a bit of such folly in my composition. Living hands set up the type and printed the words which gave me so deathly a shock; and hands, with a real purpose in them, cut it from the paper and pinned it to my cushion for me to see when I woke on that fatal morning. But whose hands? That is what I want you to discover."

I had caught the fever of her suspicions long before this and now felt justified in showing my interest.

"First, let me ask," said I, "who has access to your rooms besides your maid?"

"No one; absolutely no one."

"And what of her?"

"She is innocence itself. She is no common housemaid, but a girl my mother brought up, who for love of me consents to do such work in the household as my simple needs require."

"I should like to see her."

"There is no objection to your doing so; but you will gain nothing by it. I have already talked the subject over with her a dozen times and she is as much puzzled by it as

I am myself. She says she cannot see how any one could
have found an entrance to my room during my sleep, as the
doors were all locked. Yet, as she very naturally observes,
some one must have done so, for she was in my bedroom
herself just before I returned from the theater, and can
swear, if necessary, that no such slip of paper was to be
seen on my cushion, at that time, for her duties led her
directly to my bureau and kept her there for full five minutes."

"And you believed her?" I suggested.

"Implicitly."

"In what direction, then, do your suspicions turn?"

"Alas! in no direction. That is the trouble. I don't know
whom to mistrust. It was because I was told that you had
the credit of seeing light where others can see nothing but
darkness, but I have sought your aid in this emergency. For
the uncertainty surrounding this matter is killing me and
will make my sorrow quite unendurable if I cannot obtain relief from it."

"I do not wonder," I began, struck by the note of truth
in her tones. "And I shall certainly do what I can for you.
But before we go any further, let us examine this scrap of
newspaper and see what we can make out of it."

I had already noted two or three points in connection
with it, to which I now proceeded to direct her attention.

"Have you compared this notice," I pursued, "with such
others as you find every day in the papers?"

"No," was her eager answer. "Is it not like them all—"

"Read," was my quiet interruption. " 'On this day at the
Colonnade—' On what day? The date is usually given in
all the *bona-fide* notices I have seen."

"Is it?" she asked, her eyes moist with unshed tears, opening widely in her astonishment.

"Look in the papers on your return home and see. Then
the print. Observe that the type is identical on both sides of
this make-believe clipping, while in fact there is always a
perceptible difference between that used in the obituary
column and that to be found in the columns devoted to

other matter. Notice also," I continued, holding up the scrap of paper between her and the light, "that the alignment on one side is not exactly parallel with that on the other; a discrepancy which would not exist if both sides had been printed on a newspaper press. These facts lead me to conclude, first, that the effort to match the type exactly was the mistake of a man who tries to do too much; and secondly, that one of the sides at least, presumably that containing the obituary notice, was printed on a handpress, on the blank side of a piece of galley proof picked up in some newspaper office."

"Let me see." And stretching out her hand with the utmost eagerness, she took the slip and turned it over. Instantly a change took place in her countenance. She sank back in her seat and a blush of manifest confusion suffused her cheeks. "Oh!" she exclaimed, "what will you think of me! I brought this scrap of print into the house *myself*, and it was *I* who pinned it on the cushion with my own hands! I remember it now. The sight of those words recalls the whole occurrence."

"Then there is one mystery less for us to solve," I remarked, somewhat dryly.

"Do you think so," she protested, with a deprecatory look. "For me the mystery deepens, and becomes every minute more serious. It is true that I brought this scrap of newspaper into the house, and that it had, then as now, the notice of my husband's death upon it, but the time of my bringing it in was Tuesday night, and he was not found dead till Wednesday morning."

"A discrepancy worth noting," I remarked.

"Involving a mystery of some importance," she concluded.

I agreed to that.

"And since we have discovered how the slip came into your room, we can now proceed to the clearing up of this mystery," I observed. "You can, of course, inform me where you procured this clipping which you say you brought into the house?"

"Yes. You may think it strange, but when I alighted from the carriage that night, a man on the sidewalk put this tiny scrap of paper into my hand. It was done so mechanically that it made no more impression on my mind than the thrusting of an advertisement upon me. Indeed, I supposed it was an advertisement, and I only wonder that I retained it in my hand at all. But that I did do so, and that, in a moment of abstraction I went so far as to pin it to my cushion, is evident from the fact that a vague memory remains in my mind of having read this recipe which you see printed on the reverse side of the paper."

"It was the recipe, then, and not the obituary notice which attracted your attention the night before?"

"Probably, but in pinning it to the cushion, it was the obituary notice that chanced to come uppermost. Oh, why should I not have remembered this till now! Can you understand my forgetting a matter of so much importance?"

"Yes," I allowed, after a momentary consideration of her ingenuous countenance. "The words you read in the morning were so startling that they disconnected themselves from those you had carelessly glanced at the night before."

"That is it," she replied; "and since then I have had eyes for the one side only. How could I think of the other? But who could have printed this thing and who was the man who put it into my hand? He looked like a beggar but— Oh!" she suddenly exclaimed, her cheeks flushing scarlet and her eyes flashing with a feverish, almost alarming, glitter.

"What is it now?" I asked. "Another recollection?"

"Yes." She spoke so low I could hardly hear her. "He coughed and—"

"And what?" I encouragingly suggested, seeing that she was under some new and overwhelming emotion.

"That cough had a familiar sound, now that I think of it. It was like that of a friend who—But no, no; I will not wrong him by any false surmises. He would stoop to much, but not to that; yet—"

The flush on her cheeks had died away, but the two vivid spots which remained showed the depth of her excitement.

"Do you think," she suddenly asked, "that a man out of revenge might plan to frighten me by a false notice of my husband's death, and that God to punish him, made the notice a prophecy?"

"I think a man influenced by the spirit of revenge might do almost anything," I answered, purposely ignoring the latter part of her question.

"But I always considered him a good man. At least I never looked upon him as a wicked one. Every other beggar we meet has a cough; and yet," she added after a moment's pause, "if it was not he who gave me this mortal shock, who was it? He is the only person in the world I ever wronged."

"Had you not better tell me his name?" I suggested.

"No, I am in too great doubt. I should hate to do him a second injury."

"You cannot injure him if he is innocent. My methods are very safe."

"If I could forget his cough! but it had that peculiar catch in it that I remembered so well in the cough of John Graham. I did not pay any especial heed to it at the time. Old days and old troubles were far enough from my thoughts; but now that my suspicions are raised, that low, choking sound comes back to me in a strangely persistent way, and I seem to see a well-remembered form in the stooping figure of this beggar. Oh, I hope the good God will forgive me if I attribute to this disappointed man a wickedness he never committed."

"Who is John Graham?" I urged, "and what was the nature of the wrong you did him?"

She rose, cast me one appealing glance, and perceiving that I meant to have her whole story, turned towards the fire and stood warming her feet before the hearth, with her face turned away from my gaze.

"I was once engaged to marry him," she began. "Not because I loved him, but because we were very poor—I mean my mother and myself—and he had a home and seemed both good and generous. The day came when we were to be married—this was in the West, way out in Kansas—and

I was even dressed for the wedding, when a letter came
from my uncle here, a rich uncle, very rich, who had never
had anything to do with my mother since her marriage, and
in it he promised me fortune and everything else desirable
in life if I would come to him, unencumbered by any foolish ties. Think of it! And I within half an hour of marriage
with a man I had never loved and now suddenly hated. The
temptation was overwhelming, and heartless as my conduct
may appear to you, I succumbed to it. Telling my lover that
I had changed my mind, I dismissed the minister when he
came, and announced my intention of proceeding East as
soon as possible. Mr. Graham was simply paralyzed by his
disappointment, and during the few days which intervened
before my departure, I was haunted by his face, which was
like that of a man who had died from some overwhelming
shock. But when I was once free of the town, especially after
I arrived in New York, I forgot alike his misery and himself. Everything I saw was so beautiful! Life was so full of
charm, and my uncle so delighted with me and everything
I did! Then there was James Holmes, and after I had seen
him—But I cannot talk of that. We loved each other, and
under the surprise of this new delight how could I be expected to remember the man I had left behind me in that
barren region in which I had spent my youth? But he did
not forget the misery I had caused him. He followed me to
New York: and on the morning I was married found his
way into the house, and mixing with the wedding guests,
suddenly appeared before me just as I was receiving the
congratulations of my friends. At sight of him I experienced
all the terror he had calculated upon causing, but remembering at whose side I stood, I managed to hide my confusion under an aspect of apparent haughtiness. This irritated John Graham. Flushing with anger, and ignoring my
imploring look, he cried peremptorily, 'Present me to your
husband!' and I felt forced to present him. But his name
produced no effect upon Mr. Holmes. I had never told him
of my early experience with this man, and John Graham,
perceiving this, cast me a bitter glance of disdain and passed

on, muttering between his teeth, 'False to me and false to him! Your punishment be upon you!' and I felt as if I had been cursed."

She stopped here, moved by emotions readily to be understood. Then with quick impetuosity she caught up the thread of her story and went on.

"That was six months ago; and again I forgot. My mother died and my husband soon absorbed my every thought. How could I dream that this man, who was little more than a memory to me and scarcely that, was secretly planning mischief against me? Yet this scrap about which we have talked so much may have been the work of his hands; and even my husband's death—"

She did not finish, but her face, which was turned towards me, spoke volumes.

"Your husband's death shall be inquired into," I assured her. And she, exhausted by the excitement of her discoveries, asked that she might be excused from further discussion of the subject at that time.

As I had no wish, myself, to enter any more fully into the matter just then, I readily acceded to her request, and the pretty widow left me.

II

OBVIOUSLY THE FIRST FACT TO BE SETTLED WAS WHETHER Mr. Holmes had died from purely natural causes. I accordingly busied myself the next few days with this question, and was fortunate enough to so interest the proper authorities that an order was issued for the exhumation and examination of the body.

The result was disappointing. No traces of poison were to be found in the stomach nor was there to be seen on the body any mark of violence, with the exception of a minute prick upon one of his thumbs.

This speck was so small that it escaped every eye but my own.

The authorities assuring the widow that the doctor's certificate given her in Philadelphia was correct, he was again interred. But I was not satisfied; neither do I think she was. I was confident that his death was not a natural one, and entered upon one of those secret and prolonged investigations which have constituted the pleasure of my life for so many years. First, I visited the Colonnade in Philadelphia, and being allowed to see the room in which Mr. Holmes died, went through it carefully. As it had not been used since that time, I had some hopes of coming upon a clue.

But it was a vain hope and the only result of my journey to this place was the assurance I received that the gentleman had spent the entire evening preceding his death, in his own room, where he had been brought several letters and one small package, the latter coming by mail. With this one point gained—if it was a point—I went back to New York.

Calling on Mrs. Holmes, I asked her if, while her husband was away she had sent him anything besides letters, and upon her replying to the contrary, requested to know if in her visit to Philadelphia she had noted among her husband's effects anything that was new or unfamiliar to her. "For he received a package while there," I explained, "and though its contents may have been perfectly harmless, it is just as well for us to be assured of this, before going any further."

"Oh, you think, then, he was really the victim of some secret violence."

"We have no proof of it," I said. "On the contrary, we are assured that he died from natural causes. But the incident of the newspaper slip outweighs, in my mind, the doctor's conclusions, and until the mystery surrounding that obituary notice has been satisfactorily explained by its author, I shall hold to the theory that your husband has been made away with in some strange and seeming unaccountable manner, which it is our duty to bring to light."

"You are right! You are right! Oh, John Graham!"

She was so carried away by this plain expression of my

belief that she forgot the question I had put to her.

"You have not told whether or not you found anything among your husband's effects that can explain this mystery," I suggested.

She at once became attentive.

"Nothing," said she: "his trunks were already packed and his bag nearly so. There were a few things lying about the room which were put into the latter, but I saw nothing but what was familiar to me among them; at least, I think not; perhaps we had better look through his trunk and see. I have not had the heart to open it since I came back."

As this was exactly what I wished, I said as much, and she led me into a small room, against the wall of which stood a trunk with a traveling-bag on top of it. Opening the latter, she spread the contents out on the trunk.

"I know all these things," she sadly murmured, the tears welling in her eyes.

"This?" I inquired, lifting up a bit of coiled wire with two or three little rings dangling from it.

"No; why, what is that?"

"It looks like a puzzle of some kind."

"Then it is of no consequence. My husband was forever amusing himself over some such contrivance. All his friends knew how well he liked these toys and frequently sent them to him. This one evidently reached him in Philadelphia."

Meanwhile I was eyeing the bit of wire curiously. It was undoubtedly a puzzle, but it had appendages to it that I did not understand.

"It is more than ordinarily complicated," I observed, moving the rings up and down in a vain endeavor to work them off.

"The better he would like it," said she.

I kept on working with the rings. Suddenly I gave a painful start. A little prong in the handle of the toy had started out and pricked me.

"You had better not handle it," said I, and laid it down. But the next minute I took it up again and put it in my pocket. The prick made by this treacherous bit of mechanism was in or near the same place on my thumb as the one I had noticed on the hand of the deceased Mr. Holmes.

There was a fire in the room, and before proceeding further, I cauterized that prick with the end of a red-hot poker. Then I made my adieux to Mrs. Holmes and went immediately to a chemist friend of mine.

"Test the end of this bit of steel for me," said I. "I have reason to believe it carries with it a deadly poison."

He took the toy, promised to subject it to every test possible and let me know the result. Then I went home. I felt ill, or imagined that I did, which under the circumstances was almost as bad.

Next day, however, I was quite well, with the exception of a certain inconvenience in my thumb. But not till the following week did I receive the chemist's report. It overthrew my whole theory. He had found nothing, and returned me the bit of steel.

But I was not convinced.

"I will hunt up this John Graham," thought I, "and study him."

But this was not so easy a task as it may appear. As Mrs. Holmes possessed no clue to the whereabouts of her quondam lover, I had nothing to aid me in my search of him, save her rather vague description of his personal appearance and the fact that he was constantly interrupted in speaking by a low, choking cough. However, my natural perseverance carried me through. After seeing and interviewing a dozen John Grahams without result, I at last lit upon a man of that name who presented a figure of such vivid unrest and showed such desperate hatred of his fellows, that I began to entertain hopes of his being the person I was in search of. But determined to be sure of this before proceeding further, I confided my suspicions to Mrs. Holmes, and induced her to accompany me down to a certain spot on the "Elevated" from which I had more than once seen this man go by to his usual lounging place in Printing-house Square.

She showed great courage in doing this, for she had such

a dread of him that she was in a state of nervous excitement from the moment she left her house, feeling sure that she would attract his attention and thus risk a disagreeable encounter. But she might have spared herself these fears. He did not even glance up in passing us, and it was mainly by his walk she recognized him. But she did recognize him; and this nerved me at once to set about the formidable task of fixing upon him a crime which was not even admitted as a fact by the authorities.

He was a man-about-town, living, to all appearance, by his wits. He was to be seen mostly in the downtown portions of the city, standing for hours in front of some newspaper office, gnawing at his finger-ends, and staring at the passers-by with a hungry look that alarmed the timid and provoked alms from the benevolent. Needless to say that he rejected the latter expression of sympathy, with angry contempt.

His face was long and pallid, his cheek-bones high and his mouth bitter and resolute in expression. He wore neither beard nor mustache, but made up for their lack by an abundance of light brown hair, which hung very nearly to his shoulders. He stooped in standing, but as soon as he moved, showed decision and a certain sort of pride which caused him to hold his head high and his body more than usually erect. With all these good points his appearance was decidedly sinister, and I did not wonder that Mrs. Holmes feared him.

My next move was to accost him. Pausing before the doorway in which he stood, I addressed him some trivial question. He answered me with sufficient politeness, but with a grudging attention which betrayed the hold which his own thoughts had upon him. He coughed while speaking and his eye, which for a moment rested on mine, produced upon me an impression for which I was hardly prepared, great as was my prejudice against him. There was such an icy composure in it; the composure of an envenomed nature conscious of its superiority to all surprise. As I lingered to study him more closely, the many dangerous qualities of the man became more and more apparent to me; and convinced that to proceed further without deep and careful thought, would be to court failure where triumph would set me up for life, I gave up all present attempt at enlisting him in conversation, and went my way in an inquiring and serious mood.

In fact, my position was a peculiar one, and the problem I had set for myself one of unusual difficulty. Only by means of some extraordinary device such as is seldom resorted to by the police of this or any other nation, could I hope to arrive at the secret of this man's conduct, and triumph in a matter which to all appearance was beyond human penetration.

But what device? I knew of none, nor through two days and nights of strenuous thought did I receive the least light on the subject. Indeed, my mind seemed to grow more and more confused the more I urged it into action. I failed to get inspiration indoors or out; and feeling my health suffer from the constant irritation of my recurring disappointment, I resolved to take a day off and carry myself and my perplexities into the country.

I did so. Governed by an impulse which I did not then understand, I went to a small town in New Jersey and entered the first house on which I saw the sign "Room to Let." The result was most fortunate. No sooner had I crossed the threshold of the neat and homely apartment thrown open to my use, than it recalled a room in which I had slept two years before and in which I had read a little book I was only too glad to remember at this moment. Indeed, it seemed as if a veritable inspiration had come to me through this recollection, for though the tale to which I allude was a simple child's story written for moral purposes, it contained an idea which promised to be invaluable to me at this juncture. Indeed, by means of it, I believed myself to have solved the problem that was puzzling me, and relieved beyond expression, I paid for the night's lodging I had now determined to forego, and returned immediately to New York, having spent just fifteen minutes in the town where I had received this happy inspiration.

My first step on entering the city was to order a dozen steel coils made similar to the one which I still believed answerable for James Holmes' death. My next was to learn as far as possible all of John Graham's haunts and habits. At a week's end I had the springs and knew almost as well as he did himself where he was likely to be found at all times of the day and night. I immediately acted upon this knowledge. Assuming a slight disguise, I repeated my former stroll through Printing-house Square, looking into each doorway as I passed. John Graham was in one of them, staring in his old way at the passing crowd, but evidently seeing nothing but the images formed by his own disordered brain. A manuscript-roll stuck out of his breast-pocket, and from the way his nervous fingers fumbled with it, I began to understand the restless glitter of his eyes, which were as full of wretchedness as any eyes I have ever seen.

Entering the doorway where he stood, I dropped at his feet one of the small steel coils, with which I was provided. He did not see it. Stopping near him I directed his attention to it by saying:

"Pardon me, but did I not see something drop out of your hand?"

He started, glanced at the seeming inoffensive toy at which I pointed, and altered so suddenly and so vividly that it became instantly apparent that the surprise I had planned for him was fully as keen and searching a one as I had anticipated. Recoiling sharply, he gave me a quick look, then glanced down again at his feet as if half expecting to find the object vanished which had startled him. But, perceiving it still lying there, he crushed it viciously with his heel, and uttering some incoherent words, dashed impetuously from the building.

Confident that he would regret this hasty impulse and return, I withdrew a few steps and waited. And sure enough, in less than five minutes he came slinking back. Picking up the coil with more than one sly look about, he examined it closely. Suddenly he gave a sharp cry and went staggering out. Had he discovered that the seeming puzzle possessed the same invisible spring which had made the one handled by James Holmes so dangerous?

Certain as to the place he would be found in next, I made a short cut to an obscure little saloon in Nassau Street, where I took up my stand in a spot convenient for seeing without being seen. In ten minutes he was standing at the bar asking for a drink.

"Whiskey!" he cried, "straight."

It was given him; but as he set the empty glass down on the counter, he saw lying before him another of the steel springs, and was so confounded by the sight that the proprietor, who had put it there at my instigation, thrust out his hand toward him as if half afraid he would fall.

"Where did that—that *thing* come from?" stammered John Graham, ignoring the other's gesture and pointing with a trembling hand at the seemingly insignificant bit of wire between them.

"Didn't it drop from your coat-pocket?" inquired the proprietor. "It wasn't lying here before you came in."

With a horrible oath the unhappy man turned and fled from the place. I lost sight of him after that for three hours, then I suddenly came upon him again. He was walking up town with a set purpose in his face that made him look more dangerous than ever. Of course I followed him, expecting him to turn towards Fifty-ninth Street, but at the corner of Madison Avenue and Forty-seventh Street he changed his mind and dashed toward Third Avenue. At Park Avenue he faltered and again turned north, walking for several blocks as if the fiends were behind him. I began to think that he was but attempting to walk off his excitement, when, at a sudden rushing sound in the cut beside us, he stopped and trembled. An express train was shooting by. As it disappeared in the tunnel beyond, he looked about him with a blanched face and wandering eye; but his glance did not turn my way, or if it did, he failed to attach any meaning to my near presence.

He began to move on again and this time towards the bridge spanning the cut. I followed him very closely. In the center of it he paused and looked down at the track beneath him. Another train was approaching. As it came near he trembled from head to foot, and catching at the railing against which he leaned, was about to make a quick move forward when a puff of smoke arose from below and sent him staggering backward, gasping with a terror I could hardly understand till I saw that the smoke had taken the form of a spiral and was sailing away before him in what to his disordered imagination must have looked like a gigantic image of the coil with which twice before on this day he had found himself confronted.

It may have been chance and it may have been providence; but whichever it was it saved him. He could not face that semblance of his haunting thought; and turning away he cowered down on the neighboring curbstone, where he sat for several minutes, with his head buried in his hands; when he rose again he was his own daring and sinister self. Knowing that he was now too much master of his faculties to ignore me any longer, I walked quickly away and left him. I knew where he would be at six o'clock and had already engaged a table at the same restaurant. It was seven, however, before he put in an appearance, and by this time he was looking more composed. There was a reckless air about him, however, which was perhaps only noticeable to me; for none of the habitués of this especial restaurant were entirely without it; wild eyes and unkempt hair being in the majority.

I let him eat. The dinner he ordered was simple and I had not the heart to interrupt his enjoyment of it.

But when he had finished, and came to pay, then I allowed the shock to come. Under the bill which the waiter laid at the side of his plate was the inevitable steel coil; and it produced even more than its usual effect. I own I felt sorry for him.

He did not dash from the place, however, as he had from the liquor-saloon. A spirit of resistance had seized him and he demanded to know where this object of his fear had come from. No one could tell him (or would). Whereupon he began to rave and would certainly have done himself or somebody else an injury if he had not been calmed by a man almost as wild-looking as himself. Paying his bill, but vowing he would never enter the place again, he went out, clay-white, but with the swaggering air of a man who had just asserted himself.

He drooped, however, as soon as he reached the street, and I had no difficulty in following him to a certain gambling den where he gained three dollars and lost five. From there he went to his lodgings in West Tenth Street.

I did not follow him in. He had passed through many deep and wearing emotions since noon, and I had not the heart to add another to them.

But late the next day I returned to this house and rang the bell. It was already dusk, but there was light enough for me to notice the unrepaired condition of the iron railings on either side of the old stone stoop and to compare this abode of decayed grandeur with the spacious and elegant apartment in which pretty Mrs. Holmes mourned the loss of her young husband. Had any such comparison ever been made by the unhappy John Graham, as he hurried up these decayed steps into the dismal halls beyond?

In answer to my summons there came to the door a young woman to whom I had but to intimate my wish to see Mr. Graham for her to let me in with the short announcement:

"Top floor, back room! Door open, he's out; door shut, he's in."

As an open door meant liberty to enter, I lost no time in following the direction of her pointing finger, and presently found myself in a low attic chamber overlooking an acre of roofs. A fire had been lighted in the open grate, and the flickering red beams danced on ceiling and walls with a cheeriness greatly in contrast to the nature of the business which had led me there. As they also served to light the room I proceeded to make myself at home: and drawing up a chair, sat down at the fireplace in such a way as to conceal myself from any one entering the door.

In less than half an hour he came in.

He was in a state of high emotion. His face was flushed and his eyes burning. Stepping rapidly forward, he flung his hat on the table in the middle of the room, with a curse that was half cry and half groan. Then he stood silent and I had an opportunity of noting how haggard he had grown in the short time which had elapsed since I had seen him last. But the interval of his inaction was short, and in a moment he flung up his arms with a loud "Curse her!" that rang through the narrow room and betrayed the source of his present frenzy. Then he again stood still, grating his teeth and working his hands in a way terribly suggestive of the murderer's instinct. But not for long. He saw something that attracted his attention on the table, a something upon which my eyes had long before been fixed, and starting forward with a fresh and quite different display of emotion, he caught up what looked like a roll of manuscript and began to tear it open.

"Back again! Always back!" wailed from his lips; and he gave the roll a toss that sent from its midst a small object which he no sooner saw than he became speechless and reeled back. It was another of the steel coils.

"Good God!" fell at last from his stiff and working lips. "Am I mad or has the devil joined in the pursuit against me? I cannot eat, I cannot drink, but this diabolical spring starts up before me. It is here, there, everywhere. The visible sign of my guilt; the—the—" He had stumbled back upon my chair, and turning, saw me.

I was on my feet at once, and noting that he was dazed by the shock of my presence, I slid quietly between him and the door.

The movement roused him. Turning upon me with a sarcastic smile in which was concentrated the bitterness of years, he briefly said:

"So, I am caught! Well, there has to be an end to men as well as to things, and I am ready for mine. She turned me away from her door to-day, and after the hell of that moment I don't much fear any other."

"You had better not talk," I admonished him. "All that falls from you now will only tell against you on your trial."

He broke into a harsh laugh. "And do you think I care for that? That having been driven by a woman's perfidy into crime I am going to bridle my tongue and keep down the words which are my only safeguard from insanity? No, no; while my miserable breath lasts I will curse her, and if the halter is to cut short my words, it shall be with her name blistering my lips."

I attempted to speak, but he would not give me the opportunity. The passion of weeks had found vent and he rushed on recklessly.

"I went to her house to-day. I wanted to see her in her widow's weeds; I wanted to see her eyes red with weeping over a grief which owed its bitterness to me. But she would not grant me an admittance. She had me thrust from her door, and I shall never know how deeply the iron has sunk into her soul. But—" and here his face showed a sudden change, "I shall see her if I am tried for murder. She will be in the court-room,—on the witness stand—"

"Doubtless," I interjected; but his interruption came quickly and with vehement passion.

"Then I am ready. Welcome trial, conviction, death, even. To confront her eye to eye is all I wish. She shall never forget it, never!"

"Then you do not deny—" I began.

"I deny nothing," he returned, and held out his hands with a grim gesture. "How can I, when there falls from everything I touch, the devilish thing which took away the life I hated?"

"Have you anything more to say or do before you leave these rooms?" I asked.

He shook his head, and then, bethinking himself, pointed to the roll of paper which he had flung on the table.

"Burn that!" he cried.

I took up the roll and looked at it. It was the manuscript of a poem in blank verse.

"I have been with it into a dozen newspaper and maga-

zine offices," he explained with great bitterness. "Had I succeeded in getting a publisher for it, I might have forgotten
my wrongs and tried to build up a new life on the ruins of
the old. But they would not have it, none of them, so I say,
burn it! that no memory of me may remain in this miserable
world."

"Keep to the facts!" I severely retorted. "It was while
carrying this poem from one newspaper to another that you
secured that bit of print upon the blank side of which you
yourself printed the obituary notice with which you savored
your revenge upon the woman who had disappointed you."

"You know that? Then you know where I got the poison
with which I tipped the silly toy with which that weak man
fooled away his life?"

"No," said I, "I do not know where you got it. I merely
know it was no common poison bought at a druggist's, or
from any ordinary chemist."

"It was woorali; the deadly, secret woorali. I got it from
—but that is another man's secret. You will never hear from
me anything that will compromise a friend. I got it, that is
all. One drop, but it killed my man."

The satisfaction, the delight, which he threw into these
words are beyond description. As they left his lips a jet of
flame from the neglected fire shot up and threw his figure
for one instant into bold relief upon the lowering ceiling;
then it died out, and nothing but the twilight dusk remained
in the room and on the countenance of this doomed and
despairing man.

THE LOST SPECIAL
by Arthur Conan Doyle

THE CONFESSION OF HERBERT DE LERNAC, NOW LYING UNDER
sentence of death at Marseilles, has thrown a light upon one
of the most inexplicable crimes of the century—an incident
which is, I believe, absolutely unprecedented in the criminal
annals of any country. Although there is a reluctance to discuss the matter in official circles, and little information has
been given to the Press, there are still indications that the
statement of this arch-criminal is corroborated by the facts,
and that we have at last found a solution for a most astounding business. As the matter is eight years old, and as its importance was somewhat obscured by a political crisis which
was engaging the public attention at the time, it may be as
well to state the facts as far as we have been able to ascertain them. They are collated from the Liverpool papers of
that date, from the proceedings at the inquest upon John
Slater, the engine-driver, and from the records of the London and West Coast Railway Company, which have been
courteously put at my disposal. Briefly, they are as follows:

On the 3rd of June, 1890, a gentleman, who gave his
name as Monsieur Louis Caratal, desired an interview with
Mr. James Bland, the superintendent of the London and
West Coast Central Station in Liverpool. He was a small
man, middle-aged and dark, with a stoop which was so
marked that it suggested some deformity of the spine. He
was accompanied by a friend, a man of imposing physique,
whose deferential manner and constant attention showed
that his position was one of dependence. This friend or companion, whose name did not transpire, was certainly a for-

eigner, and probably from his swarthy complexion, either a
Spaniard or a South American. One peculiarity was observed in him. He carried in his left hand a small, black
leather dispatch-box, and it was noticed by a sharp-eyed
clerk in the Central office that this box was fastened to his
wrist by a strap. No importance was attached to the fact at
the time, but subsequent events endowed it with some significance. Monsieur Caratal was shown up to Mr. Bland's
office, while his companion remained outside.

Monsieur Caratal's business was quickly dispatched. He
had arrived that afternoon from Central America. Affairs
of the utmost importance demanded that he should be in
Paris without the loss of an unnecessary hour. He had
missed the London express. A special must be provided.
Money was of no importance. Time was everything. If the
company would speed him on his way, they might make
their own terms.

Mr. Bland struck the electric bell, summoned Mr. Potter
Hood, the traffic manager, and had the matter arranged in
five minutes. The train would start in three-quarters of an
hour. It would take that time to insure that the line should
be clear. The powerful engine called Rochdale (No. 247 on
the company's register) was attached to two carriages, with
a guard's van behind. The first carriage was solely for the
purpose of decreasing the inconvenience arising from the
oscillation. The second was divided, as usual, into four com-
partments, a first-class, a first-class smoking, a second-class,
and a second-class smoking. The first compartment, which
was nearest to the engine, was the one allotted to the travellers. The other three were empty. The guard of the special
train was James McPherson, who had been some years in
the service of the company. The stoker, William Smith, was
a new hand.

Monsieur Caratal, upon leaving the superintendent's office, rejoined his companion, and both of them manifested
extreme impatience to be off. Having paid the money asked,
which amounted to fifty pounds five shillings, at the usual
special rate of five shillings a mile, they demanded to be

shown the carriage, and at once took their seats in it, although they were assured that the better part of an hour must elapse before the line could be cleared. In the meantime a singular coincidence had occurred in the office which Monsieur Caratal had just quitted.

A request for a special is not a very uncommon circumstance in a rich commercial centre, but that two should be required upon the same afternoon was most unusual. It so happened, however, that Mr. Bland had hardly dismissed the first traveller before a second entered with a similar request. This was a Mr. Horace Moore, a gentlemanly man of military appearance, who alleged that the sudden serious illness of his wife in London made it absolutely imperative that he should not lose an instant in starting upon the journey. His distress and anxiety were so evident that Mr. Bland did all that was possible to meet his wishes. A second special was out of the question, as the ordinary local service was already somewhat deranged by the first. There was the alternative, however, that Mr. Moore should share the expense of Monsieur Caratal's train, and should travel in the other empty first-class compartment, if Monsieur Caratal objected to having him in the one which he occupied. It was difficult to see any objection to such an arrangement, and yet Monsieur Caratal, upon the suggestion being made to him by Mr. Potter Hood, absolutely refused to consider it for an instant. The train was his, he said, and he would insist upon the exclusive use of it. All argument failed to overcome his ungracious objections, and finally the plan had to be abandoned. Mr. Horace Moore left the station in great distress, after learning that his only course was to take the ordinary slow train which leaves Liverpool at six o'clock. At four thirty-one exactly by the station clock the special train, containing the crippled Monsieur Caratal and his gigantic companion, steamed out of the Liverpool station. The line was at that time clear, and there should have been no stoppage before Manchester.

The trains of the London and West Coast Railway run over the lines of another company as far as this town, which

should have been reached by the special rather before six
o'clock. At a quarter after six considerable surprise and
some consternation were caused amongst the officials at
Liverpool by the receipt of a telegram from Manchester to
say that it had not yet arrived. An inquiry directed to St.
Helens, which is a third of the way between the two cities,
elicited the following reply—

"To James Bland, Superintendent, Central L. & W. C.,
Liverpool.—Special passed here at 4.52, well up to time—
Dowser, St. Helens."

This telegram was received at six-forty. At six-fifty a second message was received from Manchester—

"No sign of special as advised by you."

And then ten minutes later a third, more bewildering—
"Presume some mistake as to proposed running of special.
Local train from St. Helens timed to follow it has just ar-
rived and has seen nothing of it. Kindly wire advices.—
Manchester."

The matter was assuming a most amazing aspect, although in some respects the last telegram was a relief to the
authorities at Liverpool. If an accident had occurred to the
special, it seemed hardly possible that the local train could
have passed down the same line without observing it. And
yet, what was the alternative? Where could the train be?
Had it possibly been sidetracked for some reason in order
to allow the slower train to go past? Such an explanation
was possible if some small repair had to be effected. A telegram was dispatched to each of the stations between St.
Helens and Manchester, and the superintendent and traffic
manager waited in the utmost suspense at the instrument
for the series of replies which would enable them to say for
certain what had become of the missing train. The answers
came back in the order of questions, which was the order
of the stations beginning at the St. Helens end—

"Special passed here five o'clock.—Collins Green."
"Special passed here six past five.—Earlstown."
"Special passed here 5.10.—Newton."
"Special passed here 5.20.—Kenyon Junction."

"No special train has passed here.—Barton Moss."

The two officials stared at each other in amazement.

"This is unique in my thirty years of experience," said Mr. Bland.

"Absolutely unprecedented and inexplicable, sir. The special has gone wrong between Kenyon Junction and Barton Moss."

"And yet there is no siding, so far as my memory serves me, between the two stations. The special must have run off the metals."

"But how could the four-fifty parliamentary pass over the same line without observing it?"

"There's no alternative, Mr. Hood. It *must* be so. Possibly the local train may have observed something which may throw some light upon the matter. We will wire to Manchester for more information, and to Kenyon Junction with instructions that the line be examined instantly as far as Barton Moss."

The answer from Manchester came within a few minutes.

"No news of missing special. Driver and guard of slow train positive no accident between Kenyon Junction and Barton Moss. Line quite clear, and no sign of anything unusual.—Manchester."

"That driver and guard will have to go," said Mr. Bland, grimly. "There has been a wreck and they have missed it. The special has obviously run off the metals without disturbing the line—how it could have done so passes my comprehension—but so it must be, and we shall have a wire from Kenyon or Barton Moss presently to say that they have found her at the bottom of an embankment."

But Mr. Bland's prophecy was not destined to be fulfilled. Half an hour passed, and then there arrived the following message from the station-master of Kenyon Junction—

"There are no traces of the missing special. It is quite certain that she passed here, and that she did not arrive at Barton Moss. We have detached engine from goods train, and I have myself ridden down the line but all is clear, and there is no sign of any accident."

Mr. Bland tore his hair in his perplexity.

"This is rank lunacy, Hood!" he cried. "Does a train vanish into thin air in England in broad daylight? The thing is preposterous. An engine, a tender, two carriages, a van, five human beings—and all lost on a straight line of railway! Unless we get something positive within the next hour, I'll take Inspector Collins, and go down myself."

And then at last something positive did occur. It took the shape of another telegram from Kenyon Junction.

"Regret to report that the dead body of John Slater, driver of the special train, has just been found among the gorse bushes at a point two and a quarter miles from the Junction. Had fallen from his engine, pitched down the embankment, and rolled among bushes. Injuries to his head, from the fall, appear to be cause of death. Ground has now been carefully examined, and there is no trace of the missing train."

The country was, as has already been stated, in the throes of a political crisis, and the attention of the public was further distracted by the important and sensational developments in Paris, where a huge scandal threatened to destroy the Government and to wreck the reputations of many of the leading men in France. The papers were full of these events, and the singular disappearance of the special train attracted less attention than would have been the case in more peaceful times. The grotesque nature of the event helped to detract from its importance, for the papers were disinclined to believe the facts as reported to them. More than one of the London journals treated the matter as an ingenious hoax, until the coroner's inquest upon the unfortunate driver (an inquest which elicited nothing of importance) convinced them of the tragedy of the incident.

Mr. Bland, accompanied by Inspector Collins, the senior detective officer in the service of the company, went down to Kenyon Junction the same evening, and their research lasted throughout the following day, but was attended with purely negative results. Not only was no trace found of the missing train, but no conjecture could be put forward which

could possibly explain the facts. At the same time, Inspector
Collins's official report (which lies before me as I write)
served to show that the possibilities were more numerous
than might have been expected.

"In the stretch of railway between these two points," said
he, "the country is dotted with ironworks and collieries. Of
these, some are being worked and some have been abandoned. There are no fewer than twelve which have small-
gauge lines which run trolley-cars down to the main line.
These can, of course, be disregarded. Besides these, however, there are seven which have, or have had, proper lines
running down and connecting with points to the main line,
so as to convey their produce from the mouth of the mine
to the great centres of distribution. In every case these lines
are only a few miles in length. Out of the seven, four be-
long to collieries which are worked out, or at least to shafts
which are no longer used. These are the Redgauntlet, Hero,
Slough of Despond, and Heartsease mines, the latter having
ten years ago been one of the principal mines in Lancashire.
These four side lines may be eliminated from our inquiry,
for, to prevent possible accidents, the rails nearest to the
main line have been taken up, and there is no longer any
connection. There remain three other sidelines leading—

   (a)   To the Carnstock Iron Works;
   (b)   To the Big Ben Colliery;
   (c)   To the Perseverance Colliery.

"Of these the Big Ben line is not more than a quarter of
a mile long, and ends at a dead wall of coal waiting removal
from the mouth of the mine. Nothing had been seen or
heard there of any special. The Carnstock Iron Works line
was blocked all day upon the 3rd of June by sixteen truck-
loads of hematite. It is a single line, and nothing could have
passed. As to the Perseverance line, it is a large double line,
which does a considerable traffic, for the output of the mine
is very large. On the 3rd of June this traffic proceeded as
usual; hundreds of men including a gang of railway plate-

layers, were working along the two miles and a quarter
which constitute the total length of the line, and it is inconceivable that an unexpected train could have come down
there without attracting universal attention. It may be remarked in conclusion that this branch line is nearer to St.
Helens than the point at which the engine-driver was discovered, so that we have every reason to believe that the
train was past that point before misfortune overtook her.

"As to John Slater, there is no clue to be gathered from
his appearance or injuries. We can only say that, so far as
we can see, he met his end by falling off his engine, though
why he fell, or what became of the engine after his fall, is
a question upon which I do not feel qualified to offer an
opinion." In conclusion, the inspector offered his resignation to the Board, being much nettled by an accusation of
incompetence in the London papers.

A month elapsed, during which both the police and the
company prosecuted their inquiries without the slightest
success. A reward was offered and a pardon promised in
case of crime, but they were both unclaimed. Every day
the public opened their papers with the conviction that so
grotesque a mystery would at last be solved, but week after
week passed by, and a solution remained as far off as ever.
In broad daylight, upon a June afternoon in the most thickly
inhabited portion of England, a train with its occupants had
disappeared as completely as if some master of subtle chem-
istry had volatilised it into gas. Indeed, among the various
conjectures which were put forward in the public press,
there were some which seriously asserted that supernatural,
or, at least preternatural, agencies had been at work, and
that the deformed Monsieur Caratal was probably a person
who was better known under a less polite name. Others
fixed upon his swarthy companion as being the author of the
mischief, but what it was exactly which he had done could
never be clearly formulated in words.

Amongst the many suggestions put forward by various
newspapers or private individuals, there were one or two
which were feasible enough to attract the attention of the

public. One which appeared in *The Times,* over the signature of an amateur reasoner of some celebrity at that date,
attempted to deal with the matter in a critical and semi-
scientific manner. An extract must suffice, although the
curious can see the whole letter in the issue of the 3rd of
July.

"It is one of the elementary principles of practical reasoning," he remarked, "that when the impossible has been
eliminated the residuum, *however improbable,* must con-
tain the truth. It is certain that the train left Kenyon Junction. It is certain that it did not reach Barton Moss. It is
in the highest degree unlikely, but still possible, that it may
have taken one of the seven available side lines. It is obviously impossible for a train to run where there are no rails,
and, therefore, we may reduce our improbables to the three
open lines, namely the Carnstock Iron Works, the Big Ben,
and the Perseverance. Is there a secret society of colliers, an
English *Camorra,* which is capable of destroying both train
and passengers? It is improbable, but it is not impossible. I
confess that I am unable to suggest any other solution. I
should certainly advise the company to direct all their ener-
gies towards the observation of those three lines, and of the
workmen at the end of them. A careful supervision of the
pawnbrokers' shops of the district might possibly bring
some suggestive facts to light."

The suggestion coming from a recognized authority upon
such matters created considerable interest, and a fierce op-
position from those who considered such a statement to be
a preposterous libel upon an honest and deserving set of
men. The only answer to this criticism was a challenge to
the objectors to lay any more feasible explanations before
the public. In reply to this two others were forthcoming
(*Times,* July 7th and 9th). The first suggested that the train
might have run off the metals and be lying submerged in the
Lancashire and Staffordshire Canal, which runs parallel to
the railway for some hundreds of yards. This suggestion was
thrown out of court by the published depth of the canal,
which was entirely insufficient to conceal so large an object.

The second correspondent wrote calling attention to the bag which appeared to be the sole luggage which the travellers had brought with them, and suggesting that some novel explosive of immense and pulverising power might have been concealed in it. The obvious absurdity, however, of supposing that the whole train might be blown to dust while the metals remained uninjured reduced any such explanation to a farce. The investigation had drifted into this hopeless position when a new and most unexpected incident occurred.

This was nothing less than the receipt by Mrs. McPherson of a letter from her husband, James McPherson, who had been the guard of the missing train. The letter, which was dated July 5th, 1890, was posted from New York and came to hand upon July 14th. Some doubts were expressed as to its genuine character, but Mrs. McPherson was positive as to the writing, and the fact that it contained a remittance of a hundred dollars in five-dollar notes was enough in itself to discount the idea of a hoax. No address was given in the letter, which ran in this way:

"My dear Wife,—

"I have been thinking a great deal, and I find it very hard to give you up. The same with Lizzie. I try to fight against it, but it will always come back to me. I send you some money which will change into twenty English pounds. This should be enough to bring both Lizzie and you across the Atlantic, and you will find the Hamburg boats which stop at Southampton very good boats, and cheaper than Liverpool. If you could come here and stop at the Johnston House I would try and send you word how to meet, but things are very difficult with me at present, and I am not very happy, finding it hard to give you both up. So no more at present, from your loving husband,

"James McPherson."

For a time it was confidently anticipated that this letter would lead to the clearing up of the whole matter, the more so as it was ascertained that a passenger who bore a close resemblance to the missing guard had travelled from South-ampton under the name of Summers in the Hamburg and New York liner *Vistula*, which started upon the 7th of June. Mrs. McPherson and her sister Lizzie Dolton went across to New York as directed and stayed for three weeks at the Johnston House, without hearing anything from the missing man. It is probable that some injudicious comments in the Press may have warned him that the police were using them as a bait. However, this may be, it is certain that he neither wrote nor came, and the women were eventually compelled to return to Liverpool.

And so the matter stood, and has continued to stand up to the present year of 1898. Incredible as it may seem, nothing has transpired during these eight years which has shed the least light upon the extraordinary disappearance of the special train which contained Monsieur Caratal and his companion. Careful inquiries into the antecedents of the two travellers have only established the fact that Monsieur Caratal was well known as a financier and political agent in Central America, and that during his voyage to Europe he had betrayed extraordinary anxiety to reach Paris. His companion, whose name was entered upon the passenger lists as Eduardo Gomez, was a man whose record was a violent one, and whose reputation was that of a bravo and a bully. There was evidence to show, however, that he was honestly devoted to the interests of Monsieur Caratal, and that the latter, being a man of puny physique, employed the other as a guard and protector. It may be added that no information came from Paris as to what the objects of Monsieur Caratal's hurried journey may have been. This com-prises all the facts of the case up to the publication in the Marseilles papers of the recent confession of Herbert de Lernac, now under sentence of death for the murder of a merchant named Bonvalot. This statement may be literally translated as follows:

"It is not out of mere pride or boasting that I give this

information, for, if that were my object, I could tell a dozen actions of mine which are quite as splendid; but I do it in order that certain gentlemen in Paris may understand that I, who am able here to tell about the fate of Monsieur Caratal, can also tell in whose interest and at whose request the deed was done, unless the reprieve which I am awaiting comes to me very quickly. Take warning, messieurs, before it is too late! You know Herbert de Lernac, and you are aware that his deeds are as ready as his words. Hasten then, or you are lost!

"At present I shall mention no names—if you only heard the names, what would you not think!—but I shall merely tell you how cleverly I did it. I was true to my employers then, and no doubt they will be true to me now. I hope so, and until I am convinced that they have betrayed me, these names, which would convulse Europe, shall not be divulged. But on that day . . . well, I say no more!

"In a word, then, there was a famous trial in Paris, in the year 1890, in connection with a monstrous scandal in politics and finance. How monstrous that scandal was can never be known save by such confidential agents as myself. The honour and careers of many of the chief men in France were at stake. You have seen a group of ninepins standing, all so rigid, and prim, and unbending. Then there comes the ball from far away and pop, pop, pop—there are your ninepins on the floor. Well, imagine some of the greatest men in France as these ninepins and then this Monsieur Caratal was the ball which could be seen coming from far away. If he arrived, then it was pop, pop, pop for all of them. It was determined that he should not arrive.

"I do not accuse them all of being conscious of what was to happen. There were, as I have said, great financial as well as political interests at stake, and a syndicate was formed to manage the business. Some subscribed to the syndicate who hardly understood what were its objects. But others understood very well, and they can rely upon it that I have not forgotten their names. They had ample warning that Monsieur Caratal was coming long before he left South

America, and they knew that the evidence which he held would certainly mean ruin to all of them. The syndicate had the command of an unlimited amount of money—absolutely unlimited, you understand. They looked around for an agent who was capable of wielding this gigantic power. The man chosen must be inventive, resolute, adaptive—a man in a million. They chose Herbert de Lernac, and I admit they were right.

"My duties were to choose my subordinates, to use freely the power which money gives, and to make certain that Monsieur Caratal should never arrive in Paris. With characteristic energy I set about my commission within an hour of receiving my instructions, and the steps which I took were the very best for the purpose which could possibly be devised.

"A man whom I could trust was dispatched instantly to South America to travel home with Monsieur Caratal. Had he arrived in time the ship would never have reached Liverpool: but alas! it had already started before my agent could reach it. I fitted out a small armed brig to intercept it, but again I was unfortunate. Like all great organizers I was, however, prepared for failure, and had a series of alternatives prepared, one or the other of which must succeed. You must not underrate the difficulties of my undertaking, or imagine that a mere commonplace assassination would meet the case. We must destroy not only Monsieur Caratal, but Monsieur Caratal's documents, and Monsieur Caratal's companions also, if we had reason to believe that he had communicated his secrets to them. And you must remember that they were on the alert, and keenly suspicious of any such attempt. It was a task which was in every way worthy of me, for I am always most masterful where another would be appalled.

"I was all ready for Monsieur Caratal's reception in Liverpool, and I was the more eager because I had reason to believe that he had made arrangements by which he would have a considerable guard from the moment that he arrived in London. Anything which was to be done must be done between the moment of his setting foot upon the Liverpool quay and that of his arrival at the London and West Coast terminus in London. We prepared six plans, each more elaborate than the last; which plan would be used would depend upon his own movements. Do what he would, we were ready for him. If he had stayed in Liverpool, we were ready. If he took an ordinary train, an express, or a special, all was ready. Everything had been foreseen and provided for.

"You may imagine that I could not do all this myself. What could I know of the English railway lines? But money can procure willing agents all the world over, and I soon had one of the acutest brains in England to assist me. I will mention no names, but it would be unjust to claim all the credit for myself. My English ally was worthy of such an alliance. He knew the London and West Coast line thoroughly, and he had the command of a band of workers who were trustworthy and intelligent. The idea was his, and my own *judgement* was only required in the details. We bought over several officials, amongst whom the most important was James McPherson, whom we had ascertained to be the guard most likely to be employed upon a special train. Smith, the stoker, was also in our employ. John Slater, the engine-driver, had been approached, but had been found to be obstinate and dangerous, so we desisted. We had no certainty that Monsieur Caratal would take a special, but we thought it very probable, for it was of the utmost importance to him that he should reach Paris without delay. It was for this contingency, therefore, that we made special preparations—preparations which were complete down to the last detail long before his steamer had sighted the shores of England. You will be amused to learn that there was one of my agents in the pilot-boat which brought that steamer to its moorings.

"The moment that Caratal arrived in Liverpool we knew that he suspected danger and was on his guard. He had brought with him as an escort a dangerous fellow, named Gomez, a man who carried weapons, and was prepared to use them. This fellow carried Caratal's confidential papers for him, and was ready to protect either them or his master. The probability was that Caratal had taken him into his counsels, and that to remove Caratal without removing Gomez would be a mere waste of energy. It was necessary that they should be involved in a common fate, and our plans to that end were much facilitated by their request for a special train. On that special train you will understand that two out of the three servants of the company were really in our employ, at a price which would make them independent for a lifetime. I do not go so far as to say that the English are more honest than any other nation, but I have found them more expensive to buy.

"I have already spoken of my English agent—who is a man with a considerable future before him, unless some complaint of the throat carries him off before his time. He had charge of all arrangements at Liverpool, whilst I was stationed at the inn at Kenyon, where I awaited a cipher signal to act. When the special was arranged for, my agent instantly telegraphed to me and warned me how soon I should have everything ready. He himself under the name of Horace Moore applied immediately for a special also, in the hope that he would be sent down with Monsieur Caratal, which might under certain circumstances have been helpful to us. If, for example, our great *coup* had failed, it would then have become the duty of my agent to have shot them both and destroyed their papers. Caratal was on his guard, however, and refused to admit any other traveller. My agent then left the station, returned by another entrance, entered the guard's van on the side farthest from the platform, and travelled down with McPherson the guard.

"In the meantime you will be interested to know what my movements were. Everything had been prepared for days before, and only the finishing touches were needed. The side line which we had chosen had once joined the main line, but it had been disconnected. We had only to replace a few rails to connect it once more. These rails had been laid down as far as could be done without danger of attracting attention, and now it was merely a case of completing a juncture with the line, and arranging the points as they had been before. The sleepers had never been removed, and the rails, fish-plates and rivets were all ready, for we had taken them from a siding on the abandoned portion of the line. With my small but competent band of workers, we had everything ready long before the special arrived. When it did arrive, it ran off upon the small side line so easily that the jolting of the points appears to have been entirely unnoticed by the two travellers.

"Our plan had been that Smith, the stoker, should chloroform John Slater, the driver, so that he should vanish with the others. In this respect, and in this respect only, our plans miscarried—I except the criminal folly of McPherson in writing home to his wife. Our stoker did his business so clumsily that Slater in his struggles fell off the engine, and though fortune was with us so far that he broke his neck in the fall, still he remained as a blot upon that which would otherwise have been one of those masterpieces which are only to be contemplated in silent admiration. The criminal expert will find in John Slater the one flaw in all our admirable combinations. A man who has had as many triumphs as I can afford to be frank, and I therefore lay my finger upon John Slater, and I proclaim him to be a flaw.

"But now I have got our special train upon the small line two kilometres, or rather more than one mile, in length, which leads, or rather used to lead, to the abandoned Heartsease mine, once one of the largest coal mines in England. You will ask how it is that no one saw the train upon this unused line. I answer that along its entire length it runs through a deep cutting, and that, unless someone had been on the edge of that cutting, he could not have seen it. There *was* someone on the edge of that cutting. I was there. And now I will tell you what I saw.

"My assistant had remained at the points in order that he might superintend the switching off of the train. He had four armed men with him, so that if the train ran off the line—we thought it probable, because the points were very rusty—we might still have resources to fall back upon. Having once seen it safely on the side line, he handed over the responsibility to me. I was waiting at a point which overlooks the mouth of the mine, and I was also armed, as were my two companions. Come what might, you see, I was always ready.

"The moment that the train was fairly on the side line, Smith, the stoker, slowed-down the engine, and then, having turned it on to the fullest speed again, he and McPherson, with my English lieutenant, sprang off before it was too late. It may be that it was this slowing-down which first attracted the attention of the travellers, but the train was running at full speed again before their heads appeared at the open window. It makes me smile to think how bewildered they must have been. Picture to yourself your own feelings if, on looking out of your luxurious carriage, you suddenly perceived that the lines upon which you ran were rusted and corroded, red and yellow with disuse and decay! What a catch must have come in their breath as in a second it flashed upon them that it was not Manchester but Death which was waiting for them at the end of that sinister line. But the train was running with frantic speed, rolling and rocking over the rotten line, while the wheels made a frightful screaming sound upon the rusted surface. I was close to them, and could see their faces. Caratal was praying, I think—there was something like a rosary dangling out of his hand. The other roared like a bull who smells the blood of the slaughter-house. He saw us standing on the bank, and he beckoned to us like a madman. Then he tore at his wrist and threw his dispatch-box out of the window in our direction. Of course, his meaning was obvious. Here was the evidence, and they would promise to be silent if their lives were spared. It would have been very agreeable if we could have done so, but business is business. Besides, the train was now as much beyond our control as theirs.

"He ceased howling when the train rattled round the curve and they saw the black mouth of the mine yawning before them. We had removed the boards which had covered it, and we had cleared the square entrance. The rails had formerly run very close to the shaft for the convenience of loading the coal, and we had only to add two or three lengths of rail in order to lead to the very brink of the shaft. In fact, as the lengths would not quite fit, our line projected about three feet over the edge. We saw the two heads at the window: Caratal below, Gomez above; but they had both been struck silent by what they saw. And yet they could not withdraw their heads. The sight seemed to have paralysed them.

"I had wondered how the train running at a great speed would take the pit into which I had guided it, and I was much interested in watching it. One of my colleagues thought that it would actually jump it, and indeed it was not very far from doing so. Fortunately, however, it fell short, and the buffers of the engine struck the other lip of the shaft with a tremendous crash. The funnel flew off into the air. The tender, carriages, and van were all smashed up into one jumble, which, with the remains of the engine, choked for a minute or so the mouth of the pit. Then something gave way in the middle, and the whole mass of green iron, smoking coals, brass fittings, wheels, wood-work, and cushions all crumbled together and crashed down into the mine. We heard the rattle, rattle, rattle, as the debris struck against the walls, and then, quite a long time afterwards, there came a deep roar as the remains of the train struck the bottom. The boiler may have burst, for a sharp crash came after the roar, and then a dense cloud of steam and smoke swirled up out of the black depths, falling in a spray as thick as rain all around us. Then the vapour shredded off into thin wisps, which floated away in the summer sunshine, and all was quiet again in the Heartsease mine.

"And now, having carried out our plans so successfully, it only remained to leave no trace behind us. Our little band

of workers at the other end had already ripped up the rails
and disconnected the side line, replacing everything as it
had been before. We were equally busy at the mine. The
funnel and other fragments were thrown in, the shaft was
planked over as it used to be, and the lines which led to it
were torn up and taken away. Then, without flurry, but without delay, we all made our way out of the country, most of
us to Paris, my English colleague to Manchester, and Mc-
Pherson to Southampton, whence he emigrated to America.
Let the English papers of that date tell how thoroughly we
had done our work, and how completely we had thrown
the cleverest of their detectives off our track.

"You will remember that Gomez threw his bag of papers
out of the window, and I need not say that I secured that
bag and brought them to my employers. It may interest my
employers now, however, to learn that out of that bag I
took one or two little papers as a souvenir of the occasion.
I have no wish to publish these papers; but, still, it is every
man for himself in this world, and what else can I do if my
friends will not come to my aid when I want them? Messieurs, you may believe that Herbert de Lernac is quite
as formidable when he is against you as when he is with
you, and that he is not a man to go to the guillotine until
he has seen that every one of you is *en route* for New Cale-
donia. For your own sake, if not for mine, make haste, Monsieur de ———, and General ———, and Baron ———
(you can fill up the blanks for yourselves as you read this).
I promise you that in the next edition there will be no blanks
to fill.

"P.S.—As I look over my statement there is only one
omission which I can see. It concerns the unfortunate man
McPherson, who was foolish enough to write to his wife
and to make an appointment with her in New York. It can
be imagined that when interests like ours were at stake, we
could not leave them to the chance of whether a man in
that class of life would or would not give away his secrets
to a woman. Having once broken his oath by writing to his

wife, we could not trust him any more. We took steps therefore to insure that he should not see his wife. I have sometimes thought that it would be a kindness to write to her and assure her that there is no impediment to her marrying again."

THE FENCHURCH
STREET MYSTERY
by Baroness Orczy

I

THE MAN IN THE CORNER PUSHED ASIDE HIS GLASS, AND leant across the table.

"Mysteries!" he commented. "There is no such thing as a mystery in connection with any crime, provided intelligence is brought to bear upon its investigation,"

Very much astonished Polly Burton looked over the top of her newspaper, and fixed a pair of very severe, coldly inquiring brown eyes upon him.

She had disapproved of the man from the instant when he shuffled across the shop and sat down opposite to her, at the same marble-topped table which already held her large coffee (3d.), her roll and butter (2d.), and plate of tongue (6d.).

Now this particular corner, this very same table, that special view of the magnificent marble hall—known as the Norfolk Street branch of the Aërated Bread Company's depots—were Polly's own corner, table, and view. Here she had partaken of eleven pennyworth of luncheon and one pennyworth of daily information ever since that glorious never-to-be-forgotten day when she was enrolled on the staff of the *Evening Observer* (we'll call it that, if you please), and became a member of that illustrious and world-famed organization known as the British Press.

She was a personality, was Miss Burton of the *Evening Observer*. Her cards were printed thus:

MISS MARY J. BURTON

Evening Observer

She had interviewed Miss Ellen Terry and the Bishop of Madagascar, Mr. Seymour Hicks and the Chief Commissioner of Police. She had been present at the last Marlborough House garden party—in the cloak-room, that is to say, where she caught sight of Lady Thingummy's hat, Miss What-you-may-call's sunshade, and of various other things modistical or fashionable, all of which were duly described under the heading "Royalty and Dress" in the early afternoon edition of the *Evening Observer*.

(The article itself is signed M.J.B., and is to be found in the files of that leading halfpennyworth.)

For these reasons—and for various others, too—Polly felt irate with the man in the corner, and told him so with her eyes, as plainly as any pair of brown eyes can speak.

She had been reading an article in the *Daily Telegraph*. The article was palpitatingly interesting. Had Polly been commenting audibly upon it? Certain it is that the man over there had spoken in direct answer to her thoughts.

She looked at him and frowned; the next moment she smiled. Miss Burton (of the *Evening Observer*) had a keen sense of humour, which two years' association with the British Press had not succeeded in destroying, and the appearance of the man was sufficient to tickle the most ultramorose fancy. Polly thought to herself that she had never seen anyone so pale, so thin, with such funny light-coloured hair, brushed very smoothly across the top of a very obviously bald crown. He looked so timid and nervous as he fidgeted incessantly with a piece of string; his long, lean, and trembling fingers tying and untying it into knots of wonderful and complicated proportions.

Having carefully studied every detail of the quaint personality Polly felt more amiable.

"And yet," she remarked kindly but authoritatively, "this

article, in an otherwise well-informed journal, will tell you
that, even within the last year, no fewer than six crimes
have completely baffled the police, and the perpetrators of
them are still at large."

"Pardon me," he said gently, "I never for a moment
ventured to suggest that there were no mysteries to the
police; I merely remarked that there were none where intelligence was brought to bear upon the investigation of
crime."

"Not even in the Fenchurch Street *mystery,* I suppose,"
she asked sarcastically.

"Least of all the so-called Fenchurch Street *mystery,*"
he replied quietly.

Now the Fenchurch Street mystery, as that extraordinary
crime had popularly been called, had puzzled—as Polly well
knew—the brains of every thinking man and woman for the
last twelve months. It had puzzled her not inconsiderably;
she had been interested, fascinated; she had studied the case,
formed her own theories, thought about it all often and
often, had even written one or two letters to the Press on the
subject—suggesting, arguing, hinting at possibilities and
probabilities, adducing proofs which other amateur detectives were equally ready to refute. The attitude of that timid
man in the corner, therefore, was peculiarly exasperating,
and she retorted with sarcasm destined to completely anni-
hilate her self-complacent interlocutor.

"What a pity it is, in that case, that you do not offer your
priceless services to our misguided though well-meaning
police."

"Isn't it?" he replied with perfect good-humour. "Well,
you know, for one thing I doubt if they would accept them;
and in the second place my inclinations and my duty would
—were I to become an active member of the detective force
—nearly always be in direct conflict. As often as not my
sympathies go to the criminal who is clever and astute
enough to lead our entire police force by the nose.

"I don't know how much of the case you remember," he
went on quietly. "It certainly, at first, began even to puzzle

me. On the 12th of last December a woman, poorly dressed, but with an unmistakable air of having seen better days, gave information at Scotland Yard of the disappearance of her husband, William Kershaw, of no occupation, and apparently of no fixed abode. She was accompanied by a friend—a fat, oily-looking German—and between them they told a tale which set the police immediately on the move.

"It appears that on the 10th of December, at about three o'clock in the afternoon, Karl Müller, the German, called on his friend, William Kershaw, for the purpose of collecting a small debt—some ten pounds or so—which the latter owed him. On arriving at the squalid lodging in Charlotte Street, Fitzroy Square, he found William Kershaw in a wild state of excitement, and his wife in tears. Müller attempted to state the object of his visit, but Kershaw, with wild gestures, waived him aside, and—in his own words—flabbergasted him by asking him point-blank for another loan of two pounds, which sum, he declared, would be the means of a speedy fortune for himself and the friend who would help him in his need.

"After a quarter of an hour spent in obscure hints, Kershaw, finding the cautious German obdurate, decided to let him into the secret plan, which, he averred, would place thousands into their hands."

Instinctively Polly had put down her paper; the mild stranger, with his nervous air and timid, watery eyes, had a peculiar way of telling his tale, which somehow fascinated her.

"I don't know," he resumed, "if you remember the story which the German told to the police, and which was corroborated in every detail by the wife or widow. Briefly it was this: Some thirty years previously, Kershaw, then twenty years of age, and a medical student at one of the London hospitals, had a chum named Barker, with whom he roomed, together with another.

"The latter, so it appears, brought home one evening a very considerable sum of money, which he had won on the turf, and the following morning he was found murdered in his bed. Kershaw, fortunately for himself, was able to prove a conclusive *alibi*; he had spent the night on duty at the hospital; as for Barker, he had disappeared, that is to say, as far as the police were concerned, but not as far as the watchful eyes of his friend Kershaw were able to spy—at least, so the latter said. Barker very cleverly contrived to get away out of the country, and, after sundry vicissitudes, finally settled down at Vladivostock, in Eastern Siberia, where, under the assumed name of Smethurst, he built up an enormous fortune by trading in furs.

"Now, mind you, every one knows Smethurst, the Siberian millionaire. Kershaw's story that he had once been called Barker, and had committed a murder thirty years ago was never proved, was it? I am merely telling you what Kershaw said to his friend the German and to his wife on that memorable afternoon of December the 10th.

"According to him Smethurst had made one gigantic mistake in his clever career—he had on four occasions written to his late friend, William Kershaw. Two of these letters had no bearing on the case, since they were written more than twenty-five years ago, and Kershaw, moreover, had lost them—so he said—long ago. According to him, however, the first of these letters was written when Smethurst, alias Barker, had spent all the money he had obtained from the crime, and found himself destitute in New York.

"Kershaw, then in fairly prosperous circumstances, sent him a £10 note for the sake of old times. The second, when the tables had turned, and Kershaw had begun to go downhill, Smethurst, as he then already called himself, sent his whilom friend £50. After that, as Müller gathered, Kershaw had made sundry demands on Smethurst's ever-increasing purse, and had accompanied these demands by various threats, which, considering the distant country in which the millionaire lived, were worse than futile.

"But now the climax had come, and Kershaw, after a final moment of hesitation, handed over to his German friend the last two letters purporting to have been written by Smethurst, and which, if you remember, played such an important part in the mysterious story of this extraordinary crime. I have a copy of both these letters here," added the man in the corner, as he took out a piece of paper from a very worn-out pocket-book, and, unfolding it very deliberately, he began to read:—

" 'Sir,—Your preposterous demands for money are wholly unwarrantable. I have already helped you quite as much as you deserve. However, for the sake of old times, and because you once helped me when I was in a terrible difficulty, I am willing to once more let you impose upon my good nature. A friend of mine here, a Russian merchant, to whom I have sold my business, starts in a few days for an extended tour to many European and Asiatic ports in his yacht, and has invited me to accompany him as far as England. Being tired of foreign parts, and desirous of seeing the old country once again after thirty years' absence, I have decided to accept his invitation. I don't know when we may actually be in Europe, but I promise you that as soon as we touch a suitable port I will write to you again, making an appointment for you to see me in London. But remember that if your demands are too preposterous I will not for a moment listen to them, and that I am the last man in the world to submit to persistent unwarrantable blackmail.

" 'I am, sir,
" 'Yours truly,
" 'Francis Smethurst'

"The second letter was dated from Southampton," continued the man in the corner calmly, "and, curiously enough, was the only letter which Kershaw professed to have received from Smethurst of which he had kept the envelope, and which was dated. It was quite brief," he added, referring once more to his piece of paper.

" 'Dear Sir,—Referring to my letter of a few weeks ago,
I wish to inform you that the *Tsarskoe Selo* will touch
at Tilbury on Tuesday next, the 10th. I shall land there,
and immediately go up to London by the first train I
can get. If you like, you may meet me at Fenchurch
Street Station, in the first-class waiting-room, in the
late afternoon. Since I surmise that after thirty years'
absence my face may not be familiar to you, I may as
well tell you that you will recognize me by a heavy
Astrakhan fur coat, which I shall wear, together with
a cap of the same. You may then introduce yourself to
me, and I will personally listen to what you may have
to say.

" 'Yours faithfully,
" 'Francis Smethurst.'

"It was this last letter which had caused William Kershaw's excitement and his wife's tears. In the German's own
words, he was walking up and down the room like a wild
beast, gesticulating wildly, and muttering sundry exclamations. Mrs. Kershaw, however, was full of apprehension.
She mistrusted the man from foreign parts—who, according to her husband's story, had already one crime upon his
conscience—who might, she feared, risk another, in order
to be rid of a dangerous enemy. Woman-like, she thought
the scheme a dishonorable one, for the law, she knew, is
severe on the blackmailer.

"The assignation might be a cunning trap, in any case
it was a curious one; why, she argued, did not Smethurst
elect to see Kershaw at his hotel the following day? A thousand whys and wherefores made her anxious, but the fat
German had been won over by Kershaw's visions of untold
gold, held tantalisingly before his eyes. He had lent the
necessary £2, with which his friend intended to tidy himself up a bit before he went to meet his friend the millionaire. Half an hour afterwards Kershaw had left his lodgings,
and that was the last the unfortunate woman saw of her husband, or Müller, the German, of his friend.

"Anxiously his wife waited that night, but he did not return; the next day she seems to have spent in making purposeless and futile inquiries about the neighborhood of Fenchurch Street; and on the 12th she went to Scotland Yard, gave what particulars she knew, and placed in the hands of the police the two letters written by Smethurst."

II

The man in the corner had finished his glass of milk. His watery blue eyes looked across at Miss Polly Burton's eager little face, from which all traces of severity had now been chased away by an obvious and intense excitement.

"It was only on the 31st," he resumed after a while, "that a body, decomposed past all recognition, was found by two lightermen in the bottom of a disused barge. She had been moored at one time at the foot of one of those dark flights of steps which lead down between tall warehouses to the river in the East End of London. I have a photograph of the place here," he added, selecting one out of his pocket, and placing it before Polly.

"The actual barge, you see, had already been removed when I took this snapshot, but you will realise what a perfect place this alley is for the purpose of one man cutting another's throat in comfort, and without fear of detection. The body, as I said, was decomposed beyond all recognition; it had probably been there eleven days, but sundry articles, such as a silver ring and a tie pin, were recognisable, and were identified by Mrs. Kershaw as belonging to her husband.

"She, of course, was loud in denouncing Smethurst, and the police had no doubt a very strong case against him, for two days after the discovery of the body in the barge, the Siberian millionaire, as he was already popularly called by enterprising interviewers, was arrested in his luxurious suite of rooms at the Hotel Cecil.

"To confess the truth, at this point I was not a little puz-

zled. Mrs. Kershaw's story and Smethurst's letters had both
found their way into the papers, and following my usual
method—mind you, I am only an amateur, I try to reason
out a case for the love of the thing—I sought about for a
motive for the crime, which the police declared Smethurst
had committed. To effectually get rid of a dangerous blackmailer was the generally accepted theory. Well! did it ever
strike you how paltry that motive really was?"

Miss Polly had to confess, however, that it had never
struck her in that light.

"Surely a man who had succeeded in building up an immense fortune by his own individual efforts, was not the sort
of fool to believe that he had anything to fear from a man
like Kershaw. He must have *known* that Kershaw held no
damning proofs against him—not enough to hang him, anyway. Have you ever seen Smethurst?" he added, as he once
more fumbled in his pocket-book.

Polly replied that she had seen Smethurst's picture in the
illustrated papers at the time. Then he added, placing a
small photograph before her:

"What strikes you most about the face?"

"Well, I think its strange, astonished expression, due to
the total absence of eyebrows, and the funny foreign cut of
the hair."

"So close that it almost looks as if it had been shaved.
Exactly. That is what struck me most when I elbowed my
way into the court that morning and first caught sight of the
millionaire in the dock. He was a tall, soldierly-looking man,
upright in stature, his face very bronzed and tanned. He
wore neither moustache nor beard, his hair was cropped
quite close to his head, like a Frenchman's; but, of course,
what was so very remarkable about him was that total absence of eyebrows and even eyelashes, which gave the face
such a peculiar appearance—as you say, a perpetually astonished look.

"He seemed, however, wonderfully calm; he had been
accommodated with a chair in the dock—being a millionaire—and chatted pleasantly with his lawyer, Sir Arthur

Inglewood, in the intervals between the calling of the several witnesses for the prosecution; whilst during the examination of these witnesses he sat quite placidly, with his head shaded by his hand.

"Müller and Mrs. Kershaw repeated the story which they had already told to the police. I think you said that you were not able, owing to pressure of work, to go to the court that day, and hear the case, so perhaps you have no recollection of Mrs. Kershaw. No? Ah, well! Here is a snapshot I managed to get of her once. That is her. Exactly as she stood in the box—over-dressed—in elaborate crape, with a bonnet which once had contained pink roses, and to which a remnant of pink petals still clung obtrusively amidst the deep black.

"She would not look at the prisoner, and turned her head resolutely towards the magistrate. I fancy she had been fond of that vagabond husband of hers: an enormous wedding-ring encircled her finger, and that, too, was swathed in black. She firmly believed that Kershaw's murderer sat there in the dock, and she literally flaunted her grief before him.

"I was indescribably sorry for her. As for Müller, he was just fat, oily, pompous, conscious of his own importance as a witness; his fat fingers, covered with brass rings, gripped the two incriminating letters, which he had identified. They were his passports, as it were, to a delightful land of importance and notoriety. Sir Arthur Inglewood, I think, disappointed him by stating that he had no questions to ask of him. Müller had been brimful of answers, ready with the most perfect indictment, the most elaborate accusations against the bloated millionaire who had destroyed his dear friend Kershaw, and murdered him in Heaven knows what an out-of-the-way corner of the East End.

"After this, however, the excitement grew apace. Müller had been dismissed, and had retired from the court altogether, leading away Mrs. Kershaw, who had completely broken down.

"Constable D21 was giving evidence as to the arrest in

the meanwhile. The prisoner, he said, had seemed completely taken by surprise, not understanding the cause or history of the accusation against him; however, when put in full possession of the facts, and realising, no doubt, the absolute futility of any resistance, he had quietly enough followed the constable into a cab. No one at the fashionable and crowded Hotel Cecil had even suspected that anything unusual had occurred.

"Then a gigantic sigh of expectancy came from every one of the spectators. The 'fun' was about to begin. James Buckland, a porter at Fenchurch Street railway station, had just sworn to tell all the truth, etc. After all, it did not amount to much. He said that at six o'clock in the afternoon of December the 10th, in the midst of one of the densest fogs he ever remembers, the 5.5 from Tilbury steamed into the station, being just about an hour late. He was on the arrival platform, and was hailed by a passenger in a first-class carriage. He could see very little of him beyond an enormous black fur coat and a travelling cap of fur also.

"The passenger had a quantity of luggage, all marked F. S., and he directed James Buckland to place it all upon a four-wheeled cab, with the exception of a small hand-bag, which he carried himself. Having seen that all his luggage was safely bestowed, the stranger in the fur coat paid the porter, and, telling the cabman to wait until he returned, he walked away in the direction of the waiting-rooms, still carrying his small hand-bag.

" 'I stayed for a bit,' added James Buckland, 'talking to the driver about the fog and that; then I went about my business, seein' that the local from Southend 'ad been signalled.'

"The prosecution insisted most strongly upon the hour when the stranger in the fur coat, having seen to his luggage, walked away towards the waiting-rooms. The porter was emphatic. 'It was not a minute later than 6.15,' he averred.

"Sir Arthur Inglewood still had no questions to ask, and the driver of the cab was called.

"He corroborated the evidence of James Buckland as to the hour when the gentleman in the fur coat had engaged him, and having filled his cab in and out with luggage, had told him to wait. And cabby did wait. He waited in the dense fog—until he was tired, until he seriously thought of depositing all the luggage in the lost-property office, and of looking out for another fare—waited until at last, at a quarter before nine, whom should he see walking hurriedly towards his cab but the gentleman in the fur coat and cap, who got in quickly and told the driver to take him at once to the Hotel Cecil. This, cabby declared, had occurred at a quarter before nine. Still Sir Arthur Inglewood made no comment, and Mr. Francis Smethurst, in the crowded, stuffy court, had calmly dropped to sleep.

"The next witness, Constable Thomas Taylor, had noticed a shabbily-dressed individual, with shaggy hair and beard, loafing about the station and waiting-rooms in the afternoon of December the 10th. He seemed to be watching the arrival platform of the Tilbury and Southend trains.

"Two separate and independent witnesses, cleverly unearthed by the police, had seen this same shabbily-dressed individual stroll into the first-class waiting-room at about 6.15 on Tuesday, December the 10th, and go straight up to a gentleman in a heavy fur coat and cap, who had also just come into the room. The two talked together for a while; no one heard what they said, but presently they walked off together. No one seemed to know in which direction.

"Francis Smethurst was rousing himself from his apathy; he whispered to his lawyer, who nodded with a bland smile of encouragement. The employes of the Hotel Cecil gave evidence as to the arrival of Mr. Smethurst at about 9:30 P.M. on Tuesday, December the 10th, in a cab, with a quantity of luggage; and this closed the case for the prosecution.

"Everybody in that court already *saw* Smethurst mounting the gallows. It was uninterested curiosity which caused the elegant audience to wait and hear what Sir Arthur Inglewood had to say. He, of course, is the most fashionable man in the law at the present moment. His lolling attitudes, his drawling speech, are quite the rage, and imitated by the gilded youth of society.

"Even at this moment, when the Siberian millionaire's neck literally and metaphorically hung in the balance, an expectant titter went round the fair spectators as Sir Arthur stretched out his long loose limbs and lounged across the table. He waited to make his effect—Sir Arthur is a born actor—and there is no doubt that he made it, when in his slowest, most drawly tones he said quietly:

" 'With regard to this alleged murder of one William Kershaw, on Wednesday, December the 10th, between 6.15 and 8.45 p.m., your Honour, I now propose to call two witnesses, who saw this same William Kershaw alive on Tuesday afternoon, December the 16th, that is to say, six days after the supposed murder.'

"It was as if a bombshell had exploded in the court. Even his Honour was aghast, and I am sure the lady next to me only recovered from the shock of surprise in order to wonder whether she need put off her dinner party after all.

"As for me," added the man in the corner, with that strange mixture of nervousness and self-complacency which had set Miss Polly Burton wondering, "well, you see, *I* had made up my mind long ago where the hitch lay in this particular case, and I was not surprised as some of the others.

"Perhaps you remember the wonderful development of the case, which so completely mystified the police—and in fact everybody except myself. Torriani and a waiter at his hotel in the Commercial Road both deposed that at about 3.30 P.M. on December the 10th a shabbily-dressed individual lolled into the coffee-room and ordered some tea. He was pleasant enough and talkative, told the waiter that his name was William Kershaw, that very soon all London would be talking about him, as he was about, through an unexpected stroke of good fortune, to become a very rich man, and so on, and so on, nonsense without end.

"When he had finished his tea he lolled out again, but no sooner had he disappeared down a turning of the road than the waiter discovered an old umbrella, left behind accidentally by the shabby, talkative individual. As is the custom in his highly respectable restaurant, Signor Torriani put the umbrella carefully away in his office, on the chance of his customer calling to claim it when he discovered his loss. And sure enough nearly a week later, on Tuesday, the 16th, at about 1 P.M., the same shabbily-dressed individual called and asked for the umbrella. He had some lunch, and chatted once again with the waiter. Signor Torriani and the waiter gave a description of William Kershaw, which coincided exactly with that given by Mrs. Kershaw of her husband.

"Oddly enough he seemed to be a very absent-minded sort of person, for on this second occasion, no sooner had he left than the waiter found a pocket-book in the coffee-room, underneath the table. It contained sundry letters and bills, all addressed to William Kershaw. This pocket-book was produced, and Karl Müller, who had returned to the court, easily identified it as having belonged to his dear and lamented friend 'Villiam.'

"This was the first blow to the case against the accused. It was a pretty stiff one, you will admit. Already it had begun to collapse like a house of cards. Still, there was the assignation, and the undisputed meeting between Smethurst and Kershaw, and those two and a half hours of a foggy evening to satisfactorily account for."

The man in the corner made a long pause keeping the girl on tenterhooks. He had fidgeted with his bit of string till there was not an inch of it free from the most complicated and elaborate knots.

"I assure you," he resumed at last, "that at that very moment the whole mystery was, to me, as clear as daylight. I only marvelled how his Honour could waste his time and mine by putting what he thought were searching questions to the accused relating to his past. Francis Smethurst, who had quite shaken off his somnolence, spoke with a curious nasal twang, and with an almost imperceptible soupçon of foreign accent. He calmly denied Kershaw's version of his past; declared that he had never been called Barker, and had certainly never been mixed up in any murder case thirty years ago.

"'But you knew this man Kershaw,' persisted his Honour, 'since you wrote to him?'

"'Pardon me, your Honour,' said the accused quietly, 'I have never, to my knowledge, seen this man Kershaw, and I can swear that I never wrote to him.'

"'Never wrote to him?' retorted his Honour warningly. 'That is a strange assertion to make when I have two of your letters to him in my hands at the present moment.'

"'I never wrote those letters, your Honour,' persisted the accused quietly, 'they are not in my handwriting.'

"'Which we can easily prove,' came in Sir Arthur Inglewood's drawly tones, as he handed up a packet to his Honour, 'here are a number of letters written by my client since he has landed in this country, and some of which were written under my very eyes.'

"As Sir Arthur Inglewood had said, this could be easily proved, and the prisoner, at his Honour's request, scribbled a few lines, together with his signature, several times upon a sheet of note-paper. It was easy to read upon the magistrate's astounded countenance, that there was not the slightest similarity in the two handwritings.

"A fresh mystery had cropped up. Who, then, had made the assignation with William Kershaw at Fenchurch Street railway station? The prisoner gave a fairly satisfactory account of the employment of his time since his landing in England.

"'I came over on the *Tsarkoe Selo*,' he said, 'a yacht belonging to a friend of mine. When we arrived at the mouth of the Thames there was such a dense fog that it was twenty-four hours before it was thought safe for me to land. My friend, who is a Russian, would not land at all; he was regularly frightened at this land of fogs. He was going on to Madeira immediately.

" 'I actually landed on Tuesday, the 10th, and took a train at once for town. I did see to my luggage and a cab, as the porter and driver told your Honour; then I tried to find my way to a refreshment-room, where I could get a glass of wine. I drifted into the waiting-room, and there I was accosted by a shabbily-dressed individual, who began telling me a piteous tale. Who he was I do not know. He *said* he was an old soldier who had served his country faithfully, and then been left to starve. He begged of me to accompany him to his lodgings, where I could see his wife and starving children, and verify the truth and piteousness of his tale.

" 'Well, your Honour,' added the prisoner with noble frankness, 'it was my first day in the old country. I had come back after thirty years with my pockets full of gold, and this was the first sad tale I had heard; but I am a business man, and did not want to be exactly "done" in the eye. I followed my man through the fog, out into the streets. He walked silently by my side for a time. I had not a notion where I was.

" 'Suddenly I turned to him with some question, and realised in a moment that my gentleman had given me the slip. Finding, probably, that I would not part with my money till I *had* seen the starving wife and children, he left me to my fate, and went in search of more willing bait.

" 'The place where I found myself was dismal and deserted. I could see no trace of cab or omnibus. I retraced my steps and tried to find my way back to the station, only to find myself in worse and more deserted neighborhoods. I became hopelessly lost and fogged. I don't wonder that two and a half hours elapsed while I thus wandered on in the dark and deserted streets; my sole astonishment is that I ever found the station at all that night, or rather close to it a policeman, who showed me the way.'

" 'But how do you account for Kershaw knowing all your

movements?' still persisted his Honour, 'and his knowing the exact date of your arrival in England? How do you account for these two letters in fact?'

" 'I cannot account for it or them, your Honour,' replied the prisoner quietly. 'I have proved to you, have I not, that I never wrote those letters, and that the man—er—Kershaw is his name?—was not murdered by me?'

" 'Can you tell me of anyone here or abroad who might have heard of your movements, and of the date of your arrival?'

" 'My late employes at Vladivostock, of course, knew of my departure, but none of them could have written these letters, since none of them know a word of English.'

" 'Then you can throw no light upon these mysterious letters? You cannot help the police in any way towards the cleaning up of this strange affair?'

" 'The affair is as mysterious to me as to your Honour, and to the police of this country.'

"Francis Smethurst was discharged, of course; there was no semblance of evidence against him sufficient to commit him for trial. The two overwhelming points of his defence which had completely routed the prosecution were, firstly, the proof that he had never written the letters making the assignation, and secondly, the fact that the man supposed to have been murdered on the 10th was seen to be alive and well on the 16th. But then, who in the world was the mysterious individual who had apprised Kershaw of the movements of Smethurst, the millionaire?"

III

The man in the corner cocked his funny thin head on one side and looked at Polly; then he took up his beloved bit of string and deliberately untied every knot he had made in it. When it was quite smooth he laid it out upon the table.

"I will take you, if you like, point by point along the line of reasoning which I followed myself, and which will inevitably lead you, as it led me, to the only possible solution of the mystery.

"First take this point," he said with nervous restlessness, once more taking up his bit of string, and forming with each point raised a series of knots which would have shamed a navigating instructor, "obviously it was *impossible* for Kershaw not to have been acquainted with Smethurst, since he was fully apprised of the latter's arrival in England by two letters. Now it was clear to me from the first that *no one* could have written those two letters except Smethurst. You will argue that those letters were proved not to have been written by the man in the dock. Exactly. Remember, Kershaw was a careless man—he had lost both envelopes. To him they were insignificant. Now it was never *disproved* that those letters were written by Smethurst."

"But—" suggested Polly.

"Wait a minute," he interrupted, while knot number two appeared upon the scene; "it was proved that six days after the murder William Kershaw was alive, and visited the Torriani Hotel, where already he was known, and where he conveniently left a pocket-book behind, so that there should be no mistake as to his identity; but it was never questioned where Mr. Francis Smethurst, the millionaire, happened to spend that very same afternoon."

"Surely, you don't mean—?" gasped the girl.

"One moment, please," he added triumphantly. "How did it come about that the landlord of the Torriani Hotel was brought into court at all? How did Sir Arthur Inglewood, or rather his client, know that William Kershaw had on those two memorable occasions visited the hotel, and that its landlord could bring such convincing evidence forward that would for ever exonerate the millionaire from the imputation of murder?"

"Surely," I argued, "the usual means, the police—"

"The police had kept the whole affair very dark until the arrest at the Hotel Cecil. They did not put into the papers the usual: 'If anyone happens to know of the whereabouts, etc., etc.' Had the landlord of that hotel heard of the dis-

appearance of Kershaw through the usual channels, he
would have put himself in communication with the police.
Sir Arthur Inglewood produced him. How did Sir Arthur
Inglewood come on his track?"

"Surely, you don't mean—?"

"Point number four," he resumed imperturbably, "Mrs.
Kershaw was never requested to produce a specimen of her
husband's handwriting. Why? Because the police, clever as
you say they are, never started on the right track. They believed William Kershaw to have been murdered; they looked
for William Kershaw."

"On December the 31st, what was presumed to be the
body of William Kershaw was found by two lightermen: I
have shown you a photograph of the place where it was
found. Dark and deserted it is in all conscience, is it not?
Just the place where a bully and a coward would decoy an
unsuspecting stranger, murder him first, then rob him of his
valuables, his papers, his very identity, and leave him there
to rot. The body was found in a disused barge which had
been moored some time against the wall, at the foot of these
steps. It was in the last stages of decomposition, and, of
course, could not be identified; but the police would have it
that it was the body of William Kershaw.

"It never entered their heads that it was the body of
*Francis Smethurst, and that William Kershaw was his mur-
derer.*

"Ah! it was cleverly, artistically conceived! Kershaw is
a genius. Think of it all! His disguise! Kershaw had a shaggy
beard, hair, and moustache. He shaved up to his very eyebrows! No wonder that even his wife did not recognise him
across the court; and remember she never saw much of his
face while he stood in the dock. Kershaw was shabby,
slouchy, he stooped. Smethurst, the millionaire, might have
served in the Prussian Army.

"Then that lovely trait about going to revisit the Torriani
Hotel. Just a few days' grace, in order to purchase moustache and beard and wig, exactly similar to what he had
himself shaved off. Making up to look like himself! Splen-

did! Then leaving the pocket-book behind! He! he! he! Kershaw was not murdered! Of course not. He called at the Torriani Hotel six days after the murder, whilst Mr. Smethurst, the millionaire, hobnobbed in the park with duchesses! Hang such a man! Fie!

He fumbled for his hat. With nervous, trembling fingers he held it deferentially in his hand whilst he rose from the table. Polly watched him as he strode up to the desk, and paid two-pence for his glass of milk and his bun. Soon he disappeared through the shop, whilst she still found herself hopelessly bewildered, with a number of snap-shot photographs before her, still staring at a long piece of string, smothered from end to end in a series of knots, as bewildering, as irritating, as puzzling as the man who had lately sat in the corner.

THE LEOPARD MAN'S STORY
by Jack London

HE HAD A DREAMY, FAR-AWAY LOOK IN HIS EYES, AND HIS sad, insistent voice, gentle-spoken as a maid's, seemed the placid embodiment of some deep-seated melancholy. He was the Leopard Man, but he did not look it. His business in life, whereby he lived, was to appear in a cage of performing leopards before vast audiences, and to thrill those audiences by certain exhibitions of nerve for which his employers rewarded him on a scale commensurate with the thrills he produced.

As I say, he did not look it. He was narrow-hipped, narrow-shouldered, and anemic, while he seemed not so much oppressed by gloom as by a sweet and gentle sadness, the weight of which was as sweetly and gently borne. For an hour I had been trying to get a story out of him, but he appeared to lack imagination. To him there was no romance in his gorgeous career, no deeds of daring, no thrills—nothing but a gray sameness and infinite boredom.

Lions? Oh, yes! he had fought with them. It was nothing. All you had to do was to stay sober. Anybody could whip a lion to a standstill with an ordinary stick. He had fought one for half an hour once. Just hit him on the nose every time he rushed, and when he got artful and rushed with his head down, why, the thing to do was to stick out your leg. When he grabbed at the leg you drew it back and hit him on the nose again. That was all.

With the far-away look in his eyes and his soft flow of words he showed me his scars. There were many of them, and one recent one where a tigress had reached for his shoulder and gone down to the bone. I could see the neatly mended rents in the coat he had on. His right arm, from the elbow down, looked as though it had gone through a threshing machine, what of the ravage wrought by claws and fangs. But it was nothing, he said, only the old wounds bothered him somewhat when rainy weather came on.

Suddenly his face brightened with a recollection, for he was really as anxious to give me a story as I was to get it.

"I suppose you've heard of the lion-tamer who was hated by another man?" he asked.

He paused and looked pensively at a sick lion in the cage opposite.

"Got the toothache," he explained. "Well, the lion-tamer's big play to the audience was putting his head in a lion's mouth. The man who hated him attended every performance in the hope sometime of seeing that lion crunch down. He followed the show about all over the country. The years went by and he grew old, and the lion-tamer grew old, and the lion grew old. And at last one day, sitting in a front seat, he saw what he had waited for. The lion crunched down, and there wasn't any need to call a doctor."

The Leopard Man glanced casually over his fingernails in a manner which would have been critical had it not been so sad.

"Now, that's what I call patience," he continued, "and it's my style. But it was not the style of a fellow I knew. He was a little, thin, sawed-off, sword-swallowing and juggling Frenchman. De Ville, he called himself, and he had a nice wife. She did trapeze work and used to dive from under the roof into a net, turning over once on the way as nice as you please.

"De Ville had a quick temper, as quick as his hand, and his hand was as quick as the paw of a tiger. One day, because the ring-master called him a frog-eater, or something like that and maybe a little worse, he shoved him against the soft pine background he used in his knife-throwing act, so quick the ring-master didn't have time to think, and there, before the audience, De Ville kept the air on fire with his knives, sinking them into the wood all around the ring-master so close that they passed through his clothes and most of them bit into his skin.

"The clowns had to pull the knives out to get him loose, for he was pinned fast. So the word went around to watch out for De Ville, and no one dared be more than barely civil to his wife. And she was a sly bit of baggage, too, only all hands were afraid of De Ville.

"But there was one man, Wallace, who was afraid of nothing. He was the lion-tamer, and he had the self-same trick of putting his head into the lion's mouth. He'd put it into the mouths of any of them, though he preferred Augustus, a big, good-natured beast who could always be depended upon.

"As I was saying, Wallace—'King' Wallace we called him—was afraid of nothing alive or dead. He was a king and no mistake. I've seen him drunk, and on a wager go into the cage of a lion that'd turned nasty, and without a stick beat him to a finish. Just did it with his fist on the nose.

"Madame de Ville—"

At an uproar behind us the Leopard Man turned quietly around. It was a divided cage, and a monkey, poking through the bars and around the partition, had had its paw seized by a big gray wolf who was trying to pull it off by main strength. The arm seemed stretching out longer and longer like a thick elastic, and the unfortunate monkey's mates were raising a terrible din. No keeper was at hand, so the Leopard Man stepped over a couple of paces, dealt the wolf a sharp blow on the nose with the light cane he carried, and returned with a sadly apologetic smile to take up his unfinished sentence as though there had been no interruption.

"—looked at King Wallace and King Wallace looked at her, while De Ville looked black. We warned Wallace, but it was no use. He laughed at us, as he laughed at De Ville one day when he shoved De Ville's head into a bucket of paste because he wanted to fight.

"De Ville was in a pretty mess—I helped to scrape him

off; but he was cool as a cucumber and made no threats at all. But I saw a glitter in his eyes which I had seen often in the eyes of wild beasts, and I went out of my way to give Wallace a final warning. He laughed, but he did not look so much in Madame de Ville's direction after that.

"Several months passed by. Nothing had happened and I was beginning to think it all a scare over nothing. We were West by that time, showing in 'Frisco. It was during the afternoon performance, and the big tent was filled with women and children, when I went looking for Red Denny, the head canvas-man, who had walked off with my pocket-knife.

"Passing by one of the dressing tents I glanced in through a hole in the canvas to see if I could locate him. He wasn't there, but directly in front of me was King Wallace, in tights, waiting for his turn to go on with his cage of performing lions. He was watching with much amusement a quarrel between a couple of trapeze artists. All the rest of the people in the dressing tent were watching the same thing, with the exception of De Ville, whom I noticed staring at Wallace with undisguised hatred. Wallace and the rest were all too busy following the quarrel to notice this or what followed.

"But I saw it through the hole in the canvas. De Ville drew his handkerchief from his pocket, made as though to mop the sweat from his face with it (it was a hot day), and at the same time walked past Wallace's back. He never stopped, but with a flirt of the handkerchief kept right on to the doorway, where he turned his head, while passing out, and shot a swift look back. The look troubled me at the time, for not only did I see hatred in it, but I saw triumph as well.

"'De Ville will bear watching,' I said to myself, and I really breathed easier when I saw him go out the entrance to the circus grounds and board an electric car for down town. A few minutes later I was in the big tent, where I had overhauled Red Denny. King Wallace was doing his turn and holding the audience spellbound. He was in a particularly vicious mood, and he kept the lions stirred up till they were all snarling, that is, all of them except old Augustus, and he was just too fat and lazy and old to get stirred up over anything.

"Finally Wallace cracked the old lion's knees with his whip and got him into position. Old Augustus, blinking good-naturedly, opened his mouth and in popped Wallace's head. Then the jaws came together, *crunch*, just like that."

The Leopard Man smiled in a sweetly wistful fashion, and the far-away look came into his eyes.

"And that was the end of King Wallace," he went on in his sad, low voice. "After the excitement cooled down I watched my chance and bent over and smelled Wallace's head. Then I sneezed."

"It . . . it was . . . ?" I queried with halting eagerness.

"Snuff—that De Ville dropped on his hair in the dressing tent. Old Augustus never meant to do it. He only sneezed."

THE PROBLEM
OF CELL 13
by Jacques Futrelle

PRACTICALLY ALL THOSE LETTERS REMAINING IN THE ALPHA-
bet after Augustus S. F. X. Van Dusen was named were
afterward acquired by that gentleman in the course of a
brilliant scientific career, and, being honorably acquired,
were tacked on to the other end. His name, therefore, taken
with all that belonged to it, was a wonderfully imposing
structure. He was a Ph.D., an LL.D., an F.R.S., an M.D.,
and an M.D.S. He was also some other things—just what he
himself couldn't say—through recognition of his ability by
various foreign educational and scientific institutions.

In appearance he was no less striking than in nomencla-
ture. He was slender with the droop of the student in his
thin shoulders and the pallor of a close, sedentary life on
his clean-shaven face. His eyes wore a perceptual, forbid-
ding squint—the squint of a man who studies little things—
and when they could be seen at all through his thick spectacles, were mere slits of watery blue. But above his eyes was
his most striking feature. This was a tall, broad brow, almost abnormal in height and width, crowned by a heavy
shock of bushy, yellow hair. All these things conspired to
give him a peculiar, almost grotesque, personality.

Professor Van Dusen was remotely German. For genera-
tions his ancestors had been noted in the sciences; he was
the logical result, the mastermind. First and above all he
was a logician. At least thirty-five years of the half century
or so of his existence had been devoted exclusively to pro-
viding that two and two always equal four, except in unusual cases, where they equal three or five, as the case may

be. He stood broadly on the general proposition that all
things that start must go somewhere, and was able to bring
the concentrated mental force of his forefathers to bear on
a given problem. Incidentally it may be remarked that Professor Van Dusen wore a No. 8 hat.

The world at large had heard vaguely of Professor Van
Dusen as The Thinking Machine. It was a newspaper catch-
phrase applied to him at the time of a remarkable exhibition
at chess; he had demonstrated then that a stranger to the
game might, by the force of inevitable logic, defeat a cham-
pion who had devoted a lifetime to its study. The Thinking
Machine! Perhaps that more nearly described him than all
his honorary initials, for he spent week after week, month
after month, in the seclusion of his small laboratory from
which had gone forth thoughts that staggered scientific associates and deeply stirred the world at large.

It was only occasionally that The Thinking Machine had
visitors, and these were usually men who, themselves high in
the sciences, dropped in to argue a point and perhaps convince themselves. Two of these men, Dr. Charles Ransome
and Alfred Fielding, called one evening to discuss some
theory which is not of consequence here.

"Such a thing is impossible," declared Dr. Ransome em-
phatically, in the course of the conversation.

"Nothing is impossible," declared The Thinking Machine
with equal emphasis. He always spoke petulantly. "The
mind is master of all things. When science fully recognizes
that fact a great advance will have been made."

"How about the airship?" asked Dr. Ransome.

"That's not impossible at all," asserted The Thinking
Machine. "It will be invented some time. I'd do it myself,
but I'm busy."

Dr. Ransome laughed tolerantly.

"I've heard you say such things before," he said. "But
they mean nothing. Mind may be master of matter, but it
hasn't yet found a way to apply itself. There are some things
that can't be *thought* out of existence, or rather which
would not yield to any amount of thinking."

"What, for instance?" demanded The Thinking Machine.

Dr. Ransome was thoughtful for a moment as he smoked.

"Well, say prison walls," he replied. "No man can *think* himself out of a cell. If he could, there would be no prisoners."

"A man can so apply his brain and ingenuity that he can leave a cell, which is the same thing," snapped The Thinking Machine.

Dr. Ransome was slightly amused.

"Let's suppose a case," he said, after a moment. "Take a cell where prisoners under sentence of death are confined— men who are desperate and, maddened by fear, would take any chance to escape—suppose you were locked in such a cell. Could you escape?"

"Certainly," declared The Thinking Machine.

"Of course," said Mr. Fielding, who entered the conversation for the first time, "you might wreck the cell with an explosive—but inside, a prisoner, you couldn't have that."

"There would be nothing of that kind," said The Thinking Machine. "You might treat me precisely as you treated prisoners under sentence of death, and I would leave the cell."

"Not unless you entered it with tools prepared to get out," said Dr. Ransome.

The Thinking Machine was visibly annoyed and his blue eyes snapped.

"Lock me in any cell in any prison anywhere at any time, wearing only what is necessary, and I'll escape in a week," he declared, sharply.

Dr. Ransome sat up straight in the chair, interested. Mr. Fielding lighted a new cigar.

"You mean you could actually *think* yourself out?" asked Dr. Ransome.

"I would get out," was the response.

"Are you serious?"

"Certainly I am serious."

Dr. Ransome and Mr. Fielding were silent for a long time.

"Would you be willing to try it?" asked Mr. Fielding, finally.

"Certainly," said Professor Van Dusen, and there was a trace of irony in his voice. "I have done more asinine things than that to convince other men of less important truths."

The tone was offensive and there was an undercurrent strongly resembling anger on both sides. Of course it was an absurd thing, but Professor Van Dusen reiterated his willingness to undertake the escape and it was decided upon.

"To begin now," added Dr. Ransome.

"I'd prefer that it begin to-morrow," said The Thinking Machine, "because—"

"No, now," said Mr. Fielding, flatly. "You are arrested, figuratively, of course, without any warning locked in a cell with no chance to communicate with friends, and left there with identically the same care and attention that would be given to a man under sentence of death. Are you willing?"

"All right, now, then," said The Thinking Machine, and he arose.

"Say, the death cell in Chisholm Prison."

"The death cell in Chisholm Prison."

"And what will you wear?"

"As little as possible," said The Thinking Machine. "Shoes, stockings, trousers and a shirt."

"You will permit yourself to be searched, of course?"

"I am to be treated precisely as all prisoners are treated," said The Thinking Machine. "No more attention and no less."

There were some preliminaries to be arranged in the matter of obtaining permission for the test, but all three were influential men and everything was done satisfactorily by telephone, albeit the prison commissioners, to whom the experiment was explained on purely scientific grounds, were sadly bewildered. Professor Van Dusen would be the most distinguished prisoner they had ever entertained.

When The Thinking Machine had donned those things which he was to wear during his incarceration, he called the little old woman who was his housekeeper, cook and maidservant all in one.

"Martha," he said, "it is now twenty-seven minutes past nine o'clock. I am going away. One week from to-night, at half past nine, these gentlemen and one, possibly two, others will take supper with me here. Remember Dr. Ransome is very fond of artichokes."

The three men were driven to Chisholm Prison, where the warden was awaiting them, having been informed of the matter by telephone. He understood merely that the eminent Professor Van Dusen was to be his prisoner, if he could keep him, for one week; that he had committed no crime, but that he was to be treated as all other prisoners were treated.

"Search him," instructed Dr. Ransome.

The Thinking Machine was searched. Nothing was found on him; the pockets of the trousers were empty; the white, stiff-bosomed shirt had no pocket. The shoes and stockings were removed, examined, then replaced. As he watched all these preliminaries, and noted the pitiful, childlike physical weakness of the man—the colorless face, and the thin, white hands—Dr. Ransome almost regretted his part in the affair.

"Are you sure you want to do this?" he asked.

"Would you be convinced if I did not?" inquired The Thinking Machine in turn.

"No."

"All right. I'll do it."

What sympathy Dr. Ransome had was dissipated by the tone. It nettled him, and he resolved to see the experiment to the end; it would be a stinging reproof to egotism.

"It will be impossible for him to communicate with anyone outside?" he asked.

"Absolutely impossible," replied the warden. "He will not be permitted writing materials of any sort."

"And your jailers, would they deliver a message from him?"

"Not one word, directly or indirectly," said the warden.

"You may rest assured of that. They will report anything he might say or turn over to me, anything he might give them."

"That seems entirely satisfactory," said Mr. Fielding, who was frankly interested in the problem.

"Of course, in the event he fails," said Dr. Ransome, "and asks for his liberty, you understand you are to set him free?"

"I understand," replied the warden.

The Thinking Machine stood listening, but had nothing to say until this was all ended, then:

"I should like to make three small requests. You may grant them or not, as you wish."

"No special favors, now," warned Mr. Fielding.

"I am asking none," was the stiff response. "I should like to have some tooth powder—buy it yourself to see that it is tooth powder—and I should like to have one five-dollar and two ten-dollar bills."

Dr. Ransome, Mr. Fielding and the warden exchanged astonished glances. They were not surprised at the request for tooth powder, but were at the request for money.

"Is there any man with whom our friend would come in contact that he could bribe with twenty-five dollars?"

"Not for twenty-five hundred dollars," was the positive reply.

"Well, let him have them," said Mr. Fielding. "I think they are harmless enough."

"And what is the third request?" asked Dr. Ransome.

"I should like to have my shoes polished."

Again the astonished glances were exchanged. This last request was the height of absurdity, so they agreed to it. These things all being attended to, The Thinking Machine was led back into the prison from which he had undertaken to escape.

"Here is Cell 13," said the warden, stopping three doors down the steel corridor. "This is where we keep condemned murderers. No one can leave it without my permission; and no one in it can communicate with the outside. I'll stake my reputation on that. It's only three doors back of my office and I can readily hear any unusual noise."

"Will this cell do, gentlemen?" asked The Thinking Machine. There was a touch of irony in his voice.

"Admirably," was the reply.

The heavy steel door was thrown open, there was a great scurrying and scampering of tiny feet, and The Thinking Machine passed into the gloom of the cell. Then the door was closed and double locked by the warden.

"What is that noise in there?" asked Dr. Ransome, through the bars.

"Rats—dozens of them," replied The Thinking Machine, tersely.

The three men, with final good nights, were turning away when The Thinking Machine called:

"What time is it exactly, Warden?"

"Eleven-seventeen," replied the warden.

"Thanks. I will join you gentlemen in your office at half past eight o'clock one week from to-night," said The Thinking Machine.

"And if you do not?"

"There is no 'if' about it."

Chisholm Prison was a great, spreading structure of granite, four stories in all, which stood in the center of acres of open space. It was surrounded by a wall of solid masonry eighteen feet high, and so smoothly finished inside and out as to offer no foothold to a climber, no matter how expert. Atop of this fence, as a further precaution, was a five-foot fence of steel rods, each terminating in a keen point. This fence in itself marked an absolute deadline between freedom and imprisonment, for, even if a man escaped from his cell, it would seem impossible for him to pass the wall.

The yard, which on all sides of the prison building was twenty-five feet wide, that being the distance from the building to the wall, was by day an exercise ground for those prisoners to whom was granted the boon of occa-

sional semi-liberty. But that was not for those in Cell 13.
At all times of the day there were armed guards in the yard,
four of them, one patrolling each side of the prison building.

By night the yard was almost as brilliantly lighted as by
day. On each of the four sides was a great arc light which
rose above the prison wall and gave to the guards a clear
sight. The lights, too, brightly illuminated the spiked top of
the wall. The wires which fed the arc lights ran up the side
of the prison building on insulators and from the top story
led out to the poles supporting the arc lights.

All these things were seen and comprehended by The
Thinking Machine, who was only enabled to see out his
closely barred cell window by standing on his bed. This was
on the morning following his incarceration. He gathered,
too, that the river lay over there beyond the wall somewhere, because he heard faintly the pulsation of a motor
boat and high up in the air saw a river bird. From that same
direction came the shouts of boys at play and the occasional
crack of a batted ball. He knew then that between the prison
wall and the river was an open space, a playground.

Chisholm Prison was regarded as absolutely safe. No man
had ever escaped from it. The Thinking Machine, from his
perch on the bed, seeing what he saw, could readily understand why. The walls of the cell, though built he judged
twenty years before, were perfectly solid, and the window
bars of new iron had not a shadow of rust on them. The
window itself, even with the bars out, would be a difficult
mode of egress because it was small.

Yet, seeing these things, The Thinking Machine was not
discouraged. Instead, he thoughtfully squinted at the great
arc light—there was bright sunlight now—and traced with
his eyes the wire which led from it to the building. That
electric wire, he reasoned, must come down the side of the
building not a great distance from his cell. That might be
worth knowing.

Cell 13 was on the same floor with the offices of the
prison—that is, not in the basement, nor yet upstairs. There
were only four steps up to the office floor, therefore the

level of the floor must be only three or four feet above the ground. He couldn't see the ground directly beneath his window, but he could see it further out toward the wall. It would be an easy drop from the window. Well and good.

Then The Thinking Machine fell to remembering how he had come to the cell. First, there was the outside guard's booth, a part of the wall. There were two heavily barred gates there, both of steel. At this gate was one man always on guard. He admitted persons to the prison after much clanking of keys and locks, and let them out when ordered to do so. The warden's office was in the prison building, and in order to reach that official from the prison yard one had to pass a gate of solid steel with only a peephole in it. Then coming from that inner office to Cell 13, where he was now, one must pass a heavy wooden door and two steel doors into the corridors of the prison; and always there was the double-locked door of Cell 13 to reckon with.

There were then, The Thinking Machine recalled, seven doors to be overcome before one could pass from Cell 13 into the outer world, a free man. But against this was the fact that he was rarely interrupted. A jailer appeared at his cell door at six in the morning with a breakfast of prison fare; he would come again at noon, and again at six in the afternoon. At nine o'clock at night would come the inspection tour. That would be all.

"It's admirably arranged, this prison system," was the mental tribute paid by The Thinking Machine. "I'll have to study it a little when I get out. I had no idea there was such great care exercised in the prisons."

There was nothing, positively nothing, in his cell, except his iron bed, so firmly put together that no man could tear it to pieces save with sledges or a file. He had neither of these. There was not even a chair, or a small table, or a bit of tin or crockery. Nothing! The jailer stood by when he ate, then took away the wooden spoon and bowl which he had used.

One by one these things sank into the brain of The Thinking Machine. When the last possibility had been considered

he began an examination of his cell. From the roof, down
the walls on all sides, he examined the stones and the cement between them. He stamped over the floor carefully
time after time, but it was cement, perfectly solid. After the
examination he sat on the edge of the iron bed and was lost
in thought for a long time. For Professor Augustus S. F. X.
Van Dusen, The Thinking Machine, had something to think
about.

He was disturbed by a rat, which ran across his foot, then
scampered away into a dark corner of the cell, frightened
at its own daring. After a while The Thinking Machine,
squinting steadily into the darkness of the corner where the
rat had gone, was able to make out in the gloom many little beady eyes staring at him. He counted six pair, and there
were perhaps others; he didn't see very well.

Then The Thinking Machine, from his seat on the bed,
noticed for the first time the bottom of his cell door. There
was an opening there of two inches between the steel bar
and floor. Still looking steadily at this opening, The Thinking Machine backed suddenly into the corner where he had
seen the beady eyes. There was a great scampering of tiny
feet, several squeaks of frightened rodents, and then silence.

None of the rats had gone out the door, yet there were
none in the cell. Therefore there must be another way out
of the cell, however small. The Thinking Machine, on hands
and knees, started a search for this spot, feeling in the darkness with his long, slender fingers.

At last his search was rewarded. He came upon a small
opening in the floor, level with the cement. It was perfectly
round and somewhat larger than a silver dollar. This was
the way the rats had gone. He put his fingers deep into the
opening; it seemed to be a disused drainage pipe and was
dry and dusty.

Having satisfied himself on this point, he sat on the bed
again for an hour, then made another inspection of his surroundings through the small cell window. One of the outside guards stood directly opposite, beside the wall, and
happened to be looking at the window of Cell 13 when the

head of The Thinking Machine appeared. But the scientist didn't notice the guard.

Noon came and the jailer appeared with the prison dinner of repulsively plain food. At home The Thinking Machine merely ate to live; here he took what was offered without comment. Occasionally he spoke to the jailer who stood outside the door watching him.

"Any improvements made here in the last few years?" he asked.

"Nothing particularly," replied the jailer. "New wall was built four years ago."

"Anything done to the prison proper?"

"Painted the woodwork outside, and I believe about seven years ago a new system of plumbing was put in."

"Ah!" said the prisoner. "How far is the river over there?"

"About three hundred feet. The boys have a baseball ground between the wall and the river."

The Thinking Machine had nothing further to say just then, but when the jailer was ready to go he asked for some water.

"I get very thirsty here," he explained. "Would it be possible for you to leave a little water in a bowl for me?"

"I'll ask the warden," replied the jailer, and he went away.

Half an hour later he returned with water in a small earthen bowl.

"The warden says you may keep this bowl," he informed the prisoner. "But you must show it to me when I ask for it. If it is broken, it will be the last."

"Thank you," said The Thinking Machine. "I shan't break it."

The jailer went on about his duties. For just the fraction of a second it seemed that The Thinking Machine wanted to ask a question, but he didn't.

Two hours later this same jailer, in passing the door of Cell No. 13, heard a noise inside and stopped. The Thinking Machine was down on his hands and knees in a corner of the cell, and from that same corner came several frightened squeaks. The jailer looked on interestedly.

"Ah, I've got you," he heard the prisoner say.

"Got what?" he asked, sharply.

"One of these rats," was the reply. "See?" And between the scientist's long fingers the jailer saw a small gray rat struggling. The prisoner brought it over to the light and looked at it closely.

"It's a water rat," he said.

"Ain't you got anything better to do than to catch rats?" asked the jailer.

"It's disgraceful that they should be here at all," was the irritated reply. "Take this one away and kill it. There are dozens more where it came from."

The jailer took the wriggling, squirmy rodent and flung it down on the floor violently. It gave one squeak and lay still. Later he reported the incident to the warden, who only smiled.

Still later that afternoon the outside armed guard on the Cell 13 side of the prison looked up again at the window and saw the prisoner looking out. He saw a hand raised to the barred window and then something white fluttered to the ground, directly under the window of Cell 13. It was a little roll of linen, evidently of white shirting material, and tied around it was a five-dollar bill. The guard looked up at the window again, but the face had disappeared.

With a grim smile he took the little linen roll and the five-dollar bill to the warden's office. There together they deciphered something which was written on it with a queer sort of ink, frequently blurred. On the outside was this:

"Finder of this please deliver to Dr. Charles Ransome."

"Ah," said the warden, with a chuckle. "Plan of escape number one has gone wrong." Then, as an afterthought: "But why did he address it to Dr. Ransome?"

"And where did he get the pen and ink to write with?" asked the guard.

The warden looked at the guard and the guard looked at the warden. There was no apparent solution of that mystery. The warden studied the writing carefully, then shook his head.

"Well, let's see what he was going to say to Dr. Ransome," he said at length, still puzzled, and he unrolled the inner piece of linen.

"Well, if that—what—what do you think of that?" he asked dazed.

The guard took the bit of linen and read this:—

"Epa cseot d'net niiy awe htto n'si sih. T."

The warden spent an hour wondering what sort of a cipher it was, and half an hour wondering why his prisoner should attempt to communicate with Dr. Ransome, who was the cause of his being there. After this the warden devoted some thought to the question of where the prisoner got writing materials, and what sort of writing materials he had. With the idea of illuminating this point, he examined the linen again. It was a torn part of a white shirt and had ragged edges.

Now it was possible to account for the linen, but what the prisoner had used to write with was another matter. The warden knew it would have been impossible for him to have either pen or pencil, and, besides, neither pen nor pencil had been used in this writing. What, then? The warden decided to investigate personally. The Thinking Machine was his prisoner; he had orders to hold his prisoners; if this one sought to escape by sending cipher messages to persons outside, he would stop it, as he would have stopped it in the case of any other prisoner.

The warden went back to Cell 13 and found The Thinking Machine on his hands and knees on the floor, engaged in nothing more alarming than catching rats. The prisoner heard the warden's step and turned to him quickly.

"It's disgraceful," he snapped, "these rats. There are scores of them."

"Other men have been able to stand them," said the

warden. "Here is another shirt for you—let me have the one you have on."

"Why?" demanded The Thinking Machine, quickly. His tone was hardly natural, his manner suggested actual perturbation.

"You have attempted to communicate with Dr. Ransome," said the warden severely. "As my prisoner, it is my duty to put a stop to it."

The Thinking Machine was silent for a moment.

"All right," he said, finally. "Do your duty."

The warden smiled grimly. The prisoner arose from the floor and removed the white shirt, putting on instead a striped convict shirt the warden had brought. The warden took the white shirt eagerly, and then and there compared the pieces of linen on which was written the cipher with certain torn places in the shirt. The Thinking Machine looked on curiously.

"The guard brought *you* those, then?" he asked.

"He certainly did," replied the warden triumphantly. "And that ends your first attempt to escape."

The Thinking Machine watched the warden as he, by comparison, established to his own satisfaction that only two pieces of linen had been torn from the white shirt.

"What did you write this with?" demanded the warden.

"I should think it a part of your duty to find out," said The Thinking Machine, irritably.

The warden started to say some harsh things, then restrained himself and made a minute search of the cell and of the prisoner instead. He found absolutely nothing; not even a match or toothpick which might have been used for a pen. The same mystery surrounded the fluid with which the cipher had been written. Although the warden left Cell 13 visibly annoyed, he took the torn shirt in triumph.

"Well, writing notes on a shirt won't get him out, that's certain," he told himself with some complacency. He put the linen scraps into his desk to await developments. "If that man escapes from that cell I'll—hang it—I'll resign."

On the third day of his incarceration The Thinking Machine openly attempted to bribe his way out. The jailer had brought his dinner and was leaning against the barred door, waiting, when The Thinking Machine began the conversation.

"The drainage pipes of the prison lead to the river, don't they?" he asked.

"Yes," said the jailer.

"I suppose they are very small."

"Too small to crawl through, if that's what you're thinking about," was the grinning response.

There was silence until The Thinking Machine finished his meal. Then:

"You know I'm not a criminal, don't you?"

"Yes."

"And that I've a perfect right to be freed if I demand it?"

"Yes."

"Well, I came here believing that I could make my escape," said the prisoner, and his squint eyes studied the face of the jailer. "Would you consider a financial reward for aiding me to escape?"

The jailer, who happened to be an honest man, looked at the slender, weak figure of the prisoner, at the large head with its mass of yellow hair, and was almost sorry.

"I guess prisons like these were not built for the likes of you to get out of," he said, at last.

"But would you consider a proposition to help me get out?" the prisoner insisted, almost beseechingly.

"No," said the jailer, shortly.

"Five hundred dollars," urged The Thinking Machine. "I am not a criminal."

"No," said the jailer.

"A thousand?"

"No," again said the jailer, and he started away hurriedly to escape further temptation. Then he turned back. "If you should give me ten thousand dollars I couldn't get you out. You'd have to pass through seven doors, and I only have the keys to two."

Then he told the warden all about it.

"Plan number two fails," said the warden, smiling grimly. "First a cipher, then bribery."

When the jailer was on his way to Cell 13 at six o'clock, again bearing food to The Thinking Machine, he paused, startled by the unmistakable scrape, scrape of steel against steel. It stopped at the sound of his steps, then craftily the jailer, who was beyond the prisoner's range of vision, resumed his tramping, the sound being apparently that of a man going away from Cell 13. As a matter of fact he was in the same spot.

After a moment there came again the steady scrape, scrape, and the jailer crept cautiously on tiptoes to the door and peered between the bars. The Thinking Machine was standing on the iron bed working at the bars of the little window. He was using a file, judging from the backward and forward swing of his arms.

Cautiously the jailer crept back to the office, summoned the warden in person, and they returned to Cell 13 on tiptoes. The steady scrape was still audible. The warden listened to satisfy himself and then suddenly appeared at the door.

"Well?" he demanded, and there was a smile on his face.

The Thinking Machine glanced back from his perch on the bed and leaped suddenly to the floor, making frantic efforts to hide something. The warden went in, with hand extended.

"Give it up," he said.

"No," said the prisoner, sharply.

"Come, give it up," urged the warden. "I don't want to have to search you again."

"No," repeated the prisoner.

"What was it—a file?" asked the warden.

The Thinking Machine was silent and stood squinting at the warden with something very nearly approaching disappointment on his face—nearly, but not quite. The warden was almost sympathetic.

"Plan number three fails, eh?" he asked, good-naturedly. "Too bad, isn't it?"

The prisoner didn't say.

"Search him," instructed the warden.

The jailer searched the prisoner carefully. At last, artfully concealed in the waistband of the trousers, he found a piece of steel about two inches long, with one side curved like a half moon.

"Ah," said the warden, as he received it from the jailer. "From your shoe heel," and he smiled pleasantly.

The jailer continued his search and on the other side of the trousers waistband found another piece of steel identical with the first. The edges showed where they had been worn against the bars of the window.

"You couldn't saw a way through those bars with these," said the warden.

"I could have," said The Thinking Machine firmly.

"In six months, perhaps," said the warden, good-naturedly.

The warden shook his head slowly as he gazed into the slightly flushed face of his prisoner.

"Ready to give it up?" he asked.

"I haven't started yet," was the prompt reply.

Then came another exhaustive search of the cell. Carefully the two men went over it, finally turning out the bed and searching that. Nothing. The warden in person climbed upon the bed and examined the bars of the window where the prisoner had been sawing. When he looked he was amused.

"Just made it a little bright by hard rubbing," he said to the prisoner, who stood looking on with a somewhat crestfallen air. The warden grasped the iron bars in his strong hands and tried to shake them. They were immovable, set firmly in the solid granite. He examined each in turn and found them all satisfactory. Finally he climbed down from the bed.

"Give it up, Professor," he advised.

The Thinking Machine shook his head and the warden and jailer passed on again. As they disappeared down the

corridor The Thinking Machine sat on the edge of the bed
with his head in his hands.

"He's crazy to try to get out of that cell," commented the
jailer.

"Of course he can't get out," said the warden. "But he's
clever. I would like to know what he wrote that cipher with."

It was four o'clock next morning when an awful, heart-
racking shriek of terror resounded through the great prison.
It came from a cell, somewhere about the center, and its
tone told a tale of horror, agony, terrible fear. The warden
heard and with three of his men rushed into the long corridor leading to Cell 13.

As they ran there came again that awful cry. It died
away in a sort of wail. The white faces of prisoners appeared
at cell doors upstairs and down, staring out wonderingly,
frightened.

"It's that fool in Cell 13," grumbled the warden.

He stopped and stared in as one of the jailers flashed a
lantern. "That fool in Cell 13" lay comfortably on his cot,
flat on his back with his mouth open, snoring. Even as they
looked there came again the piercing cry, from somewhere
above. The warden's face blanched a little as he started up
the stairs. There on the top floor he found a man in Cell 43,
directly above Cell 13, but two floors higher, cowering in a
corner of his cell.

"What's the matter?" demanded the warden.

"Thank God you've come," exclaimed the prisoner, and
he cast himself against the bars of his cell.

"What is it?" demanded the warden again.

He threw open the door and went in. The prisoner
dropped on his knees and clasped the warden about the
body. His face was white with terror, his eyes were widely
distended, and he was shuddering. His hands, icy cold,
clutched at the warden's.

"Take me out of this cell, please take me out," he pleaded.

"What's the matter with you, anyhow?" insisted the warden, impatiently.

"I heard something—something," said the prisoner, and his eyes roved nervously around the cell.

"What did you hear?"

"I—I can't tell you," stammered the prisoner. Then, in a sudden burst of terror: "Take me out of this cell—put me anywhere—but take me out of here."

The warden and the three jailers exchanged glances.

"Who is this fellow? What's he accused of?" asked the warden.

"Joseph Ballard," said one of the jailers. "He's accused of throwing acid in a woman's face. She died from it."

"But they can't prove it," gasped the prisoner. "They can't prove it. Please put me in some other cell."

He was still clinging to the warden, and that official threw his arms off roughly. Then for a time he stood looking at the cowering wretch, who seemed possessed of all the wild, unreasoning terror of a child.

"Look here, Ballard," said the warden, finally, "if you heard anything, I want to know what it was. Now tell me."

"I can't, I can't," was the reply. He was sobbing.

"Where did it come from?"

"I don't know. Everywhere—nowhere. I just heard it."

"What was it—a voice?"

"Please don't make me answer," pleaded the prisoner.

"You must answer," said the warden, sharply.

"It was a voice—but—but it wasn't human," was the sobbing reply.

"Voice, but not human?" repeated the warden, puzzled.

"It sounded muffled and—and far away—and ghostly," explained the man.

"Did it come from inside or outside the prison?"

"It didn't seem to come from anywhere—it was just here, here, everywhere. I heard it. I heard it."

For an hour the warden tried to get the story, but Ballard had become suddenly obstinate and would say nothing—only pleaded to be placed in another cell, or to have one of the jailers remain near him until daylight. These requests were gruffly refused.

"And see here," said the warden, in conclusion, "if there's any more of this screaming I'll put you in the padded cell."

Then the warden went his way, a sadly puzzled man. Ballard sat at his cell door until daylight, his face, drawn and white with terror, pressed against the bars, and looked out into the prison with wide, staring eyes.

That day, the fourth since the incarceration of The Thinking Machine, was enlivened considerably by the volunteer prisoner, who spent most of his time at the little window of his cell. He began proceedings by throwing another piece of linen down to the guard, who picked it up dutifully and took it to the warden. On it was written:

"Only three days more."

The warden was in no way surprised at what he read; he understood that The Thinking Machine meant only three days more of his imprisonment, and he regarded the note as a boast. But how was the thing written? Where had The Thinking Machine found this new piece of linen? Where? How? He carefully examined the linen. It was white, of fine texture, shirting material. He took the shirt which he had taken and carefully fitted the two original pieces of the linen to the torn places. This third piece was entirely superfluous; it didn't fit anywhere, and yet it was unmistakably the same goods.

"And where—where does he get anything to write with?" demanded the warden of the world at large.

Still later on the fourth day The Thinking Machine, through the window of his cell, spoke to the armed guard outside.

"What day of the month is it?" he asked.

"The fifteenth," was the answer.

The Thinking Machine made a mental astronomical calculation and satisfied himself that the moon would not rise until after nine o'clock that night. Then he asked another question:

"Who attends to those arc lights?"

"Man from the company."

"You have no electricians in the building?"

"No."

"I should think you could save money if you had your own man."

"None of my business," replied the guard.

The guard noticed The Thinking Machine at the cell window frequently during that day, but always the face seemed listless and there was a certain wistfulness in the squint eyes behind the glasses. After a while he accepted the presence of the leonine head as a matter of course. He had seen other prisoners do the same thing; it was the longing for the outside world.

That afternoon, just before the day guard was relieved, the head appeared at the window again, and The Thinking Machine's hand held something out between the bars. It fluttered to the ground and the guard picked it up. It was a five-dollar bill.

"That's for you," called the prisoner.

As usual, the guard took it to the warden. That gentleman looked at it suspiciously; he looked at everything that came from Cell 13 with suspicion.

"He said it was for me," explained the guard.

"It's a sort of a tip, I suppose," said the warden. "I see no particular reason why you shouldn't accept—"

Suddenly he stopped. He had remembered that The Thinking Machine had gone into Cell 13 with one five-dollar bill and two ten-dollar bills; twenty-five dollars in all. Now a five dollar bill had been tied around the first pieces of linen that came from the cell. The warden still had it, and to convince himself he took it out and looked at it. It was five dollars; yet here was another five dollars, and The Thinking Machine had only had ten-dollar bills.

"Perhaps somebody changed one of the bills for him," he thought at last, with a sigh of relief.

But then and there he made up his mind. He would search Cell 13 as a cell was never before searched in this world. When a man could write at will, and change money, and do other wholly inexplicable things, there was something radically wrong with his prison. He planned to enter the cell at night—three o'clock would be an excellent time. The Thinking Machine must do all the weird things he did sometime. Night seemed the most reasonable.

Thus it happened that the warden stealthily descended upon Cell 13 that night at three o'clock. He paused at the door and listened. There was no sound save the steady, regular breathing of the prisoner. The keys unfastened the double locks with scarcely a clank, and the warden entered, locking the door behind him. Suddenly he flashed his dark lantern in the face of the recumbent figure.

If the warden had planned to startle The Thinking Machine he was mistaken, for that individual merely opened his eyes quietly, reached for his glasses and inquired, in a most matter-of-fact tone: "Who is it?"

It would be useless to describe the search that the warden made. It was minute. Not one inch of the cell or the bed was overlooked. He found the round hole in the floor, and with a flash of inspiration thrust his thick fingers into it. After a moment of fumbling there he drew up something and looked at it in the light of his lantern.

"Ugh!" he exclaimed.

The thing he had taken out was a rat—a dead rat. His inspiration fled as a mist before the sun. But he continued the search. The Thinking Machine, without a word, arose and kicked the rat out of the cell into the corridor.

The warden climbed on the bed and tried the steel bars in the tiny window. They were perfectly rigid; every bar of the door was the same.

Then the warden searched the prisoner's clothing, beginning at the shoes. Nothing hidden in them! Then the trousers waistband. Still nothing! Then the pockets of the trousers. From one side he drew out some paper money and examined it.

"Five one-dollar bills," he gasped.

"That's right," said the prisoner.

"But the—you had two tens and a five—what the—how do you do it?"

"That's my business," said The Thinking Machine.

"Did any of my men change this money for you—on your word of honor?"

The Thinking Machine paused just a fraction of a second. "No," he said.

"Well, do you make it?" asked the warden. He was prepared to believe anything.

"That's my business," again said the prisoner.

The warden glared at the eminent scientist fiercely. He felt—he knew—that this man was making a fool of him, yet he didn't know how. If he were a real prisoner he would get the truth—but, then, perhaps, those inexplicable things which had happened would not have been brought before him so sharply. Neither of the men spoke for a long time, then suddenly the warden turned fiercely and left the cell, slamming the door behind him. He didn't dare to speak then.

He glanced at the clock. It was ten minutes to four. He had hardly settled himself in bed when again came that heart-breaking shriek through the prison. With a few muttered words, which, while not elegant, were highly expressive, he relighted his lantern and rushed through the prison again to the cell on the upper floor.

Again Ballard was crushing himself against the steel door, shrieking, shrieking at the top of his voice. He stopped only when the warden flashed his lamp in the cell.

"Take me out, take me out," he screamed. "I did it, I did it, I killed her. Take it away."

"Take what away?" asked the warden.

"I threw the acid in her face—I did it—I confess. Take me out of here."

Ballard's condition was pitiable; it was only an act of mercy to let him out into the corridor. There he crouched in a corner, like an animal at bay, and clasped his hands to his ears. It took half an hour to calm him sufficiently for him to speak. Then he told incoherently what had happened. On the night before at four o'clock he had heard a voice—a sepulchral voice, muffled and wailing in tone.

"What did it say?" asked the warden, curiously.

"Acid—acid—acid!" gasped the prisoner. "It accused me. Acid! I threw the acid, and the woman died. Oh!" It was a long, shuddering wail of terror.

"Acid?" echoed the warden, puzzled. The case was beyond him.

"Acid. That's all I heard—that one word, repeated several times. There were other things, too, but I didn't hear them."

"That was last night, eh?" asked the warden. "What happened to-night—what frightened you just now?"

"It was the same thing," gasped the prisoner. "Acid—acid—acid!" He covered his face with his hands and sat shivering. "It was acid I used on her, but I didn't mean to kill her. I just heard the words. It was something accusing me—accusing me." He mumbled, and was silent.

"Did you hear anything else?"

"Yes—but I couldn't understand—only a little bit—just a word or two."

"Well, what was it?"

"I heard 'acid' three times, then I heard a long, moaning sound, then—then—I heard 'No. 8 hat.' I heard that twice."

"No. 8 hat," repeated the warden. "What the devil—No. 8 hat? Accusing voices of conscience have never talked about No. 8 hats, so far as I ever heard."

"He's insane," said one of the jailers, with an air of finality.

"I believe you," said the warden. "He must be. He probably heard something and got frightened. He's trembling now. No. 8 hat! What the—"

When the fifth day of The Thinking Machine's imprisonment rolled around the warden was wearing a hunted look. He was anxious for the end of the thing. He could not help but feel that his distinguished prisoner had been amusing himself. And if this were so, The Thinking Machine had lost none of his sense of humor. For on this fifth day he flung down another linen note to the outside guard, bearing the words: "Only two days more." Also he flung down half a dollar.

Now the warden knew—he *knew*—that the man in Cell 13 didn't have any half dollars—he *couldn't* have any half dollars, no more than he could have pen and ink and linen, and yet he did have them. It was a condition, not a theory; that is one reason why the warden was wearing a hunted look.

That ghastly, uncanny thing, too, about "Acid" and "No. 8 hat" clung to him tenaciously. They didn't mean anything, of course, merely the ravings of an insane murderer who had been driven by fear to confess his crime, still there were so many things that "didn't mean anything" happening in the prison now since The Thinking Machine was there.

On the sixth day the warden received a card stating that Dr. Ransome and Mr. Fielding would be at Chisholm Prison on the following evening, Thursday, and in the event Professor Van Dusen had not yet escaped—and they presumed he had not because they had not heard from him—they would meet him there.

"In the event he had not yet escaped!" The warden smiled grimly. Escaped!

The Thinking Machine enlivened this day for the warden with three notes. They were on the usual linen and bore generally on the appointment at half past eight o'clock Thursday night, which appointment the scientist had made at the time of his imprisonment.

On the afternoon of the seventh day the warden passed Cell 13 and glanced in. The Thinking Machine was lying on the iron bed, apparently sleeping lightly. The cell appeared precisely as it always did from a casual glance. The warden would swear that no man was going to leave it between that hour—it was then four o'clock—and half past eight o'clock that evening.

On his way back past the cell the warden heard the steady breathing again, and coming close to the door looked in.

He wouldn't have done so if The Thinking Machine had been looking, but now—well, it was different.

A ray of light came through the high window and fell on the face of the sleeping man. It occurred to the warden for the first time that his prisoner appeared haggard and weary. Just then The Thinking Machine stirred slightly and the warden hurried on up the corridor guiltily. That evening after six o'clock he saw the jailer.

"Everything all right in Cell 13?" he asked.

"Yes, sir," replied the jailer. "He didn't eat much, though."

It was with a feeling of having done his duty that the warden received Dr. Ransome and Mr. Fielding shortly after seven o'clock. He intended to show them the linen notes and lay before them the full story of his woes, which was a long one. But before this came to pass the guard from the river side of the prison yard entered the office.

"The arc light in my side of the yard won't light," he informed the warden.

"Confound it, that man's a hoodoo," thundered the official. "Everything has happened since he's been here."

The guard went back to his post in the darkness, and the warden phoned to the electric light company.

"This is Chisholm Prison," he said through the phone. "Send three or four men down here quick, to fix an arc light."

The reply was evidently satisfactory, for the warden hung up the receiver and passed out into the yard. While Dr. Ransome and Mr. Fielding sat waiting, the guard at the outer gate came in with a special-delivery letter. Dr. Ransome happened to notice the address, and, when the guard went out, looked at the letter more closely.

"By George!" he exclaimed.

"What is it?" asked Mr. Fielding.

Silently the doctor offered the letter. Mr. Fielding examined it closely.

"Coincidence," he said. "It must be."

It was nearly eight o'clock when the warden returned to

his office. The electricians had arrived in a wagon, and were now at work. The warden pressed the buzz-button communicating with the man at the outer gate in the wall.

"How many electricians came in?" he asked, over the short phone. "Four? Three workmen in jumpers and overalls and the manager? Frock coat and silk hat? All right. Be certain that only four go out. That's all."

He turned to Dr. Ransome and Mr. Fielding.

"We have to be careful here—particularly," and there was broad sarcasm in his tone, "since we have scientists locked up."

The warden picked up the special delivery letter carelessly, and then began to open it.

"When I read this I want to tell you gentlemen something about how—Great Caesar!" he ended, suddenly, as he glanced at the letter. He sat with mouth open, motionless, from astonishment.

"What is it?" asked Mr. Fielding.

"A special delivery letter from Cell 13," gasped the warden. "An invitation to supper."

"What?" and the two others arose, unanimously.

The warden sat dazed, staring at the letter for a moment, then called sharply to a guard outside the corridor.

"Run down to Cell 13 and see if that man's in there."

The guard went as directed, while Dr. Ransome and Mr. Fielding examined the letter.

"It's Van Dusen's handwriting; there's no question of that," said Dr. Ransome. "I've seen too much of it."

Just then the buzz on the telephone from the outer gate sounded, and the warden, in a semi-trance, picked up the receiver.

"Hello! Two reporters, eh? Let 'em come in." He turned suddenly to the doctor and Mr. Fielding. "Why, the man *can't* be out. He must be in his cell."

Just at that moment the guard returned.

"He's still in his cell, sir," he reported, "I saw him. He's lying down."

"There, I told you so," said the warden, and he breathed

freely again. "But how did he mail that letter?"

There was a rap on the steel door which led from the jail yard into the warden's office.

"It's the reporters," said the warden. "Let them in," he instructed the guard; then to the two other gentlemen: "Don't say anything about this before them, because I'd never hear the last of it."

The door opened, and the two men from the front gate entered.

"Good-evening, gentlemen," said one. That was Hutchinson Hatch; the warden knew him well.

"Well?" demanded the other, irritably. "I'm here."

That was The Thinking Machine.

He squinted belligerently at the warden, who sat with mouth agape. For the moment that official had nothing to say. Dr. Ransome and Mr. Fielding were amazed, but they didn't know what the warden knew. They were only amazed; he was paralyzed. Hutchinson Hatch, the reporter, took in the scene with greedy eyes.

"How—how—how did you do it?" gasped the warden, finally.

"Come back to the cell," said The Thinking Machine, in the irritated voice which his scientific associates knew so well.

The warden, still in a condition bordering on trance, led the way.

"Flash your light in there," directed The Thinking Machine.

The warden did so. There was nothing unusual in the appearance of the cell, and there—there on the bed lay the figure of The Thinking Machine. Certainly! There was the yellow hair! Again the warden looked at the man beside him and wondered at the strangeness of his own dreams.

With trembling hands he unlocked the cell door and The Thinking Machine passed inside.

"See here," he said.

He kicked at the steel bars in the bottom of the cell door

and three of them were pushed out of place. A fourth broke off and rolled away in the corridor.

"And here, too," directed the erstwhile prisoner as he stood on the bed to reach the small window. He swept his hand across the opening and every bar came out.

"What's this in bed?" demanded the warden, who was slowly recovering. ·

"A wig," was the reply. "Turn down the cover."

The warden did so. Beneath it lay a large coil of strong rope, thirty feet or more, a dagger, three files, ten feet of electric wire, a thin, powerful pair of steel pliers, a small tack hammer with its handle, and—and a derringer pistol.

"How did you do it?" demanded the warden.

"You gentlemen have a engagement to supper with me at half past nine o'clock," said The Thinking Machine. "Come on, or we shall be late."

"But how did you do it?" insisted the warden.

"Don't ever think you can hold any man who can use his brain," said The Thinking Machine. "Come on; we shall be late."

It was an impatient supper party in the rooms of Professor Van Dusen and a somewhat silent one. The guests were Dr. Ransome, Alfred Fielding, the warden, and Hutchinson Hatch, reporter. The meal was served to the minute, in accordance with Professor Van Dusen's instructions of one week before; Dr. Ransome found the artichokes delicious. At last the supper was finished and The Thinking Machine turned on Dr. Ransome and squinted at him fiercely.

"Do you believe it now?" he demanded.

"I do," replied Dr. Ransome.

"Do you admit that it was a fair test?"

"I do."

With the others, particularly the warden, he was waiting anxiously for the explanation.

"Suppose you tell us how—" began Mr. Fielding.

"Yes, tell us how," said the warden.

The Thinking Machine readjusted his glasses, took a couple of preparatory squints at his audience, and began the story. He told it from the beginning logically; and no man ever talked to more interested listeners.

"My agreement was," he began, "to go into a cell, carrying nothing except what was necessary to wear, and to leave that cell within a week. I had never seen Chisholm Prison. When I went into the cell I asked for tooth powder, two ten- and one five-dollar bills, and also to have my shoes blacked. Even if these requests had been refused it would not have mattered seriously. But you agreed to them.

"I knew there would be nothing in the cell which you thought I might use to advantage. So when the warden locked the door on me I was apparently helpless, unless I could turn three seemingly innocent things to use. They were things which would have been permitted any prisoner under sentence of death, were they not, warden?"

"Tooth powder and polished shoes, yes, but not money," replied the warden.

"Anything is dangerous in the hands of a man who knows how to use it," went on The Thinking Machine. "I did nothing that first night but sleep and chase rats." He glared at the warden. "When the matter was broached I knew I could do nothing that night, so suggested next day. You gentlemen thought I wanted time to arrange an escape with outside assistance, but this was not true. I knew I could communicate with whom I pleased, when I pleased."

The warden stared at him a moment, then went on smoking solemnly.

"I was aroused next morning at six o'clock by the jailer with my breakfast," continued the scientist. "He told me dinner was at twelve and supper at six. Between these times, I gathered, I would be pretty much to myself. So immediately after breakfast I examined my outside surroundings from my cell window. One look told me it would be useless to try to scale the wall, even should I decide to leave my cell by the window, for my purpose was to leave not only the cell, but the prison. Of course, I could have gone over the wall, but it would have taken me longer to lay my plans that way. Therefore, for the moment, I dismissed all idea of that.

"From this first observation I knew the river was on that side of the prison, and that there was also a playground there. Subsequently these surmises were verified by a keeper. I knew then one important thing—that anyone might approach the prison wall from that side if necessary without attracting any particular attention. That was well to remember. I remembered it.

"But the outside thing which most attracted my attention was the feed wire to the arc light which ran within a few feet—probably three or four—of my cell window. I knew that would be valuable in the event I found it necessary to cut off that arc light."

"Oh, you shut it off to-night, then?" asked the warden.

"Having learned all I could from that window," resumed The Thinking Machine, without heeding the interruption, "I considered the idea of escaping through the prison proper. I recalled just how I had come into the cell, which I knew would be the only way. Seven doors lay between me and the outside. So, also for the time being, I gave up the idea of escaping that way. And I couldn't go through the solid granite walls of the cell."

The Thinking Machine paused for a moment and Dr. Ransome lighted a new cigar. For several minutes there was silence, then the scientific jailbreaker went on:

"While I was thinking about these things a rat ran across my foot. It suggested a new line of thought. There were at least half a dozen rats in the cell—I could see their beady eyes. Yet I had noticed none come under the cell door. I frightened them purposely and watched the cell door to see if they went out that way. They did not, but they were gone. Obviously they went another way. Another way meant another opening.

"I searched for this opening and found it. It was an old drain pipe, long unused and partly choked with dirt and dust. But this was the way the rats had come. They came from somewhere. Where? Drain pipes usually lead outside prison grounds. This one probably led to the river, or near it. The rats must therefore come from that direction. If they came a part of the way, I reasoned that they came all the way, because it was extremely unlikely that a solid iron or lead pipe would have any hole in it except at the exit.

"When the jailer came with my luncheon he told me two important things, although he didn't know it. One was that a new system of plumbing had been put in the prison seven years before; another that the river was only three hundred feet away. Then I knew positively that the pipe was a part, of an old system; I knew, too, that it slanted generally toward the river. But did the pipe end in the water or on land?

"This was the next question to be decided. I decided it by catching several of the rats in the cell. My jailer was surprised to see me engaged in this work. I examined at least a dozen of them. They were perfectly dry; they had come through the pipe, and, most important of all, they were *not house rats, but field rats*. The other end of the pipe was on land, then, outside the prison walls. So far, so good.

"Then, I knew that if I worked freely from this point I must attract the warden's attention in another direction. You see, by telling the warden that I had come there to escape you made the test more severe, because I had to trick him by false scents."

The warden looked up with a sad expression in his eyes.

"The first thing was to make him think I was trying to communicate with you, Dr. Ransome. So I wrote a note on a piece of linen I tore from my shirt, addressed it to Dr. Ransome, tied a five dollar bill around it and threw it out the window. I knew the guard would take it to the warden, but I rather hoped the warden would send it as addressed. Have you that first linen note, warden?"

The warden produced the cipher.

"What the deuce does it mean, anyhow?" he asked.

"Read it backward, beginning with the "T" signature and disregard the division into words," instructed The Thinking Machine.

The warden did so.

"T-h-i-s, this," he spelled, studied it for a moment, then read it off, grinning:

"This is not the way I intend to escape."

"Well, now what do you think o' that?" he demanded, still grinning.

"I knew that would attract your attention, just as it did," said The Thinking Machine, "and if you really found out what it was it would be a sort of gentle rebuke."

"What did you write it with?" asked Dr. Ransome, after he had examined the linen and passed it to Mr. Fielding.

"This," said the erstwhile prisoner, and he extended his foot. On it was the shoe he had worn in prison, though the polish was gone—scraped off clean. "The shoe blacking, moistened with water, was my ink; the metal tip of the shoe lace made a fairly good pen."

The warden looked up and suddenly burst into a laugh, half of relief, half of amusement.

"You're a wonder," he said, admiringly. "Go on."

"That precipitated a search of my cell by the warden, as I had intended," continued The Thinking Machine. "I was anxious to get the warden into the habit of searching my cell, so that finally, constantly finding nothing, he would get disgusted and quit. This at last happened, practically."

The warden blushed.

"He then took my white shirt away and gave me a prison shirt. He was satisfied that those two pieces of the shirt were all that was missing. But while he was searching my cell I had another piece of that same shirt, about nine inches square, rolled up into a small ball in my mouth."

"Nine inches of that shirt?" demanded the warden. "Where did it come from?"

"The bosoms of all stiff white shirts are of triple thickness," was the explanation. "I tore out the inside thickness, leaving the bosom only two thicknesses. I knew you wouldn't see it. So much for that."

There was a little pause, and the warden looked from one to another of the men with a sheepish grin.

"Having disposed of the warden for the time being by

giving him something else to think about, I took my first
serious step toward freedom," said Professor Van Dusen. "I
knew, within reason, that the pipe led somewhere to the
playground outside; I knew a great many boys played
there; I knew the rats came into my cell from out there.
Could I communicate with some one outside with these
things at hand?

"First was necessary, I saw, a long and fairly reliable
thread, so—but here," he pulled up his trousers legs and
showed that the tops of both stockings, of fine, strong lisle,
were gone. "I unraveled those—after I got them started it
wasn't difficult—and I had easily a quarter of a mile of
thread that I could depend on.

"Then on half of my remaining linen I wrote, laboriously
enough I assure you, a letter explaining my situation to this
gentleman here," and he indicated Hutchinson Hatch. "I
knew he would assist me—for the value of the newspaper
story. I tied firmly to this linen letter a ten-dollar bill—
there is no surer way of attracting the eye of anyone—and
wrote on the linen: 'Finder of this deliver to Hutchinson
Hatch, *Daily American*, who will give another ten dollars
for the information.'

"The next thing was to get this note outside on that playground where a boy might find it. There were two ways, but
I chose the best. I took one of the rats—I became adept in
catching them—tied the linen and money firmly to one leg,
fastened my lisle thread to another, and turned him loose
in the drain pipe. I reasoned that the natural fright of the
rodent would make him run until he was outside the pipe
and then out on earth he would probably stop to gnaw off
the linen and money.

"From the moment the rat disappeared into that dusty
pipe I became anxious. I was taking so many chances. The
rat might gnaw the string, of which I held one end; other
rats might gnaw it; the rat might run out of the pipe and
leave the linen and money where they would never be found;
a thousand other things might have happened. So began
some nervous hours, but the fact that the rat ran on until

only a few feet of the string remained in my cell made me think he was outside the pipe. I had carefully instructed Mr. Hatch what to do in case the note reached him. The question was: Would it reach him?

"This done, I could only wait and make other plans in case this one failed. I openly attempted to bribe my jailer, and learned from him that he held the keys to only two of seven doors between me and freedom. Then I did something else to make the warden nervous. I took the steel supports out of the heels of my shoes and made a pretense of sawing the bars of my cell window. The warden raised a pretty row about that. He developed, too, the habit of shaking the bars of my cell window to see if they were solid. They were—then."

Again the warden grinned. He had ceased being astonished.

"With this one plan I had done all I could and could only wait to see what happened," the scientist went on. "I couldn't know whether my note had been delivered or even found, or whether the mouse had gnawed it up. And I didn't dare to draw back through the pipe that one slender thread which connected me with the outside.

"When I went to bed that night I didn't sleep, for fear there would come the slight signal twitch at the thread which was to tell me that Mr. Hatch had received the note. At half past three o'clock, I judge, I felt this twitch, and no prisoner actually under sentence of death ever welcomed a thing more heartily."

The Thinking Machine stopped and turned to the reporter.

"You'd better explain just what you did," he said.

"The linen note was brought to me by a small boy who had been playing baseball," said Mr. Hatch. "I immediately saw a big story in it, so I gave the boy another ten dollars, and got several spools of silk, some twine, and a roll of light, pliable wire. The professor's note suggested that I have the finder of the note show me just where it was picked up, and told me to make my search from there, beginning at

two o'clock in the morning. If I found the other end of the
thread, I was to twitch it gently three times, then a fourth.

"I began the search with a small-bulb electric light. It
was an hour and twenty minutes before I found the end of
the drain pipe, half hidden in weeds. The pipe was very
large there, say twelve inches across. Then I found the end
of the lisle thread, twitched it as directed and immediately I
got an answering twitch.

"Then I fastened the silk to this and Professor Van Dusen
began to pull it into his cell. I nearly had heart disease for
fear the string would break. To the end of the silk I fastened
the twine, and when that had been pulled in I tied on the
wire. Then that was drawn into the pipe and we had a sub-
stantial line, which rats couldn't gnaw, from the mouth of
the drain into the cell."

The Thinking Machine raised his hand and Hatch
stopped.

"All this was done in absolute silence," said the scientist.
"But when the wire reached my hand I could have shouted.
Then we tried another experiment, which Mr. Hatch was
prepared for. I tested the pipe as a speaking tube. Neither
of us could hear very clearly, but I dared not speak loud
for fear of attracting attention in the prison. At last I made
him understand what I wanted immediately. He seemed to
have great difficulty in understanding when I asked for nitric
acid, and I repeated the word 'acid' several times.

"Then I heard a shriek from a cell above me. I knew instantly that someone had overheard, and when I heard you
coming, Mr. Warden, I feigned sleep. If you had entered
my cell at that moment that whole plan of escape would
have ended there. But you passed on. That was the nearest
I ever came to being caught.

"Having established this improvised trolley it is easy to
see how I got things in the cell and made them disappear
at will. I merely dropped them back into the pipe. You,
Mr. Warden, could not have reached the connecting wire
with your fingers; they are too large. My fingers, you see,

are longer and more slender. In addition I guarded the top
of that pipe with a rat—you remember how."

"I remember," said the warden, with a grimace.

"I thought that if anyone were tempted to investigate
that hole the rat would dampen his ardor. Mr. Hatch could
not send me anything useful through the pipe until next
night, although he did send me change for ten dollars as a
test, so I proceeded with other parts of my plan. Then I
evolved the method of escape which I finally employed.

"In order to carry this out successfully it was necessary
for the guard in the yard to get accustomed to seeing me at
the cell window. I arranged this by dropping linen notes to
him, boastful in tone, to make the warden believe, if possible, one of his assistants was communicating with the outside for me. I would stand at my window for hours gazing
out, so the guard could see, and occasionally I spoke to him.
In that way I learned that the prison had no electricians of
its own, but was dependent upon the lighting company if
anything should go wrong.

"That cleared the way to freedom perfectly. Early in the
evening of the last day of my imprisonment, when it was
dark, I planned to cut the feed wire which was only a few
feet from my window, reaching it with an acid-tipped wire
I had. That would make that side of the prison perfectly
dark while the electricians were searching for the break.
That would also bring Mr. Hatch into the prison yard.

"There was only one more thing to do before I actually
began the work of setting myself free. This was to arrange
final details with Mr. Hatch through our speaking tube. I
did this within half an hour after the warden left my cell on
the fourth night of my imprisonment. Mr. Hatch again had
serious difficulty in understanding me, and I repeated the
word 'acid' to him several times, and later on the words:
'No. 8 hat'—that's my size—and these were the things which
made a prisoner upstairs confess to murder, so one of the
jailers told me next day. This prisoner heard our voices,
confused of course, through the pipe, which also went to his

cell. The cell directly over me was not occupied, hence no one else heard.

"Of course the actual work of cutting the steel bars out of the window and door was comparatively easy with nitric acid, which I got through the pipe in tin bottles, but it took time. Hour after hour on the fifth and sixth and seventh days the guard below was looking at me as I worked on the bars of the window with the acid on a piece of wire. I used the tooth powder to prevent the acid spreading. I looked away abstractedly as I worked and each minute the acid cut deeper into the metal. I noticed that the jailers always tried the door by shaking the upper part, never the lower bars, therefore I cut the lower bars, leaving them hanging in place by thin strips of metal. But that was a bit of dare-deviltry. I could not have gone that way so easily."

The Thinking Machine sat silent for several minutes.

"I think that makes everything clear," he went on. "Whatever points I have not explained were merely to confuse the warden and jailers. These things in my bed I brought in to please Mr. Hatch, who wanted to improve the story. Of course, the wig was necessary in my plan. The special-delivery letter I wrote and directed in my cell with Mr. Hatch's fountain pen, then sent it out to him and he mailed it. That's all, I think."

"But your actually leaving the prison grounds and then coming in through the outer gate to my office?" asked the warden.

"Perfectly simple," said the scientist. "I cut the electric light wire with acid, as I said, when the current was off. Therefore when the current was turned on the arc didn't light. I knew it would take some time to find out what was the matter and make repairs. When the guard went to report to you the yard was dark. I crept out the window—it was a tight fit, too—replaced the bars by standing on a narrow ledge and remained in a shadow until the force of electricians arrived. Mr. Hatch was one of them.

"When I saw him I spoke and he handed me a cap, a jumper and overalls, which I put on within ten feet of you,

Mr. Warden, while you were in the yard. Later Mr. Hatch called me, presumably as a workman, and together we went out the gate to get something out of the wagon. The late guard let us pass out readily as two workmen who had just passed in. We changed our clothing and reappeared, asking to see you. We saw you. That's all."

There was silence for several minutes. Dr. Ransome was first to speak.

"Wonderful!" he exclaimed. "Perfectly amazing."

"How did Mr. Hatch happen to come with the electricians?" asked Mr. Fielding.

"His father is manager of the company," replied The Thinking Machine.

"But what if there had been no Mr. Hatch outside to help?"

"Every prisoner has one friend outside who would help him escape if he could."

"Suppose—just suppose—there had been no old plumbing system there?" asked the warden, curiously.

"There were two other ways out," said The Thinking Machine, enigmatically.

Ten minutes later the telephone bell rang. It was a request for the warden.

"Light all right, eh?" the warden asked, through the phone. "Good. Wire cut beside Cell 13? Yes, I know. One electrician too many? What's that? Two came out?"

The warden turned to the others with a puzzled expression.

"He only let in four electricians, he has let out two and says there are three left."

"I was the odd one," said The Thinking Machine.

"Oh," said the warden. "I see." Then through the phone: "Let the fifth man go. He's all right."

THE ALUMINUM DAGGER
by R. A. Freeman

THE "URGENT CALL"—THE INSTANT, PEREMPTORY SUMMONS to professional duty—is an experience that appertains to the medical rather than the legal practitioner, and I had supposed, when I abandoned the clinical side of my profession in favour of the forensic, that henceforth I should know it no more; that the interrupted meal, the broken leisure, and the jangle of the night-bell were things of the past; but in practice it was otherwise. The medical jurist, is, so to speak, on the borderland of the two professions, and exposed to the vicissitudes of each calling, and so it happened from time to time that the professional services of my colleague or myself were demanded at a moment's notice. And thus it was in the case that I am about to relate.

The sacred rite of the "tub" had been duly performed, and the freshly-dried person of the present narrator was about to be insinuated into the first instalment of clothing, when a hurried step was heard upon the stair, and the voice of our laboratory assistant, Polton, arose at my colleague's door.

"There's a gentleman downstairs, sir, who says he must see you instantly on most urgent business. He seems to be in a rare twitter, sir—"

Polton was proceeding to descriptive particulars, when a second and more hurried step became audible, and a strange voice addressed Thorndyke.

"I have come to beg your immediate assistance, sir; a most dreadful thing has happened. A horrible murder has been committed. Can you come with me now?"

"I will be with you almost immediately," said Thorndyke. "Is the victim quite dead?"

"Quite. Cold and stiff. The police think—"

"Do the police know that you have come for me?" interrupted Thorndyke.

"Yes. Nothing is to be done until you arrive."

"Very well. I will be ready in a few minutes."

"And if you would wait downstairs, sir," Polton added persuasively, "I could help the doctor to get ready."

With this crafty appeal, he lured the intruder back to the sitting-room, and shortly after stole softly up the stairs with a small breakfast-tray, the contents of which he deposited firmly in our respective rooms, with a few timely words on the folly of "undertaking murders on an empty stomach." Thorndyke and I had meanwhile clothed ourselves with a celerity known only to medical practitioners and quick-change artists, and in a few minutes descended the stairs together, calling in at the laboratory for a few appliances that Thorndyke usually took with him on a visit of investigation.

As we entered the sitting-room, our visitor, who was feverishly pacing up and down, seized his hat with a gasp of relief. "You are ready to come?" he asked. "My carriage is at the door"; and, without waiting for an answer, he hurried out, and rapidly preceded us down the stairs.

The carriage was a roomy brougham which fortunately accomodated the three of us, and as soon as we had entered and shut the door, the coachman whipped up his horse and drove off at a smart trot.

"I had better give you some account of the circumstances, as we go," said our agitated friend. "In the first place my name is Curtis, Henry Curtis; here is my card. Ah! and here is another card, which I should have given you before. My solicitor, Mr. Marchmont, was with me when I made this dreadful discovery, and he sent me to you. He remained in the rooms to see that nothing is disturbed until you arrive."

"That was wise of him," said Thorndyke. "But now tell us exactly what has occurred."

"I will," said Mr. Curtis. "The murdered man was my brother-in-law, Alfred Hartridge, and I am sorry to say he was—well, he was a bad man. It grieves me to speak of him thus—*de mortuis,* you know—but, still, we must deal with the facts, even though they be painful."

"Undoubtedly," agreed Thorndyke.

"I have had a great deal of very unpleasant correspondence with him—Marchmont will tell you about that—and yesterday I left a note for him, asking for an interview, to settle the business, naming eight o'clock this morning as the hour, because I had to leave town before noon. He replied, in a very singular letter, that he would see me at that hour, and Mr. Marchmont very kindly consented to accompany me. Accordingly, we went to his chambers together this morning, arriving punctually at eight o'clock. We rang the bell several times and knocked loudly at the door, but as there was no response, we went down and spoke to the hall-porter. This man, it seems, had already noticed, from the courtyard, that the electric lights were full on in Mr. Hart-ridge's sitting-room, as they had been all night, according to the statement of the night-porter; so now, suspecting that something was wrong, he came up with us, and rang the bell and battered on the door. Then, as there was still no sign of life within, he inserted his duplicate key and tried to open the door—unsuccessfully, however, as it proved to be bolted on the inside. Thereupon the porter fetched a constable, and, after a consultation, we decided that we were justified in breaking open the door; the porter produced a crowbar, and by our united efforts the door was eventually burst open. We entered, and—my God! Dr. Thorndyke, what a terrible sight it was that met our eyes! My brother-in-law was lying dead on the floor of the sitting-room. He had been stabbed—stabbed to death; and the dagger had not even been withdrawn. It was still sticking out of his back."

He mopped his face with his handkerchief, and was about to continue his account of the catastrophe when the carriage entered a quiet side-street between Westminister and Vic-

toria, and drew up before a block of tall, new, red-brick
buildings. A flurried hall-porter ran out to open the door,
and we alighted opposite the main entrance.

"My brother-in-law's chambers are on the second floor,"
said Mr. Curtis. "We can go up in the lift."

The porter had hurried before us, and already stood
with his hand upon the rope. We entered the lift, and in a
few seconds were discharged on to the second floor, the
porter, with furtive curiosity, following us down the corridor. At the end of the passage was a half-open door, considerably battered and bruised. Above the door, painted in
white lettering, was the inscription, "Mr. Hartridge"; and
through the doorway protruded the rather foxy countenance of Inspector Badger.

"I am glad you have come, sir," said he, as he recognised
my colleague. "Mr. Marchmont is sitting inside like a
watch-dog, and he growls if any of us even walks across the
room."

The words formed a complaint, but there was a certain
geniality in the speaker's manner which made me suspect
that Inspector Badger was already navigating his craft on
a lee shore.

We entered a small lobby or hall, and from thence passed
into the sitting-room, where we found Mr. Marchmont keeping his vigil, in company with a constable and a uniformed
inspector. The three rose softly as we entered, and greeted
us in a whisper; and then, with one accord, we all looked
towards the other end of the room, and so remained for a
time without speaking.

There was, in the entire aspect of the room, something
very grim and dreadful. An atmosphere of tragic mystery
enveloped the most commonplace objects; and sinister suggestions lurked in the most familiar appearances. Especially
impressive was the air of suspense—of ordinary, every-day
life suddenly arrested—cut short in the twinkling of an eye.
The electric lamps, still burning dim and red, though the
summer sunshine streamed in through the windows; the
half-emptied tumbler and open book by the empty chair,

had each its whispered message of swift and sudden disaster, as had the hushed voices and stealthy movements of the waiting men, and, above all, an awesome shape that was but a few hours since a living man, and that now sprawled, prone and motionless, on the floor.

"This is a mysterious affair," observed Inspector Badger, breaking the silence at length, "though it is clear enough up to a certain point. The body tells its own story."

We stepped across and looked down at the corpse. It was that of a somewhat elderly man, and lay, on an open space of floor before the fireplace, face downwards, with the arms extended. The slender hilt of a dagger projected from the back below the left shoulder, and, with the exception of a trace of blood upon the lips, this was the only indication of the mode of death. A little way from the body a clock-key lay on the carpet, and, glancing up at the clock on the mantelpiece, I perceived that the glass front was open.

"You see," pursued the inspector, noting my glance, "he was standing in front of the fireplace, winding the clock. Then the murderer stole up behind him—the noise of the turning key must have covered his movements—and stabbed him. And as you see, from the position of the dagger on the left side of the back, that the murderer must have been left-handed. That is all clear enough. What is not clear is how he got in, and how he got out again."

"The body has not been moved, I suppose," said Thorndyke.

"No. We sent for Dr. Egerton, the police-surgeon, and he certified that the man was dead. He will be back presently to see you and arrange about the post-mortem."

"Then," said Thorndyke, "we will not disturb the body till he comes, except to take the temperature and dust the dagger-hilt."

He took from his bag a long, registering chemical thermometer and an insufflator or powder-blower. The former he introduced under the dead man's clothing against the abdomen, and with the latter blew a stream of fine yellow powder on to the black leather handle of the dagger. Inspector Badger stooped eagerly to examine the handle, as Thorndyke blew away the powder that had settled evenly on the surface.

"No finger-prints," said he, in a disappointed tone. "He must have worn gloves. But that inscription gives a pretty broad hint."

He pointed, as he spoke, to the metal guard of the dagger, on which was engraved, in clumsy lettering, the single word, "TRADITORE."

"That's the Italian for 'traitor,'" continued the inspector, "and I got some information from the porter that fits in with that suggestion. We'll have him in presently, and you shall hear."

"Meanwhile," said Thorndyke, "as the position of the body may be of importance in the inquiry, I will take one or two photographs and make a rough plan to scale. Nothing has been moved, you say? Who opened the windows?"

"They were open when we came in," said Mr. Marchmont. "Last night was very hot, you remember. Nothing whatever has been moved."

Thorndyke produced from his bag a small folding camera, a telescopic tripod, a surveyor's measuring-tape, a boxwood scale, and a sketch-block. He set up the camera in a corner, and exposed a plate, taking a general view of the room, and including the corpse. Then he moved to the door and made a second exposure.

"Will you stand in front of the clock, Jervis," he said, "and raise your hand as if winding it? Thanks; keep like that while I expose a plate."

I remained thus, in the position that the dead man was assumed to have occupied at the moment of the murder, while the plate was exposed, and then, before I moved, Thorndyke marked the position of my feet with a blackboard chalk. He next set up the tripod over the chalk marks, and took two photographs from that position, and finally photographed the body itself.

The photographic operations being concluded, he next proceeded, with remarkable skill and rapidity, to lay out on the sketch-block a ground-plan of the room, showing the exact position of the various objects, on a scale of a quarter of an inch to the foot—a process that the inspector was inclined to view with some impatience.

"You don't spare trouble, doctor," he remarked; "nor time either," he added, with a significant glance at his watch.

"No," answered Thorndyke, as he detached the finished sketch from the block; "I try to collect all the facts that may bear on a case. They may prove worthless, or they may turn out of vital importance; one never knows beforehand, so I collect them all. But here, I think, is Dr. Egerton."

The police-surgeon greeted Thorndyke with respectful cordiality, and we proceeded at once to the examination of the body. Drawing out the thermometer, my colleague noted the reading, and passed the instrument to Dr. Egerton.

"Dead about ten hours," remarked the latter, after a glance at it. "This was a very determined and mysterious murder."

"Very," said Thorndyke. "Feel that dagger, Jervis."

I touched the hilt, and felt the characteristic grating of bone.

"It is through the edge of a rib!" I exclaimed.

"Yes; it must have been used with extraordinary force. And you notice that the clothing is screwed up slightly, as if the blade had been rotated as it was driven in. That is a very peculiar feature, especially when taken together with the violence of the blow."

"It is singular, certainly," said Dr. Egerton, "though I don't know that it helps us much. Shall we withdraw the dagger before moving the body?"

"Certainly," replied Thorndyke, "or the movement may produce fresh injuries. But wait." He took a piece of string from his pocket, and, having drawn the dagger out a couple of inches, stretched the string in a line parallel to the flat of the blade. Then, giving me the ends to hold, he drew the weapon out completely. As the blade emerged, the twist in the clothing disappeared. "Observe," said he, "that the string gives the direction of the wound, and that the cut in the clothing no longer coincides with it. There is quite a considerable angle, which is the measure of the rotation of the blade."

"Yes, it is odd," said Dr. Egerton, "though, as I said, I doubt that it helps us."

"At present," Thorndyke rejoined dryly, "we are noting the facts."

"Quite so," agreed the other, reddening slightly; "and perhaps we had better move the body to the bedroom, and make a preliminary inspection of the wound."

We carried the corpse into the bedroom, and, having examined the wound without eliciting anything new, covered the remains with a sheet, and returned to the sitting-room.

"Well, gentlemen," said the Inspector, "you have examined the body and the wound, and you have measured the floor and the furniture, and taken photographs, and made a plan, but we don't seem much more forward. Here's a man murdered in his rooms. There is only one entrance to the flat, and that was bolted on the inside at the time of the murder. The windows are some forty feet from the ground; there is no rain-pipe near any of them; they are set flush in the wall, and there isn't a foothold for a fly on any part of that wall. The grates are modern, and there isn't room for a good-sized cat to crawl up any of the chimneys. Now, the question is, How did the murderer get in, and how did he get out again?"

"Still," said Mr. Marchmont, "the fact is that he did get in and that he is not here now; and therefore he must have got out; and therefore it must have been possible for him to get out. And, further, it must be possible to discover how he got out."

The inspector smiled sourly, but made no reply.

"The circumstances," said Thorndyke, "appear to have been these: The deceased seems to have been alone; there is no trace of a second occupant of the room, and only one half-emptied tumbler on the table. He was sitting reading when apparently he noticed that the clock had stopped—at ten minutes to twelve; he laid his book, face downwards, on the table, and rose to wind the clock, and as he was winding it he met his death."

"By a stab dealt by a left-handed man, who crept up behind him on tiptoe," added the inspector.

Thorndyke nodded. "That would seem to be so," he said. "But now let us call in the porter, and hear what he has to tell us."

The custodian was not difficult to find, being, in fact, engaged at that moment in a survey of the premises through the slit in the letter-box.

"Do you know what persons visited these rooms last night?" Thorndyke asked him, when he entered, looking somewhat sheepish.

"A good many were in and out of the building," was the answer, "but I can't say if any of them came to this flat. I saw Miss Curtis pass in about nine."

"My daughter!" exclaimed Mr. Curtis, with a start. "I didn't know that."

"She left about nine-thirty," the porter added.

"Do you know what she came about?" asked the inspector.

"I can guess," replied Mr. Curtis.

"Then don't say," interrupted Mr. Marchmont. "Answer no questions."

"You're very close, Mr. Marchmont," said the inspector; "we are not suspecting the young lady. We don't ask, for instance, if she is left-handed."

He glanced craftily at Mr. Curtis as he made this remark, and I noticed that our client suddenly turned deathly pale, whereupon the inspector looked away again quickly, as though he had not observed the change.

"Tell us about those Italians again," he said, addressing the porter. "When did the first of them come here?"

"About a week ago," was the reply. "He was a common-looking man—looked like an organ-grinder—and he brought a note to my lodge. It was in a dirty envelope, and was addressed 'Mr. Hartridge, Esq., Brackenhurst Mansions,' in a very bad handwriting. The man gave me the note and asked me to give it to Mr. Hartridge; then he went away, and I took the note up and dropped it into the letter-box."

"What happened next?"

"Why, the very next day an old hag of an Italian woman —one of them fortune-telling swines with a cage of birds on a stand—came and set up just by the main doorway. I soon sent her packing, but, bless you! she was back again in ten minutes, birds and all. I sent her off again—I kept on sending her off, and she kept on coming back, until I was reg'lar wore to a thread."

"You seem to have picked up a bit since then," remarked the inspector with a grin and a glance at the sufferer's very pronounced bow-window.

"Perhaps I have," the custodian replied haughtily. "Well, the next day there was a ice-cream man—a reg'lar waster, *he* was. Stuck outside as if he was froze to the pavement. Kept giving the errand-boys tasters, and when I tried to move him on, he told me not to obstruct his business. Business, indeed! Well, there them boys stuck, one after the other, wiping their tongues round the bottoms of them glasses, until I was fit to bust with aggravation. And *he* kept me going all day.

"Then, the day after that there was a barrel-organ, with a mangy-looking monkey on it. He was the worst of all. Profane, too *he* was. Kept mixing up sacred tunes and comic songs: 'Rock of Ages,' 'Bill Bailey,' 'Cujus Animal,' and 'Over the Garden Wall.' And when I tried to move him on, that little blighter of a monkey made a run at my leg; and then the man grinned and started playing, 'Wait till the Clouds roll by.' I tell you, it was fair sickening."

He wiped his brow at the recollection, and the inspector smiled appreciatively.

"And that was the last of them?" said the latter; and as the porter nodded sulkily, he asked: "Should you recognise the note that the Italian gave you?"

"I should," answered the porter with frosty dignity.

The inspector bustled out of the room, and returned a minute later with a letter-case in his hand.

"This was in his breast-pocket," said he, laying the bulging case on the table, and drawing up a chair. "Now, here are three letters tied together. Ah! this will be the one." He untied the tape, and held out a dirty envelope addressed in a sprawling, illiterate hand to "Mr. Hartridge, Esq." "Is that the note the Italian gave you?"

The porter examined it critically. "Yes," said he; "that is the one."

The inspector drew the letter out of the envelope and, as he opened it, his eyebrows went up.

"What do you make of that, doctor?" he said, handing the sheet to Thorndyke.

Thorndyke regarded it for a while in silence, with deep attention. Then he carried it to a window, and, taking his lens from his pocket, examined the paper closely, first with the low power, and then with the highly magnifying Coddington attachment.

"I should have thought you could see that with the naked eye," said the inspector, with a sly grin at me. "It's a pretty bold design."

"Yes," replied Thorndyke; "a very interesting production. What do you say, Mr. Marchmont?"

The solicitor took the note, and I looked over his shoulder. It was certainly a curious production. Written in red ink, on the commonest notepaper, and in the same sprawling hand as the address, was the following message: "You are given six days to do what is just. By the sign above, know what to expect if you fail." The sign referred to was a skull and crossbones, very neatly, but rather unskillfully, drawn at the top of the paper.

"This," said Mr. Marchmont, handing the document to Mr. Curtis, "explains the singular letter that he wrote yesterday. You have it with you, I think?"

"Yes," replied Mr. Curtis; "here it is."

He produced a letter from his pocket, and read aloud:

" 'Yes: come if you like, though it is an ungodly hour. Your threatening letters have caused me great amusement. They are worthy of Sadler's Wells in its prime.

" 'Alfred Hartridge.' "

"Was Mr. Hartridge ever in Italy?" asked Inspector Badger.

"Oh yes," replied Mr. Curtis. "He stayed at Capri nearly the whole of last year."

"Why, then, that gives us our clue. Look here. Here are these two other letters; E.C. postmark—Saffron Hill is E.C. And just look at that!"

He spread out the last of the mysterious letters, and we saw that, besides the *memento mori,* it contained only three words: "Beware! Remember Capri!"

"If you have finished, doctor, I'll be off and have a look round Little Italy. Those four Italians oughtn't to be difficult to find, and we've got the porter here to identify them."

"Before you go," said Thorndyke, "there are two little matters that I should like to settle. One is the dagger: it is in your pocket, I think. May I have a look at it?"

The inspector rather reluctantly produced the dagger and handed it to my colleague.

"A very singular weapon, this," said Thorndyke, regarding the dagger thoughtfully, and turning it about to view its different parts. "Singular both in shape and material. I have never seen an aluminium hilt before, and bookbinder's morocco is a little unusual."

"The aluminium was for lightness," explained the inspector, "and it was made narrow to carry up the sleeve, I expect."

"Perhaps so," said Thorndyke.

He continued his examination, and presently, to the inspector's delight, brought forth his pocket lens.

"I never saw such a man!" exclaimed the jocose detective. "His motto ought to be, 'We magnify thee.' I suppose he'll measure it next."

The inspector was not mistaken. Having made a rough

sketch of the weapon on his block, Thorndyke produced from his bag a folding rule and a delicate calliper-gauge. With these instruments he proceeded, with extraordinary care and precision, to take the dimensions of the various parts of the dagger, entering each measurement in its place on the sketch, with a few brief, descriptive details.

"The other matter," said he at length, handing the dagger back to the inspector, "refers to the houses opposite."

He walked to the window, and looked out at the backs of a row of tall buildings similar to the one we were in. They were about thirty yards distant, and were separated from us by a piece of ground, planted with shrubs and intersected by gravel paths.

"If any of those rooms were occupied last night," continued Thorndyke, "we might obtain an actual eyewitness of the crime. This room was brilliantly lighted, and all the blinds were up, so that an observer at any of those windows could see right into the room, and very distinctly, too. It might be worth inquiring into."

"Yes, that's true," said the inspector; "though I expect, if any of them have seen anything, they will come forward quick enough when they read the report in the papers. But I must be off now, and I shall have to lock you out of the rooms."

As we went down the stairs, Mr. Marchmont announced his intention of calling on us in the evening, "unless," he added, "you want any information from me now."

"I do," said Thorndyke. "I want to know who is interested in this man's death."

"That," replied Marchmont, "is rather a queer story. Let us take a turn in that garden that we saw from the window. We shall be quite private there."

He beckoned to Mr. Curtis, and, when the inspector had departed with the police-surgeon, we induced the porter to let us into the garden.

"The question that you asked," Mr. Marchmont began, looking up curiously at the tall houses opposite, "is very simply answered." The only person immediately interested

in the death of Alfred Hartridge is his executor and sole
legatee, a man named Leonard Wolfe. He is no relation of
the deceased, merely a friend, but he inherits the entire estate—about twenty thousand pounds. The circumstances
are these: Alfred Hartridge was the elder of two brothers,
of whom the younger, Charles, died before his father, leaving a widow and three children. Fifteen years ago the father
died, leaving the whole of his property to Alfred, with the
understanding that he should support his brother's family
and make the children his heirs."

"Was there no will?" asked Thorndyke.

"Under great pressure from the friends of his son's
widow, the old man made a will shortly before he died; but
he was then very old and rather childish, so the will was
contested by Alfred, on the grounds of undue influence, and
was ultimately set aside. Since then Alfred Hartridge has
not paid a penny towards the support of his brother's family.
If it had not been for my client, Mr. Curtis, they might have
starved; the whole burden of the support of the widow and
the education of the children has fallen upon him.

"Well, just lately the matter has assumed an acute form,
for two reasons. The first is that Charles's eldest son, Edmund, has come of age. Mr. Curtis had him articled to a
solicitor, and, as he is now fully qualified, and a most ad-
vantageous proposal for a partnership has been made, we
have been putting pressure on Alfred to supply the necessary capital in accordance with his father's wishes. This he
had refused to do, and it was with reference to this matter
that we were calling on him this morning. The second reason involves a curious and disgraceful story. There is a certain Leonard Wolfe, who has been an intimate friend of the
deceased. He is, I may say, a man of bad character, and
their association has been of a kind creditable to neither.
There is also a certain woman named Hester Greene, who
had certain claims upon the deceased, which we need not
go into at present. Now, Leonard Wolfe and the deceased,
Alfred Hartridge, entered into an agreement, the terms of
which were these: (1) Wolfe was to marry Hester Greene,

and in consideration of this service (2) Alfred Hartridge was to assign to Wolfe the whole of his property, absolutely, the actual transfer to take place on the death of Hartridge."

"And has this transaction been completed?" asked Thorndyke.

"Yes, it has, unfortunately. But we wished to see if anything could be done for the widow and the children during Hartridge's lifetime. No doubt, my client's daughter Miss Curtis called last night on a similar mission—very indiscreetly, since the matter was in our hands; but, you know, she is engaged to Edmund Hartridge—and I expect the interview was a pretty stormy one."

Thorndyke remained silent for a while, pacing slowly along the gravel path, with his eyes bent on the ground: not abstractedly, however, but with a searching, attentive glance that roved amongst the shrubs and bushes, as though he were looking for something.

"What sort of man," he asked presently, "is this Leonard Wolfe? Obviously he is a low scoundrel, but what is he like in other respects? Is he a fool, for instance?"

"Not at all, I should say," said Mr. Curtis. "He was formerly an engineer, and, I believe, a very capable mechanician. Latterly he has lived on some property that came to him, and has spent both his time and his money in gambling and dissipation. Consequently, I expect he is pretty short of funds at present."

"And in appearance?"

"I only saw him once," replied Mr. Curtis, "and all I can remember of him is that he is rather short, fair, thin, and clean-shaven, and that he has lost the middle finger of his left hand."

"And he lives at—?"

"Eltham, in Kent. Morton Grange, Eltham," said Mr. Marchmont. "And now, if you have all the information that you require, I must really be off, and so must Mr. Curtis."

The two men shook our hands and hurried away, leaving Thorndyke gazing meditatively at the dingy flower-beds.

"A strange and interesting case, this, Jervis," said he,

stooping to peer under a laurel-bush. "The inspector is on a
hot scent—a most palpable red herring on a most obvious
string; but that is his business. Ah, here comes the porter,
intent, no doubt, on pumping us, whereas—" He smiled
genially at the approaching custodian, and asked: "Where
did you say those houses fronted?"

"Cotman Street, sir," answered the porter. "They are
nearly all offices."

"And the numbers? That open second-floor window, for
instance?"

"That is number six; but the house opposite Mr. Hartridge's rooms is number eight."

"Thank you."

Thorndyke was moving away, but suddenly turned again
to the porter.

"By the way," said he, "I dropped something out of the
window just now—a small flat piece of metal, like this." He
made on the back of his visiting card a neat sketch of a circular disc, with a hexagonal hole through it, and handed
the card to the porter. "I can't say where it fell," he continued; "these flat things scale about so; but you might ask
the gardener to look for it. I will give him a sovereign if he
brings it to my chambers, for, although it is of no value to
anyone else, it is of considerable value to me."

The porter touched his hat briskly, and as we turned out
at the gate, I looked back and saw him already wading
among the shrubs.

The object of the porter's quest gave me considerable
mental occupation. I had not seen Thorndyke drop anything, and it was not his way to finger carelessly any object
of value. I was about to question him on the subject, when,
turning sharply round into Cotman Street, he drew up at
the doorway of number six, and began attentively to read
the names of the occupants.

" 'Third floor,' " he read out, " 'Mr. Thomas Barlow,
Commission Agent.' Hum! I think we will look in on Mr.
Barlow."

He stepped quickly up the stone stairs, and I followed,

until we arrived, somewhat out of breath, on the third floor. Outside the Commission Agent's door he paused for a moment, and we both listened curiously to an irregular sound of shuffling feet from within. Then he softly opened the door and looked into the room. After remaining thus for nearly a minute, he looked round at me with a broad smile, and noiselessly set the door wide open. Inside, a lanky youth of fourteen was practising, with no mean skill, the manipulation of an appliance known by the appropriate name of diabolo; and so absorbed was he in his occupation that we entered and shut the door without being observed. At length the shuttle missed the string and flew into a large waste-paper basket; the boy turned and confronted us, and was instantly covered with confusion.

"Allow me," said Thorndyke, rooting rather unnecessarily in the waste-paper basket, and handing the toy to its owner. "I need not ask if Mr. Barlow is in," he added, "nor if he is likely to return shortly."

"He won't be back to-day," said the boy, perspiring with embarrassment; "he left before I came. I was rather late."

"I see," said Thorndyke. "The early bird catches the worm, but the late bird catches the diabolo. How did you know he would not be back?"

"He left a note. Here it is."

He exhibited the document, which was neatly written in red ink. Thorndyke examined it attentively, and then asked:

"Did you break the inkstand yesterday?"

The boy stared at him in amazement. "Yes, I did," he answered. "How did you know?"

"I didn't, or I should not have asked. But I see that he has used his stylo to write this note."

The boy regarded Thorndyke distrustfully, as he continued:

"I really called to see if your Mr. Barlow was a gentleman whom I used to know; but I expect you can tell me. My friend was tall and thin, dark, and clean-shaved."

"This ain't him, then," said the boy. "He's thin, but he ain't tall or dark. He's got a sandy beard, and he wears

spectacles and a wig. I know a wig when I see one," he
added cunningly, " 'cause my father wears one. He puts it
on a peg to comb it, and he swears at me when I larf."

"My friend had injured his left hand," pursued Thorndyke.

"I dunno about that," said the youth. "Mr. Barlow nearly
always wears gloves; he always wears one on his left hand,
anyhow."

"Ah well! I'll just write him a note on the chance, if you
will give me a piece of notepaper. Have you any ink?"

"There's some in the bottle. I'll dip the pen in for you."

He produced, from the cupboard, an opened packet of
cheap notepaper and a packet of similar envelopes, and,
having dipped the pen to the bottom of the ink-bottle,
handed it to Thorndyke, who sat down and hastily scribbled
a short note. He had folded the paper, and was about to address the envelope, when he appeared suddenly to alter his
mind.

"I don't think I will leave it, after all," he said, slipping
the folded paper into his pocket. "No. Tell him I called—
Mr. Horace Budge—and say I will look in again in a day
or two."

The youth watched our exit with an air of perplexity,
and he even came out on to the landing, the better to observe us over the balusters; until, unexpectedly catching
Thorndyke's eye, he withdrew his head with remarkable
suddenness, and retired in disorder.

To tell the truth, I was now little less perplexed than the
office-boy by Thorndyke's proceedings; in which I could
discover no relevancy to the investigation that I presumed
he was engaged upon: and the last straw was laid upon the
burden of my curiosity when he stopped at a staircase window, drew the note out of his pocket, examined it with his
lens, held it up to the light, and chuckled aloud.

"Luck," he observed, "though no substitute for care and
intelligence, is a very pleasant addition. Really, my learned
brother, we are doing uncommonly well."

When we reached the hall, Thorndyke stopped at the

housekeeper's box, and looked in with a genial nod.

"I have just been up to see Mr. Barlow," said he. "He seems to have left quite early."

"Yes, sir," the man replied. "He went away about half-past eight."

"That was very early; and presumably he came earlier still?"

"I suppose so," the man assented, with a grin; "but I had only just come on when he left."

"Had he any luggage with him?"

"Yes, sir. There was two cases, a square one and a long, narrow one, about five foot long. I helped him to carry them down to the cab."

"Which was a four-wheeler, I suppose?"

"Yes, sir."

"Mr. Barlow hasn't been here very long, has he?" Thorndyke inquired.

"No. He only came in last quarter-day—about six weeks ago."

"Ah well! I must call another day. Good-morning"; and Thorndyke strode out of the building, and made directly for the cab-rank in the adjoining street. Here he stopped for a minute or two to parley with the driver of a four-wheeled cab, whom he finally commissioned to convey us to a shop in New Oxford Street. Having dismissed the cabman with his blessing and a half-sovereign, he vanished into the shop, leaving me to gaze at the lathes, drills, and bars of metal displayed in the window. Presently he emerged with a small parcel, and explained, in answer to my inquiring look: "A strip of tool steel and a block of metal for Polton."

His next purchase was rather more eccentric. We were proceeding along Holborn when his attention was suddenly arrested by the window of a furniture shop, in which was displayed a collection of obsolete French small-arms—relics of the tragedy of 1870—which were being sold for decorative purposes. After a brief inspection, he entered the shop, and shortly reappeared carrying a long sword-bayonet and an old Chassepot rifle.

"What may be the meaning of this martial display?" I asked, as we turned down Fetter Lane.

"House protection," he replied promptly. "You will agree that a discharge of musketry, followed by a bayonet charge, would disconcert the boldest of burglars."

I laughed at the absurd picture thus drawn of the strenuous house-protector, but nevertheless continued to speculate on the meaning of my friend's eccentric proceedings, which I felt sure were in some way related to the murder in Brackenhurst Chambers, though I could not trace the connection.

After a late lunch, I hurried out to transact such of my business as had been interrupted by the stirring events of the morning, leaving Thorndyke busy with a drawing-board, squares, scale, and compasses, making accurate, scaled drawings from his rough sketches; while Polton, with the brown-paper parcel in his hand, looked on at him with an air of anxious expectation.

As I was returning homeward in the evening by way of Mitre Court, I overtook Mr. Marchmont, who was also bound for our chambers, and we walked on together.

"I had a note from Thorndyke," he explained, "asking for a specimen of handwriting, so I thought I would bring it along myself, and hear if he has any news."

When we entered the chambers, we found Thorndyke in earnest consultation with Polton, and on the table before them I observed, to my great surprise, the dagger with which the murder had been committed.

"I have got you the specimen that you asked for," said Marchmont. "I didn't think I should be able to, but, by a

THE ALUMINUM DAGGER

lucky chance, Curtis kept the only letter he ever received from the party in question."

He drew the letter from his wallet, and handed it to Thorndyke, who looked at it attentively and with evident satisfaction.

"By the way," said Marchmont, taking up the dagger, "I thought the inspector took this away with him."

"He took the original," replied Thorndyke. "This is a duplicate, which Polton has made, for experimental purposes, from my drawings."

"Really!" exclaimed Marchmont, with a glance of respectful admiration at Polton; "it is a perfect replica—and you have made it so quickly, too."

"It was quite easy to make," said Polton, "to a man accustomed to work in metal."

"Which," added Thorndyke, "is a fact of some evidential value."

At this moment a hansom drew up outside. A moment later flying footsteps were heard on the stairs. There was a furious battering at the door, and, as Polton threw it open, Mr. Curtis burst wildly into the room.

"Here is a frightful thing, Marchmont!" he gasped. "Edith—my daughter—arrested for the murder. Inspector Badger came to our house and took her. My God! I shall go mad!"

Thorndyke laid his hand on the excited man's shoulder. "Don't distress yourself, Mr. Curtis," said he. "There is no occasion, I assure you. I suppose," he added, "your daughter is left-handed?"

"Yes, she is, by a most disastrous coincidence. But what are we to do? Good God! Dr. Thorndyke, they have taken her to prison—to prison—think of it! My poor Edith!"

"We'll soon have her out," said Thorndyke. "But listen; there is someone at the door."

A brisk rat-tat confirmed his statement, and when I rose to open the door, I found myself confronted by Inspector Badger. There was a moment of extreme awkwardness, and then both the detective and Mr. Curtis proposed to retire in favour of the other.

"Don't go, inspector," said Thorndyke; "I want to have a word with you. Perhaps Mr. Curtis would look in again, say, in an hour. Will you? We shall have news for you by then, I hope."

Mr. Curtis agreed hastily, and dashed out of the room with his characteristic impetuosity When he had gone, Thorndyke turned to the detective, and remarked dryly:

"You seem to have been busy, inspector?"

"Yes," replied Badger; "I haven't let the grass grow under my feet; and I've got a pretty strong case against Miss Curtis already. You see, she was the last person seen in the company of the deceased; she had a grievance against him; she is left-handed, and you remember that the murder was committed by a left-handed person."

"Anything else?"

"Yes. I have seen those Italians, and the whole thing was a put-up job. A woman, in a widow's dress and veil, paid them to go and play the fool outside the building, and she gave them the letter that was left with the porter. They haven't identified her yet, but she seems to agree in size with Miss Curtis."

"And how did she get out of the chambers, with the door bolted on the inside?"

"Ah, there you are! That's a mystery at present—unless you can give us an explanation." The inspector made this qualification with a faint grin, and added: "As there was no one in the place when we broke into it, the murderer must have got out somehow. You can't deny that."

"I do deny it, nevertheless," said Thorndyke. "You look surprised," he continued (which was undoubtedly true), "but yet the whole thing is exceedingly obvious. The explanation struck me directly I looked at the body. There was evidently no practicable exit from the flat, and there was certainly no one in it when you entered. Clearly, then, *the murderer had never been in the place at all.*"

"I don't follow you in the least," said the inspector.

"Well," said Thorndyke, "as I have finished with the case, and am handing it over to you, I will put the evidence before you *seriatim*. Now, I think we are agreed that, at the moment when the blow was struck, the deceased was standing before the fireplace, winding the clock. The dagger entered obliquely from the left, and, if you recall its position, you will remember that its hilt pointed directly towards an open window."

"Which was forty feet from the ground."

"Yes. And now we will consider the very peculiar character of the weapon with which the crime was committed."

He had placed his hand upon the knob of a drawer, when we were interrupted by a knock at the door. I sprang up, and, opening it, admitted no less a person than the porter of Brackenhurst Chambers. The man looked somewhat surprised on recognising our visitors, but advanced to Thorndyke, drawing a folded paper from his pocket.

"I've found the article you were looking for, sir," said he, "and a rare hunt I had for it. It had stuck in the leaves of one of them shrubs."

Thorndyke opened the packet, and, having glanced inside, laid it on the table.

"Thank you," said he, pushing a sovereign across to the gratified official. "The inspector has your name, I think?"

"He have, sir," replied the porter; and, pocketing his fee, he departed, beaming.

"To return to the dagger," said Thorndyke, opening the drawer. "It was a very peculiar one, as I have said, and as you will see from this model, which is an exact duplicate." Here he exhibited Polton's production to the astonished detective. "You see that it is extraordinarily slender, and free from projections, and of unusual materials. You also see that it was obviously not made by an ordinary dagger-maker; that, in spite of the Italian word scrawled on it, there is plainly written all over it, 'British mechanic.' The blade is made from a strip of common three-quarter-inch tool steel; the hilt is turned from an aluminium rod; and there is not a line of engraving on it that could not be produced in a lathe by any engineer's apprentice. Even the boss at the top is mechanical, for it is just like an ordinary hexagon nut. Then, notice the dimensions, as shown on my drawing. The parts A and B, which just project beyond the blade, are exactly similar in diameter—and such exactness could hardly be accidental. They are each parts of a circle having a diameter of 10.9 millimetres—a dimension which happens, by a singular coincidence, to be exactly the calibre of the old Chassepot rifle, specimens of which are now on sale at several shops in London. Here is one, for instance."

He fetched the rifle that he had bought, from the corner in which it was standing, and, lifting the dagger by its point, slipped the hilt into the muzzle. When he let go, the dagger slid quietly down the barrel, until its hilt appeared in the open breech.

"Good God!" exclaimed Marchmont. "You don't suggest that the dagger was shot from a gun?"

"I do, indeed; and you now see the reason for the aluminium hilt—to diminish the weight of the already heavy projectile—and also for this hexagonal boss on the end?"

"No, I do not," said the inspector; "but I say that you are suggesting an impossibility."

"Then," replied Thorndyke, "I must explain and demonstrate. To begin with, this projectile had to travel point foremost; therefore it had to be made to spin—and it certainly was spinning when it entered the body, as the clothing and the wound showed us. Now, to make it spin, it had to be fired from a rifled barrel; but as the hilt would not engage in the rifling, it had to be fitted with something that would. That something was evidently a soft metal washer, which fitted on to this hexagon, and which would be pressed into the grooves of the rifling, and so spin the dagger, but would drop off as soon as the weapon left the barrel. Here is such a washer, which Polton has made for us."

He laid on the table a metal disc, with a hexagonal hole through it.

"This is all very ingenious," said the inspector, "but I say it is impossible and fantastic."

"It certainly sounds rather improbable," Marchmont agreed.

"We will see," said Thorndyke. "Here is a makeshift cartridge of Polton's manufacture, containing an eighth charge of smokeless powder for a 20-bore gun."

He fitted the washer on to the boss of the dagger in the open breech of the rifle, pushed it into the barrel, inserted the cartridge, and closed the breech. Then, opening the office, he displayed a target of padded strawboard against the wall.

"The length of the two rooms," said he, "gives us a distance of thirty-two feet. Will you shut the windows, Jervis?"

I complied, and he then pointed the rifle at the target. There was a dull report—much less loud than I had expected—and when we looked at the target, we saw the dagger driven in up to its hilt at the margin of the bull's-eye.

"You see," said Thorndyke, laying down the rifle, "that the thing is practicable. Now for the evidence as to the actual occurrence. First, on the original dagger there are linear scratches which exactly correspond with the grooves of the rifling. Then there is the fact that the dagger was certainly spinning from left to right—in the direction of the rifling, that is—when it entered the body. And then there is this, which, as you heard, the porter found in the garden."

He opened the paper packet. In it lay a metal disc, perforated by a hexagonal hole. Stepping into the office, he picked up from the floor the washer that he had put on the dagger, and laid it on the paper beside the other. The two discs were identical in size, and the margin of each was indented with identical markings, corresponding to the rifling of the barrel.

The inspector gazed at the two discs in silence for a while; then, looking up at Thorndyke, he said:

"I give in, doctor. You're right, beyond all doubt; but how you came to think of it beats me into fits. The only question now is, Who fired the gun, and why wasn't the report heard?"

"As to the latter," said Thorndyke, "it is probable that he used a compressed-air attachment, not only to diminish the noise, but also to prevent any traces of the explosive from being left on the dagger. As to the former, I think I can give you the murderer's name; but we had better take the evidence in order. You may remember," he continued, "that when Dr. Jervis stood as if winding the clock, I chalked a mark on the floor where he stood. Now, standing on that marked spot, and looking out of the open window, I could see two of the windows of a house nearly opposite. They were the second- and third-floor windows of No. 6 Cotman Street. The second floor is occupied by a firm of architects; the third floor by a commission agent named Thomas Barlow. I called on Mr. Barlow, but before describing my visit, I will refer to another matter. You haven't those threatening letters about you, I suppose?"

"Yes, I have," said the inspector; and he drew forth a wallet from his breast-pocket.

"Let us take the first one, then," said Thorndyke. "You see that the paper and envelope are of the very commonest, and the writing illiterate. But the ink does not agree with this. Illiterate people usually buy their ink in penny bottles. Now, this envelope is addressed with Draper's dichroic—a superior office ink, sold only in large bottles—and the red ink in which the note is written is an unfixed, scarlet ink, such as is used by draughtsmen, and has been used, as you can see, in a stylographic pen. But the most interesting thing about this letter is the design drawn at the top. In an artistic sense, the man could not draw, and the anatomical details of the skull are ridiculous. Yet the drawing is very neat. It has the clean, wiry line of a machine drawing, and is done with a steady, practised hand. It is also perfectly symmetrical; the skull, for instance, is exactly in the centre, and, when we examine it through a lens, we see why it is so, for we discover traces of a pencilled centre-line and ruled cross-lines. Moreover, the lens reveals a tiny particle of draughtsmen's soft, red rubber, with which the pencil lines were taken out; and all these facts, taken together, suggest that the drawing was made by someone accustomed to making accurate mechanical drawings. And now we will return to Mr. Barlow. He was out when I called, but I took the liberty of glancing round the office, and this is what I saw. On the mantelshelf was a twelve-inch flat boxwood rule, such as engineers use, a piece of soft, red rubber, and a stone bottle of Draper's dichroic ink. I obtained, by a simple ruse, a specimen of the office notepaper and the ink. We will examine it presently. I found that Mr. Barlow is a new tenant, that he is rather short, wears a wig and spectacles, and always wears a glove on his left hand. He left the office at 8:30 this morning, and no one saw him arrive. He had with him a square case, and a narrow, oblong one about five feet in length; and he took a cab to Victoria, and apparently caught the 8:51 train to Chatham."

"Ah!" exclaimed the inspector.

"But," continued Thorndyke, "now examine those three letters, and compare them with this note that I wrote in Mr. Barlow's office. You see that the paper is of the same make, with the same water-mark, but that is of no great significance. What is of crucial importance is this: You see, in each of these letters, two tiny indentations near the bottom corner. Somebody has used compasses or drawing-pins over the packet of notepaper, and the points have made little indentations, which have marked several of the sheets. Now, notepaper is cut to its size after it is folded, and if you stick a pin into the top sheet of a section, the indentations on all the underlying sheets will be at exactly similar distances from the edges and corners of the sheet. But you see that these little dents are all at the same distance from the edges and the corner." He demonstrated the fact with a pair of compasses. "And now look at this sheet, which I obtained at Mr. Barlow's office. There are two little indentations—rather faint, but quite visible—near the bottom corner, and when we measure them with the compasses, we find that they are exactly the same distance apart as the others, and the same distance from the edges and the bottom corner. The irresistible conclusion is that these four sheets came from the same packet."

The inspector started up from his chair, and faced Thorndyke. "Who is this Mr. Barlow?" he asked.

"That," replied Thorndyke, "is for you to determine; but I can give you a useful hint. There is only one person who benefits by the death of Alfred Hartridge, but he benefits to the extent of twenty thousand pounds. His name is Leonard Wolfe, and I learn from Mr. Marchmont that he is a man of indifferent character—a gambler, and a spendthrift. By profession he is an engineer, and he is a capable mechanician. In appearance he is thin, short, fair, and clean-shaven, and he has lost the middle finger of his left hand. Mr. Barlow is also short, thin, and fair, but wears a wig, a beard, and spectacles, and always wears a glove on his left hand. I have seen the handwriting of both these gentlemen, and should say that it would be difficult to distinguish one from the other."

"That's good enough for me," said the inspector. "Give me his address, and I'll have Miss Curtis released at once."

The same night Leonard Wolfe was arrested at Eltham, in the very act of burying in his garden a large and powerful compressed-air rifle. He was never brought to trial, however, for he had in his pocket a more portable weapon—a large-bore Derringer pistol—with which he managed to terminate an exceedingly ill spent life.

"And, after all," was Thorndyke's comment, when he heard of the event, "he had his uses. He has relieved society of two very bad men, and he has given us a most instructive case. He has shown us how a clever and ingenious criminal may take endless pains to mislead and delude the police, and yet, by inattention to trivial details, may scatter clues broadcast. We can only say to the criminal class generally, in both respects, 'Go thou and do likewise.' "

THE SECRET GARDEN
by G. K. Chesterton

ARISTIDE VALENTIN, CHIEF OF THE PARIS POLICE, WAS LATE
for his dinner, and some of his guests began to arrive before
him. These were, however, reassured by his confidential
servant, Ivan, the old man with a scar, and a face almost as
grey as his moustaches, who always sat at a table in the entrance hall—a hall hung with weapons. Valentin's house was
perhaps as peculiar and celebrated as its master. It was an
old house, with high walls and tall poplars almost overhang-
ing the Seine; but the oddity—and perhaps the police value
—of its architecture was this: that there was no ultimate
exit at all except through this front door, which was guarded by Ivan and the armoury. The garden was large and elaborate, and there were many exits from the house into the
garden. But there was no exit from the garden into the world
outside; all round it ran a tall, smooth, unscalable wall with
special spikes at the top; no bad garden, perhaps, for a man
to reflect in whom some hundred criminals had sworn to
kill.

As Ivan explained to the guests, their host had telephoned
that he was detained for ten minutes. He was, in truth, making some last arrangements about executions and such ugly
things; and though these duties were rootedly repulsive to
him, he always performed them with precision. Ruthless in
the pursuit of criminals, he was very mild about their punishment. Since he had been supreme over French—and
largely over European—political methods, his great influence had been honourably used for the mitigation of sen-
tences and the purification of prisons. He was one of the

great humanitarian French freethinkers; and the only thing wrong with them is that they make mercy even colder than justice.

When Valentin arrived he was already dressed in black clothes and the red rosette—an elegant figure, his dark beard already streaked with grey. He went straight through his house to his study, which opened on the grounds behind. The garden door of it was open, and after he had carefully locked his box in its official place, he stood for a few seconds at the open door looking out upon the garden. A sharp moon was fighting with the flying rags and tatters of a storm, and Valentin regarded it with a wistfulness unusual in such scientific natures as his. Perhaps such scientific natures have some psychic prevision of the most tremendous problem of their lives. From any such occult mood, at least, he quickly recovered, for he knew he was late and that his guests had already begun to arrive. A glance at his drawing-room when he entered it was enough to make certain that his principal guest was not there, at any rate. He saw all the other pillars of the little party; he saw Lord Galloway, the English Ambassador—a choleric old man with a russet face like an apple, wearing the blue ribbon of the Garter. He saw Lady Galloway, slim and threadlike, with silver hair and a face sensitive and superior. He saw her daughter, Lady Margaret Graham, a pale and pretty girl with an elfish face and copper-coloured hair. He saw the Duchess of Mont St. Michel, black-eyed and opulent, and with her her two daughters, black-eyed and opulent also. He saw Dr. Simon, a typical French scientist, with glasses, a pointed brown beard, and a forehead barred with those parallel wrinkles which are the penalty of superciliousness, since they come through constantly elevating the eyebrows. He saw Father Brown, of Cobhole, in Essex, whom he had recently met in England. He saw—perhaps with more interest than any of these—a tall man in uniform, who had bowed to the Galloways without receiving any very hearty acknowledgment, and who now advanced alone to pay his respects to his host. This was Commandant

O'Brien, of the French Foreign Legion. He was a slim yet
somewhat swaggering figure, clean-shaven, dark-haired, and
blue-eyed, and, as seemed natural in an officer of that famous regiment of victorious failures and successful suicides,
he had an air at once dashing and melancholy. He was by
birth an Irish gentleman, and in boyhood had known the
Galloways—especially Margaret Graham. He had left his
country after some crash of debts, and now expressed his
complete freedom from British etiquette by swinging about
in uniform, sabre and spurs. When he bowed to the Ambassador's family, Lord and Lady Galloway bent stiffly, and
Lady Margaret looked away.

But for whatever old causes such people might be interested in each other, their distinguished host was not special-
ly interested in them. No one of them at least was in his eyes
the guest of the evening. Valentin was expecting, for special
reasons, a man of world-wide fame, whose friendship he
had secured during some of his great detective tours and
triumphs in the United States. He was expecting Julius K.
Brayne, that multimillionaire whose colossal and even crushing endowments of small religions have occasioned so much
easy sport and easier solemnity for the American and English papers. Nobody could quite make out whether Mr.
Brayne was an atheist or a Mormon or a Christian Scientist;
but he was ready to pour money into any intellectual vessel,
so long as it was an untried vessel. One of his hobbies was
to wait for the American Shakespeare—a hobby more pa-
tient than angling. He admired Walt Whitman, but thought
that Luke P. Tanner, of Paris, Pa., was more "progressive"
than Whitman any day. He liked anything that he thought
"progressive." He thought Valentin "progressive," thereby
doing him a grave injustice.

The solid appearance of Julius K. Brayne in the room
was as decisive as a dinner bell. He had this great quality,
which very few of us can claim, that his presence was as
big as his absence. He was a huge fellow, as fat as he was
tall, clad in complete evening black, without so much relief
as a watch-chain or a ring. His hair was white and well

brushed back like a German's; his face was red, fierce and cherubic, with one dark tuft under the lower lip that threw up that otherwise infantile visage with an effect theatrical and even Mephistophelean. Not long, however, did that *salon* merely stare at the celebrated American; his lateness had already become a domestic problem, and he was sent with all speed into the dining-room with Lady Galloway upon his arm.

Except on one point the Galloways were genial and casual enough. So long as Lady Margaret did not take the arm of that adventurer O'Brien, her father was quite satisfied; and she had not done so, she had decorously gone in with Dr. Simon. Nevertheless, old Lord Galloway was restless and almost rude. He was diplomatic enough during dinner, but when, over the cigars, three of the younger men— Simon the doctor, Brown the priest, and the detrimental O'Brien, the exile in a foreign uniform—all melted away to mix with the ladies or smoke in the conservatory, then the English diplomatist grew very undiplomatic indeed. He was stung every sixty seconds with the thought that the scamp O'Brien might be signalling to Margaret somehow; he did not attempt to imagine how. He was left over the coffee with Brayne, the hoary Yankee who believed in all religions, and Valentin, the grizzled Frenchman who believed in none. They could argue with each other, but neither could appeal to him. After a time this "progressive" logomachy had reached a crisis of tedium; Lord Galloway got up also and sought the drawing-room. He lost his way in long passages for some six or eight minutes: till he heard the high-pitched, didactic voice of the doctor, and then the dull voice of the priest, followed by general laughter. They also, he thought with a curse, were probably arguing about "science and religion." But the instant he opened the *salon* door he saw only one thing—he saw what was not there. He saw that Commandant O'Brien was absent, and that Lady Margaret was absent too.

Rising impatiently from the drawing-room, as he had from the dining-room, he stamped along the passage once more. His notion of protecting his daughter from the Irish-Algerian ne'er-do-weel had become something central and even mad in his mind. As he went towards the back of the house, where was Valentin's study, he was surprised to meet his daughter, who swept past with a white scornful face, which was a second enigma. If she had been with O'Brien, where was O'Brien? If she had not been with O'Brien, where had she been? With a sort of senile and passionate suspicion he groped his way to the dark back parts of the mansion, and eventually found a servant's entrance that opened on to the garden. The moon with her scimitar had now ripped up and rolled away all the storm-wrack. The argent light lit up all four corners of the garden. A tall figure in blue was striding across the lawn towards the study door; a glint of moonlit silver on his facings picked him out as Commandant O'Brien.

He vanished through the French windows into the house, leaving Lord Galloway in an indescribable temper, at once virulent and vague. The blue-and-silver garden, like a scene in a theatre, seemed to taunt him with all that tyrannic tenderness against which his worldly authority was at war. The length and grace of the Irishman's stride enraged him as if he were a rival instead of a father; the moonlight maddened him. He was trapped as if by magic into a garden of troubadours, a Watteau fairyland; and, willing to shake off such amorous imbecilities by speech, he stepped briskly after his enemy. As he did so he tripped over some tree or stone in the grass; looked down at it first with irritation and then a second time with curiostiy. The next instant the moon and the tall poplars looked at an unusual sight—an elderly English diplomatist running hard and crying or bellowing as he ran.

His hoarse shouts brought a pale face to the study door, the beaming glasses and worried brow of Dr. Simon, who heard the nobleman's first clear words. Lord Galloway was crying: "A corpse in the grass—a blood-stained corpse." O'Brien at least had gone utterly out of his mind.

"We must tell Valentin at once," said the doctor, when

the other had brokenly described all that he had dared to examine. "It is fortunate that he is here"; and even as he spoke the great detective entered the study, attracted by the cry. It was almost amusing to note his typical transformation; he had come with the common concern of a host and a gentleman, fearing that some guest or servant was ill. When he was told the gory fact, he turned with all his gravity instantly bright and business-like; for this, however abrupt and awful, was his business.

"Strange, gentlemen," he said as they hurried out into the garden, "that I should have hunted mysteries all over the earth, and now one comes and settles in my own back-yard. But where is the place?" They crossed the lawn less easily, as a slight mist had begun to rise from the river; but under the guidance of the shaken Galloway they found the body sunken in deep grass—the body of a very tall and broad-shouldered man. He lay face downwards, so they could only see that his big shoulders were clad in black cloth, and that his big head was bald, except for a wisp or two of brown hair that clung to his skull like wet seaweed. A scarlet serpent of blood crawled from under his fallen face.

"At least," said Simon, with a deep and singular intonation; "he is none of our party."

"Examine him, doctor," cried Valentin rather sharply. "He may not be dead."

The doctor bent down. "He is not quite cold, but I am afraid he is dead enough," he answered. "Just help me to lift him up."

They lifted him carefully an inch from the ground, and all doubts as to him being really dead were settled at once and frightfully. The head fell away. It had been entirely sundered from the body; whoever had cut his throat had managed to sever the neck as well. Even Valentin was slightly shocked. "He must have been as strong as a gorilla," he muttered.

Not without a shiver, though he was used to anatomical abortions, Dr. Simon lifted the head. It was slightly slashed

about the neck and jaw, but the face was substantially un-
hurt. It was a ponderous, yellow face, at once sunken and
swollen, with a hawk-like nose and heavy lids—the face
of a wicked Roman Emperor, with, perhaps, a distant
touch of a Chinese emperor. All present seemed to look
at it with the coldest eye of ignorance. Nothing else could
be noted about the man except that, as they had lifted his
body, they had seen underneath it the white gleam of a
shirt-front defaced with a red gleam of blood. As Dr.
Simon said, the man had never been of their party. But
he might very well have been trying to join it, for he had
come dressed for such an occasion.

Valentin went down on his hands and knees and examined with his closest professional attention the grass and
ground for some twenty yards round the body, in which
he was assisted less skilfully by the doctor, and quite vaguely by the English lord. Nothing rewarded their grovellings
except a few twigs, snapped or chopped into very small
lengths, which Valentin lifted for an instant's examination
and then tossed away.

"Twigs," he said gravely; "twigs, and a total stranger
with his head cut off; that is all there is on this lawn."

There was an almost creepy stillness, and then the unnerved Galloway called out sharply:

"Who's that? Who's that over there by the garden wall?"

A small figure with a foolishly large head drew waver-
ingly near them in the moonlit haze; looked for an instant
like a goblin, but turned out to be the harmless little priest
whom they had left in the drawing-room.

"I say," he said meekly, "there are no gates to this garden, do you know."

Valentin's black brows had come together somewhat
crossly, as they did on principle at the sight of the cassock.
But he was far too just a man to deny the relevance of the
remark. "You are right," he said. "Before we find out how
he came to be killed, we may have to find out how he came
to be here. Now listen to me, gentlemen. If it can be done
without prejudice to my position and duty, we shall all

agree that certain distinguished names might well be kept out of this. There are ladies, gentlemen, and there is a foreign ambassador. If we must mark it down as a crime, then it must be followed up as a crime. But till then I can use my own discretion. I am the head of the police; I am so public that I can afford to be private. Please Heaven, I will clear every one of my own guests before I call in my men to look for anybody else. Gentlemen, upon your honour, you will none of you leave the house till to-morrow at noon; there are bedrooms for all. Simon, I think you know where to find my man, Ivan, in the front hall; he is a confidential man. Tell him to leave another servant on guard and come to me at once. Lord Galloway, you are certainly the best person to tell the ladies what has happened, and prevent a panic. They also must stay. Father Brown and I will remain with the body."

When this spirit of the captain spoke in Valentin he was obeyed like a bugle. Dr. Simon went through to the armoury and routed out Ivan, the public detective's private detective. Galloway went to the drawing-room and told the terrible news tactfully enough, so that by the time the company assembled there the ladies were already startled and already soothed. Meanwhile the good priest and the good atheist stood at the head and foot of the dead man motionless in the moonlight, like symbolic statues of their two philosophies of death.

Ivan, the confidential man with the scar and the moustaches, came out of the house like a cannon ball, and came racing across the lawn to Valentin like a dog to his master. His livid face was quite lively with the glow of this domestic detective story, and it was with almost unpleasant eagerness that he asked his master's permission to examine the remains.

"Yes; look, if you like, Ivan," said Valentin; "but don't be long. We must go in and thrash this out in the house."

Ivan lifted his head, and then almost let it drop.

"Why," he gasped, "it's—no, it isn't; it can't be. Do you know this man, sir?"

"No," said Valentin indifferently; "we had better go inside."

Between them they carried the corpse to a sofa in the study, and then all made their way to the drawing-room.

The detective sat down at a desk quietly, and even with hesitation; but his eye was the iron eye of a judge at assize. He made a few rapid notes upon paper in front of him, and then said shortly: "Is everybody here?"

"Not Mr. Brayne," said the Duchess of Mont St. Michel, looking round.

"No," said Lord Galloway in a hoarse, harsh voice. "And not Mr. Neil O'Brien, I fancy. I saw that gentleman walking in the garden when the corpse was still warm."

"Ivan," said the detective, "go and fetch Commandant O'Brien and Mr. Brayne. Mr. Brayne, I know, is finishing a cigar in the dining-room; Commandant O'Brien, I think, is walking up and down the conservatory. I am not sure."

The faithful attendant flashed from the room, and before anyone could stir or speak Valentin went on with the same soldierly swiftness of exposition.

"Everyone here knows that a dead man has been found in the garden, his head cut clean from his body. Dr. Simon, you have examined it. Do you think that to cut a man's throat like that would need great force? Or, perhaps, only a very sharp knife?"

"I should say that it could not be done with a knife at all," said the pale doctor.

"Have you any thought," resumed Valentin, "of a tool with which it could be done?"

"Speaking within modern probabilities, I really haven't," said the doctor, arching his painful brows. "It's not easy to hack a neck through even clumsily, and this was a very clean cut. It could be done with a battle-axe or an old headsman's axe, or an old two-handed sword."

"But, good heavens!" cried the Duchess, almost in hysterics, "there aren't any two-handed swords and battle-axes round here."

Valentin was still busy with the paper in front of him.

"Tell me," he said, still writing rapidly, "could it have been done with a long French cavalry sabre?"

A low knocking came at the door, which, for some unreasonable reason, curdled everyone's blood like the knocking in *Macbeth*. Amid that frozen silence Dr. Simon managed to say: "A sabre—yes, I suppose it could."

"Thank you," said Valentin. "Come in, Ivan."

The confidential Ivan opened the door and ushered in Commandant Neil O'Brien, whom he had found at last pacing the garden again.

The Irish officer stood disordered and defiant on the threshold. "What do you want with me?" he cried.

"Please sit down," said Valentin in pleasant, level tones. "Why, you aren't wearing your sword. Where is it?"

"I left it on the library table," said O'Brien, his brogue deepening in his disturbed mood. "It was a nuisance, it was getting—"

"Ivan," said Valentin, "please go and get the Commandant's sword from the library." Then, as the servant vanished, "Lord Galloway says he saw you leaving the garden just before he found the corpse. What were you doing in the garden?"

The Commandant flung himself recklessly into a chair. "Oh," he cried in pure Irish, "admirin' the moon. Communing with Nature, me bhoy."

A heavy silence sank and endured, and at the end of it came again that trivial and terrible knocking. Ivan reappeared, carrying an empty steel scabbard. "This is all I can find," he said.

"Put it on the table," said Valentin, without looking up.

There was an inhuman silence in the room, like that sea of inhuman silence round the dock of the condemned murderer. The Duchess's weak exclamations had long ago died away. Lord Galloway's swollen hatred was satisfied and even sobered. The voice that came was quite unexpected.

"I think I can tell you," cried Lady Margaret, in that clear quivering voice with which a courageous woman speaks publicly. "I can tell you what Mr. O'Brien was doing in the

garden, since he is bound to silence. He was going to ask
me to marry him. I refused; I said in my family circumstances I could give him nothing but my respect. He was a
little angry at that; he did not seem to think much of my
respect. I wonder," she added, with rather a wan smile, "if
he will care at all for it now. For I offer it him now. I will
swear anywhere that he never did a thing like this."

Lord Galloway had edged up to his daughter, and was
intimidating her in what he imagined to be an undertone.
"Hold your tongue, Maggie," he said in a thunderous whisper. "Why should you shield the fellow? Where's his sword?
Where's his confounded cavalry——"

He stopped because of the singular stare with which his
daughter was regarding him, a look that was indeed a lurid
magnet for the whole group.

"You old fool!" she said, in a low voice without pretence
of piety, "what do you suppose you are trying to prove? I
tell you this man was innocent while with me. But if he
wasn't innocent, he was still with me. If he murdered a man
in the garden, who was it who must have seen——who must
at least have known? Do you hate Neil so much as to put
your own daughter——"

Lady Galloway screamed. Everyone else sat tingling at
the touch of those satanic tragedies that have been between
lovers before now. They saw the proud, white face of the
Scotch aristocrat and her lover, the Irish adventurer, like
old portraits in a dark house. The long silence was full of
formless historical memories of murdered husbands and
poisonous paramours.

In the centre of this morbid silence an innocent voice
said: "Was it a very long cigar?"

The change of thought was so sharp that they had to look
round to see who had spoken.

"I mean," said little Father Brown, from the corner of
the room, "I mean that cigar Mr. Brayne is finishing. It
seems nearly as long as a walking-stick."

Despite the irrelevance there was assent as well as irritation in Valentin's face as he lifted his head.

"Quite right," he remarked sharply. "Ivan, go and see about Mr. Brayne again, and bring him here at once."

The instant the factotum had closed the door, Valentin addressed the girl with an entirely new earnestness.

"Lady Margaret," he said, "we all feel, I am sure, both gratitude and admiration for your act in rising above your lower dignity and explaining the Commandant's conduct. But there is a hiatus still. Lord Galloway, I understand, met you passing from the study to the drawing-room, and it was only some minutes afterwards that he found the garden and the Commandant still walking there."

"You have to remember," replied Margaret, with a faint irony in her voice, "that I had just refused him, so we should scarcely have come back arm in arm. He is a gentleman, anyhow; and he loitered behind—and so got charged with murder."

"In those few moments," said Valentin gravely, "he might really—"

The knock came again, and Ivan put in his scarred face.

"Beg pardon, sir," he said, "but Mr. Brayne has left the house."

"Left!" cried Valentin, and rose for the first time to his feet.

"Gone. Scooted. Evaporated," replied Ivan, in humorous French. "His hat and coat are gone, too, and I'll tell you something to cap it all. I ran outside the house to find any traces of him, and I found one, and a big trace, too."

"What do you mean?" asked Valentin.

"I'll show you," said his servant, and reappeared with a flashing naked cavalry sabre, streaked with blood about the point and edge. Everyone in the room eyed it as if it were a thunderbolt; but the experienced Ivan went on quite quietly:

"I found this," he said, "flung among the bushes fifty yards up the road to Paris. In other words, I found it just where your respectable Mr. Brayne threw it when he ran away."

There was again a silence, but of a new sort. Valentin

took the sabre, examined it, reflected with unaffected concentration of thought, and then turned a respectable face to O'Brien. "Commandant," he said, "we trust you will always produce this weapon if it is wanted for police examination. Meanwhile," he added, slapping the steel back in the ringing scabbard, "let me return you your sword."

At the military symbolism of the action the audience could hardly refrain from applause.

For Neil O'Brien, indeed, that gesture was the turning-point of existence. By the time he was wandering in the mysterious garden again in the colours of the morning the tragic futility of his ordinary mien had fallen from him; he was a man with many reasons for happiness. Lord Galloway was a gentleman, and had offered him an apology. Lady Margaret was something better than a lady, a woman at least, and had perhaps given him something better than an apology, as they drifted among the old flower-beds before breakfast. The whole company was more light-hearted and humane, for though the riddle of the death remained, the load of suspicion was lifted off them all, and sent flying off to Paris with the strange millionaire—a man they hardly knew. The devil was cast out of the house—he had cast himself out.

Still, the riddle remained; and when O'Brien threw himself on a garden seat beside Dr. Simon, that keenly scientific person at once resumed it. He did not get much talk out of O'Brien, whose thoughts were on pleasanter things.

"I can't say it interests me much," said the Irishman frankly, "especially as it seems pretty plain now. Apparently Brayne hated this stranger for some reason; lured him into the garden, and killed him with my sword. Then he fled to the city, tossing the sword away as he went. By the way, Ivan tells me the dead man had a Yankee dollar in his pocket. So he was a countryman of Brayne's, and that seems to clinch it. I don't see any difficulties about the business."

"There are five colossal difficulties," said the doctor quietly; "like high walls within walls. Don't mistake me. I don't doubt that Brayne did it; his flight, I fancy, proves that. But as to how he did it. First difficulty: Why should a man kill another man with a great hulking sabre, when he can almost kill him with a pocket knife and put it back in his pocket? Second difficulty: Why was there no noise or outcry? Does a man commonly see another come up waving a scimitar and offer no remarks? Third difficulty: A servant watched the front door all evening; and a rat cannot get into Valentin's garden anywhere. How did the dead man get into the garden? Fourth difficulty: Given the same conditions, how did Brayne get out of the garden?"

"And the fifth," said Neil, with eyes fixed on the English priest who was coming slowly up the path.

"Is a trifle, I suppose," said the doctor, "but I think an odd one. When I first saw how the head had been slashed, I supposed the assassin had struck more than once. But on examination I found many cuts across the truncated section; in other words, they were struck *after* the head was off. Did Brayne hate his foe so fiendishly that he stood sabring his body in the moonlight?"

"Horrible!" said O'Brien, and shuddered.

The little priest, Brown, had arrived while they were talking, and had waited, with characteristic shyness, till they had finished. Then he said awkwardly:

"I say, I'm sorry to interrupt. But I was sent to tell you the news!"

"News?" repeated Simon, and stared at him rather painfully through his glasses.

"Yes, I'm sorry," said Father Brown mildly. "There's been another murder, you know."

Both men on the seat sprang up, leaving it rocking.

"And, what's stranger still," continued the priest, with his dull eye on the rhododendrons, "it's the same disgusting sort; it's another beheading. They found the second head actually bleeding in the river, a few yards along Brayne's road to Paris; so they suppose that he—"

"Great Heaven!" cried O'Brien. "Is Brayne a mono-maniac?"

"There are American vendettas," said the priest impassively. Then he added: "They want you to come to the library and see it."

Commandant O'Brien followed the others towards the inquest, feeling decidedly sick. As a soldier, he loathed all this secretive carnage; where were these extravagant amputations going to stop? First one head was hacked off, and then another; in this case (he told himself bitterly) it was not true that two heads were better than one. As he crossed the study he almost staggered at a shocking coincidence. Upon Valentin's table lay the coloured picture of yet a third bleeding head; and it was the head of Valentin himself. A second glance showed him it was only a Nationalist paper, called *The Guillotine,* which every week showed one of its political opponents with rolling eyes and writhing features just after execution; for Valentin was an anti-clerical of some note. But O'Brien was an Irishman, with a kind of chastity even in his sins; and his gorge rose against that great brutality of the intellect which belongs only to France. He felt Paris as a whole, from the grotesques on the Gothic churches to the gross caricatures in the newspapers. He remembered the gigantic jests of the Revolution. He saw the whole city as one ugly energy, from the sanguinary sketch lying on Valentin's table up to where, above a mountain and forest of gargoyles, the great devil grins on Notre Dame.

The library was long, low, and dark; what light entered it shot from under low blinds and had still some of the ruddy tinge of morning. Valentin and his servant Ivan were waiting for them at the upper end of a long, slightly-sloping desk, on which lay the mortal remains, looking enormous in the twilight. The big black figure and yellow face of the man found in the garden confronted them essentially unchanged. The second head, which had been fished from among the river reeds that morning, lay streaming and dripping beside it; Valentin's men were still seeking to recover the rest of this second corpse, which was supposed to be afloat. Father Brown, who did not seem to share O'Brien's sensibilities in the least, went up to the second head and examined it with his blinking care. It was little more than a mop of wet, white hair, fringed with silver fire in the red and level morning light; the face, which seemed of an ugly, empurpled and perhaps criminal type, had been much battered against trees or stones as it tossed in the water.

"Good morning, Commandant O'Brien," said Valentin, with quiet cordiality. "You have heard of Brayne's last experiment in butchery, I suppose?"

Father Brown was still bending over the head with white hair, and he said, without looking up:

"I suppose it is quite certain that Brayne cut off this head, too."

"Well, it seems common sense," said Valentin, with his hands in his pockets. "Killed in the same way as the other. Found within a few yards of the other. And sliced by the same weapon which we know he carried away."

"Yes, yes; I know," replied Father Brown submissively. "Yet, you know, I doubt whether Brayne could have cut off this head."

"Why not?" inquired Dr. Simon, with a rational stare.

"Well, doctor," said the priest, looking up blinking, "can a man cut off his own head? I don't know."

O'Brien felt an insane universe crashing about his ears; but the doctor sprang forward with impetuous practicality and pushed back the wet white hair.

"Oh, there's no doubt it's Brayne," said the priest quietly. "He had exactly that chip in the left ear."

The detective, who had been regarding the priest with steady and glittering eyes, opened his clenched mouth and said sharply: "You seem to know a lot about him, Father Brown."

"I do," said the little man simply. "I've been about with him for some weeks. He was thinking of joining our church."

The star of the fanatic sprang into Valentin's eyes; he strode towards the priest with clenched hands. "And, perhaps," he cried, with a blasting sneer, "perhaps he was also thinking of leaving all his money to your church."

"Perhaps he was," said Brown stolidly; "it is possible."

"In that case," cried Valentin, with a dreadful smile, "you may indeed know a great deal about him. About his life and about his—"

Commandant O'Brien laid a hand on Valentin's arm. "Drop that slanderous rubbish, Valentin," he said, "or there may be more swords yet."

But Valentin (under the steady, humble gaze of the priest) had already recovered himself. "Well," he said shortly, "people's private opinions can wait. You gentlemen are still bound by your promise to stay; you must enforce it on yourselves—and on each other. Ivan here will tell you anything more you want to know; I must get to business and write to the authorities. We can't keep this quiet any longer. I shall be writing in my study if there is any more news."

"Is there any more news, Ivan?" asked Dr. Simon, as the chief of police strode out of the room.

"Only one more thing, I think, sir," said Ivan, wrinkling up his grey old face, "but that's important, too, in its way. There's that old buffer you found on the lawn," and he pointed without pretence of reverence at the big black body with the yellow head. "We've found out who he is, anyhow."

"Indeed!" cried the astonished doctor, "and who is he?"

"His name was Arnold Becker," said the under-detective, "though he went by many aliases. He was a wandering sort of scamp, and is known to have been in America; so that was where Brayne got his knife into him. We didn't have much to do with him ourselves, for he worked mostly in Germany. We've communicated, of course, with the German police. But, oddly enough, there was a twin brother of his, named Louis Becker, whom we had a great deal to do with. In fact, we found it necessary to guillotine him only yesterday. Well, it's a rum thing, gentlemen, but when I saw that fellow flat on the lawn I had the greatest jump of my life. If I hadn't seen Louis Becker guillotined with my own eyes, I'd have sworn it was Louis Becker lying there in the grass. Then, of course, I remembered his twin brother in Germany, and following up the clue—"

The explanatory Ivan stopped, for the excellent reason

that nobody was listening to him. The Commandant and the doctor were both staring at Father Brown, who had sprung stiffly to his feet, and was holding his temples tight like a man in sudden and violent pain.

"Stop, stop, stop!" he cried; "stop talking a minute, for I see half. Will God give me strength? Will my brain make the one jump and see all? Heaven help me! I used to be fairly good at thinking. I could paraphrase any page in Aquinas once. Will my head split—or will it see? I see half —I only see half."

He buried his head in his hands, and stood in a sort of rigid torture of thought or prayer, while the other three could only go on staring at this last prodigy of their wild twelve hours.

When Father Brown's hands fell they showed a face quite fresh and serious, like a child's. He heaved a huge sigh, and said: "Let us get this said and done with as quickly as possible. Look here, this will be the quickest way to convince you all of the truth." He turned to the doctor. "Dr. Simon," he said, "you have a strong head-piece, and I heard you this morning asking the five hardest questions about this business. Well, if you will now ask them again, I will answer them."

Simon's pince-nez dropped from his nose in his doubt and wonder, but he answered at once. "Well, the first question, you know, is why a man should kill another with a clumsy sabre at all when a man can kill with a bodkin?"

"A man cannot behead with a bodkin," said Brown calmly, "and for *this* murder beheading was absolutely necessary."

"Why?" asked O'Brien, with interest.

"And the next question?" asked Father Brown.

"Well, why didn't the man cry out or anything?" asked the doctor; "sabres in gardens are certainly unusual."

"Twigs," said the priest gloomily, and turned to the window which looked on the scene of death. "No one saw the point of the twigs. Why should they lie on that lawn (look at it) so far from any tree? They were not snapped off; they were chopped off. The murderer occupied his enemy with some tricks with the sabre, showing how he could cut a branch in mid-air, or what not. Then, while his enemy bent down to see the result, a silent slash, and the head fell."

"Well," said the doctor slowly, "that seems plausible enough. But my next two questions will stump anyone."

The priest still stood looking critically out of the window and waited.

"You know how all the garden was sealed up like an air-tight chamber," went on the doctor. "Well, how did the strange man get into the garden?"

Without turning round, the little priest answered: "There never was any strange man in the garden."

There was a silence, and then a sudden cackle of almost childish laughter relieved the strain. The absurdity of Brown's remark moved Ivan to open taunts.

"Oh!" he cried; "then we didn't lug a great fat corpse on to a sofa last night? He hadn't got into the garden, I suppose?"

"Got into the garden?" repeated Brown reflectively. "No, not entirely."

"Hang it all," cried Simon, "a man gets into a garden, or he doesn't."

"Not necessarily," said the priest, with a faint smile. "What is the next question, doctor?"

"I fancy you're ill," exclaimed Dr. Simon sharply; "but I'll ask the next question if you like. How did Brayne get out of the garden?"

"He didn't get out of the garden," said the priest, still looking out of the window.

"Didn't get out of the garden?" exploded Simon.

"Not completely," said Father Brown.

Simon shook his fists in a frenzy of French logic. "A man gets out of a garden, or he doesn't," he cried.

"Not always," said Father Brown.

Dr. Simon sprang to his feet impatiently. "I have no time to spare on such senseless talk," he cried angrily. "If you can't understand a man being on one side of a wall or the other, I won't trouble you further."

"Doctor," said the cleric very gently, "we have always got on very pleasantly together. If only for the sake of old friendship, stop and tell me your fifth question."

The impatient Simon sank into a chair by the door and said briefly: "The head and shoulders were cut about in a queer way. It seemed to be done after death."

"Yes," said the motionless priest, "it was done so as to make you assume exactly the one simple falsehood that you did assume. It was done to make you take for granted that the head belonged to the body."

The borderland of the brain, where all the monsters are made, moved horribly in the Gaelic O'Brien. He felt the chaotic presence of all the horse-men and fish-women that man's unnatural fancy has begotten. A voice older than his first fathers seemed saying in his ear: "Keep out of the monstrous garden where grows the tree with double fruit. Avoid the evil garden where died the man with two heads." Yet, while these shameful symbolic shapes passed across the ancient mirror of his Irish soul, his Frenchified intellect was quite alert, and was watching the odd priest as closely and incredulously as all the rest.

Father Brown had turned round at last, and stood against the window with his face in dense shadow; but even in that shadow they could see it was pale as ashes. Nevertheless, he spoke quite sensibly, as if there were no Gaelic souls on earth.

"Gentlemen," he said, "you did not find the strange body of Becker in the garden. You did not find any strange body in the garden. In face of Dr. Simon's rationalism, I still affirm that Becker was only partly present. Look here!" (pointing to the black bulk of the mysterious corpse) "you never saw that man in your lives. Did you ever see this man?"

He rapidly rolled away the bald, yellow head of the unknown, and put in its place the white-maned head beside it. And there, complete, unified, unmistakable, lay Julius K. Brayne.

"The murderer," went on Brown quietly, "hacked off his enemy's head and flung the sword far over the wall. But he was too clever to fling the sword only. He flung the *head* over the wall also. Then he had only to clap on another head to the corpse, and (as he insisted on a private inquest) you all imagined a totally new man."

"Clap on another head!" said O'Brien, staring. "What other head? Heads don't grow on garden bushes, do they?"

"No," said Father Brown huskily, and looking at his boots; "there is only one place where they grow. They grow in the basket of the guillotine, beside which the Chief of Police, Aristide Valentin, was standing not an hour before the murder. Oh, my friends, hear me a minute more before you tear me in pieces. Valentin is an honest man, if being mad for an arguable cause is honesty. But did you never see in that cold, grey eye of his that he is mad? He would do anything, *anything,* to break what he calls the superstition of the Cross. He has fought for it and starved for it, and now he has murdered for it. Brayne's crazy millions had hitherto been scattered among so many sects that they did little to alter the balance of things. But Valentin heard a whisper that Brayne, like so many scatter-brained sceptics, was drifting to us; and that was quite a different thing. Brayne would pour supplies into the impoverished and pugnacious Church of France; he would support six Nationalist newspapers like *The Guillotine.* The battle was already balanced on a point, and the fanatic took flame at the risk. He resolved to destroy the millionaire, and he did it as one would expect the greatest of detectives to commit his only crime. He abstracted the severed head of Becker on some criminological excuse, and took it home in his official box. He had that last argument with Brayne, that Lord Galloway did not hear the end of; that failing, he led him out into the sealed garden, talked about swordsmanship, used twigs and a sabre for illustration and—"

Ivan of the Scar sprang up. "You lunatic," he yelled; "you'll go to my master now, if I take you by—"

"Why, I was going there," said Brown heavily; "I must ask him to confess, and all that."

Driving the unhappy Brown before them like a hostage or sacrifice, they rushed together into the sudden stillness of Valentin's study.

The great detective sat at his desk apparently too occupied to hear their turbulent entrance. They paused a moment, and then something in the look of that upright and elegant back made the doctor run forward slightly. A touch and a glance showed him that there was a small box of pills at Valentin's elbow, and that Valentin was dead in his chair; and on the blind face of the suicide was more than the pride of Cato.

THE ANGEL OF THE LORD
by Melville D. Post

I ALWAYS THOUGHT MY FATHER TOOK A LONG CHANCE, BUT somebody had to take it and certainly I was the one least likely to be suspected. It was a wild country. There were no banks. We had to pay for the cattle, and somebody had to carry the money. My father and my uncle were always being watched. My father was right, I think.

"Abner," he said, "I'm going to send Martin. No one will ever suppose that we would trust this money to a child."

My uncle drummed on the table and rapped his heels on the floor. He was a bachelor, stern and silent. But he could talk . . . and when he did, he began at the beginning and you heard him through; and what he said—well, he stood behind it.

"To stop Martin," my father went on, "would be only to lose the money; but to stop you would be to get somebody killed."

I knew what my father meant. He meant that no one would undertake to rob Abner until after he had shot him to death.

I ought to say a word about my Uncle Abner. He was one of those austere, deeply religious men who were the product of the Reformation. He always carried a Bible in his pocket and he read it where he pleased. Once the crowd at Roy's Tavern tried to make sport of him when he got his book out by the fire; but they never tried it again. When the fight was over Abner paid Roy eighteen silver dollars for the broken chairs and the table—and he was the only

man in the tavern who could ride a horse. Abner belonged
to the church militant, and his God was a war lord.

So that is how they came to send me. The money was in
greenbacks in packages. They wrapped it up in newspaper and put in into a pair of saddle-bags, and I set out.
I was about nine years old. No, it was not as bad as you
think. I could ride a horse all day when I was nine years old
—most any kind of a horse. I was tough as whit'-leather, and
I knew the country I was going into. You must not picture
a little boy rolling a hoop in the park.

It was an afternoon in early autumn. The clay roads
froze in the night; they thawed out in the day and they
were a bit sticky. I was to stop at Roy's Tavern, south of
the river, and go on in the morning. Now and then I passed
some cattle driver, but no one overtook me on the road
until almost sundown; then I heard a horse behind me and
a man came up. I knew him. He was a cattle man named
Dix. He had once been a shipper, but he had come in for
a good deal of bad luck. His partner, Alkire, had ab-
sconded with a big sum of money due the grazers. This
had ruined Dix; he had given up his land, which wasn't
very much, to the grazers. After that he had gone over the
mountain to his people, got together a pretty big sum of
money and bought a large tract of grazing land. Foreign
claimants had sued him in the courts on some old title and
he had lost the whole tract and the money that he had paid
for it. He had married a remote cousin of ours and he had
always lived on her lands, adjoining those of my Uncle
Abner.

Dix seemed surprised to see me on the road.

"So it's you, Martin," he said; "I thought Abner would
be going into the upcountry."

One gets to be a pretty cunning youngster, even at this
age, and I told no one what I was about.

"Father wants the cattle over the river to run a month,"
I returned easily, "and I'm going up there to give his orders
to the grazers."

He looked me over, then he rapped the saddlebags with

his knuckles. "You carry a good deal of baggage, my lad."

I laughed. "Horse feed," I said. "You know my father! A horse must be fed at dinner time, but a man can go till he gets it."

One was always glad of any company on the road, and we fell into an idle talk. Dix said he was going out into the Ten Mile country; and I have always thought that was, in fact, his intention. The road turned south about a mile our side of the tavern. I never liked Dix; he was of an apologetic manner, with a cunning, irresolute face.

A little later a man passed us at a gallop. He was a drover named Marks, who lived beyond my Uncle Abner, and he was riding hard to get in before night. He hailed us, but he did not stop; we got a shower of mud and Dix cursed him. I have never seen a more evil face. I suppose it was because Dix usually had a grin about his mouth, and when that sort of face gets twisted there's nothing like it.

After that he was silent. He rode with his head down and his fingers plucking at his jaw, like a man in some perplexity. At the crossroads he stopped and sat for some time in the saddle, looking before him. I left him there, but at the bridge he overtook me. He said he had concluded to get some supper and go on after that.

Roy's Tavern consisted of a single big room, with a loft above it for sleeping quarters. A narrow covered way connected this room with the house in which Roy and his family lived. We used to hang our saddles on wooden pegs in this covered way. I have seen that wall so hung with saddles that you could not find a place for another stirrup. But tonight Dix and I were alone in the tavern. He looked cunningly at me when I took the saddle-bags with me into the big room and when I went with them up the ladder into the loft. But he said nothing—in fact, he had scarely spoken. It was cold; the road had begun to freeze when we got in. Roy had lighted a big fire. I left Dix before it. I did not take off my clothes, because Roy's beds were mattresses of wheat straw covered with heifer skins—good enough for summer but pretty cold on such a night, even with the heavy, hand-woven coverlet in big white and black checks.

I put the saddle-bags under my head and lay down. I went at once to sleep, but I suddenly awaked. I thought there was a candle in the loft, but it was a gleam of light from the fire below, shining through a crack in the floor. I lay and watched it, the coverlet pulled up to my chin. Then I began to wonder why the fire burned so brightly. Dix ought to be on his way some time and it was a custom for the last man to rake out the fire. There was not a sound. The light streamed steadily through the crack.

Presently it occurred to me that Dix had forgotten the fire and that I ought to go down and rake it out. Roy always warned us about the fire when he went to bed. I got up, wrapped the great coverlet around me, went over to the gleam of light and looked down through the crack in the floor. I had to lie out at full length to get my eye against the board. The hickory logs had turned to great embers and glowed like a furnace of red coals.

Before the fire stood Dix. He was holding out his hands and turning himself about as though he were cold to the marrow; but with all that chill upon him, when the man's face came into the light I saw it covered with a sprinkling of sweat.

I shall carry the memory of that face. The grin was there at the mouth, but it was pulled about; the eyelids were drawn in; the teeth were clamped together. I have seen a dog poisoned with strychnine look like that.

I lay there and watched the thing. It was as though something potent and evil dwelling within the man were in travail to re-form his face upon its image. You cannot realize how that devilish labor held me—the face worked as though it were some plastic stuff, and the sweat oozed through. And all the time the man was cold; and he was crowding into the fire and turning himself about and putting out his hands. And it was as though the heat would no more enter in and warm him than it will enter in and warm the ice.

It seemed to scorch him and leave him cold—and he was fearfully and desperately cold! I could smell the singe of

the fire on him, but it had no power against this diabolic
chill. I began myself to shiver, although I had the heavy
coverlet wrapped around me.

The thing was a fascinating horror; I seemed to be looking down into the chamber of some abominable maternity.
The room was filled with the steady red light of the fire. Not
a shadow moved in it. And there was silence. The man had
taken off his boots and he twisted before the fire without a
sound. It was like the shuddering tales of possession or
transformation by a drug. I thought the man would burn
himself to death. His clothes smoked. How could he be so
cold?

Then, finally the thing was over! I did not see it for his
face was in the fire. But suddenly he grew composed and
stepped back into the room. I tell you I was afraid to look!
I do not know what thing I expected to see there, but I did
not think it would be Dix.

Well, it was Dix; but not the Dix that any of us knew.
There was a certain apology, a certain indecision, a certain
servility in that other Dix, and these things showed about
his face. But there was none of these weaknesses in this
man.

His face had been pulled into planes of firmness and decision; the slack in his features had been taken up; the furtive moving of the eye had gone. He stood now squarely on
his feet and he was full of courage. But I was afraid of him
as I have never been afraid of any human creature in this
world! Something that had been servile in him, that had
skulked behind disguises, that had worn the habiliments of
subterfuge, had now come forth; and it had molded the
features of the man to its abominable courage.

Presently he began to move swiftly about the room. He
looked out at the window and he listened at the door; then
he went softly into the covered way. I thought he was going
on his journey; but then he could not be going with his boots
there beside the fire. In a moment he returned with a saddle
blanket in his hand and came softly across the room to the
ladder.

Then I understood the thing that he intended, and I was motionless with fear. I tried to get up, but I could not. I could only lie there with my eye strained to the crack in the floor. His foot was on the ladder, and I could already feel his hand on my throat and that blanket on my face, and the suffocation of death in me, when far away on the hard road I heard a horse!

He heard it, too, for he stopped on the ladder and turned his evil face about toward the door. The horse was on the long hill beyond the bridge, and he was coming as though the devil rode in his saddle. It was a hard, dark night. The frozen road was like flint; I could hear the iron of the shoes ring. Whoever rode that horse rode for his life or for something more than his life, or he was mad. I heard the horse strike the bridge and thunder across it. And all the while Dix hung there on the ladder by his hands and listened. Now he sprang softly down, pulled on his boots and stood up before the fire, his face—this new face—gleaming with its evil courage. The next moment the horse stopped.

I could hear him plunge under the bit, his iron shoes ripping the frozen road; then the door leaped back and my Uncle Abner was in the room. I was so glad that my heart almost choked me and for a moment I could hardly see—everything was in a sort of mist.

Abner swept the room in a glance, then he stopped.

"Thank God!" he said; "I'm in time." And he drew his hand down over his face with the fingers hard and close as though he pulled something away.

"In time for what?" said Dix.

Abner looked him over. And I could see the muscles of his big shoulders stiffen as he looked. And again he looked him over. Then he spoke and his voice was strange.

"Dix," he said, "is it you?"

"Who would it be but me?" said Dix.

"It might be the devil," said Abner. "Do you know what your face looks like?"

"No matter what it looks like!" said Dix.

"And so," said Abner, "we have got courage with this new face."

Dix drew up his head.

"Now, look here, Abner," he said, "I've had about enough of your big manner. You ride a horse to death and you come plunging in here; what the devil's wrong with you?"

"There's nothing wrong with me," replied Abner, and his voice was low. "But there's something damnably wrong with you, Dix."

"The devil take you," said Dix, and I saw him measure Abner with his eye. It was not fear that held him back; fear was gone out of the creature; I think it was a kind of prudence.

Abner's eyes kindled, but his voice remained low and steady.

"Those are big words," he said.

"Well," cried Dix, "get out of the door then and let me pass!"

"Not just yet," said Abner; "I have something to say to you."

"Say it then," cried Dix, "and get out of the door."

"Why hurry?" said Abner. "It's a long time until daylight, and I have a good deal to say."

"You'll not say it to me," said Dix. "I've got a trip to make tonight; get out of the door."

Abner did not move. "You've got a longer trip to make tonight than you think, Dix," he said; "but you're going to hear what I have to say before you set out on it."

I saw Dix rise on his toes and I knew what he wished for. He wished for a weapon; and he wished for the bulk of bone and muscle that would have a chance against Abner. But he had neither the one nor the other. And he stood there on his toes and began to curse—low, vicious, withering oaths, that were like the swish of a knife.

Abner was looking at the man with a curious interest.

"It is strange," he said, as though speaking to himself, "but it explains the thing. While one is the servant of neither,

one has the courage of neither; but when he finally makes
his choice he gets what his master has to give him."

Then he spoke to Dix.

"Sit down!" he said; and it was in that deep, level voice
that Abner used when he was standing close behind his
words. Every man in the hills knew that voice; one had only
a moment to decide after he heard it. Dix knew that, and
yet for one instant he hung there on his toes, his eyes shim-
mering like a weasel's, his mouth twisting. He was not
afraid! If he had had the ghost of a chance against Abner
he would have taken it. But he knew he had not, and with
an oath he threw the saddle blanket into a corner and sat
down by the fire.

Abner came away from the door then. He took off his
great coat. He put a log on the fire and he sat down across
the hearth from Dix. The new hickory sprang crackling into flames. For a good while there was silence; the two men
sat at either end of the hearth without a word. Abner seemed
to have fallen into a study of the man before him. Finally
he spoke:

"Dix," he said, "do you believe in the providence of
God?"

Dix flung up his head.

"Abner," he cried, "if you are going to talk nonsense I
promise you on my oath that I will not stay to listen."

Abner did not at once reply. He seemed to begin now at
another point.

"Dix," he said, "you've had a good deal of bad luck . . .
Perhaps you wish it put that way."

"Now, Abner," he cried, "you speak the truth; I have had
hell's luck."

"Hell's luck you have had," replied Abner. "It is a good
word. I accept it. Your partner disappeared with all the
money of your grazers on the other side of the river; you
lost the land in your lawsuit; and you are to-night without
a dollar. That was a big tract of land to lose. Where did you
get so great a sum of money?"

"I have told you a hundred times," replied Dix. "I got it

from my people over the mountains. You know where I got it."

"Yes," said Abner. "I know where you got it, Dix. And I know another thing. But first I want to show you this," and he took a little penknife out of his pocket. "And I want to tell you that I believe in the providence of God, Dix."

"I don't care a fiddler's damn what you believe in," said Dix.

"But you do care what I know," replied Abner.

"What do you know?" said Dix.

"I know where your partner is," replied Abner.

I was uncertain about what Dix was going to do, but finally he answered with a sneer.

"Then you know something that nobody else knows."

"Yes," replied Abner, "there is another man who knows."

"Who?" said Dix.

"You," said Abner.

Dix leaned over in his chair and looked at Abner closely.

"Abner," he cried, "you are talking nonsense. Nobody knows where Alkire is. If I knew I'd go after him."

"Dix," Abner answered, and it was again in that deep, level voice, "if I had got here five minutes later you would have gone after him. I can promise you that, Dix.

"Now, listen! I was in the upcountry when I got your word about the partnership; and I was on my way back when at Big Run I broke a stirrup-leather. I had no knife and I went into the store and bought this one; then the store-keeper told me that Alkire had gone to see you. I didn't want to interfere with him and I turned back. . . . So I did not become your partner. And so I did not disappear . . . What was it that prevented? The broken stirrup-leather? The knife? In old times, Dix, men were so blind that God had to open their eyes before they could see His angel in the way before them. . . . They are still blind, but they ought not to be that blind. . . . Well, on the night that Alkire disappeared I met him on his way to your house. It was out there at the bridge. He had broken a stirrup-leather and he was trying to fasten it with a nail. He asked me if I had a knife, and I gave him this one. It was beginning to rain and I went on, leaving him there in the road with the knife in his hand."

Abner paused; the muscles of his great iron jaw contracted.

"God forgive me," he said; "it was His angel again! I never saw Alkire after that."

"Nobody ever saw him after that," said Dix. "He got out of the hills that night."

"No," replied Abner; "it was not in the night when Alkire started on his journey; it was in the day."

"Abner," said Dix, "you talk like a fool. If Alkire had traveled the road in the day somebody would have seen him."

"Nobody could see him on the road he traveled," replied Abner.

"What road?" said Dix.

"Dix," replied Abner, "you will learn that soon enough."

Abner looked hard at the man.

"You saw Alkire when he started on his journey," he continued; "but did you see who it was that went with him?"

"Nobody went with him," replied Dix; "Alkire rode alone."

"Not alone," said Abner; "there was another."

"I didn't see him," said Dix.

"And yet," continued Abner, "you made Alkire go with him."

I saw cunning enter Dix's face. He was puzzled, but he thought Abner off the scent.

"And I made Alkire go with somebody, did I? Well, who was it? Did you see him?"

"Nobody ever saw him."

"He must be a stranger."

"No," replied Abner, "he rode the hills before we came into them."

"Indeed!" said Dix. "And what kind of a horse did he ride?"

"White!" said Abner.

Dix got some inkling of what Abner meant now, and his face grew livid.

"What are you driving at?" he cried. "You sit here beating around the bush. If you know anything, say it out; let's hear it. What is it?"

Abner put out his big sinewy hand as though to thrust Dix back into his chair.

"Listen!" he said. "Two days after that I wanted to get out into the Ten Mile country and I went through your lands; I rode a path through the narrow valley west of your house. At a point on the path where there is an apple tree something caught my eye and I stopped. Five minutes later I knew exactly what had happened under that apple tree. . . . Someone had ridden there; he had stopped under that tree; then something happened and the horse had run away—I knew that by the tracks of a horse on this path. I knew that the horse had a rider and that it had stopped under this tree, because there was a limb cut from the tree at a certain height. I knew the horse had remained there, because the small twigs of the apple limb had been pared off, and they lay in a heap on the path. I knew that something had frightened the horse and that it had run away, because the sod was torn up where it had jumped. . . . Ten minutes later I knew that the rider had not been in the saddle when the horse jumped; I knew what it was that had frightened the horse; and I knew that the thing had occurred the day before. Now, how did I know that?

"Listen! I put my horse into the tracks of that other horse under the tree and studied the ground. Immediately I saw where the weeds beside the path had been crushed, as though some animal had been lying down there, and in the very center of that bed I saw a little heap of fresh earth. That was strange, Dix, that fresh earth where the animal had been lying down! It had come there after the animal had got up, or else it would have been pressed flat. But where had it come from?

"I got off and walked around the apple tree, moving out from it in an ever-widening circle. Finally I found an ant

heap, the top of which had been scraped away as though
one had taken up the loose earth in his hands. Then I went
back and plucked up some of the earth. The under clods of
it were colored as with red paint. . . . No, it wasn't paint.

"There was a brush fence some fifty yards away. I went
over to it and followed it down.

"Opposite the apple tree the weeds were again crushed
as though some animal had lain there. I sat down in that
place and drew a line with my eye across a log of the fence
to a limb of the apple tree. Then I got on my horse and again
put him in the tracks of that other horse under the tree; the
imaginary line passed through the pit of my stomach! . . . I
am four inches taller than Alkire."

It was then that Dix began to curse. I had seen his face
work while Abner was speaking and that spray of sweat had
reappeared. But he kept the courage he had got.

"Lord Almighty, man!" he cried. "How prettily you sum
it up! We shall presently have Lawyer Abner with his brief.
Because my renters have killed a calf; because one of their
horses frightened at the blood has bolted, and because they
cover the blood with earth so the other horses traveling the
path may not do the like; straightway I have shot Alkire out
of his saddle. . . . Man! What a mare's nest! And now,
Lawyer Abner, with your neat little conclusions, what did I
do with Alkire after I had killed him? Did I cause him to
vanish into the air with a smell of sulphur or did I cause the
earth to yawn and Alkire to descend into its bowels?"

"Dix," replied Abner, "your words move somewhat near
the truth."

"Upon my soul," cried Dix, "you compliment me. If I
had that trick of magic, believe me, you would be already
some distance down."

Abner remained a moment silent.

"Dix," he said, "what does it mean when one finds a plot
of earth resodded?"

"Is that a riddle?" cried Dix. "Well, confound me, if I
don't answer it! You charge me with murder and then you
fling in this neat conundrum. Now, what could be the answer

MELVILLE D. POST

to that riddle, Abner? If one had done a murder this sod would overlie a grave and Alkire would be in it in his bloody shirt. Do I give the answer?"

"You do not," replied Abner.

"No!" cried Dix. "Your sodded plot no grave, and Alkire not within it waiting for the trump of Gabriel! Why, man, where are your little damned conclusions?"

"Dix," said Abner, "you do not deceive me in the least; Alkire is not sleeping in a grave."

"Then in the air," sneered Dix, "with the smell of sulphur?"

"Nor in the air," said Abner.

"Then consumed with fire, like the priests of Baal?"

"Nor in the air," said Abner.

Dix had got back the quiet of his face; this banter had put him where he was when Abner entered. "This is all fools' talk," he said; "if I had killed Alkire, what could I have done with the body? And the horse! What could I have done with the horse? Remember, no man has ever seen Alkire's horse any more than he has seen Alkire—and for the reason that Alkire rode him out of the hills that night. Now, look here, Abner, you have asked me a good many questions. I will ask you one. Among your little conclusions do you find that I did this thing alone or with the aid of others?"

"Dix," replied Abner, "I will answer that upon my own belief you had no accomplice."

"Then," said Dix, "how could I have carried off the horse? Alkire I might carry; but his horse weighed thirteen hundred pounds!"

"Dix," said Abner, "no man helped you do this thing; but there were men who helped you to conceal it."

"And now," cried Dix, "the man is going mad! Who could I trust with such work, I ask you? Have I a renter that would not tell it when he moved on to another's land, or when he got a quart of cider in him? Where are the men who helped me?"

"Dix," said Abner, "they have been dead these fifty years."

I heard Dix laugh then, and his evil face lighted as though a candle were behind it. And, in truth, I thought he had got Abner silenced.

"In the name of Heaven!" he cried. "With such proofs it is a wonder that you did not have me hanged."

"And hanged you should have been," said Abner.

"Well," cried Dix, "go and tell the sheriff, and mind you lay before him those little, neat conclusions: How from a horse track and the place where a calf was butchered you have reasoned on Alkire's murder, and to conceal the body and the horse you have reasoned on the aid of men who were rotting in their graves when I was born; and see how he will receive you!"

Abner gave no attention to the man's flippant speech. He got his great silver watch out of his pocket, pressed the stem and looked. Then he spoke in his deep, even voice.

"Dix," he said, "it is nearly midnight; in an hour you must be on your journey, and I have something more to say. Listen! I knew this thing had been done the previous day because it had rained on the night that I met Alkire, and the earth of this ant heap had been disturbed after that. Moreover, this earth had been frozen, and that showed a night had passed since it had been placed there. And I knew the rider of that horse was Alkire because, beside the path near the severed twigs lay my knife, where it had fallen from his hand. This much I learned in some fifteen minutes; the rest took somewhat longer.

" I followed the track of the horse until it stopped in the little valley below. It was easy to follow while the horse ran, because the sod was torn; but when it ceased to run there was no track that I could follow. There was a little stream threading the valley, and I began at the wood and came slowly up to see if I could find where the horse had crossed. Finally I found a horse track and there was also a man's track, which meant that you had caught the horse and were leading it away. But where?

"On the rising ground above there was an old orchard where there had once been a house. The work about that house had been done a hundred years. It was rotted down now. You had opened this orchard into the pasture. I rode all over the face of this hill and finally I entered this orchard. There was a great, flat, moss-covered stone lying a few steps from where the house had stood. As I looked I noticed that the moss growing from it into the earth had been broken along the edges of the stone, and then I noticed that for a few feet about the stone the ground had been re-sodded. I got down and lifted up some of this new sod. Under it the earth had been soaked with that . . . red paint.

"It was clever of you, Dix, to resod the ground; that took only a little time and it effectually concealed the place where you had killed the horse; but it was foolish of you to forget that the broken moss around the edges of the great flat stone could not be mended."

"Abner!" cried Dix. "Stop!" And I saw that spray of sweat, and his face working like kneaded bread, and the shiver of that abominable chill on him.

Abner was silent for a moment and then he went on, but from another quarter.

"Twice," said Abner, "the Angel of the Lord stood before me and I did not know it; but the third time I knew it. It is not in the cry of the wind, nor in the voice of many waters that His presence is made known to us. That man in Israel had only the sign that the beast under him would not go on. Twice I had as good a sign, and tonight, when Marks broke a stirrup-leather before my house and called me to the door and asked me for a knife to mend it, I saw and I came!"

The log that Abner had thrown on was burned down, and the fire was again a mass of embers; the room was filled with that dull red light. Dix had got to his feet, and he stood now twisting before the fire, his hands reaching out to it, and that cold creeping in his bones, and the smell of the fire on him.

Abner rose. And when he spoke his voice was like a thing that has dimensions and weight.

"Dix," he said, "you robbed the grazers; you shot Alkire out of his saddle; and a child you would have murdered!"

And I saw the sleeve of Abner's coat begin to move, then it stopped. He stood staring at something against the wall. I looked to see what the thing was, but I did not see it. Abner was looking beyond the wall, as though it had been moved away.

And all the time Dix had been shaking with that hellish cold, and twisting on the hearth and crowding into the fire. Then he fell back, and he was the Dix I knew—his face was slack; his eye was furtive; and he was full of terror.

It was his weak whine that awakened Abner. He put up his hand and brought the fingers hard down over his face, and then he looked at this new creature, cringing and beset with fears.

"Dix," he said, "Alkire was a just man; he sleeps as peacefully in that abandoned well under his horse as he would sleep in the churchyard. My hand has been held back; you may go. Vengeance is mine, I will repay, saith the Lord."

"But where shall I go, Abner?" the creature wailed; "I have no money and I am cold."

Abner took out his leather wallet and flung it toward the door.

"There is money," he said—"a hundred dollars—and there is my coat. Go! But if I find you in the hills to-morrow, or if I ever find you, I warn you in the name of the living God that I will stamp you out of life!"

I saw the loathsome thing writhe into Abner's coat and seize the wallet and slip out through the door; and a moment later I heard a horse. And I crept back on to Roy's heifer skin.

When I came down at daylight my Uncle Abner was reading by the fire.

THE PLYMOUTH EXPRESS
by Agatha Christie

ALEC SIMPSON, R.N., STEPPED FROM THE PLATFORM AT
Newton Abbot into a first-class compartment of the Plymouth Express. A porter followed him with a heavy suitcase.
He was about to swing it up to the rack, but the young sailor
stopped him.

"No—leave it on the seat. I'll put it up later. Here you
are."

"Thank you, sir." The porter, generously tipped, withdrew.

Doors banged; a stentorian voice shouted: "Plymouth
only. Change for Torquay. Plymouth next stop." Then a
whistle blew, and the train drew slowly out of the station.

Lieutenant Simpson had the carriage to himself. The
December air was chilly, and he pulled up the window.
Then he sniffed vaguely, and frowned. What a smell there
was! Reminded him of that time in hospital, and the operation on his leg. Yes, chloroform; that was it!

He let the window down again, changing his seat to one
with its back to the engine. He pulled a pipe out of his pocket and lit it. For a little time he sat inactive, looking out into
the night and smoking.

At last he roused himself, and opening the suitcase, took
out some papers and magazines, then closed the suitcase
again and endeavored to shove it under the opposite seat—
without success. Some hidden obstacle resisted it. He shoved
harder with rising impatience, but it still stuck out halfway
into the carriage.

"Why the devil won't it go in?" he muttered, and hauling

it out completely, he stooped down and peered under the seat. . . .

A moment later a cry rang out into the night, and the great train came to an unwilling halt in obedience to the imperative jerking of the communication-cord.

"Mon ami," said Poirot, "you have, I know, been deeply involved in this mystery of the Plymouth Express. Read this."

I picked up the note he flicked across the table to me. It was brief and to the point.

Dear Sir:

I shall be obliged if you will call upon me at your earliest convenience.

Yours faithfully,
Ebenezer Halliday

The connection was not clear to my mind, and I looked inquiringly at Poirot.

For answer he took up the newspaper and read aloud:

" 'A sensational discovery was made last night. A young naval officer returning to Plymouth found under the seat of his compartment the body of a woman, stabbed through the heart. The officer at once pulled the communication-cord, and the train was brought to a standstill. The woman, who was about thirty years of age, and richly dressed, has not yet been identified.'

"And later we have this: 'The woman found dead in the Plymouth Express has been identified as the Honorable Mrs. Rupert Carrington.' You see now, my friend? Or if you do not, I will add this—Mrs. Rupert Carrington was, before her marriage, Flossie Halliday, daughter of old man Halliday, the steel king of America."

"And he has sent for you? Splendid!"

"I did him a little service in the past—an affair of bearer bonds. And once, when I was in Paris for a royal visit, I had Mademoiselle Flossie pointed out to me. *La jolie petite*

pensionnaire! She had the *jolie dot* too! It caused trouble.
She nearly made a bad affair."

"How was that?"

"A certain Count de la Rochefour. *Un bien mauvais sujet!*
A bad hat, as you would say. An adventurer pure and simple, who knew how to appeal to a romantic young girl.
Luckily her father got wind of it in time. He took her back
to America in haste. I heard of her marriage some years
later, but I know nothing of her husband."

"H'm," I said. "The Honorable Rupert Carrington is no
beauty, by all accounts. He'd pretty well run through his
own money on the turf, and I should imagine old man Halliday's dollars came along in the nick of time. I should say
that for a good-looking, well-mannered, utterly unscrupu-
lous young scoundrel, it would be hard to find his match!"

"Ah, the poor little lady! *Elle n'est pas bien tombée!*"

"I fancy he made it pretty obvious at once that it was her
money, and not she, that had attracted him. I believe they
drifted apart almost at once. I have heard rumors lately that
there was to be a definite legal separation."

"Old man Halliday is no fool. He would tie up her money
pretty tight."

"I dare say. Anyway, I know as a fact that the Honorable
Rupert is said to be extremely hard up."

"Ah-ha! I wonder—"

"You wonder what?"

"My good friend, do not jump down my throat like that.
You are interested, I see. Supposing you accompany me to
see Mr. Halliday. There is a taxi stand at the corner."

A few minutes sufficed to whirl us to the superb house in
Park Lane rented by the American magnate. We were shown
into the library, and almost immediately we were joined by
a large, stout man, with piercing eyes and an aggressive chin.

"M. Poirot?" said Mr. Halliday. "I guess I don't need to
tell you what I want you for. You've read the papers, and
I'm never one to let the grass grow under my feet. I happened to hear you were in London, and I remembered the

good work you did over those bonds. Never forget a name. I've got the pick of Scotland Yard, but I'll have my own man as well. Money no object. All the dollars were made for my little girl—and now she's gone, I'll spend my last cent to catch the damned scoundrel that did it! See? So it's up to you to deliver the goods."

Poirot bowed.

"I accept, monsieur, all the more willingly that I saw your daughter in Paris several times. And now I will ask you to tell me the circumstances of her journey to Plymouth and any other details that seem to you to bear upon the case."

"Well, to begin with," responded Halliday, "she wasn't going to Plymouth. She was going to join a house-party at Avonmead Court, the Duchess of Swansea's place. She left London by the twelve-fourteen from Paddington, arriving at Bristol (where she had to change) at two-fifty. The principal Plymouth expresses, of course, run via Westbury, and do not go near Bristol at all. The twelve-fourteen does a nonstop run to Bristol, afterward stopping at Weston, Taunton, Exeter and Newton Abbot. My daughter traveled alone in her carriage, which was reserved as far as Bristol, her maid being in a third-class carriage in the next coach."

Poirot nodded, and Mr. Halliday went on: "The party at Avonmead Court was to be a very gay one, with several balls, and in consequence my daughter had with her nearly all her jewels—amounting in value, perhaps, to about a hundred thousand dollars."

"*Un moment,*" interrupted Poirot. "Who had charge of the jewels? Your daughter, or the maid?"

"My daughter always took charge of them herself, carrying them in a small blue morocco case."

"Continue, monsieur."

"At Bristol the maid, Jane Mason, collected her mistress' dressing-bag, and wraps, which were with her, and came to the door of Flossie's compartment. To her surprise, my daughter told her that she was not getting out at Bristol, but was going on farther. She directed Mason to get out the luggage and put it in the cloak-room. She could have tea in the refreshment-room, but she was to wait at the station for her mistress, who would return to Bristol by an up-train in the course of the afternoon. The maid, although very much astonished, did as she was told. She put the luggage in the cloak-room and had some tea. But up-train after up-train came in, and her mistress did not appear. After the arrival of the last train, she left the luggage where it was, and went to a hotel near the station for the night. This morning she read of the tragedy, and returned to town by the first available train."

"Is there nothing to account for your daughter's sudden change of plan?"

"Well, there is this: According to Jane Mason, at Bristol, Flossie was no longer alone in her carriage. There was a man in it who stood looking out of the farther window so that she could not see his face."

"The train was a corridor one, of course?"

"Yes."

"Which side was the corridor?"

"On the platform side. My daughter was standing in the corridor as she talked to Mason."

"And there is no doubt in your mind—excuse me!" He got up, and carefully straightened the inkstand which was a little askew. *"Je vous demande pardon,"* he continued, reseating himself. "It affects my nerves to see anything crooked. Strange, is it not? I was saying, monsieur, that there is no doubt in your mind, as to this probably unexpected meeting being the cause of your daughter's sudden change of plan?"

"It seems the only reasonable supposition."

"You have no idea as to who the gentleman in question might be?"

The millionaire hesitated for a moment, and then replied:

"No—I do not know at all."

"Now—as to the discovery of the body?"

"It was discovered by a young naval officer who at once gave the alarm. There was a doctor on the train. He examined the body. She had been first chloroformed, and then stabbed. He gave it as his opinion that she had been dead about four hours, so it must have been done not long after leaving Bristol—probably between there and Weston, possibly between Weston and Taunton."

"And the jewel-case?"

"The jewel-case, M. Poirot, was missing."

"One thing more, monsieur. Your daughter's fortune—to whom does it pass at her death?"

"Flossie made a will soon after her marriage, leaving everything to her husband." He hesitated for a minute, and then went on: "I may as well tell you, Monsieur Poirot, that I regard my son-in-law as an unprincipled scoundrel, and that, by my advice, my daughter was on the eve of freeing herself from him by legal means—no difficult matter. I settled her money upon her in such a way that he could not touch it during her lifetime, but although they have lived entirely apart for some years, she had frequently acceded to his demands for money, rather than face an open scandal. However, I was determined to put an end to this. At last Flossie agreed, and my lawyers were instructed to take proceedings."

"And where is Monsieur Carrington?"

"In town. I believe he was away in the country yesterday, but he returned last night."

Poirot considered a little while. Then he said: "I think that is all, monsieur."

"You would like to see the maid, Jane Mason?"

"If you please."

Halliday rang the bell, and gave a short order to the footman.

A few minutes later Jane Mason entered the room, a respectable, hard-featured woman, as emotionless in the face of tragedy as only a good servant can be.

"You will permit me to put a few questions? Your mistress, she was quite as usual before starting yesterday morning? Not excited or flurried?"

"Oh, no, sir!"

"But at Bristol she was quite different?"

"Yes, sir, regular upset—so nervous she didn't seem to know what she was saying."

"What did she say exactly?"

"Well, sir, as near as I can remember, she said: 'Mason, I've got to alter my plans. Something has happened—I mean, I'm not getting out here after all. I must go on. Get out the luggage and put it in the cloak-room; then have some tea, and wait for me in the station.'

" 'Wait for you here, ma'am?' I asked.

" 'Yes, yes. Don't leave the station. I shall return by a later train. I don't know when. It mayn't be until quite late.'

" 'Very well, ma'am,' I says. It wasn't my place to ask questions, but I thought it very strange."

"It was unlike your mistress, eh?"

"Very unlike her, sir."

"What did you think?"

"Well, sir, I thought it was to do with the gentleman in the carriage. She didn't speak to him, but she turned round once or twice as though to ask him if she was doing right."

"But you didn't see the gentleman's face?"

"No sir; he stood with his back to me all the time."

"Can you describe him at all?"

"He had on a light fawn overcoat, and a traveling-cap. He was tall and slender, like, and the back of his head was dark."

"You didn't know him?"

"Oh, no, I don't think so, sir."

"It was not your master, Mr. Carrington, by any chance?" Mason looked rather startled.

"Oh! I don't think so, sir!"

"But you are not *sure?*"

"It was about the master's build, sir—but I never thought of it being him. We so seldom saw him . . . I couldn't say it *wasn't* him!"

Poirot picked up a pin from the carpet, and frowned at it severely; then he continued: "Would it be possible for the man to have entered the train at Bristol before you reached the carriage?"

Mason considered.

"Yes, sir, I think it would. My compartment was very crowded, and it was some minutes before I could get out—and then there was a very large crowd on the platform, and that delayed me too. But he'd only have had a minute or two to speak to the mistress, that way. I took it for granted that he'd come along the corridor."

"That is more probable, certainly."

He paused, still frowning.

"You know how the mistress was dressed, sir?"

"The papers gave a few details, but I would like you to confirm them."

"She was wearing a white fox fur toque, sir, with a white spotted veil, and a blue frieze coat and skirt—the shade of blue they call electric."

"H'm, rather striking."

"Yes," remarked Mr. Halliday. "Inspector Japp is in hopes that that may help us to fix the spot where the crime took place. Anyone who saw her would remember her."

"*Précisément!*—Thank you, mademoiselle."

The maid left the room.

"Well!" Poirot got up briskly. "That is all I can do here—except, monsieur, that I would ask you to tell me everything—but *everything!*"

"I have done so."

"You are sure?"

"Absolutely."

"Then there is nothing more to be said. I must decline the case."

"Why?"

"Because you have not been frank with me."

"I assure you—"

"No, you are keeping something back."

There was a moment's pause, and then Halliday drew a paper from his pocket and handed it to my friend.

"I guess that's what you're after, Monsieur Poirot—

though how you know about it fairly gets my goat!"

Poirot smiled, and unfolded the paper. It was a letter written in thin sloping handwriting. Poirot read it aloud.

" 'Chère Madame:

" 'It is with infinite pleasure that I look forward to the felicity of meeting you again. After your so amiable reply to my letter, I can hardly restrain my impatience. I have never forgotten those days in Paris. It is most cruel that you should be leaving London tomorrow. However, before very long, and perhaps sooner than you think, I shall have the joy of beholding once more the lady whose image has ever reigned supreme in my heart.

" 'Believe, chère madame, all the assurances of my most devoted and unaltered sentiments—

" 'Armand de la Rochefour.' "

Poirot handed the letter back to Halliday with a bow.

"I fancy, monsieur, that you did not know that your daughter intended renewing her acquaintance with the Count de la Rochefour?"

"It came as a thunderbolt to me! I found this letter in my daughter's handbag. As you probably know, Monsieur Poirot, this so-called count is an adventurer of the worst type."

Poirot nodded.

"But I want to know how you knew of the existence of this letter?"

My friend smiled. "Monsieur, I did not. But to track foot-marks and recognize cigarette-ash is not sufficient for a detective. He must also be a good psychologist! I knew that you disliked and mistrusted your son-in-law. He benefits by your daughter's death; the maid's description of the mysterious man bears a sufficient resemblance to him. Yet you are not keen on his track! Why? Surely because your suspicions lie in another direction. Therefore you were keeping something back."

"You're right, Monsieur Poirot. I was sure of Rupert's

guilt until I found this letter. It unsettled me horribly."

"Yes. The Count says: 'Before very long, and perhaps sooner than you think.' Obviously he would not want to wait until you should get wind of his reappearance. Was it he who traveled down from London by the twelve-fourteen, and came along the corridor to your daughter's compartment? The Count de la Rochefour is also, if I remember rightly, tall and dark!"

The millionaire nodded.

"Well, monsieur, I will wish you good day. Scotland Yard has, I presume, a list of the jewels?"

"Yes. I believe Inspector Japp is here now if you would like to see him."

Japp was an old friend of ours, and greeted Poirot with a sort of affectionate contempt.

"And how are you, monsieur? No bad feeling between us, though we *have* got our different ways of looking at things. How are the 'little gray cells,' eh? Going strong?"

Poirot beamed upon him. "They function, my good Japp; assuredly they do!"

"Then that's all right. Think it was the Honorable Rupert, or a crook? We're keeping an eye on all the regular places, of course. We shall know if the shiners are disposed of, and of course whoever did it isn't going to keep them to admire their sparkle. Not likely! I'm trying to find out where Rupert Carrington was yesterday. Seems a bit of a mystery about it. I've got a man watching him."

"A great precaution, but perhaps a day late," suggested Poirot gently.

"You always will have your joke, Monsieur Poirot. Well, I'm off to Paddington. Bristol, Weston, Taunton, that's my beat. So long."

"You will come around and see me this evening, and tell me the result?"

"Sure thing, if I'm back."

"That good Inspector believes in matter in motion," murmured Poirot as our friend departed. "He travels; he

measures footprints; he collects mud and cigarette-ash! He
is extremely busy! He is zealous beyond words! And if I
mentioned psychology to him, do you know what he would
do, my friend? He would smile! He would say to himself:
'Poor old Poirot! He ages! He grows senile!' Japp is the
'younger generation knocking on the door.' And *ma foi!*
They are so busy knocking that they do not notice that the
door is open!"

"And what are you going to do?"

"As we have *carte blanche,* I shall expend threepence in
ringing up the Ritz—where you may have noticed our
Count is staying. After that, as my feet are a little damp,
and I have sneezed twice, I shall return to my rooms and
make myself a *tisane* over the spirit lamp!"

I did not see Poirot again until the following morning. I
found him placidly finishing his breakfast.

"Well?" I inquired eagerly. "What has happened?"

"Nothing."

"But Japp?"

"I have not seen him."

"The Count?"

"He left the Ritz the day before yesterday."

"The day of the murder?"

"Yes."

"Then that settles it! Rupert Carrington is cleared."

"Because the Count de la Rochefour has left the Ritz?
You go too fast, my friend."

"Anyway, he must be followed, arrested! But what could
be his motive?"

"One hundred thousand dollars' worth of jewelry is a
very good motive for anyone. No, the question to my mind
is: why kill her? Why not simply steal the jewels? She would
not prosecute."

"Why not?"

"Because she is a woman, *mon ami.* She once loved this
man. Therefore she would suffer her loss in silence. And the
Count, who is an extremely good psychologist where women

are concerned—hence his successes—would know that perfectly well! On the other hand, if Rupert Carrington killed her, why take the jewels, which would incriminate him fatally?”

“As a blind.”

“Perhaps you are right, my friend. Ah, here is Japp! I recognize his knock.”

The inspector was beaming good-humoredly.

“Morning, Poirot. Only just got back. I’ve done some good work! And you?”

“Me, I have arranged my ideas,” replied Poirot placidly.

Japp laughed heartily.

“Old chap’s getting on in years,” he observed beneath his breath to me. “That won’t do for us young folk,” he said aloud.

“*Quel dommage?*” Poirot inquired.

“Well, do you want to hear what I’ve done?”

“You permit me to make a guess? You have found the knife with which the crime was committed, by the side of the line between Weston and Taunton, and you have interviewed the paper-boy who spoke to Mrs. Carrington at Weston!”

Japp’s jaw fell. “How on earth did you know? Don’t tell me it was those almighty ‘little gray cells’ of yours!”

“I am glad you admit for once that they are *all mighty!* Tell me, did she give the paper-boy a shilling for himself?”

“No, it was a half a crown!” Japp had recovered his temper and grinned. “Pretty extravagant, these rich Americans!”

“And in consequence the boy did not forget her?”

“Not he. Half-crowns don’t come his way every day. She hailed him and bought two magazines. One had a picture of a girl in blue on the cover. ‘That’ll match me’, she said. Oh! He remembered her perfectly. Well, that was enough for me. By the doctor’s evidence, the crime *must* have been committed before Taunton. I guessed they’d throw the knife away at once, and I walked down the line looking for it; and sure enough, there it was. I made inquiries at Taunton about our man, but of course it’s a big station, and it wasn’t likely they'd notice him. He probably got back to London by a later train."

Poirot nodded. "Very likely."

"But I found another bit of news when I got back. They're passing the jewels, all right! That large emerald was pawned last night—by one of the regular lot. Who do you think it was?"

"I don't know—except that he was a short man."

Japp stared. "Well, you're right there. He's short enough. It was Red Narky."

"Who is Red Narky?" I asked.

"A particularly sharp jewel-thief, sir. And not one to stick at murder. Usually works with a woman—Gracie Kidd; but she doesn't seem to be in it this time—unless she's got off to Holland with the rest of the swag."

"You've arrested Narky?"

"Sure thing. But mind you, it's the other man we want— the man who went down with Mrs. Carrington in the train. He was the one who planned the job, right enough. But Narky won't squeal on a pal!"

I noticed that Poirot's eyes had become very green.

"I think," he said gently, "that I can find Narky's pal for you, all right."

"One of your little ideas, eh?" Japp eyed Poirot sharply. "Wonderful how you manage to deliver the goods sometimes, at your age and all, Devil's own luck, of course."

"Perhaps, perhaps," murmured my friend. "Hastings, my hat. And the brush. So! My galoshes, if it still rains! We must not undo the good work of that *tisane*. *Au revoir*, Japp!"

"Good luck to you, Poirot."

Poirot hailed the first taxi we met, and directed the driver to Park Lane.

When we drew up before Halliday's house, he skipped out nimbly, paid the driver and rang the bell. To the footman who opened the door he made a request in a low voice, and we were immediately taken upstairs. We went up to the top of the house, and were shown into a small neat bedroom.

Poirot's eyes roved round the room and fastened themselves on a small black trunk. He knelt in front of it, scrutinized the labels on it, and took a small twist of wire from his pocket.

"Ask Mr. Halliday if he will be so kind as to mount to me here," he said over his shoulder to the footman.

The man departed, and Poirot gently coaxed the lock of the trunk with a practiced hand. In a few minutes the lock gave, and he raised the lid of the trunk. Swiftly he began rummaging among the clothes it contained, flinging them out on the floor.

There was a heavy step on the stairs, and Halliday entered the room.

"What in hell are you doing here?" he demanded, staring.

"I was looking, monsieur, for *this*." Poirot withdrew from the trunk a coat and skirt of bright blue frieze, and a small toque of white fox fur.

"What are you doing with my trunk?" I turned to see that the maid, Jane Mason, had entered the room.

"If you will just shut the door, Hastings. Thank you. Yes, and stand with your back against it. Now, Mr. Halliday, let me introduce you to Gracie Kidd, otherwise Jane Mason, who will shortly rejoin her accomplice, Red Narky, under the kind escort of Inspector Japp."

Poirot waved a deprecating hand. "It was of the most simple!" He helped himself to more caviar.

"It was the maid's insistence on the clothes that her mistress was wearing that first struck me. Why was she so anxious that our attention should be directed to them? I reflected that we had only the maid's word for the mysterious man in the carriage at Bristol. As far as the doctor's evidence went, Mrs. Carrington might easily have been murdered *before* reaching Bristol. But if so, then the maid must be an accomplice. And if she were an accomplice, she would not wish this point to rest on her evidence alone. The clothes

Mrs. Carrington was wearing were of a striking nature. A maid usually has a good deal of choice as to what her mistress shall wear. Now if, after Bristol, anyone saw a lady in a bright blue coat and skirt, and a fur toque, he will be quite ready to swear he has seen Mrs. Carrington.

"I began to reconstruct. The maid would provide herself with duplicate clothes. She and her accomplice chloroform and stab Mrs. Carrington between London and Bristol, probably taking advantage of a tunnel. Her body is rolled under the seat; and the maid takes her place. At Weston she must make herself noticed. How? In all probability, a newspaper-boy will be selected. She will insure his remembering her by giving him a large tip. She also drew his attention to the color of her dress by a remark about one of the magazines. After leaving Weston, she throws the knife out of the window to mark the place where the crime presumably occurred, and changes her clothes, or buttons a long mackintosh over them. At Taunton she leaves the train and returns to Bristol as soon as possible, where her accomplice has duly left the luggage in the cloak-room. He hands over the ticket and himself returns to London. She waits on the platform, carrying out her role, goes to a hotel for the night and returns to town in the morning, exactly as she had said.

"When Japp returned from his expedition, he confirmed all my deductions. He also told me that a well-known crook was passing the jewels. I knew that whoever it was would be the exact opposite of the man Jane Mason described. When I heard that it was Red Narky, who always worked with Gracie Kidd—well, I knew just where to find her."

"And the Count?"

"The more I thought of it, the more I was convinced that he had nothing to do with it. That gentleman is much too careful of his own skin to risk murder. It would be out of keeping with his character."

"Well, Monsieur Poirot," said Halliday, "I owe you a big debt. And the check I write after lunch won't go near to settling it."

Poirot smiled modestly, and murmured to me: "The good

Japp, he shall get the official credit, all right, but though he has got his Gracie Kidd, I think that I, as the Americans say, have got his goat!"

MIRACLES DO HAPPEN
by Ellery Queen

THE MOMENT HENRY PECKED HER CHEEK THAT NIGHT, Claire knew something was wrong. But all she said was a wifely, "How did it go at the office today, dear?"

"All right," Henry Witter said, and Claire knew it was not the office. "What kind of a day did Jody have?"

"About the same, dear."

Henry put his coat, hat, and rubbers in the hall closet while the other three children hunted through his pockets for the candy bars he always brought home on paydays.

"It's the teentsy size again," little Sal lisped indignantly.

"I wanna big one!" five-year-old Pete wailed.

Eddie, who was ten and knew the financial facts of life, merely scuttled off with his share of the loot.

"Aren't you two ashamed?" Claire said to Sal and Pete.

But Henry said in a queer voice, "Why should they be? It's true," and he went into the back bedroom to see Jody, who had been lying there for the last three of her eight years.

After dinner, which was beans baked around an irreducible minimum of Mr. Scholte's cheapest shortribs, Claire put Sal and Pete to bed, parked Eddie at the TV set, fixed Jody for the night, and hurried back to the kitchen. She helped Henry finish the dishes, and then the Witters sat down at the kitchen table for their weekly session—Claire with her budget notes, Henry with paper and pencil and his paycheck between them.

Claire read off the items in a loud and casual voice, and Henry wrote them down in his bookkeeper's copperplate.

The prorated expenses—rent, gas, electricity, telephone, TV installment, life insurance, health plan, personal loans. The running expenses—food, laundry, Henry's allowance. The "extras"—new shoes for Pete, school notebook for Eddie, repairs for the vacuum cleaner. And then—in that dread separate column headed "Jody"—medicines, therapist, installment on surgeon's fee for last operation . . .

Henry added the two columns in silence.

"Expenses, $89.61. Take-home pay, $82.25. Debit balance, $7.36." And Henry's tic began to act up.

Claire started to say something, but she swallowed it. It was the Jody column again. Without the Jody column they would be in the black, have a small savings account, and the children could get the clothes they desperately needed. . . . Claire shut *those* thoughts off.

Henry cleared his throat. "Claire," he began.

"No," Claire cried. "*No,* Henry! Maybe you've given up hope on Jody, but I haven't. I'm *not* going to send a child of mine to a state institution, no matter what. She needs her family—the love and help we can give her—and maybe some day . . . Hen, we'll have the phone taken out, or send the TV back. You're due for another raise in a few months. We can hold out."

"Who said anything about sending Jody away?" Henry's voice was very queer indeed, and Claire felt a chill. "It's not that, Claire."

"Then what is it? I knew there was something wrong the minute you came home."

"It's Tully. He phoned me at the office this afternoon."

"Tully." Claire sat still. Last year, when Jody had needed her second operation and they had exhausted the annual health-plan benefits, Henry had been forced to go to a loan shark for the money. "What's he want?"

"I don't know." Henry reached for his cigarettes. But then he remembered that he had smoked his quota for the day, and he put the pack back in his pocket. "He just said for me to be at his office tomorrow night—at seven o'clock."

"But you paid him last month's interest on the loan. Or
—did you, Henry?"

"Of course I did!"

"Then why—?"

"I don't know, I tell you!"

Dear God, Claire thought, nothing more *now*, please. She
got up to go over to Henry and put her cracked and red-
dened hands on his thin shoulders.

"Darling . . . don't worry."

Henry said, "Who's worrying?" But he wished his tic
would stop.

"Sit down, Witter." Tully indicated the only other chair
in the dingy office. He had Henry's folder on his desk and
was leafing through it.

Henry sat down. The room held nothing but an old desk
and swivel chair, a filing cabinet, a big metal wastebasket,
a costumer, and the "client's chair"—yet it always managed
to seem crowded. Everything looked cheap, used hard,
rubbed off, like Tully himself. The loan shark was a paper-
thin man with eyes like rusty razor blades.

"Nice clean file," Tully said, tossing it aside.

"I try to meet my payments on time." Henry thought of
all the empty-stomached lunch hours, the cigarette rations,
Claire's incredible economies, the children's patched clothes,
and he felt a gust of anger. "Just what is it you want, Mr.
Tully?"

"The principal," Tully said indifferently.

"The . . . "Henry found himself half standing.

The moneylender leaned back with a swivelly creak that
crawled up Henry's spine. "I've run into a little recession,
you might call it. You know? Over-extended. So I'm calling
my loans in. Sorry."

"But when I took the loan, Mr. Tully, you assured me—"

"Now don't give me that." Tully flicked some papers from
the folder, his murderous eyes suddenly intent. "There's a
demand clause in these notes, friend. Want to read it over?"

Henry did not try to focus. He knew what the fine print

said. But last year he would have signed anything; he had borrowed the limit from legitimate loan companies and Tully had been his last resort.

Tully lit a big cigar. "You've got forty-eight hours to hand me a certified check for $490."

Henry put his finger on the tic. "I haven't got it, Mr. Tully."

"Borrow it."

"I can't. I can't get any more loans. I have a crippled child —the operations, a therapist who comes in every day—"

The moneylender picked up a letter-opener with a sharp point and began to clean his fingernails. "Look, Witter, you got your troubles and I got mine. Be here Thursday night nine o'clock with your check, or I take action."

Henry stumbled out.

Ellery was watching "The Late Show" on TV Thursday night when his doorbell rang. He opened the door and a woman with a worn cloth coat thrown over her housedress fell into his arms. Her eyes were wild.

"Mr. Queen? I'm Claire Witter, Mrs. Henry Witter. I live in the neighborhood—left the children with a neighbor —ran all the way. They say you help people in trouble—"

"Get your breath, Mrs. Witter," Ellery said, supporting her. "Just what kind of trouble are you in?"

"My husband's just been picked up by the police. I understand an Inspector Queen is in charge. He's your father, I'm told. But Henry didn't do it, Mr. Queen—"

"What didn't Henry do?"

"Kill that moneylender! They've taken Henry to the office where Tully's body was found. I don't know what to do." And Claire Witter sobbed like a little girl.

"Now, now," Ellery said. "I'll get my hat."

The Inspector had invited Ellery to trail along when the homicide call came in about 10:30, and Ellery had pleaded fatigue; so the old man was surprised when his son showed up nearly two hours later.

"I'm representing Mrs. Witter," Ellery told him. "What's the charge against her husband?"

"Suspicion of murder."

"As pat as all that, Dad?" Ellery glanced around the crowded office. He had left Claire Witter in the hall in the care of a patrolman. "Is that my client?"

A white-faced man with clerical shoulders was leaning against the wall, his eyes shut, and with Sergeant Velie's beef between him and the possibly tempting open window. Nearby huddled a frowsy old lady, a dumpy woman in a smart suit, and an Italian-looking man with a big gray mustache.

Inspector Queen nodded. "The one next to Velie. And don't tell me Witter doesn't look the type."

"He doesn't."

"Just goes to show. It's Witter, all right."

The basket crew were crating the remains of Mr. Tully. Ellery glimpsed the back of a tan jacket splattered with blood.

"I don't see the weapon. Knife?"

"Tully's letter-opener. We couldn't seem to raise a print, so we sent it down to the lab."

Ellery looked around at the bare room, the bare floor. "Those empty desk and file drawers were found open, the way they are now?"

"Nothing's been changed or removed except the letter-opener. By the way, the heat was on Tully for a usury charge and he must have got wind of it. He was getting set to skip. Anyway, here's the run-down. Prouty says Tully was knifed tonight between 8:30 and 9:30—"

The Inspector paused; Mr. Tully was leaving. Ellery hoped Claire Witter would be crying on the patrolman's shoulder when the basket passed her in the hall. There was blood on it.

"Three people entered this office during that hour," the Inspector resumed. "That dumpy woman next to the man with the mustache—her name is Mrs. Lester. Mr. Mustache came next—he's a barber named Dominini. Finally, Witter."

"Who's the old lady beside Mrs. Lester?"

"The cleaning woman of the building. She found the body." The Inspector raised his voice. "Mrs. Bogan?"

The old woman shuffled forward on her shapeless shoes. She still had her work-apron on and a dust cloth bound around her lifeless white hair.

"Tell your story again, Mrs. Bogan."

"Couple minutes after ten I comes in here to clean." She had badly fitted false teeth, and her words came bubbling and hissing out like water from a rusty faucet. "What do I see but Mr. Tully laying with his face on the desk and a knife sticking outen his back. There was all blood . . ." Her bleary eyes rolled. But there was nothing on the desk now.

"Did you touch anything, Mrs. Bogan?" Ellery asked.

"Me? I run out yelling me head off. Found a cop in the street and that's all I know, Mister. I'll be seeing that knife sticking outen his back in me dreams."

"You didn't hear anything—a fight, an argument—between half-past eight and half-past nine?"

"I wasn't on this floor then. I was cleaning two floors down."

"Mrs. Lester," Inspector Queen called out.

The dumpy woman in the smart suit blanched under her heavy makeup. She was well into her forties, her hair hennaed to a screaming red, her figure fighting a corset. She kept biting her lips, but Ellery saw under her nervousness the expression of chronic restlessness so often worn by women with too little to do.

"You were one of Tully's victim's, too?" he asked her.

"Don't tell my husband," Mrs. Lester said in a rapid-fire falsetto. "He'd kick me out, no kidding. I had to get a loan on the q.t. see, because of—well, a bunch of us girls have a little afternoon poker club. We started out sociable, but I don't know, the limit kept getting higher. . . . The thing is, I went into the hole for a lot of money, mostly to that Mrs. Carson. If my husband Phil knew—he's a nut against gambling. . . . Anyway, she says if I don't pay up she'll go to Phil. So I took a $600 loan from this shark Tully."

"And Tully called the loan in, Mrs. Lester?"

The woman's gloved hands began to writhe. "He said I had to pay off the whole thing by half-past eight tonight. Meantime I'd lost more—I swear to God those harpies play with marked cards! So I came here at half-past eight and I hand Tully two hundred dollars—all I could scrape up between what I could sneak off my household money and a ring I hocked that I told Phil I lost. But Tully says nothing doing. So I start begging him to give me more time, and all he does, the rat, is sit here emptying desk drawers and throwing away papers and ignoring me like I was dirt!"

"Why was he doing that, Mrs. Lester?"

"How should I know? He takes my money and says either I have the other four hundred for him by tomorrow morning or he goes to my husband. I left him still tearing up papers."

"Alive, of course," Ellery smiled.

"Are you kidding? Say, you don't think—" Her bloated eyes began to look terrified.

"Mr. Dominini," Inspector Queen cut in.

The barber bounded forward in bitter excitement. It took a great many haircuts and shaves to keep his ten children in *pasta* and shoe leather, he exclaimed. He had a small neighborhood shop that could accommodate only so many. The neighborhood had run down, lots of people had moved in, Mr. Dominini said, and even with the higher prices barbers had to charge these days things got worse and worse. Finally, he had faced the possible loss of his shop.

"I go to bank, bank say Dominini no good risk no more," the barber shouted, brandishing his clean hairy hands. "What can I do? I go to Tully, the blood suck'!"

For a year he had managed to meet Tully's usurious interest charges. Then, on Tuesday, the loan shark had phoned him and demanded payment in full by Thursday night. He named a quarter to nine as the deadline.

"Where Dominini get fifteen hundred dollar?" the mustachioed barber cried. "I bring him five hundred sixty-five, it's a best I can do. He say, Dominini, that's a no good. I

say okay, Mr. Tully, you run barber shop. I work for you.
He call me bad name, take my money, say get out, I sue you.
Couple hour later, the policeman he pick me up. For what?
My wife she cry, *bambini* run under bed. . . . I no kill Tully!"

"Then he was alive when you left this office tonight, Mr.
Dominini?" Ellery said. "That's your story?"

"It's a true!"

"Clearing Mrs. Lester," Inspector Queen murmured.

Ellery frowned. "What was Tully doing, if anything,"
he asked the barber, "while you were here?"

"Like a that lady say. He take a things out of file cabinet.
Tear up paper, folder."

"Bringing us," the Inspector said, "to Henry Witter."

Sergeant Velie had to assist Henry forward. The bookkeeper sank into the chair, his tic working overtime. Suddenly his nostrils expanded. He looked up. Ellery was lighting a cigarette.

"Might I have one?" Henry asked. "I've run out."

"Sure. No, that's all right. Keep the pack."

"Oh, no—"

"I have another, Mr. Witter."

"Thanks. Thanks a million." Henry inhaled hungrily. "I
should have cut them out long ago." He puffed and puffed.

"Mr. Witter, you found Tully alive at nine?"

"Oh, yes," Henry said.

"Alive and alone?"

Henry nodded.

"Clearing Dominini," the Inspector murmured. "Neat?"

"Even gaudy," Ellery murmured back. "Tell me just what
happened, Mr. Witter, after you got here."

Henry lit a fresh cigarette from the butt of the old one,
looked around, hesitated, then tossed the smoldering butt
into the wastebasket.

"I told Tully I hadn't been able to raise the money. I
said, you can do what you want, Mr. Tully, sue me, have me
arrested, beaten up, killed, it won't do you any good, you
can't get blood from a stone. He kept sitting there behind

the desk tearing up papers and records as if he didn't hear me. But he was paying attention, all right." Henry gulped in a lungful of smoke. "Because as soon as I got through he started to chew me out. What he called me—"

Henry choked over the smoke. After a moment Ellery said, "Yes, Mr. Witter?"

"I never raised my hand in anger to anybody in my life. But Tully said some things to me no man could take. Real nasty things. And while he was saying them I kept getting sorer and sorer." Henry's tic was hopping around now like a flea. "I thought of all the months we'd scrimped to pay his blood money and at the same time pay for the medical care my little girl Jody needs so maybe some day she'll walk again. I thought of the stockings my wife couldn't buy, the baseball cards my Eddie couldn't collect, the complaints we didn't make to the Health Department about the cockroaches because the landlord might get mad and somehow chisel us out of the apartment and we'd have to rent another place at a bigger rent. . . . I thought of a lot of things like that, and then I leaned over the desk and let Tully have it."

"With the paper-knife?" Ellery asked gently.

"Huh?" Henry Witter came back to the present. "No, with this." Henry made a skinny fist and looked at it. "I pasted him one right on the button. Socko!" The memory of it gave him a momentary pleasure; a spark of life came into his eyes. "I didn't know I could hit that hard. He went out like a light."

"How did he fall, Mr. Witter?"

"On his face on the desk. I certainly was surprised. But I felt better, too. So then I walked out."

"Leaving Tully unconscious but alive?"

"Sure. He was breathing like a walrus."

"Did you notice anyone in the hall, or downstairs?"

"Just the night man mopping in the lobby."

"And that's how we know," Inspector Queen said to his son, "that nobody else entered the building between Witter's leaving and Mrs. Bogan's finding the body. The porter saw

Witter come and go, and he was in the lobby working the whole time afterward. Yes, Velie?"

The Sergeant, who had been summoned into the hall, came back to rumble into the Inspector's ear.

"That cinches it," the Inspector snapped. "The lab's found three partially smeared prints on Tully's letter-knife. One is Tully's. The other two have been identified, Witter, as yours."

Henry Witter sat there with his mouth open. But then he yelped as the cigarette burned his fingers. He flung it into the wastebasket and covered his face with his hands. Ellery, fearing a fire, walked over to the basket, but he saw that it was empty except for the two butts.

"So, Witter," Inspector Queen began.

"Hold it, Dad." Ellery stooped over Henry. "Mr. Witter, while you were seated here across the desk from Tully, did you happen to handle the letter-knife?"

Henry looked up dully. "I must have, if my fingerprints are on it. I don't remember. But I didn't use it on Tully. I'd remember that. God, yes. Don't you believe me, Inspector?"

"No," Inspector Queen said. "No, Witter, I don't. Take my advice and come clean. Maybe the D.A. would consent to a lesser plea—"

"Maybe the D.A. would, but I won't," Ellery said. "My client will plead not guilty."

Sergeant Velie remarked with some bitterness to no one in particular, "And the beauty of it is, he does it all with his little sleeves rolled up."

The Inspector's glance at the Sergeant was a terrible thing. "How come, Ellery?"

"Because they aren't here," Ellery said, waving vaguely.

"Because *what* aren't here?"

"The papers."

"*What* papers?"

"Look," Ellery said. "Mrs. Lester, Dominini, Witter— all three say Tully was cleaning out his desk and file, throwing away papers and records. You told me, Dad, that nothing has been removed from this office except Tully's letter-knife. Yet the file and desk drawers are cleaned out, the floor is bare, there's nothing on the desk—*and the waste-basket is empty*. I ask you: Where are all the papers and records Tully was throwing out?"

His father looked as if he had been struck by lightning. He turned toward the old cleaning woman cowering in her corner, but Ellery was there before him. "You'd been inside this office earlier tonight than you claimed, Mrs. Bogan," Ellery was saying "—right after Witter left, in fact. And you found Tully just recovering from Witter's haymaker."

The old woman blinked.

"You owed Tully money, too, didn't you, Mrs. Bogan? And he put the screws on you tonight as well, while you were cleaning his offiice—right? You'd already emptied the wastebasket and taken the contents outside when you killed him. By the way, how did you come to owe Tully money?"

The old woman blinked and blinked. Finally she touched her liverish old lips with her old tongue, and she said, "Me boy Jim. Jim's a three-times loser. Next time he gets sent up, it's for life. And then what's he do but hook a wad outen the till in the garage where he's working. The boss says he won't send Jimmy up if I pays back the money, so I borries it offen Tully. . . . I paid him his interest faithful.

"But tonight Tully says he wants all the money or he'll have me pinched. I didn't care about meself, I've had it, but if I wasn't around to keep an eye on Jim. . . . I had me cleaning gloves on. . . . I sees the knife on Tully's desk. . . . I was in back of him. . . . Her old face settled, but it was hard to tell whether the lines told of remorse, resignation, or indifference. But then she said, "Now who'll be keeping me Jimmy out of trouble?"

Inspector Queen said furiously, "Maybe you, Mother, maybe you. Just tell that story to a jury."

When they had taken the old lady out, Ellery nudged Henry Witter, whose mouth was open. "You still here? Don't you know there's a lady waiting for you in the hall?"

"Claire." Henry hauled himself out of the chair.

"Oh, and you might remember," Ellery said severely, "—I'm thinking of your little girl, Mr. Witter—that miracles do happen."

Henry shook himself like a dog coming out of a mud hole. "You bet, Mr. Queen," he said. Thanks for reminding me."

THE STOLEN
WHITE ELEPHANT[1]
by Mark Twain

THE FOLLOWING CURIOUS HISTORY WAS RELATED TO ME BY
a chance railway acquaintance. He was a gentleman more
than seventy years of age, and his thoroughly good and
gentle face and earnest and sincere manner imprinted the
unmistakable stamp of truth upon every statement which
fell from his lips. He said:

You know in what reverence the royal white elephant
of Siam is held by the people of that country. You know
it is sacred to kings, only Kings may possess it, and that it
is, indeed, in a measure even superior to kings, since it re-
ceives not merely honor but worship. Very well; five years
ago, when the troubles concerning the frontier line arose
between Great Britian and Siam, it was presently manifest
that Siam had been in the wrong. Therefore every repara-
tion was quickly made, and the British representative stated
that he was satisfied and the past should be forgotten. This
greatly relieved the King of Siam, and partly as a token of
gratitude, but partly also, perhaps, to wipe out any little
remaining vestige of unpleasantness which England might
feel toward him, he wished to send the Queen a present
—the sole sure way of propitiating an enemy, according to Oriental ideas. This present ought not only to be a
royal one, but transcendently royal. Wherefore, what offer-

[1] Left out of *A Tramp Abroad*, because it was feared that
some of the particulars had been exaggerated, and that others
were not true. Before these suspicions had been proven
groundless, the book had gone to press.—M. T.

ing could be so meet as that of a white elephant? My position in the Indian civil service was such that I was deemed peculiarly worthy of the honor of conveying the present to her Majesty. A ship was fitted out for me and my servants and the officers and attendants of the elephant, and in due time I arrived in New York harbor and placed my royal charge in admirable quarters in Jersey City. It was necessary to remain awhile in order to recruit the animal's health before resuming the voyage.

All went well during a fortnight—then my calamities began. The white elephant was stolen! I was called up at dead of night and informed of this fearful misfortune. For some moments I was beside myself with terror and anxiety; I was helpless. Then I grew calmer and collected my faculties. I soon saw my course—for, indeed, there was but the one course for an intelligent man to pursue. Late as it was, I flew to New York and got a policeman to conduct me to the headquarters of the detective force. Fortunately I arrived in time, though the chief of the force, the celebrated Inspector Blunt, was just on the point of leaving for his home. He was a man of middle size and compact frame, and when he was thinking deeply he had a way of knitting his brows and tapping his forehead reflectively with his finger, which impressed you at once with the conviction that you stood in the presence of a person of no common order. The very sight of him gave me confidence and made me hopeful. I stated my errand. It did not flurry him in the least; it had no more visible effect upon his iron self-possession than if I had told him somebody had stolen my dog. He motioned me to a seat, and said, calmly:

"Allow me to think a moment, please."

So saying, he sat down at his office table and leaned his head upon his hand. Several clerks were at work at the other end of the room; the scratching of their pens was all the sound I heard during the next six or seven minutes. Meantime the inspector sat there, buried in thought. Finally he raised his head, and there was that in the firm lines of his face which showed me that his brain had done its work and his plan was made. Said he—and his voice was low and impressive:

"This is no ordinary case. Every step must be warily taken; each step must be made sure before the next is ventured. And secrecy must be observed—secrecy profound and absolute. Speak to no one about the matter, not even the reporters. I will take care of *them;* I will see that they get only what it may suit my ends to let them know." He touched a bell; a youth appeared. "Alaric, tell the reporters to remain for the present." The boy retired. "Now let us proceed to business—and systematically. Nothing can be accomplished in this trade of mine without strict and minute method."

He took a pen and some paper. "Now—name of the elephant?"

"Hassan Ben Ali Ben Selim Abdallah Mohammed Moisé Alhammal Jamsetjejeebhoy Dhuleep Sultan Ebu Bhudpoor."

"Very well. Given name?"

"Jumbo."

"Very well. Place of birth?"

"The capital city of Siam."

"Parents living?"

"No—dead."

"Had they any other issue besides this one?"

"None. He was an only child."

"Very well. These matters are sufficient under that head. Now please describe the elephant, and leave out no particular, however insignificant—that is, insignificant from *your* point of view. To men in my profession there *are* no insignificant particulars; they do not exist."

I described—he wrote. When I was done, he said:

"Now listen. If I have made any mistakes, correct me."

He read as follows:

"Height, 19 feet; length from apex of forehead to insertion of tail, 26 feet; length of trunk, 16 feet; length of tail, 6 feet; total length, including trunk and tail, 48 feet; length of tusks, 9½ feet; ears in keeping with these dimensions; footprint resembles the mark left when one up-ends a barrel in the snow; color of the elephant, a dull white; has a hole the size of a plate in each ear for the insertion of jewelry, and possesses the habit in a remarkable degree of squirting water upon spectators and of maltreating with his trunk not only such persons as he is acquainted with, but even entire strangers; limps slightly with his right leg, and has a small scar in his left armpit caused by a former boil; had on, when stolen, a castle containing seats for fifteen persons, and a gold-cloth saddle blanket the size of an ordinary carpet."

There were no mistakes. The inspector touched the bell, handed the description to Alaric, and said:

"Have fifty thousand copies of this printed at once and mailed to every detective office and pawnbroker's shop on the continent." Alaric retired. "There—so far, so good. Next, I must have a photograph of the property."

I gave him one. He examined it critically, and said:

"It must do, since we can do no better; but he has his trunk curled up and tucked into his mouth. That is unfortunate, and is calculated to mislead, for of course he does not usually have it in that position." He touched his bell.

"Alaric, have fifty thousand copies of this photograph made the first thing in the morning, and mail them with the descriptive circulars."

Alaric retired to execute his orders. The inspector said:

"It will be necessary to offer a reward, of course. Now as to the amount?"

"What sum would you suggest?"

"To *begin* with, I should say—well, twenty-five thousand dollars. It is an intricate and difficult business; there are a thousand avenues of escape and opportunities of concealment. These thieves have friends and pals everywhere—"

"Bless me, do you know who they are?"

The wary face, practised in concealing the thoughts and feelings within, gave me no token, nor yet the replying words, so quietly uttered:

"Never mind about that. I may, and I may not. We generally gather a pretty shrewd inkling of who our man is by the manner of his work and the size of the game he goes after. We are not dealing with a pickpocket or a hall thief now, make up your mind to that. This property was not 'lifted' by a novice. But, as I was saying, considering the amount of travel which will have to be done, and the diligence with which the thieves will cover up their traces as they move along, twenty-five thousand may be too small a sum to offer, yet I think it worth while to start with that."

So we determined upon that figure as a beginning. Then this man, whom nothing escaped which could by any possibility be made to serve as a clue, said:

"There are cases in detective history to show that criminals have been detected through peculiarities in their appetites. Now, what does this elephant eat, and how much?"

"Well, as to *what* he eats—he will eat *anything*. He will eat a man, he will eat a Bible—he will eat anything *between* a man and a Bible."

"Good—very good, indeed, but too general. Details are necessary—details are the only valuable things in our trade. Very well—as to men. At one meal—or, if you prefer, during one day—how many men will he eat, if fresh?"

"He would not care whether they were fresh or not; at a single meal he would eat five ordinary men."

"Very good; five men; we will put that down. What nationalities would he prefer?"

"He is indifferent about nationalities. He prefers acquaintances, but is not prejudiced against strangers."

"Very good. Now, as to Bibles. How many Bibles would he eat at a meal?"

"He would eat an entire edition."

"It is hardly succinct enough. Do you mean the ordinary octavo, or the family illustrated?"

"I think he would be indifferent to illustrations; that is, I think he would not value illustrations above simple letter-press."

"No, you do not get my idea. I refer to bulk. The ordinary octavo Bible weighs about two pounds and a half, while the great quarto with the illustrations weighs ten or twelve.

How many Doré Bibles would he eat at a meal?"

"If you knew this elephant, you could not ask. He would take what they had."

"Well, put it in dollars and cents, then. We must get at it somehow. The Doré costs a hundred dollars a copy, Russia leather, beveled."

"He would require about fifty thousand dollars' worth —say an edition of five hundred copies."

"Now that is more exact. I will put that down. Very well; he likes men and Bibles; so far, so good. What else will he eat? I want particulars."

"He will leave Bibles to eat bricks, he will leave bricks to eat bottles, he will leave bottles to eat clothing, he will leave clothing to eat cats, he will leave cats to eat oysters, he will leave oysters to eat ham, he will leave ham to eat sugar, he will leave sugar to eat pie, he will leave pie to eat potatoes, he will leave potatoes to eat bran, he will leave bran to eat hay, he will leave hay to eat oats, he will leave oats to eat rice, for he was mainly raised on it. There is nothing whatever that he will not eat but European butter, and he would eat that if he could taste it."

"Very good. General quantity at a meal—say about—"

"Well, anywhere from a quarter to half a ton."

"And he drinks—"

"Everything that is fluid. Milk, water, whisky, molasses, castor oil, camphene, carbolic acid—it is no use to go into particulars; whatever fluid occurs to you set it down. He will drink anything that is fluid, except European coffee."

"Very good. As to quantity?"

"Put it down five to fifteen barrels—his thirst varies; his other appetites do not."

"These things are unusual. They ought to furnish quite good clues toward tracing him."

He touched the bell.

"Alaric, summon Captain Burns."

Burns appeared. Inspector Blunt unfolded the whole matter to him, detail by detail. Then he said in the clear, decisive tones of a man whose plans are clearly defined in his head and who is accustomed to command:

"Captain Burns, detail Detectives Jones, Dakin, Halsey, Bates, and Hackett to shadow the elephant.

"Yes, sir."

"Detail Detectives Moses, Dakin, Murphy, Rogers, Tupper, Higgins, and Batholomew to shadow the thieves."

"Yes, sir."

"Place a strong guard—a guard of thirty picked men, with a relief of thirty—over the place from whence the elephant was stolen, to keep strict watch there night and day, and allow none to approach—except reporters—without written authority from me."

"Yes, sir."

"Place detectives in plain clothes in the railway, steamship, and ferry depots, and upon all roadways leading out of Jersey City, with orders to search all suspicious persons."

"Yes, sir."

"Furnish all these men with photograph and accompanying description of the elephant, and instruct them to search all trains and outgoing ferryboats and other vessels."

"Yes, sir."

"If the elephant should be found, let him be seized, and the information forwarded to me by telegraph."

"Yes, sir."

"Let me be informed at once if any clues should be found—footprints of the animal, or anything of that kind."

"Yes, sir."

"Get an order commanding the harbor police to patrol the frontages vigilantly."

"Yes, sir."

"Despatch detectives in plain clothes over all the railways, north as far as Canada, west as far as Ohio, south as far as Washington."

"Yes, sir."

"Place experts in all the telegraph offices to listen to all messages; and let them require that all cipher despatches be interpreted to them."

"Yes, sir."

"Let all these things be done with the utmost secrecy— mind, the most impenetrable secrecy."

"Yes, sir."

"Report to me promptly at the usual hour."

"Yes, sir."

"Go!"

"Yes, sir."

He was gone.

Inspector Blunt was silent and thoughtful a moment, while the fire in his eye cooled down and faded out. Then he turned to me and said in a placid voice:

"I am not given to boasting, it is not my habit; but—we shall find the elephant."

I shook him warmly by the hand and thanked him; and I *felt* my thanks, too. The more I had seen of the man the more I liked him and the more I admired him and marveled over the mysterious wonders of his profession. Then we parted for the night, and I went home with a far happier heart than I had carried with me to his office.

II

Next morning it was all in the newspapers, in the minutest detail. It even had additions—consisting of Detective This, Detective That, and Detective The Other's "Theory" as to how the robbery was done, who the robbers were, and whither they had flown with their booty. There were eleven of these theories, and they covered all the possibilities; and this single fact shows what independent thinkers detectives are. No two theories were alike, or even much resembled each other, save in one striking particular, and in that one all the other eleven theories were absolutely agreed. That was, that although the rear of my building was torn out and the only door remained locked, the elephant had not been removed through the rent, but by some other (undiscovered) outlet. All agreed that the robbers had made that rent only to mislead the detectives. That never would have occurred to me or to any other layman, perhaps, but it had not deceived the detectives for a moment. Thus, what I had supposed was the only thing that had no mystery about it was in fact the very thing I had gone furthest astray in. The eleven theories all named the supposed robbers, but no two named the same robbers; the total number of suspected persons was thirty-seven. The various newspaper accounts all closed with the most important opinion of all—that of Chief Inspector Blunt. A portion of this statement read as follows:

"The chief knows who the two principals are, namely 'Brick' Duffy and 'Red' McFadden. Ten days before the robbery was achieved he was already aware that it was to be attempted, and had quietly proceeded to shadow these two noted villians; but unfortunately on the night in question their track was lost, and before it could be found again the bird was flown—that is, the elephant.

"Duffy and McFadden are the boldest scoundrels in the profession; the chief has reasons for believing that they are the men who stole the stove out of the detective headquarters on a bitter night last winter—in consequence of which the chief and every detective present were in the hands of the physicians before morning, some with frozen feet, others with frozen fingers, ears, and other members."

When I read the first half of that I was more astonished than ever at the wonderful sagacity of this strange man. He not only saw everything in the present with a clear eye, but even the future could not be hidden from him. I was soon at his office, and said I could not help wishing he had had those men arrested, and so prevented the trouble and loss; but his reply was simple and unanswerable:

"It is not our province to prevent crime, but to punish it. We cannot punish it until it is committed."

I remarked that the secrecy with which we had begun had been marred by the newspapers; not only all our facts but all our plans and purposes had been revealed; even all the suspected persons had been named; those would doubtless disguise themselves now, or go into hiding.

"Let them. They will find that when I am ready for them my hand will descend upon them, in their secret places, as unerringly as the hand of fate. As to the newspapers, we *must* keep in with them. Fame, reputation, constant public mention—these are the detective's bread and butter. He must publish his facts, else he will be supposed to have none; he must publish his theory, for nothing is so strange or striking as a detective's theory, or brings him so much wonderful respect; we must publish our plans, for these the journals insist upon having, and we could not deny them without offending. We must constantly show the public what we are doing, or they will believe we are doing nothing. It is much pleasanter to have a newspaper say, 'Inspector Blunt's ingenious and extraordinary theory is as follows,' than to have it say some harsh thing, or, worse still, some sarcastic one."

"I see the force of what you say. But I noticed that in one part of your remarks in the papers this morning you refused to reveal your opinion upon a certain minor point."

"Yes, we always do that; it has a good effect. Besides, I had not formed any opinion on that point, anyway."

I deposited a considerable sum of money with the inspector, to meet current expenses, and sat down to wait for news. We were expecting the telegrams to begin to arrive at any moment now. Meantime I reread the newspapers and also our descriptive circular, and observed that our twenty-five thousand dollars reward seemed to be offered only to detectives. I said I thought it ought to be offered to anybody who would catch the elephant. The inspector said:

"It is the detectives who will find the elephant, hence the reward will go to the right place. If other people found the animal, it would only be by watching the detectives and taking advantage of clues and indications stolen from them,

and that would entitle the detectives to the reward, after all.
The proper office of a reward is to stimulate the men who
deliver up their time and their trained sagacities to this
sort of work, and not to confer benefits upon chance citizens
who stumble upon a capture without having earned the
benefits by their own merits and labors."

This was reasonable enough, certainly. Now the telegraphic machine in the corner began to click, and the following despatch was the result:

"Flower Station, N. Y., 7.30 A.M.
Have got a clue. Found a succession of deep tracks
across a farm near here. Followed them two miles east
without result; think elephant went west. Shall now
shadow him in that direction.
"Darley, *Detective.*"

"Darley's one of the best men on the force," said the
inspector. "We shall hear from him again before long."
Telegram No. 2 came:

"Barker's, N. J., 7.40 A.M.
"Just arrived. Glass factory broken open here during night, and eight hundred bottles taken. Only water
in large quantity near here is five miles distant. Shall
strike for there. Elephant will be thirsty. Bottles were
empty.   Baker, *Detective.*"

"That promises well, too," said the inspector. "I told you
the creature's appetites would not be bad clues."
Telegram No. 3:

Taylorville, L. I., 8.15 A.M.
"A haystack near here disappeared during the night.
Probably eaten. Have got a clue, and am off.
Hubbard, *Detective.*"

"How he does move around!" said the inspector. "I knew
we had a difficult job on hand, but we shall catch him yet."

Flower Station, N. Y., 9 A.M.

"Shadowed the tracks three miles westward. Large, deep, and ragged. Have just met a farmer who says they are not elephant tracks. Says they are holes where he dug up saplings for shade-trees when ground was frozen last winter. Give me orders how to proceed.

"Darley, *Detective.*"

"Aha! a confederate of the thieves! The thing grows warm," said the inspector.

He dictated the following telegram to Darley:

"Arrest the man and force him to name his pals. Continue to follow the tracks—to the Pacific, if necessary.   "*Chief* Blunt."

Next telegram:

"Coney Point, Pa., 8.45 A.M.

"Gas office broken open here during night and three months' unpaid gas bills taken. Have got a clue and am away.   "Murphy, *Detective.*"

"Heavens!" said the inspector; "would he eat gas bills?"

"Through ignorance—yes; but they cannot support life. At least, unassisted."

Now came this exciting telegram:

Ironville, N. Y., 9.30 A.M.

"Just arrived. This village in consternation. Elephant passed through here at five this morning. Some say he went east, some say west, some north, some south—but all say they did not wait to notice particularly. He killed a horse; have secured a piece of it for a clue. Killed it with his trunk; from style of blow, think he struck it left-handed. From position in which horsē lies, think elephant traveled northward along line of Berkley Railway. Has four and a half hour's start, but I move on his track at once.   Hawes, *Detective.*"

I uttered exclamations of joy. The inspector was as self-contained as a graven image. He calmly touched the bell.

"Alaric, send Captain Burns here."

Burns appeared.

"How many men are ready for instant orders?"

"Ninety-six, sir."

"Send them north at once. Let them concentrate along the line of the Berkley road north of Ironville."

"Yes, sir."

"Let them conduct their movements with the utmost secrecy. As fast as others are at liberty, hold them for orders."

"Yes, sir."

"Go!"

"Yes, sir."

Presently came another telegram:

> "Sage Corners, N. Y., 10.30.
> "Just arrived. Elephant passed through here at 8.15. All escaped from the town but a policeman. Apparently elephant did not strike at policeman, but at the lamp-post. Got both. I have secured a portion of the policeman as clue.   "Stumm, *Detective*."

"So the elephant has turned westward," said the inspector. "However, he will not escape, for my men are scattered all over that region."

The next telegram said:

> "Glover's, 11.15.
> "Just arrived. Village deserted, except sick and aged. Elephant passed through three-quarters of an hour ago. The anti-temperance mass-meeting was in session; he put his trunk in at a window and washed it out with water from cistern. Some swallowed it—since dead; several drowned. Detectives Cross and O'Shaughnessy were passing through town, but going south— so missed elephant. Whole region for many miles

around in terror—people flying from their homes. Wherever they turn they meet elephant, and many are killed. Brant, *Detective.*"

I could have shed tears, this havoc so distressed me. But the inspector only said:

"You see—we are closing in on him. He feels our presence; he has turned eastward again."

Yet further troublous news was in store for us. The telegraph brought this:

Hogansport, 12.19.

"Just arrived. Elephant passed through half an hour ago, creating wildest fright and excitement. Elephant raged around streets; two plumbers going by, killed one—other escaped. Regret general.

O'Flaherty, *Detective.*"

"Now he is right in the midst of my men," said the inspector. "Nothing can save him."

A succession of telegrams came from detectives who were scattered through New Jersey and Pennsylvania, and who were following clues consisting of ravaged barns, factories, and Sunday-school libraries, with high hopes—hopes amounting to certainties, indeed. The inspector said:

"I wish I could communicate with them and order them north, but that is impossible. A detective only visits a telegraph office to send his report; then he is off again, and you don't know where to put your hand on him."

Now came the despatch:

Bridgeport, Conn., 12.15.

"Barnum offers rate of $4,000 a year for exclusive privilege of using elephant as traveling advertising medium from now till detectives find him. Wants to paste circus-posters on him. Desires immediate answer.

Boggs, *Detective.*"

"That is perfectly absurd!" I exclaimed.

"Of course it is," said the inspector. "Evidently Mr. Barnum, who thinks he is so sharp, does not know me—but I know him."

Then he indicated this answer to the despatch:

"Mr. Barnum's offer declined. Make it $7,000 or nothing.   *Chief* Blunt."

"There. We shall not have to wait long for an answer. Mr. Barnum is not at home; he is in the telegraph office— it is his way when he has business on hand. Inside of three—"

"Done.—P. T. Barnum".

So interrupted the clicking telegraphic instrument. Before I could make a comment upon this extraordinary episode, the following despatch carried my thoughts into another and very distressing channel:

Bolivia, N. Y., 12.50.

"Elephant arrived here from the south and passed through toward the forest at 11.50, dispersing a funeral on the way, and diminishing the mourners by two. Citizens fired some small cannon-balls into him, and then fled. Detective Burke and I arrived ten minutes later, from the north, but mistook some excavations for footprints, and so lost a good deal of time; but at last we struck the right trail and followed it to the woods. We then got down on our hands and knees and continued to keep a sharp eye on the track, and so shadowed it into the brush. Burke was in advance. Unfortunately the animal had stopped to rest; therefore, Burke having his head down, intent upon the track, butted up against the elephant's hind legs before he was aware of his vicinity. Burke instantly arose to

his feet, seized the tail, and exclaimed joyfully, "I claim
the re——" but got no further, for a single blow of the
huge trunk laid the brave fellow's fragments low in
death. I fled rearward, and the elephant turned and
shadowed me to the edge of the wood, making tremendous speed, and I should inevitably have been lost,
but the remains of the funeral providentially intervened again and diverted his attention. I have just
learned that nothing of that funeral is now left; but
this is no loss, for there is abundance of material for
another. Meantime, the elephant has disappeared again.

Mulrooney, *Detective*."

We heard no news except from the diligent and confident detectives scattered about New Jersey, Pennsylvania,
Delaware, and Virginia—who were all following fresh and
encouraging clues—until shortly after 2 P.M., when this
telegram came:

"Baxter Center, 2.15.
"Elephant been here plastered over with circus-
bills, and broke up a revival, striking down and damag-
ing many who were on the point of entering upon a
better life. Citizens penned him up and established a
guard. When Detective Brown and I arrived, some
time after, we entered inclosure and proceeded to identify elephant by photograph and description. All marks
tallied exactly except one, which we could not see—
the boil-scar under armpit. To make sure, Brown crept
under to look, and was immediately brained—that is
head crushed and destroyed, though nothing issued
from debris. All fled; so did elephant, striking right and
left with much effect. Has escaped, but left bold blood-
track from cannon-wounds. Rediscovery certain. He
broke southward, through a dense forest.

"Brant, *Detective*."

That was the last telegram. At nightfall a fog shut down

which was so dense that objects but three feet away could not be discerned. This lasted all night. The ferry-boats and even the omnibuses had to stop running.

III

Next morning the papers were as full of detective theories as before; they had all our tragic facts in detail also, and a great many more which they had received from their telegraphic correspondents. Column after column was occupied, a third of its way down, with glaring head-lines, which it made my heart sick to read. Their general tone was like this:

"THE WHITE ELEPHANT AT LARGE! HE MOVES UPON HIS FATAL MARCH! WHOLE VILLAGES DESERTED BY THEIR FRIGHT-STRICKEN OCCUPANTS! PALE TERROR GOES BEFORE HIM, DEATH AND DEVASTATION FOLLOW AFTER! AFTER THESE, THE DETECTIVES! BARNS DESTROYED, FACTORIES GUTTED, HARVESTS DEVOURED, PUBLIC ASSEMBLAGES DISPERSED, ACCOMPANIED BY SCENES OF CARNAGE IMPOSSIBLE TO DESCRIBE! THEORIES OF THIRTY-FOUR OF THE MOST DISTINGUISHED DETECTIVES ON THE FORCE! THEORY OF CHIEF BLUNT!"

"There!" said Inspector Blunt, almost betrayed into excitement, "this is magnificent! This is the greatest windfall that any detective organization ever had. The fame of it will travel to the ends of the earth, and endure to the end of time, and my name with it."

But there was no joy for me. I felt as if I had committed all those red crimes, and that the elephant was only my irresponsible agent. And how the list had grown! In one place he had "interfered with an election and killed five repeaters." He had followed this act with the destruction of two poor fellows, named O'Donohue and McFlannigan, who had "found a refuge in the home of the oppressed of all lands only the day before, and were in the act of exercising for the first time the noble right of American citizens at the polls, when stricken down by the relentless hand of the Scourge of Siam." In another, he had "found a crazy sensation-preacher preparing his next season's heroic attacks on the dance, the theater, and other things which can't strike back, and had stepped on him." And in still another place he had "killed a lightning-rod agent." And so the list went on, growing redder and redder, and more and more heartbreaking. Sixty persons had been killed, and two hundred and forty wounded. All the accounts bore just testimony to the activity and devotion of the detectives, and all closed with the remark that "three hundred thousand citizens and four detectives saw the dread creature, and two of the latter he destroyed."

I dreaded to hear the telegraphic instrument begin to click again. By and by the messages began to pour in, but I was happily disappointed in their nature. It was soon apparent that all trace of the elephant was lost. The fog had enabled him to search out a good hiding-place unobserved. Telegrams from the most absurdly distant points reported that a dim vast mass had been glimpsed there through the fog at such and such an hour, and was "undoubtedly the elephant." This dim vast mass had been glimpsed in New Haven, in New Jersey, in Pennsylvania, in interior New York, in Brooklyn, and even in the city of New York itself! But in all cases the dim vast mass had vanished quickly and left no trace. Every detective of the large force scattered over this huge extent of country sent his hourly report, and each and every one of them had a clue, and was shadowing something, and was hot upon the heels of it.

But the day passed without other result.

The next day the same.

The next just the same.

The newspaper reports began to grow monotonous with facts that amounted to nothing, clues which led to nothing, and theories which had nearly exhausted the elements which surprise and delight and dazzle.

By advice of the inspector I doubled the reward.

Four more dull days followed. Then came a bitter blow to the poor, hard-working detectives—the journalists declined to print their theories, and coldly said, "Give us a rest."

Two weeks after the elephant's disappearance I raised the reward to seventy-five thousand dollars by the inspector's advice. It was a great sum, but I felt that I would rather sacrifice my whole private fortune than lose my credit with my government. Now that the detectives were in adversity, the newspapers turned upon them, and began to fling the most stinging sarcasms at them. This gave the minstrels an idea, and they dressed themselves as detectives and hunted the elephant on the stage in the most extravagant way. The caricaturists made pictures of detectives scanning the country with spy-glasses, while the elephant, at their backs, stole apples out of their pockets. And they made all sorts of ridiculous pictures of the detective badge—you have seen that badge printed in gold on the back of detective novels, no doubt—it is a wide-staring eye, with the legend, "WE NEVER SLEEP." When detectives called for a drink, the would-be facetious barkeeper resurrected an obsolete form of expression and said, "Will you have an eye-opener?" All the air was thick with sarcasms.

But there was one man who moved calm, untouched, unaffected, through it all. It was that heart of oak, the chief inspector. His brave eye never drooped, his serene confidence never wavered. He always said:

"Let them rail on; he laughs best who laughs last."

My admiration for the man grew into a species of worship. I was at his side always. His office had become an unpleasant place to me, and now became daily more and more so. Yet if he could endure it I meant to do so also— at least, as long as I could. So I came regularly, and stayed —the only outsider who seemed to be capable of it. Everybody wondered how I could; and often it seemed to me that I must desert, but at such times I looked into that calm and apparently unconscious face, and held my ground.

About three weeks after the elephant's disappearance I was about to say, one morning, that I should *have* to strike my colors and retire, when the great detective arrested the thought by proposing one more superb and masterly move.

This was to compromise with the robbers. The fertility of this man's invention exceeded anything I have ever seen, and I have had a wide intercourse with the world's finest minds. He said he was confident he could compromise for one hundred thousand dollars and recover the elephant. I said I believed I could scrape the amount together, but what would become of the poor detectives who had worked so faithfully? He said:

"In compromises they always get half."

This removed my only objection. So the inspector wrote two notes, in this form:

> "Dear Madam,—Your husband can make a large sum of money (and be entirely protected from the law) by making an immediate appointment with me.
> *Chief* Blunt."

He sent one of these by his confidential messenger to the "reputed wife" of Brick Duffy, and the other to the reputed wife of Red McFadden.

Within the hour these offensive answers came:

> "Ye Owld fool: brick Duffy's bin ded 2 yere.
> "Bridget Mahoney."

> "Chief Bat,—Red McFadden is hung and in heving 18 month. Any Ass but a detective knose that.
> "Mary O'Hooligan."

"I had long suspected these facts," said the inspector; "this testimoney proves the unerring accuracy of my instinct."

The moment one resource failed him he was ready with another. He immediately wrote an advertisement for the morning papers, and I kept a copy of it:

"A.—xwblv. 242 N. Tjnd—fz328wmlg. Ozpo,—; 2
m! ogw. Mum."

He said that if the thief was alive this would bring him
to the usual rendezvous. He further explained that the usual
rendezvous was a place where all business affairs between
detectives and criminals were conducted. This meeting
would take place at twelve the next night.

We could do nothing till then, and I lost no time in getting out of the office, and was grateful indeed for the
privilege.

At eleven the next night I brought one hundred thousand
dollars in bank-notes and put them into the chief's hands,
and shortly afterward he took his leave, with the brave old
undimmed confidence in his eye. An almost intolerable
hour dragged to a close; then I heard his welcome tread,
and rose gasping and tottered to meet him. How his fine
eyes flamed with triumph! He said:

"We've compromised. The jokers will sing a different
tune to-morrow! Follow me!"

He took a lighted candle and strode down into the vast
vaulted basement where sixty detectives always slept, and
where a score were now playing cards to while the time. I
followed close after him. He walked swiftly down to the
dim and remote end of the place, and just as I succumbed
to the pangs of suffocation and was swooning away he
stumbled and fell over the outlying members of a mighty
object, and I heard him exclaim as he went down:

"Our noble profession is vindicated. Here is your elephant!"

I was carried to the office above and restored with carbolic acid. The whole detective force swarmed in, and such
another season of triumphant rejoicing ensued as I had
never witnessed before. The reporters were called, baskets of
champagne were opened, toasts were drunk, the handshak-
ings and congratulations were continuous and enthusiastic.
Naturally the chief was the hero of the hour, and his happiness was so complete and had been so patiently and

worthily and bravely won that it made me happy to see it, though I stood there a homeless beggar, my priceless charge dead, and my position in my country's service lost to me through what would always seem my fatally careless execution of a great trust. Many an eloquent eye testified its deep admiration for the chief, and many a detective's voice murmured, "Look at him—just the king of the profession; only give him a clue, it's all he wants, and there ain't anything hid that he can't find." The dividing of the fifty thousand dollars made great pleasure; when it was finished the chief made a little speech while he put his share in his pocket, in which he said, "Enjoy it, boys, for you've earned it; and, more than that, you've earned for the detective profession undying fame."

A telegram arrived, which read:

"Monroe, Mich., 10 P.M.

"First time I've struck a telegraph office in over three weeks. Have followed those footprints, horseback, through the woods, a thousand miles to here, and they get stronger and bigger and fresher every day. Don't worry—inside of another week I'll have the elephant. This is dead sure.   Darley, *Detective*."

The chief ordered three cheers for "Darley, one of the finest minds on the force," and then commanded that he be telegraphed to come home and receive his share of the reward.

So ended that marvelous episode of the stolen elephant. The newspapers were pleasant with praises once more, the next day, with one contemptible exception. This sheet said, "Great is the detective! He may be a little slow in finding a little thing like a mislaid elephant—he may hunt him all day and sleep with his rotting carcass all night for three weeks, but he will find him at last—if he can get the man who mislaid him to show him the place!"

Poor Hassan was lost to me forever. The cannon-shots had wounded him fatally, he had crept to that unfriendly place in the fog, and there, surrounded by his enemies and in constant danger of detection he had wasted away with hunger and suffering till death gave him peace.

The compromise cost me one hundred thousand dollars; my detective expenses were forty-two thousand dollars more; I never applied for a place again under my government; I am a ruined man and a wanderer on the earth—but my admiration for that man, whom I believe to be the greatest detective the world has ever produced, remains undimmed to this day, and will so remain unto the end.

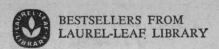

BESTSELLERS FROM
LAUREL-LEAF LIBRARY

A Revealing Novel about Teenagers—
by a Teenager

THE OUTSIDERS

by S. E. Hinton

"The Outsiders" are a rough and swinging gang of long-haired teen-agers from the wrong side of the tracks. They have little hope for the Mustangs and the madras shirts and all the rest of the material pleasures of American life. Their mode of expression is violence—directed toward the group of privileged kids who are at once objects of their envy and their hatred.

"Taut with tension, filled with drama."

—*Chicago Tribune*

"Written by a most perceptive teenager . . . it attempts to speak for all teenagers who find it so difficult to communicate to adults their doubts, their dreams, and their needs."

—*Book Week*

A DELL BOOK 95c

If you cannot obtain copies of this title from your local bookseller, just send the price (plus 35¢ per copy for handling and postage) to Dell Books, Post Office Box 1000, Pinebrook, N. J. 07058.

Share the strange adventures of an
orphaned boy after the Civil War!

The Fool Killer

HELEN EUSTIS

George woke up with a jump. More footsteps creaking
up the stairs. He knew it was Mr. Galt walkin' easy so's
not to wake anyone; but at the same time, with his heart
in his throat, he thought: *"That's the Fool Killer, eight
foot tall with his chopper in his hand, licking his lips
and his mouth watering. Come on!"* He said to him inside his head: *"Come on and get me! Looks like however I do is the wrong way anyhow!"*

"The book is nearly as prodigal of amazing characters as
one by Dickens and it rises to a climax as violent and
breathtaking as Stevenson could have devised."

—*San Francisco Chronicle*